Courting

Hope

Book 4 of
The Courtship Saga

A.R. Kaufer

ISBN 979-8-8693632-6-8
Cover image & design by: A.R. Kaufer
Background, *Courting the Stars,* & Moon Phase on spine by Cassie Evans
Courting Books Publishing
First edition, June 15th, 2024.

Quote from *Bruised Melodies* by Mia Sanchez used with permission from the author.

DEDICATED TO RYAN REYNOLDS

THANK YOU FOR CHOOSING EARTH

How far could I fall

Until the ends nears

Tell me how much more

Could the pain last now

Love, just a punishment

Tell me when it would end?

-Mia Sanchez, *Fall*

(Bruised Melodies)

Chapter 1

Rafe looks down and finds a spot in the woods where he can rest for a moment. He lowers to the ground and can't help but wonder how Ana is doing. Though he wants nothing more than to fly straight through and get back to her, he knows he has to do this right, take his time, and be careful.

A snapping branch catches his attention. He scans the woods and listens intently. Hearing and seeing nothing, he hastily gets back into the air, knowing it's the safest place for him to be. He grows cold the further south he goes, which is wrong for him, as it should get warmer instead. He continues, wanting to search for the camp before it gets dark. Approaching MoonFrost, he gives it a wide berth so no scouts will see him flying past.

South of MoonFrost, he lowers down. He stops and listens, closing his eyes as he focuses on finding Ana. His body grows cold. Something inside him snaps suddenly, as if broken in half. His breathing becomes erratic, and his lungs burn with every breath. He gasps softly as his eyes fly open.

He reaches out, trying again to feel for Ana, but nothingness consumes him. The realization collides with him like a freight train. There is no camp. It was a trap, and like a fool, he fell for it. He collects himself, preparing to fly harder and faster than he ever has. The ache in his chest wants to paralyze him, but he pushes it down and focuses on returning to Ana.

I'm coming, mia estrela. Please, please forgive me for what I've done. More importantly, please be alive. I'm sorry. I'm so sorry.

Rafe rushes into the palace, nearly colliding with Melian.

"There you are! Wait," she calls out as he runs for the stairway. "She's not here!"

Rafe halts at her words before turning to face her. He flies to her and grips her arms. "Then where is she?" he demands.

"We… we don't know. Kara is in the Medical Center and—" Before she can finish, Rafe releases her and runs up the stairs and through the corridor, ignoring the looks he gets.

He slams open the doors to the center. Winslow is passing by, reading a patient's chart. Rafe rushes to him.

"Where is everyone? Where is Ana?" His voice hitches at her name.

Winslow shakes his head. "Come with me, Rafe," he says softly.

"What is going on?" Rafe asks as they walk through the hallway. His exasperation grows when Winslow doesn't respond, but he opens a door and gestures for Rafe to go inside.

Rafe sees Kara lying in a hospital bed with Evren by her side, clasping her hand.

"Evren, what happened? Where is Ana?"

"Kara was… Kara was stabbed as she fought off their attackers. The queen is… gone."

Rafe's breath catches in his throat. "What do you mean, she's gone?"

"We don't know where she is. I'm sorry. Kara tried to stop them—"

"NightFall," Rafe murmurs. "Remus took Ana there to execute his plan. I have to stop him. When did the attack occur?"

Evren glances at the clock. "About three hours ago."

"Does Bela know about the attack?"

"No, we have no way to reach him."

"I thought he was still here?"

"Shortly after you left, he received an urgent message. He and Joph left immediately."

"Then I'll message Bela before I leave."

"Rafe, you need to rest," Evren says, getting to her feet and approaching him. "I see how weary you are."

"No, Evren. There's no time. I have to go."

"Take a few guardians with you, at least."

"I will."

He heads to the Communications Lounge, messaging Bela to let him know what has transpired. He finds Melian in the barracks.

"I am sorry about earlier, but this is urgent. The camp was a false lead so they could take Ana. I am going to NightFall. Who can accompany me?"

"I will send two with you then assemble a small battalion to follow."

"Thank you."

"Roesh, Aylin, on deck!" Melian calls out.

They approach and salute Rafe, before he explains to them where they are going and the mission before them. He explains that Remus is a priority but the most important objective is to protect the queen.

They fly straight through, grateful it is under the cover of darkness. Rafe observes the guards on the wall before signaling Roesh and Aylin to follow behind him. They make their way to the center, grateful there is enough light around the door. Rafe tries the knob.

"Locked."

Aylin smiles and nudges him aside, before she quickly manages to pick the lock. Rafe glances around along with Roesh, keeping their eyes and ears peeled for any patrolling guards or passers-by.

The door squeaks open, and the trio rush in before slamming it shut behind them. They wait a moment, giving their eyes time to adjust to the dim light.

"Remus should have her in the sublevel, where Joph has his laboratory set up. Follow me."

A door opens at the end of the hall but quickly closes again. Rafe takes a deep breath before continuing. They take the elevator down to the sublevel. As soon as the doors open, they are greeted by Ana's screams.

Rafe can barely contain his rage as he charges into the room. Ana is bound to the exam table with a metal collar wrapped around her neck. Joph is on the table beside her, restrained in a similar manner.

Remus approaches Ana. "Abomination! Both of you. It is disgusting that we have to share this realm. Neither of you should've been born!" He presses a button on the machine, and Ana's piercing shrieks fill the room once more. She can only writhe as pain rocks her body.

"Get the queen!" Roesh says to Rafe as he charges forward, trying to distract Remus so he can apprehend him.

Rafe debates for a moment, wanting nothing more than to go after Remus, but he is pulled from his thoughts by Ana. He rushes to her side, smashing the large red button, causing the machine to power down. Bile rises in his throat at the sight of her. Tubes and wires are in her legs and arms, and her color is completely gone, except for the blue of her lips.

As gently as he can, he removes everything from her before freeing her from the bindings. He turns, when Aylin screams, watching as Roesh is gravely wounded by Remus's blade. Blood spatters across the floor, and Roesh crumples in a heap.

Rafe frees Joph as quickly as he can. "Help Roesh," he instructs.

Joph nods before grabbing his bag and rushing to his side, watching for a moment as Aylin and Remus duel. She leads Remus away from them, so Joph can tend to his wounds. Rafe watches Remus rush into the elevator. He turns to give chase, but Ana grabs his arm.

"Please, stay with me," she says with a whimper. "I… I don't know how much time I have left."

"Ana—"

"It's okay. Remove my collar, and I'll heal myself. I'll be okay. I promise." She gives him a pitiful smile.

Rafe shakes his head, knowing she doesn't have the strength. "Ana, please, let me do this for you."

"I can see how tired you are from your travels. There's no need to risk you, too."

"All right. I'll remove the collar, then let you heal yourself," he says as he lifts the keys from the console.

He removes the cold metal from her neck, tossing it to the floor as he envelops her in his arms.

"Rafe, no! I command—"

He kisses her, cutting off her words with his mouth as he heals her. They lose consciousness together before landing on the cold, hard floor.

⁂

Ana opens her eyes, realizing she is in Rafe's arms and in a private room. Anger floods through her, and she pulls away.

"Where are you going?" Rafe mumbles, still half-asleep.

"Washroom," she responds as she jerks herself free of his hold.

After she's done, she washes her hands when the shower catches her eye. She strips down and turns on the tap. As she steps in, she relishes the hot water washing over her.

She nearly screams when Rafe grips her shoulder. "You didn't tell me you were getting a shower."

"I didn't plan on it. I saw it and got in. Now, what are you doing in here?"

Rafe grows concerned when she keeps her back to him, running her hands through her hair under the water. "Are you mad at me?"

She scoffs as she faces him. "You're damn right I am! Where do I begin? I told you something was wrong, literally got on my knees and begged you not to go! Are you happy now?"

"I had to go after him! He has to be stopped, and I had to take the chance. The way you did when you left to save Bela, even though I begged you to stay."

"I went to save an ally and prevent another war. You left to scout for information, something any guardian could've done. It didn't have to be you."

"Wait, is that really what you believe? Yes, I left to protect you, because it had to be me."

"Really?" She studies him for a moment before gasping as the realization creeps in. "You didn't leave on a scouting trip. You were going to kill him yourself, weren't you?"

"Ana—"

"I command you to speak the truth!"

His hands clench. "Yes. I was going to kill him, no matter the cost. Not if it meant saving you from him."

She scoffs. "And how did that work out?"

"I nearly lost you," he admits quietly as he turns away. He collects himself before meeting her gaze. "I'm sorry. For everything. I honestly thought I could end this before it got out of hand. I did it for you."

"I know you believe you did."

"What does that mean?"

"Rafe, tell me exactly what you intended to do when you left the palace."

His jaw tightens. "I was going to find Remus, sneak into his camp, and slit his throat. I intended to stop him before he gained any more supporters, before he had an army to march on you with." He is unable to hide the anger blazing in his eyes. "Rescind your command now, before I say something I may regret."

"Oh, like what?" she asks.

"That you are being a spoiled brat for using this on me!" he spits out. "I hate how it makes me feel. That you would treat me this way. It's not fair."

"And if I were to command you again?" She watches his hands clench open and shut. "Rafe?"

"I would be pissed beyond words, but I would still love you."

"Fine, I rescind my commands. Now leave the shower."

"No."

She maintains his gaze as her index finger pokes his torso. "I am the queen, and you are my guardian. You have dishonored me. Therefore, you do not deserve to be in here with me." A gasp flies from her lips when he falls to his knees before her.

"You're right. I was scared and angry. I told you not to give in to yours, but the truth is, that's exactly what I did. I risked everything because I blame myself for what happened to you in MoonFrost. For what I have done, I forfeit my life."

"No!" Ana cries out, grabbing his hands and pulling him to his feet. "What happened in MoonFrost was not your fault." Her arms wrap around her stomach as she thinks over her words carefully. "I am angry about everything you did, but do not blame yourself for that."

"I am your guardian, your protector, the one who is dedicated solely to your safety. It is what I am born and trained to do. It is who I am."

Ana shakes her head. "Funny, I thought you were my lover." She gives a half-bow. "Apologies, Guardian. Please, continue with your duties."

Her voice cuts through his heart. He shakes his head, unable to bear the pain of it. "That's not… Ana, please…"

"Then what do you mean?"

"I have failed you twice because of Remus. I only meant, I…" He closes his eyes.

"Why did you kiss me?" she demands. "I was perfectly capable of healing myself!"

"I could see how bad of shape you were in. You did not have the strength to do it."

"What else?"

"What do you mean?"

"No. I could see it in your eyes. There was another reason you didn't want me to. Tell me, or I will go out there and demand a separate room."

"You wouldn't," he murmurs in surprise.

"I haven't even forgiven you for what you did. So yes, I most certainly will. Tell me!"

"The book Kara read said the more you use your wings of fire, the stronger you will become. However, that power comes with a price, and in using it, you could… you could undo your immortality. I couldn't take that chance."

"You lied to me again, after you said you wouldn't keep things from me anymore?"

"Ana, you aren't really mad at me. You're doing it so I won't be mad at you, after the fight we had. You're doing this to protect yourself. Please, don't push me away."

"Rafe, do you not understand how badly I want to climb into your arms, to let your warmth overtake me? After what you said, and the way you left—" She shakes her head.

"I can't do this. Not anymore." She stands under the shower head, letting the water rain over her as tears stream down her cheeks.

Rafe wraps his arm around her waist then gently pulls her against his chest. "Please, mia estrela. I need to have you in my arms. Forgive me for everything, please. I beg of you."

"You left me!" she screams as she jerks away. "How could you?" Her voice is but a whisper.

"Because I will do whatever I must to keep you alive, even if that means having you angry with me. I knew the risk I took when I left you. If you choose not to love me anymore, I'll understand. But as long as you are alive to make that choice, that is what matters to me."

"I know I was angry in the closet, but how can you even say that?"

"You told me if I left, not to come back."

"You were leaving me! I was terrified, and hurt, and it reminded me of our first day here."

"Ana—" He reaches for her, only to see her recoil from his touch. "Please."

She turns off the water and steps out from the shower. Snatching the towel from the rack, she promptly dries, then slips back into her gown. Rafe wraps a towel around his waist.

"Ana, please," he tries again.

"I can't... I can't do this. You promised me you would never leave me, then you went out the door the first chance you had! What am I supposed to believe?"

He finishes drying off and dresses. "I told you why."

"I don't care. Do you?"

"What do you mean?"

"He tortured me, cut me, hurt me, and it's your fault!"

"You... you told me what happened to you in MoonFrost wasn't my fault."

"I'm talking about today!" She leaves the room and goes for the door. Two of Bela's guards are stationed outside. "Will one of you get me Joph, please?"

"Yes, Majesty."

Ana steps back in but refuses to look at Rafe when he joins her by the bed. "I sent for Joph. I'm getting clothes, then I'm leaving."

"You need to rest. You are in no shape to travel."

"You no longer dictate what I do. I have let you for so long because you know the customs here, you know what to do. I am tired of it. Besides, I'm fine!" she yells as she falls unconscious.

Rafe catches her and puts her on the bed. He kisses her forehead. "My warrior queen."

"How is everyone?" Joph asks as he enters the room.

"We're all right. She's resting." Rafe tries to hide his concern, knowing Ana overdid it. "How is Roesh?"

"For now, he is also resting. I am still unsure if he will survive, as his wounds are not healing as they should." Joph clears his throat. "Also, Bela wanted me to ask if you will be up for joining us for dinner or if he should have it brought in for you?"

"I don't even know what time it is," Rafe admits.

"A little after three," Joph responds.

"We should be able to join you for dinner, but I don't believe Ana has any clothes."

"That is being taken care of."

"Thank you." Rafe glances at Ana before turning to Joph. "Can I ask?"

"Ask about what?"

"What all did Remus do to her before we arrived?"

Joph clears his throat as he shifts where he stands. "I believe I will leave that between the two of you."

"I understand. Sorry."

"Do either of you need anything?"

"Other than to rest, I don't believe we do."

"I will be back to check on you both."

Rafe watches him leave then clasps Ana's hand. He kisses it softly. "You were right. In every way that mattered. I never should've left." He wipes his tears as they fall. "Regardless of what you said, all of this is my fault. I am not worthy of you. I have never been, and especially not now. Please, find it in your heart to forgive me. And if you tell me to go, I will. Though it would be the hardest thing I've ever done, it's the least I can do after everything."

"Hmm, Rafe?"

"I'm right here."

"Do you… do you still love me?" she asks quietly, a small hitch in her voice as she bites back tears.

He climbs into bed and holds her taut against his chest. "With every fiber of my being."

"It hurts."

"Where, Ana? Where do you hurt?"

"My heart. Did you shut off our bond?"

"No. I still feel it—"

"I meant earlier, when you were scouting for his camp."

"No, I didn't. I couldn't feel you, either. Something interrupted it."

"I love you, and because of that, I want to forgive you. But I'm so afraid. I can't… I can't do this again."

"Command me to speak the truth."

"What?"

"I mean it. Command me."

"Uh, okay. Rafe, I command you to speak the truth."

"I swear to you, here and now, if you forgive me, I will never leave you again. I will stay by your side, hold you, comfort you, and love you. Never again will I doubt you or make you feel small. I promise to continue working on my anger, so I can become the man you deserve. Will you give me the chance?"

"Why do you deserve one?"

"I don't, but I'll beg for it anyway."

"I rescind my last command."

"But?"

She shakes her head. "I can't forgive you."

"I understand. When we return to the palace, I'll get my things, and we can see about—"

"No, please." The thought of losing him completely sends her head swimming.

"I don't understand?"

"I can't forgive you. It hurts too much. But even so, I would hope…" Her voice trails off. "I would hope you would at least stay on, as my guardian."

"If that is your command."

"I don't deserve your forgiveness, either," she blurts out, wiping her tears.

His brow furrows. "Why not?"

"Telling you not to come back, for banishing you from the palace." She weeps into his shirt. "I was so hurt and angry."

"We both said things we didn't mean."

"I am the queen, and as such, I am held to a higher standard of behavior. I was whiny and hurtful."

"Yes, you are the queen. You are also human, and that means having human emotions."

Ana scoffs. "Not anymore."

Rafe sighs as he debates his next question. "What you said to me, that you hate what you are. Did you mean that?"

"Yes and no. I don't hate myself. I only hated myself because it gave Remus the excuse to hurt me, but I know you're right. I have to acknowledge it was because I am the queen and had the information he wanted, not because of my wings. They were hurting, and I was looking for an excuse to hate them. I'm so sorry."

"Ana, I forgave you for everything the moment I saw you on that table. Will you forgive me now?"

She pulls away and sits on the edge of the bed. "I want to, I really do."

"What's wrong?"

She meets his gaze. "Rafe, I laid down and died as wings grew out of my back. Yet, that isn't the most painful experience of my life. Our first day here, you told me I was your mission, that you didn't love me. I never thought anything would hurt as much as that." Her head goes down to hide her tears.

"Ana—"

"Then for you to walk out the door, after I had been tortured…" Her hands clench, and she swallows hard. "You didn't break my heart. You shattered it. I don't know what it will take to make it whole again."

Rafe gently grips her arm and lifts her onto his lap, enveloping her tightly against his chest. "Mia estrela, I will do whatever you ask. I will spend the rest of my immortal life making this up to you, if that's what it takes. Please, give me the chance."

His warmth and love flow in, and she moves away, nearly falling from the bed. "Stop," she says as she stands up.

"Stop what?"

"You know what physical touch does for us. I don't want to be manipulated into forgiving you."

"I swear, that wasn't what I was doing. I need to hold you. I need to be with you."

"Maybe you should've thought about that before leaving me."

Rafe jumps to his feet. "You told me to go."

Her head whips around as she stares daggers at him. "After you said you were!"

"What do you want me to do, Ana? We are going in circles! How can I make this right?"

She opens her mouth but shuts it immediately when Joph enters with clothing in his arms. "Mi'lady, how do you feel?"

"Better," she answers, taking the clothing. "Thank you. I'm sure I'll find something suitable for dinner."

She doesn't look at Rafe as she goes into the washroom and shuts the door. In her heart, she wants desperately to forgive him. She doesn't see how she can, though. How can she trust him again?

I know he believes he was acting in my defense. He doesn't realize how badly he hurt me, or he doesn't care. She shakes her head. *No, I know better than that. He does care, but how can I get him to see exactly what he did?*

The gown slips over her head, and she focuses on looking herself over in the mirror. It is rose pink with layers in the skirt. She expands her wings, happy that they have plenty of room, before stepping out.

"Thank you, Joph. This is lovely."

"You are most welcome. Dinner will be ready shortly. I will check on a few patients then return to escort you myself."

"Thanks," Rafe says, grabbing his bag and getting out clothes.

When the door closes behind Joph, Rafe dresses, then approaches Ana. "You look beautiful in that gown."

She turns away, clutching her chest, trying to hide the tears threatening to spill down her face. "Thanks," she manages.

"Are you in pain?"

"I'm fine."

"Please, talk to me."

She sits on the edge. Her eyes stay down, refusing to meet his gaze. "I think I will ask for a separate room after dinner."

"Ana—"

"I need space, and time to think, after what you've done to me. I will sleep in another room tonight, then we will talk in the morning."

"It hurts me to be away from you. Why are you so unwilling to forgive me?"

"You really don't know what you did? I would rather be tortured again than to watch you walk out the door."

Rafe freezes in place, unable to comprehend what he is hearing. "You don't mean that."

She lifts her hand. "Feel for yourself. Don't push your emotions into me, but feel what I am."

He takes her hand, delicately kisses it, then closes his eyes as he does what she requested. His mouth opens, and his breathing runs ragged. He pulls away. "How are you so calm while feeling like this?"

"Because I learned a long time ago how to push past the pain, to do what needed to be done regardless. Same as you. I want to get through dinner with Bela and Joph then be alone for the rest of the night." She glances at the clock. "Joph will be back any moment."

"Ana, please—" he tries again.

"You will behave during dinner, do you hear me?"

"You're going to treat me like a child?" he asks in utter disbelief.

"I'm treating you better than you deserve at the moment. Be grateful for that."

Joph walks in. "Dinner is ready."

"Thank you," Ana says, lacing her arm with his. He blushes slightly then smiles at Rafe, who gives a small scowl. Joph swallows. "First, may we check on Roesh?"

"Of course, Majesty."

He leads them to another private room, where Aylin sits beside Roesh, his hand clasped firmly in her own.

Joph turns to Ana. "We asked her to stand guard outside your room, but she insisted on staying with him."

Aylin jumps to her feet. "Majesty, forgive me. I know I have disobeyed—"

"Aylin, it's okay. You nearly lost him. Please, do not apologize."

"Thank you. I can't..." She closes her eyes. "I got him back. I don't want to be away from him. But if you need me, I am here for you."

"I appreciate that, but he needs you more than I do. Now, how is he doing?"

Joph steps up to Roesh and takes his vitals before inspecting his wounds. "His accelerated healing has finally kicked in, and he is recovering."

"We are going to dinner. Aylin, let us know if you need anything."

"Thank you, Majesty." She bows before she resumes her vigil at Roesh's side.

Ana's heart aches at the sight. She pushes it down as she follows Joph and Rafe to the banquet room.

Chapter 2

Ana sits beside Bela, smiling politely at him. "Thank you for inviting us to join you."

"Any time, mi'lady."

Their plates are set down, and Ana stares at her meal. Bela notices when she hasn't touched her food.

"Is something the matter, Ana?"

Rafe stops and watches her. Ana keeps her head down. "I'm fine," she says, taking a bite. "Just needed a moment." She looks at Bela. "I am sorry for everything that is happening because of Remus."

"He is every bit as tenacious as his brother."

"Roban or Regan?"

"Kane."

The fork slips from Ana's hand. "I beg your pardon?"

Bela glances at Rafe before returning his attention to Ana. "Then you did not know?"

"Know what?"

"Kane was half-brother to Remus, Regan, and Roban. We found out after he tried to ally with our council. It was a setup, to use our army to gain the throne, then turn on us and wipe us out. Kane pretended to ally with our council, to offer information to help us in battle but, all the while, they were working together to bring us down from the inside."

"Mi'lady, are you all right?" Joph asks. "You look rather pale."

"I'm fine."

"Are you having any after effects from the machine?"

"No, Joph."

"What did the machine to do her?" Rafe asks.

Joph looks from Ana to Rafe. "As I previously stated, I will let her tell you when she is ready."

"I don't wish to discuss it now. Not while we are eating." She clears her throat. "Bela, are we staying in your medical wing tonight?" she asks, hoping to change the topic. She understands how important the discussion is, but she is in no shape for it at the moment.

"I have quarters arranged for you."

"Will you set a room aside for Rafe, as well?"

Bela is taken aback by her request, but upon seeing the anger on Rafe's face, decides it best not to pursue it. "We can, Ana. That is fine."

Rafe notices the look Bela and Joph exchange. His skin flushes with humiliation. "Excuse me." He abruptly leaves the table.

Ana takes another bite of her meal. Bela's concern grows when she keeps her head down. "Ana, I know it is not my place, but are the two of you okay?"

"You know how he left, how things were between us. He wants me to forgive him, but I don't see how I can."

Bela pats her hand before taking a drink. "You will. I've seen how the two of you are, and everything will be okay."

"Thank you."

They finish their meal, and Ana grows concerned when Rafe hasn't returned. She follows Bela to her quarters. The room has dark floors, contrasting the pale blue walls. There is a poster bed and fireplace, with a small sofa to sit on.

"It's lovely." She smiles at Bela. "If you see Rafe," she clears her throat, "please show him here, so he may stay with me tonight."

"Mi'lady, are you sure?" Bela asks.

"I am. Thank you."

She watches them leave, then goes to the dresser, happy to find a nightgown ready for her. After holding it up to be sure it looks all right, she goes into the washroom and gets ready for bed. As she's returning to the main chamber, Rafe steps in. Her eyes immediately go down.

"Bela said you wanted to see me?" His voice is emotionless, his demeanor betraying nothing of how he feels.

"I wanted to talk with you."

"I think you've said enough."

Ana steps forward but stops when her body runs cold. "You shut off the bond?"

"Yes. God forbid I manipulate you with it, though I have no clue how to do that."

"I was ready to talk, to work through this. Why are you being so distant now?"

"I went for a flight to cool off, after you requested separate rooms. I thought about what we discussed earlier. If you choose to deny me, to deny our bond, and not forgive me, that is your right to do so. But I will not suffer in this purgatory, while you try to decide what you want. That isn't fair to me."

"Rafe—"

"Tell me here and now, what you want."

"I… I don't know," she admits. "It's why I thought we should talk. I, at least, wanted to try."

"We talked earlier. It did not do any good."

"Rafe, you're scaring me. I don't like this side of you, so cold! Please, I have done nothing to deserve this."

"Really, you call toying with my emotions, toying with my heart, nothing? After all we have been through together?"

She pushes past her fear and approaches him. Her palm rests on his chest as she meets his gaze. "Give me a chance. Can we please talk?"

"Talk."

She shakes her head. "Not like this. I want Rafe, I want *my* Rafe. The one who is loving, protective, and sweet. Where is he?" Her hand pats his torso. "I know he is still in here. Please."

He grips her hand, removing it, then stepping back. "I want to work things out. I want us to be together, but not if we are going to fight all the time. Not if you are going to get angry with me and tell me to leave."

"I didn't tell you to leave! You made that decision all on your own." Her voice cracks. "Rafe, please. My heart can't take much more."

"Ana, I begged your forgiveness in the shower. I even offered you my life."

"I know, but—"

"Let me speak!"

Her breath sucks in, as she takes a step away from him while glancing around the room. "I'm sorry."

He reaches for her, and she falls backwards, landing against the dresser. She buries her face in her legs.

"Please, don't hurt me!" she cries out, trembling as tears stream down her face.

Everything crashes in on him as he realizes what he has done. He rushes to her side, lifting her in his arms as he opens the bond.

"I'm here, mia estrela. I'm right here, and I would never hurt you that way. You're safe. It's okay now."

She clings to him. "Please," she whispers, wiping her tears.

"What do you need?"

"A shower."

He takes her into the washroom, gently placing her on the vanity. He pulls back the satin curtain. "Shit."

"What's wrong?" she asks.

He faces her. "There is only a tub. No shower." Slowly, he approaches her, gently cupping her chin in his hand. "Could I fix you a bath? If I were with you, would that help? You don't have to."

"It would be a first for us. If you don't mind?"

"I'll fix it right up. If at any point, you are uncomfortable or don't want to, say the word. Am I clear?"

"Yes, thank you."

He drops the stopper in and starts the water. "Do you want me in here with you."

"I don't want to be alone."

"I mean in the tub."

Her breath sucks in. "Oh."

"I have more shorts. I can stay dressed."

"Please?"

"Of course."

He fills the tub, adding soap that was on the shelf. He helps her undress as he removes his pajama pants and shirt. They lay everything on the vanity. Taking her hand, they step in. He sits down, gently pulling her with him. She tries to relax in the warm water, while fighting her fears. When she lies against his chest, his arm comes around her waist, startling her.

"Ana, are you—"

"I'm okay."

"Your heart is racing, and your fear is flowing in."

"I'm sorry, I'm trying to be calm." She grips his arm, then gently rubs her hand over it. "You're right, I'm sorry I wasn't ready to forgive you. I was trying, and I thought I could." She swallows down her tears. "But I do forgive you. I only pray you never do anything like that again."

"I swear to you, Ana, I will never leave your side. I will work on my anger, and we will work on our communication." He shifts to get comfortable, and she nearly jumps from the bath. "Shh. You're safe. Let the warm water relax you. Just imagine we're on vacation in Paris, staying at a quaint little bed and breakfast."

She smiles. "With croissants and coffee for breakfast?"

"What else?"

"We go to the Louvre, see the Eiffel Tower, cruise on the Seine."

"It sounds wonderful."

"Thank you, Rafe. Between my foster father and Remus, I never thought I would be able to take another bath. This is really nice."

"You're very welcome. Now, what else would you do in Paris?"

"Go the cafés, people watch, visit Notré Dame."

"You always wanted to go there, didn't you?"

"It was a dream of mine."

"Ana, why are you feeling sad?"

"Because now I'll never get to go. Even if the portal weren't closed, I couldn't go because of my wings."

"Oh, Ana, I'm so sorry."

"It's okay."

"Close your eyes."

"Yes, Rafe."

"Picture the Eiffel Tower. Can you imagine riding the elevator up? You anxiously await, as the gate slowly opens. You step out, the city alight all around you, a breathtaking view." He stops when a tear lands on his arm. "Ana?"

"Please, don't stop."

"The boats are on the river as cars come around the arch, lit up for the night. Do you see it?"

"I do. Thank you." She leans up, kissing him. "That was perfect."

"You are happy and relaxed. That makes me feel better, as I was worried about you."

"That's your job, isn't it?"

He laughs. "Yes, it is."

"I'm ready to get out."

He helps her to her feet. She grabs a towel and dries off, slipping back into her undergarments and nightgown.

He changes into dry shorts, before putting his pajamas back on. Climbing into bed, he smiles as she snuggles in his arms.

"Thank you, love, for another amazing first."

He kisses her forehead. "I love you, mia estrela. Now sleep."

"I love you, too."

He grips her arm, his love and warmth flowing into her. When she falls asleep, clutching his shirt, he can't help but smile. He strokes his hand through her hair, singing into her ear as he falls asleep as well.

"Joph, please come in," Rafe offers as he opens the door further.

"I only stopped by to inform you breakfast is at eight in the banquet room."

"We will be there. How are Aylin and Roesh?"

Joph looks down for a moment. "They are fine."

"And?"

"I, hmm, I did not know they are a couple. I went in to check on him, and they were kissing."

Rafe chuckles. "It's okay, Joph. As you've seen, we are a little more open with our feelings."

"No, Rafe. They had no clothing on."

He stifles the laugh. "You're a doctor. I'm sure you've seen worse."

"Yes, Rafe."

"We will see you at eight for breakfast."

"Until then."

Rafe steps back in as Ana is leaving the washroom, softly giggling as she pins in her tiara.

"You heard that?" Rafe asks.

"Yes. Poor Joph, he can't catch a break."

"I didn't know they were a couple."

"I did. You can see how much they care for each other."

"Yes, and Joph did as well."

They burst out laughing. "Rafe, what is wrong with you?"

"I couldn't help it." He glances at the clock. "We have a little time until breakfast. Would you like to snuggle in front of the fireplace?"

"That would be wonderful."

He leads her to the sofa and sits with her, his arm around her shoulder. "Ana, I am sorry for what happened. I was blinded with anger, and I wanted to make sure he could never hurt you again. In doing so, I was the one to cause you pain."

"Rafe, you've already apologized."

"I know, but I want everything out in the open. I'm sorry I broke my promise. I will always be here with you, by your side."

"Thank you, love. I promise to work on my anger, as well, and that we will talk about the issue, discuss it together. You and I are a team, and we need to approach the problem that way, instead of seeing each other as the issue."

"Very well put."

"What was it like, flying south of MoonFrost? Is it vast and empty, or are there inhabitants?"

"There are forests and a few fields."

"I'd love to see it sometime, maybe even one day be able to visit MoonFrost."

"You said you didn't travel when you were on Earth?"

"No, other than going from one small town to another."

"So you never saw the beach?"

She sighs. "No. I desperately wanted to."

"We'll go one day."

"What? What are you talking about?"

"You haven't learned about MorningStella in your studies?" His nose scrunches in confusion.

"Only that it's a metropolis in the southeast, and that

it's where most of the factories are."

"It's on the coast. There are beaches there."

"Are you serious?" she asks, sitting up and bouncing in excitement. "I want to see them!"

"Let's get Remus taken care of, then you and I will travel there, I promise you." The clock chimes. "Oh, we need to head out or we'll be late for breakfast."

***

"Majesty, how are you this morning?" Bela asks.

Ana sits beside him. "We are both well, thank you, and our quarters are lovely!"

"I am glad you like them. We can set that as your quarters for when you return, if you would like. Will you be leaving after breakfast?"

"If Roesh is up for it," Rafe answers, watching Joph approach them.

"I apologize for being late," he offers as he sits.

"Quite all right," Ana responds. "How are my guardians doing?"

"They are well. Roesh has recovered and says he is up for travel when you are."

"Did you knock this time?" Rafe asks with a sly grin.

"Rafe!" Ana exclaims as he and Bela laugh uncontrollably, causing a few diners to glance over at them. "Joph, I am so sorry. He really thinks he's funny."

"I am funny," Rafe says.

"I swear, I cannot take you anywhere."

"Ana, now I see why you and I get along so well."

"Yes, Count."

***

"Are you ready to return home?" Rafe asks as he checks his bag one more time.

"I am."

"How do you feel? From what he… from the machine?"

Ana's head goes down. "I'm fine."

"I thought we were going to be open from now on."

"I am fine, I mean it. I'll tell you about the machine itself once we are back at the palace. I promise."

Reluctantly, Rafe nods. "All right."

They follow Bela to the entrance, where they meet Joph, Aylin, and Roesh.

Ana studies him for a moment. "Roesh, are you sure you are up to travel?"

"I am, Majesty."

They say their goodbyes then take off, Roesh and Aylin scouting ahead with Ana in Rafe's arms.

"I would like to fly some."

"Ana, you are still recovering."

"I didn't mean fly all the way there. Just, maybe a few minutes before we set up camp? Please?"

"We'll see."

After a few hours, they stop to eat a snack and rest for a moment. Ana takes a drink from the canteen Bela had sent with her. Rafe glances around, scanning the area.

"Rafe, why don't you join me?"

He gives her a gentle smile before he resumes searching the woods. "I have to keep my guard up."

Ana sighs. "We have two guardians with us."

"Yes, and I am your third."

She closes the canteen, places it in her bag, and marches to him. Her hands grip his face as she kisses him hard, her arms wrapping around his neck.

"Love, I know you are my guardian, but that is not all you are to me. I want to be with you, as my friend, as my love, as my everything."

He kisses her softly. "I will try."

Roesh and Aylin land beside them. "We scouted ahead. No threats in sight."

"Thank you, Roesh," Ana says.

Rafe scoops her into his arms, and they take off for the sky. Her arms tighten when a shift in the wind blows him slightly off course.

"Are you all right?" he asks.

"I'm fine."

"You know, I love carrying you like this."

"I love it, too, but I still want to fly a little."

After a few hours, they land to eat a snack and rest for a moment. Ana grips Rafe's arm, when they are about to take off.

"Love, please?"

He turns to Aylin and Roesh. "We'll set up camp shortly. Ana wants to fly but is still learning and self-conscious. Fly ahead and scout the area."

"Yes, Rafe," Roesh responds.

"Thank you."

Roesh and Aylin hold hands as they go into the air. Ana gasps as she watches them. "They are great together."

"Yes, they are. Now, stretch your wings."

She furls and unfurls them, then smiles when Rafe takes her hand and leads her upward. He holds her hand tightly as they fly.

After half an hour spent focusing on her entire body, the wind, and all the things Rafe told her she should concentrate on as a new flyer, exhaustion washes over her.

"Rafe, I'm fine," she protests when he pulls her into his arms.

"I feel how tired you are."

She doesn't argue, instead wrapping her arms tighter around his neck. He catches up to Aylin and Roesh, gesturing for them to land in a small clearing.

Roesh helps Aylin, while Rafe is unloading his pack. "Ana, I only have one sleeping bag."

"Whatever will we do?" she asks playfully, biting her lower lip. Her face goes flush when Roesh and Aylin laugh. "I'm sorry, I didn't know you could hear me."

"Do not worry, Your Majesty."

Ana turns back to Rafe, shivering as the evening air begins to chill. "Are we lighting a fire?"

"It's too dangerous. We'll be warm enough."

They get ready to settle in for the night. Roesh is on one side, Aylin the other, with Rafe and Ana in the middle. Rafe climbs into the sleeping bag first, then holds it open for Ana.

"Oh, you're right, it is warm. We should do this more often," she says as he fastens it up. When she snuggles up against him, he gasps. "Are you all right?"

He grinds his teeth. "It's okay. Just… go to sleep."

"Yes, love."

Ana has never been happier to see the palace. Rafe escorts her inside, and they immediately head to the Medical Center, while Aylin takes their things to their quarters.

Roesh scans for any danger. They walk in and are greeted by a nurse.

"We're here to see—"

"Your Majesty, we are grateful you have returned."

Ana turns to Winslow, giving him a reassuring smile. "Thank you. How is Kara doing?"

"She is much better and in her own quarters."

Ana sighs in relief. "Then that is where we are heading. Thank you."

Rafe keeps his arm around Ana as they head for their quarters. The corridor is mostly empty, as it is still early yet. Rafe knocks on Kara's door when they arrive.

"Who is it?" Kara asks from the other side. She opens the door, dropping the bundle of fabric and rushing to Ana, clutching her tightly. Rafe steps back to give her room. "Oh, I thought I had lost you!"

"I'm right here. Thank you for defending me. How do you feel?"

"I'm recovered. Evren worked a little magic to help.

How are you? What happened in NightFall?" Regret washes over her, when she sees the tears forming in Ana's eyes. "I'm sorry, don't cry!"

Rafe wraps his arm around Ana's waist, kissing her forehead softly. "Is something wrong?"

"I'm still tired from everything. I think I need to lay down."

"Of course. Plus, all of the traveling you guys did. Take it easy, and we'll be over shortly with lunch."

"Kara, I know you are still recovering, too."

"I'm fine. Besides, I want to see you and Rafe."

"You must be in worse shape than you think."

Kara's nose crinkles. "What do you mean?"

Ana laughs. "You said you want to see me and Rafe."

Kara shakes her head and chuckles. "Ana, don't be mean. We'll be over soon."

"All right." Ana follows Rafe as they go inside. Seeing the crate by the fireplace, Ana runs to Smaug. "My poor little dragon! I bet you missed me. I'll play with you soon."

She goes into the closet, getting clean clothes, then goes to the washroom. She's setting them on the vanity when Rafe enters. The pain in her eyes causes him to stop in his tracks.

"Do you want to shower by yourself?" he offers.

"No. I'm okay but really tired." She turns on the tap and strips down. "We'll get cleaned up, then I'll answer any questions you have."

"Right now, I only have one."

"What?" she asks as she meets his gaze.

"Can I kiss you?"

Flooded with tears, she can only nod in response. His lips brush hers, gentle at first, then his kiss grows in hunger. He explores her mouth, taking her in as if he hasn't seen her in a thousand years. When she wraps her arms around his neck, something clicks inside him, as if the piece of him that had been missing has finally snapped into place.

"Never stop," she begs when he pulls away.

"You need to rest now," he says as he leads her into the shower. He washes and rinses her off as she clings to him. They dry off together and dress, then he carries her to the chaise.

"Rafe, I need you. Please."

"We'll have lunch shortly, then you will go to sleep. I can feel how tired you are. Tomorrow, we'll do whatever you want. I promise you. I love you, and I'm grateful to have you back with me."

"I love you, too."

"What's wrong?"

"You do have me. You have every broken piece of me. It seems like I finally start to heal, only to get broken all over again. It's not fair to you."

"Ana, telling you I love you has meant more to me than anything I have done in over five hundred years. If it takes every single day of my immortal life to make you whole, then I make this vow to you. I will do whatever it takes, to protect you, to keep you, to love you."

"Rafe, I love you. I know now, fate and destiny has this in store for us. They gave us eternity, when I thought I wouldn't live to see another day. I was always meant to be yours, the way you were meant to be mine. I'm sorry I ever cursed fate."

"What do you mean?"

"I… I want to lay down."

He carries her to bed, gets her settled in, then climbs in. Her hand grips his shirt.

"I'm right here, mia estrela."

<hr>

"Ana, sorry to barge in," Kara says as she enters their quarters. "I knocked, but no one answered."

Ana yawns as she sits up. "Sorry, still waking up. Will lunch be here soon?"

Kara clears her throat. "Um, actually, it's five

o'clock."

"What?" Rafe asks as he sits up beside Ana.

"We came over at noon, but you were both pretty out of it, so we thought it best to let you sleep."

"Thank you," Ana says as she and Rafe get to their feet. She follows him into the closet.

He watches as she slips on a rose-pink gown with a silver tiara. He takes her hand and kisses it softly. "Every day, you grow more into your beauty."

"Thank you." She smiles at him. "Your eyes are my favorite. They light up when you're happy, more so than your mouth."

"Especially when I'm looking at you."

He leans down, pressing his lips to hers as her body folds into him.

"Love, they're waiting for us."

He chuckles softly before getting dressed. They walk to the table, both happy to see the food has been served. Ana's stomach rumbles.

"Are you hungry?"

She blushes in response. "I didn't realize how hungry I am." Her eyes trail to Kara. "How are you feeling?"

"I'm fully healed."

"Do we know how Remus got in?" Ana asks, tearing her roll in half.

"No. How he got in again, you mean. We're looking into it."

"Did you know Kane was his brother?"

Kara sets down her glass, before looking at Ana. "What are you talking about?"

"Bela told us," Rafe explains. "Kane was the oldest. He was a half-brother to Remus, Roban, and Regan."

"How did we not know that?" Evren asks.

"Simply put, he lied. He claimed to be an only child, and nobody questioned it. Same father, different mother. No one here knew."

Ana decides to change the subject. "Kara, I would

like to spend the day with Rafe tomorrow, but Thursday I want to do something, you and me. Can we do that?"

"Yes, Ana. Do you know what you would like to do?"

"Maybe we could cook something?" she asks timidly.

"If that's what you want to do."

"Yay!" Ana beams at Rafe, who returns her smile.

"Kara, I think you made her day."

"Good. One of us has to."

"Kara, that is not nice," Ana exclaims.

"Right. Sorry, Rafe."

He laughs. "It's okay. I'm glad you two are getting along."

"We will disagree, but Kara, I don't want us to fight again."

"I don't, either. I pledged my duty to you, on our first day here. I try to honor that, but in doing so, I sometimes put it above you, if that makes sense."

"Our first day here. God, that seems ages ago. Kara, do you think they'll ever reopen the portal to Earth?"

"They never closed it," Kara says as Rafe's fork slips from his hand.

"Rafe, you lied to me?"

"Ana, please understand. At the time, I had to. You had to stay here, it was too important."

"What are you two talking about?" Kara asks.

"After Rafe told me the truth about his mission to find me on Earth, I begged him to take me back there. He said he couldn't, because they sealed off the portal."

Kara gasps. "Rafe!"

"I had to," he says, slamming his drink on the table. "You know how important it was to get her here and restore the throne. She was our only hope to end the war!" There is a noticeable hitch in his voice as he speaks. "I didn't want to lie to you, Ana. We didn't know each other as well back then, and I was thinking of the kingdom. Believe me, I wish I had never lied to you about any of it."

"Am I angry you lied to me? Yes. I also understand you were doing your job, trying to protect me and the people of this realm. What was it you said to me? Sometimes we must put our duty above ourselves. We have both had to do that."

"I never wanted to hurt you, but hearing you beg to go back to Earth, I was afraid you would command me to take you. I couldn't take that risk. Still, I should've sat down and talked about it with you, instead of lying."

"Rafe, you had lost your father, too. Suddenly, everything was on your shoulders. Honestly, I'm glad you lied."

"What, why?" he asks.

"Because being here with you, knowing you didn't love me, while trying to fight off Kane, I would've been tempted to leave. I know now, the reason I had to come here and suffer what I did. Everything we have endured, not only to bring peace, but it has also brought us closer."

Ana finishes her meal and goes to the window, her mind racing over everything that has happened since her first day in this new realm. Kara and Evren quietly gather dishes and slip away.

Rafe approaches, taking Ana's hand. "If I had asked you at the Snowflake Ball—"

She pulls away, hugging herself tightly. "Please, don't ask about that."

"What's wrong?"

"Thinking now, about everything I've been through, and it's hard for me to talk about the future when I don't even know if we'll have one."

He swallows hard. "What does that mean?"

"I've been poisoned, shot, stabbed, tortured, literally killed. At this rate, I don't even know how much longer I'll be here! Is this what I have to look forward to? A future without hope, knowing my life isn't my own?"

"You have survived all of that, coming out even stronger. We will be together forever, you have no reason to be so afraid now."

"Remus is still out there."

"We will get him."

"Don't touch her!" Rafe screams, nearly knocking Ana out of bed. She jerks away from him and realizes he is having a nightmare.

"Rafe," she cries out as she makes her way to him. "Love, it's okay. Wake up."

His eyes fly open at her words. "Ana?" He grabs her tight against his chest as he weeps into the crook of her neck.

"What happened?"

"A nightmare. I won't… I can't lose you."

"I'm right here. We're both perfectly safe, love. I promise."

"It was so real, I thought I had lost you for good. Ana, please, don't ever let me leave your side again. Even if you have to command me to stay!"

"It won't come to that. We are learning from our mistakes, and this was a nightmare." She kisses his cheek as her fingertips trace his jawline. "We're okay," she assures him.

"I'm so grateful you open up to me," he says as he sits up, pulling her with him and positioning her on his lap.

"What do you mean?"

"If we hadn't talked about what happened in MoonFrost, I wouldn't have known to go to NightFall. Because you opened up, I was able to find you. This is why it's so important we keep doing it, when you are up for it."

Chapter 3

Ana smiles as Rafe sets up dinner. "Thank you for this wonderful day with you. Watching the rain, playing cheshire, we needed this break."

He returns her smile. "I agree." Once she is in her seat, he joins her. "Would you like a bath after dinner?"

Her hand freezes midair, and she nearly spills her drink. She carefully sets it back down. "I know I enjoyed the one in NightFall with you, but I'm not ready."

"All right." He can't help but notice her hand shaking as she lifts her fork. "What's wrong?"

She sets it on her plate before looking at him. "I… I can't. It's… I'm not ready."

"You know you can tell me anything."

"I wrote in my statement that he nearly drowned me in the tub. That is the truth, but it's not all he did."

Rafe braces himself. "Ana, what else did he do?"

Her hand clenches in her lap. "He had a cloth and washed me… all over." She hangs her head. "I'm so ashamed!"

"You're safe now," Rafe assures her as he caresses her neck and chin. "I won't let him touch you again, I give you my word."

"I'm so disgusted, with him and myself."

Rafe stands up and takes her to the chaise. "Ana, you did nothing wrong. You are safe now. I will find him and kill him myself."

"No, don't leave me!" Her grip tightens.

"It's okay. I'm not going anywhere. I'm sorry I said that." He comforts her as best he can. "We will get him, I promise you." His hand lowers to her wing. "How do these feel today?"

Her shoulders sag. "They hurt." She looks at him.

"But I want to continue flying lessons, especially so we can teach Smaug."

"I'm curious to see how that goes," Rafe says, smiling when she giggles in response. His finger trails over her hand and down her wrist. He brings it to his mouth, kissing her scar. "You are so beautiful."

She moves from him and stands before the fire. "That's the last thing I feel right now."

He's instantly beside her. "What do you mean?"

"Before you found me in MoonFrost, I had already started to heal. I... I have more scars now." Her hand trails over her stomach. "They hurt, and—"

"Ana, it's okay. Your scars are badges to wear, showing you went through hell and came out the other side. They are something to be proud of, not ashamed of."

"You're perfect."

"I beg your pardon?"

She laughs softly. "No, I mean with your accelerated healing, your wounds close up. You don't have any scars, despite having been a warrior for over five hundred years."

"Ana, I am full of scars. They aren't visible."

"I'm so sorry. I didn't mean—"

"I know. Believe me when I tell you, you are perfect how you are. My soul is made for yours, my body is made for yours."

"I noticed you in the coffee shop."

"Really?"

"I tried not to stare. I couldn't get over how gorgeous you are. Honestly, I think the barista felt the same way. She's never messed up my order before. I felt a pull to you, and I almost approached you, but I was too shy. If we had spoken, maybe things would've been different."

"Let's focus on the future, the one we have ahead of us. I know it's hard for you to see, but I promise you, it's there."

"How do you know?"

"Close your eyes." He chuckles when she gives him

a worried look. "Trust me, please." She takes a breath and closes them. "Do you see us sitting side by side on the thrones? We attend the briefings, tour the palace, visit Bela and Joph. We will go to MorningStella, go to the beach. We will go into the closet, lying together on our ottoman, nothing between us, our bodies entwining. Can you see this future?" He wipes away a tear that rolls down her cheek.

"I desperately want to. What do I have to do?"

"Ana, be here with me, and that's what we can have, when you are ready."

"My walls. I know we are working on those. The bath in NightFall was a big hurdle for me to overcome. Growing up, reading love stories, and wishing for one of my own, I never saw you coming."

"It was my duty to the queen." His chin nuzzles the back of her hair. "It's my pleasure to serve."

"Rafe!" Ana cries out, laughing. "We are taking it easy today."

"Yes, mia estrela." He walks to the window with her, watching the rain. "I want to lie with you under the sea of stars. You and me, staring up into the eternal night sky. I want us baring our souls, opening our hearts, hand in hand. Can we do that one night?"

"Set up camp in our battlement?"

"Yes."

"That would be wonderful. Yes, please!"

"We have to wait," he says, nodding towards the window. "Don't want to get caught out in that, do we?"

"No, of course not."

"I want to say something to you, something very important."

"Go ahead."

"I want every sunrise with you, every sunset. I want you in my arms, in my heart, for the rest of our lives. I want to tell you every day how much I love you."

"I want the same things," she assures him with a smile.

"Why are you worried?"

"I… I'm excited to spend the day with Kara tomorrow, but I hate how I feel, being away from you."

"I know, but you're right. The two of you do need the time together."

"It's the least I can do for her. She has taken on so much responsibility around here. I miss Kara, the Kara I knew on Earth. She was protective of me there, but we still had fun, too. We'd dance in our pajamas while eating ice cream, playing video games, or watching movies. Now, she's so serious. I hate what this place has done to her."

"Remind her what it's like to have fun, to let loose. I think that will be good for the both of you."

"Thank you for understanding." Smaug squawks, causing Ana to jump. "I almost forgot about you!" She laughs as she cuts him up some fruit.

Rafe goes to her desk, while she feeds him. "It's so organized over here, I'm almost afraid to touch anything."

"Evren must've done that." She gives her attention back to Smaug, opening and closing her wings and laughing when he does the same. He curls up and falls asleep.

Ana goes into the closet to get fresh clothes, then goes into the washroom to get ready for bed. Rafe finishes at her desk, then does the same. His smile falls when he takes her hand.

"What's the matter?"

"I looked at my scars while I was changing." He takes her to the bed. "I'm okay now."

"I'll use the washroom, then we'll snuggle. Deal?"

"Deal." She watches him go in. Her head hits the pillow, and she brings up her arm to inspect where her scar had once been. She wonders about her healing, if it would work anywhere on her.

"Ana, no."

"What do you mean?"

"I agreed to help you with the scar on your wrist, but that's the only one we're doing."

"Rafe, please, they—"

"No, Ana. End of discussion!" He crawls up beside her, lifting her gown, and planting soft kisses along her stomach. "I told you, you are perfect how you are. Now, get some sleep."

She clutches his shirt as he holds her against his chest. He kisses the top of her head, praying she sleeps through the night.

Rafe wakes up when he hears Kara. "Are you guys awake?" she asks, knocking.

"Come in," he calls out. He caresses Ana's face. "Are you ready for breakfast?"

She smiles and stretches. "No, I need more sleep."

Rafe laughs as Kara and Evren take the trays to the table. "Ana, food is here. We need to get up."

"Ugh, fine."

"Are you okay?"

"Yes, love. Just a little tired."

He stands up, then takes her hand and helps her out of bed. He studies her for a moment. "Is that blood on your gown?"

She looks down. "No," she says, turning away. Rafe grabs her hand and gently places her on the bed. He unbuttons her nightgown. "Kara, stop him!" Ana cries out.

Kara runs to them. "Rafe, what are—"

They watch as he opens the gown, revealing Ana's smooth, flawless stomach. Rafe turns away, running his hand through his hair. He takes a breath, then leans down, his face inches from her own.

"What did you do?" he demands.

"You said you wouldn't do it, so I did."

"Your wings of fire?" His hands clench when she nods in confirmation. "What were you thinking? What if you had bled out?"

"I'm fine," she says, getting to her feet and buttoning her gown back up. "See?"

"That's not the point," he snarls. "Sit!" He points at the bed. "After what you did, you need to rest."

"Why are you so angry about this? It's something I did for myself. You have no right—"

"I honestly don't even know what to say. Why didn't you at least talk to me about this?"

"I tried!" she yells, collapsing onto the bed. "You ended the discussion before I even had a chance. How could I talk to you after that, when you made the ultimatum?"

Evren brings her a plate. "Please, eat. I know you need this."

Rafe watches her intently, so Ana takes it. "Thank you, Evren." She eats every bite, then sets the plate on the nightstand. "Please, talk to me now."

"I can't." He turns for the door.

"Rafe, please!" Ana jumps to her feet. "I... I command you to stay!"

"Let me leave, before I say something I will regret."

"You promised you wouldn't leave me!"

"I am leaving because I need to think about this. I am not leaving you."

"Same thing."

"Ana—"

"Fine, I rescind my command." She runs to him and falls to her knees before him. "But I am begging you, stay here and talk to me about this."

"I have nothing to say to you."

Kara gasps. "Rafe! Being angry does not excuse being rude. The queen herself is on her knees, begging your forgiveness. At the very least, you can hear her out."

Rafe bends down to pick Ana up off the floor. They sit on the chaise. "Why did you do it?"

"My scars were hurting again. I pushed it down for so long, then for Remus to... after what he did... everything came to the surface."

Rafe shakes his head. "We were close, so close." He scoffs. "I guess it doesn't matter now."

"What are you talking about?" Realization sinks in, causing a chill to run down her spine. "No, love. Please." She sees the tears in his eyes. "We're feeding off each other's hurt. You need to shut it off. I can't, so it has to be you. I'll be okay, I promise."

He closes his eyes, pushing down his anger, and focusing on his love for her. Her warmth, her pure heart, her kindness, take over and fill him with her joy instead. "Is that better?"

"Yes, love."

He takes her hand. "You should be exhausted after what you did."

"I know, but I'm not."

"I'm worried. Do I need to take you to see Joph?"

"Winslow can run my blood." She runs her fingers over his hand. "Will you forgive me?"

"I already have. I know about painful scars and being desperate to escape them."

"What do you mean?"

"I was on Earth about two weeks, and I was in agony from having my wings removed. I could hardly breathe, the pain was so intense. I tried to focus on my mission, but one night, the pain became too much. I drank an entire bottle of bourbon, trying to numb myself."

"But your guardian abilities?"

"You have to remember, the way Earth is, I was basically a human there. I nearly died from alcohol poisoning."

"I'm so sorry you had to go through that alone."

"While I am still angry about what you did, I understand why you did it. I am going to ask you a question, and I would appreciate an honest answer."

"All right."

"Were you feeling more self-conscious about them because I kissed them?"

"I'm so sorry, but yes."

"I thought I was helping you."

"I know."

"How did you even do this? How did you not wake me up?"

"I didn't plan to do it. I went in to use the washroom, and as I was standing in front of the vanity, I saw the blades. I decided to try it with my wrist, to see if it would work the same way you healed me." Her voice hitches as unshed tears glimmer in her eyes. "I don't know what I was thinking."

"You were traumatized." He looks at Kara and Evren, who are finishing their meal. "Why don't you two go on? We'll see you at lunch."

Kara steps forward to argue, but Evren grips her elbow. "We'll be back after the briefing," she says.

Ana watches them leave. "Is this what I have to look forward to? A future of torture and pain?"

"No, Ana. We've already discussed this. You have a happy future to look forward to. This was a setback, but we are okay now. I think getting cleaned up will do you some good."

"Yes, love. That does sound nice."

"Stay here." He fetches clothing, then meets her in the washroom.

They strip down and step under the hot water. She trembles against him when he reaches for the cloth, so he leaves it hanging up. Like before, he washes her with his hands, his anger growing as he trails over her stomach.

"Rafe, please."

"What's wrong?"

"You're getting angry again."

"I didn't mean to. I just, I think about you hurting yourself and—"

"It didn't hurt."

"What?"

"There was no pain. When I battled Everard, my wings were fire nearly the whole time. He stabbed me in the shoulder, shocked when the wound healed immediately. It didn't hurt. Last night was the same."

"Really?"

"I swear."

"That's the biggest reason I was angry, thinking you hated yourself, or what you are, and that you could hurt yourself because of that."

"It was nothing like that. I needed the scars to go away, to no longer have the reminders of my trauma."

Ana steps in front of the mirror, completely undressed. Her head stays down as she collects herself. Rafe joins her and takes her hand.

"I'm right here. Look when you are ready."

She takes a breath before studying her reflection. "Oh," she murmurs.

"Are you happy with what you see?"

"Yes, I am."

"There was never anything wrong with having scars, you know that, right?"

"Every time I saw them, I was back in that house with my foster brothers. I was back in MoonFrost, chained to the floor and tortured. It was too much."

"I had no idea."

Her shoulders sag. "Because I didn't tell you." She looks at her reflection again, blushing at the sight. Her gown swishes softly against her as she lifts it up in an attempt to cover herself.

Rafe gently takes it from her. "Ana, you have no reason to be embarrassed or ashamed of your body." He kisses her softly. "Every part of you, inside and out, is absolutely breathtaking." His arm wraps around her stomach.

"Rafe, what are we doing?" she asks as his passion flows into her.

"Whatever you want, mia estrela."

A knock at the door interrupts her attempt to kiss him. Rafe groans, while Ana giggles. Another knock.

"Are you guys in here?" Kara asks.

"We'll be out in a moment," Ana responds.

"Food is ready."

"Thanks, Kara."

Ana presses her chest against his stomach. "This evening, we will have all the time together we want."

She slips on a pink gown while he changes, then they join Kara and Evren at the table.

Rafe turns to Evren. "Excited about going to the market with me?"

Evren laughs softly, about to respond when Ana interrupts. "You're letting me have the afternoon with Kara?"

"Ana, you are the queen. I don't let you do anything."

"Thank you." She looks at Kara. "How was the briefing?"

Kara swallows hard. "Okay," she mumbles.

"Kara, what's wrong?" Ana asks.

"Just... we're getting more reports of Remus, and I don't want a repeat of last time."

"What are your scouts telling you?" Rafe asks.

"He did escape NightFall shortly after you arrived there, and we hear that he set up a temporary camp in the forest nearby. I have scouts out investigating. Neither one of you are getting personally involved in this. Am I clear?"

"I'm already personally involved," Ana says as she traces her fingers over her stomach. "Don't worry, we won't get involved."

"You two are going to be the death of me." She smiles at Ana. "Now, to happier things. What are we making in the kitchen?"

"It's a surprise!" Ana says with a grin. Kara grumbles something as she takes a drink. The smile falls from Ana's face. "Do you not want to?" Ana asks, her voice not much above a whisper.

"You know, cooking really isn't my thing." Rafe shoots Kara an angry look. "But I am looking forward to doing it with you today."

"Great!" Ana exclaims with a laugh. "You'll like what we're making, I promise."

"I'm sure I will."

Ana squeezes Rafe's hand. "You and Evren will meet us in the kitchen at four o'clock."

"We'll be there."

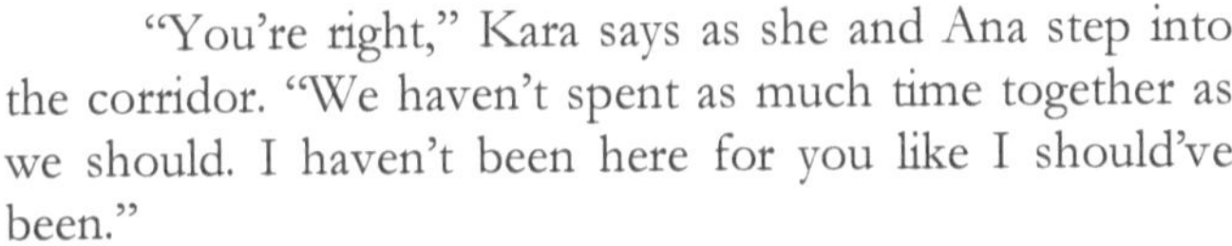

"You're right," Kara says as she and Ana step into the corridor. "We haven't spent as much time together as we should. I haven't been here for you like I should've been."

"Kara, you were literally running the kingdom while I was going through everything. You have put so much responsibility on your own shoulders, it's a wonder you can even walk! I'm back, and I'm ready to help wherever I can."

They arrive at the kitchen, where Yeona and two other members of kitchen staff greet them.

"Mi'lady, as you requested. What are we making?"

"Ingredients, first. Do you have yeast?"

"Mi'lady?"

"What do you use to make your bread with, the rising agent?"

"We call that leaven."

"Ok. We need that." She goes over her list of ingredients, checking out various spices.

"Ana, are you… seriously? Are we making pizza?"

"Yes, Kara." She startles when Kara doubles over with laughter. "What?"

"All of the foods to try, and that's what we're making? It's great!"

Ana smiles, seeing her old friend again. "Told you that

you'd like it."

They prepare the dough, then let it sit to rise. While waiting for it, they make petit cakes. Ana reads the recipe card.

"Is something wrong, mi'lady?" Yeona asks.

"No eggs in the recipe?" She gets two eggs, cracking and adding them in with one hand. Seeing the look on Yeona's face, she smiles at her. She tosses the shells away and smells the liquid flavors. "Ah, this is as close to vanilla as we're going to get." She adds in a splash.

"That is called sugar beanen. It comes from MorningStella."

"Thank you." She puts the petit cakes in the oven. She checks the dough, then splits it in two, kneading it and working it with Kara.

"Mi'lady, you are very good at that!" Yeona beams.

"Thank you. As I said, I loved cooking back on Earth."

"You said this is pizza? I believe I've heard of that. It's quite popular in the country of New York?"

Ana laughs. "New York is a state, and yes, it's very popular there."

"Will you tell us what it was like, growing up on Earth?"

Kara sees the look on Ana's face. "Maybe instead we should—"

"It's okay, Kara." She nods at her. "Um, what would you like to know?"

"What is it like there?"

"Very different from here. There are different climates, different architecture, from farms and plains to cities with buildings that touch the sky. The forests are beautiful, but the beaches seem to be most people's favorite places to visit."

"Where did you grow up?" Maena asks.

"A small town in the middle of nowhere," she answers, laughing. "It was a nice town, I miss it sometimes."

"Mi'lady, that's understandable."

Ana takes the dough, putting it on the bread paddle. Kara strains the tomastes for making the sauce. Ana goes to the wheels of white cheese to try various pieces. She looks at Kara, who joins her.

"This one," Kara says, handing her a piece.

Ana eats it. "Ooh! It's like a mozzarella and provolone mix!" She laughs. "I love cheese!"

"Obviously." They both laugh.

She grates the cheese on, finishing by adding the seasoning. She slides it into the wood oven, then turns back to the second ball of dough, kneading it out and shaping it.

"Ana, now what are you making?"

She grins at Kara as she finishes, brushing butter on and adding the cheese.

"Mi'lady, is that a type of cheese bread?" Yeona asks.

"Yes. We'll cut them into breadsticks."

Kara laughs. "You really miss that, don't you?"

"I miss sitting at our table, eating pizza and cracking jokes."

"Mi'lady, how do you crack a joke?"

"It's a phrase, Yeona."

"I see."

She adds the cheesesticks to the fire oven, checking the pizza, then pulls out the petit cakes, seeing if they are done.

"Dinner and dessert. I must be special," Kara says.

"Sis, you know you are."

"How long have you been wanting to do this?"

"Um, since our first day here," Ana admits as her cheeks flush.

"Why am I not surprised?" They laugh as she removes the pizza and sets it on a plate. Ana checks the cheesesticks, seeing they are nearly done. "Okay, this was fun. You were right, Ana."

Ana notices it's almost four. "Rafe and Evren will be joining us shortly."

"Mi'lady, what do you mean, joining us?"

"To eat here. Is that okay?"

"This is just a simple kitchen. You deserve—"

"Stop, please. There is nothing simple about this kitchen. The wonders you have created here, the amazing dishes. Believe me, it's more than okay."

Yeona bows. "Thank you, mi'lady." She watches Ana get out the plates, setting them on the island they are standing around. She gets the saucepan, spooning sauce onto each plate. "Milady, if I may, what are you doing?"

Ana laughs. "It's okay. You'll see." She takes the cheesesticks out, slicing everything up, as Rafe and Evren walk in. He kisses her forehead.

"You girls have fun today?"

"Yes!" Kara beams.

Rafe smiles at her. "Good. What did we… pizza? I should've known."

Ana starts serving when Yeona runs to her. "Mi'lady, I insist—"

"Yeona, please. It's okay. Really."

"Yes, mi'lady."

"Thank you."

Ana hands everyone a plate with a slice of pizza and a cheesestick. She realizes Yeona and the girls are watching her, so she picks up her cheesestick, dipping it in the sauce before eating it. They follow suit.

"Oh, my! This is delicious. If I may, how did you do this without a recipe?"

"I have it memorized. Believe me, I can make it in my sleep."

Rafe devours his piece. "You did great. It tastes amazing."

"Thank you, love. Did you have fun in the village?"

"We did. Evren bought a few pieces for their quarters while I ran my errand."

"It was fun!" Evren agrees. "Kara, you're going to love what I got."

"As long as it's not a green couch." Yeona and the kitchen staff are confused as the three of them laugh. "Long story," Ana explains.

"Yes, mi'lady." She gasps when she is gathering dishes. "Oh, no. I insist we take care of this."

"All right. We are heading back to our quarters."

Yeona and the two girls bow. "Thank you for this wonderful Earth treat."

"You are very welcome."

"Just when you get a moment, would you give me a recipe card?"

"Yes," Ana answers as Rafe takes her hand.

"How was your trip into the village?" Kara asks.

Rafe smiles. "We had a nice time."

"He ate one of those poultry legs."

Ana and Kara burst out laughing. "Then had room for pizza, too?" Ana asks, shaking her head.

"I have a big appetite."

Kara gags. "Now we are in public!"

Rafe smirks at Ana, who blushes and turns away. They arrive at their quarters, stopping outside the door. She hugs Kara.

"Sis, we needed this. We need to do it more often."

"I agree. Would you like us to bring breakfast in the morning?"

"Yes, please."

"We'll see you then."

They say their goodnights and go inside. Noticing Smaug trying to jump out of his crate, Ana goes to him.

"Here, baby." She lifts him out. He follows her as she walks around. Her wings extend out. She opens and closes them, giggling softly as he does the same before he starts jumping. "Well, I guess Rafe was right about that!"

"About what?" he asks as he joins her.

"Jumping before flying."

Rafe extends his wings, then flies up towards the ceiling. "Wanna try, little man?"

Smaug huffs at him, then looks at Ana. "Oh, no. I'm still learning." She laughs when he squawks at her. "Okay."

She focuses on curving her wings, slowly rising off the ground. Smaug jumps as he flaps his wings. Rafe watches, fascinated.

"How are you doing that? I can't believe what I'm seeing!"

Lowering down, she smiles at him, then steps up to him and takes his hand. "I don't know. I just… do it."

"It's amazing!"

She snuggles into his chest. "I'm going to use the washroom, then I'll meet you in the closet."

Smaug follows her in, and Rafe can only laugh. When they come out a few minutes later, Ana places him gently in the crate.

"I'll be waiting for you."

Rafe's heart speeds up. "I'll be right there."

Ana strips down as she walks to the ottoman. She sits down, crossing her legs as her body trembles in anticipation. When Rafe comes in, she starts to stand, but he gestures for her to stay seated. He sits beside her, trailing kisses from her chin down to the crook of her neck. She pulls onto his lap, her lips meeting his.

Chapter 4

Ana leaves the washroom. When her eyes meet Rafe's, she steps back and lowers her head. He rushes to her and takes her hand.

"What's the matter?" he asks softly, a slight tremble in his voice. Fear and shame pour into him.

"I… I was thinking about this morning."

"It was a bad morning, but everything is okay now."

"I want to ask a question, but I'm afraid of the answer."

"Please, Ana. Ask me anything."

"What did you mean when you said we were so close? That it didn't matter anymore? Close to what? Do you… do you not want…" Her lip quivers as she is unable to continue.

"I was angry and hurt. I gave in to my feelings and said something I shouldn't have said. Believe me, we are okay now, I promise you."

She meets his gaze, noting the sincerity in his eyes, the softness of his expression. "Rafe, I love you more than my words could ever say. I am so deeply, desperately, madly in love with you."

His mouth collides with hers. "I love you, my star. You know how much I do." He leads her to the chaise. "What else am I feeling?"

"I'm missing Earth."

"Do you want to talk about it?"

"Are you sure?"

"Yes, mia estrela."

"All right. I miss going to the café, having the world at my fingertips with my phone. Waiting for news here can sometimes be unbearable. I miss blue jeans and sweatshirts. I miss… being normal. I don't mean my wings but being the queen. I miss being Ana."

"Even if you had been born on Earth, you would never be just anything. You are so special, incredible, amazing." He cocks his head when she laughs. "What's funny?"

"Gee, are you going to yell at me that you love me?"

He joins in the laughter. "I didn't mean to do it that way. I was only trying to convince you of how special you are."

"Thank you."

"Aren't you going to tell me how special I am?"

"No, cause you're a jerk!" she says as she punches his shoulder. In a flash, he has her in his arms and up to the ceiling.

Her laughter makes his skin tingle, as warmth crawls through him along with her joy. "I do have my good moments, right?" he asks as they lower back down.

She kisses him softly. "Of course you do." She yawns. "I am ready for bed."

"Yes, Majesty."

He places her softly on the mattress, tucking her in under the blanket before joining her. She waits and watches him fall asleep. After an hour, she leans up so her mouth is nearly on his ear.

"Rafe?" No response. She tries again, then whispers until she falls asleep in his arms.

Ana jerks awake, covered in a cold sweat. Taking a breath, she sees Rafe sleeping peacefully beside her. She slips away to the washroom, where she sits on the edge of the tub and cries softly into her hands.

This is one of those times she should wake him up, but her shame is overpowering. She cleans off her face at the vanity, her reflection staring back at her. Shame dissolves into anger at the sight of her wings. After retracting them in as tightly as she can, she leaves the washroom as Kara is knocking.

"Are you guys up?"

Ana opens the door, smiling at Kara and Evren as they walk inside. Rafe is instantly beside her. "Ready to get dressed?"

"Yes, love." Ana turns to Kara. "We'll be out in a moment."

"No rush."

"Thanks, sis." Ana goes with Rafe into the closet, sighing as she looks through her gowns.

"What's wrong?" Rafe asks as he buttons his shirt.

"I love these gowns, but I long to take a break from them."

"You said last night you miss jeans. I'm sure you miss your yoga pants, too?"

"Anything to be comfortable, yes." She rummages through the dresser, finding a soft pair of pants with a matching blouse. "Hmm, are these clothes or pajamas?"

Rafe shakes his head. "I'm not sure. You'll have to ask Evren."

"Big help you are," Ana says with a laugh as she places them back in the drawer. "I'll put on a gown."

"Just not that silver-blue one. You look positively hideous in it." Rafe smirks at her.

She stifles her giggle, trying to appear serious. "How dare you?" She holds up a royal blue gown. "Then I shall wear this instead."

"Be that way."

They finish dressing and join Kara and Evren at the table. "Thank you, Evren. I believe you have mended nearly every gown in there. I deeply appreciate your hard work."

"You are most welcome, mi'lady."

Breakfast goes smoothly, then Ana and Evren go into the closet. Ana pulls out the outfit from earlier. "Is this an everyday outfit or pajamas?"

"Those are day pajamas."

Ana tosses them back inside. "I will never learn all of this, I swear."

"You will. We can resume your lessons any time you like."

"Really?"

"Of course, Ana."

"Thank you. That will be nice, to get back into the routine. I long to feel normal again."

"Is that possible for you?" Kara asks as she enters the closet.

"Probably not," Ana answers with a laugh.

"Tired of wearing gowns?"

"A little," Ana responds.

"I'm sorry. I tease you about your yoga pants, but I know you miss the comfort."

Ana sits on the ottoman. "Of all things for me to complain about. It's petty, I know."

"It's not petty. You're already uncomfortable because of your wings. Speaking of which, how do they feel today?"

"Why are you so obsessed with them?"

Kara chuckles. "I'm not! But they are absolutely beautiful."

Ana stands and extends them out. Kara runs to her. "You are obsessed."

"Maybe a little. I think they are amazing! So why don't you love them yet?"

Ana tucks them in, ignoring the gasp from Evren as she steps up to Kara's face. "How dare you ask me that?"

"Ana, I—"

"I died that day. I came back as fire was erupting from my back. It was traumatic and terrifying! But right, they are beautiful and amazing, and that's all you care about." She flees the closet, rushing into the washroom and slamming the door.

"Ana, please come out," Rafe begs from the other side. "Come talk to us."

"I can't. I'm so angry and ashamed. I don't want you feeling any of this."

"Sis, please. Talk to us." Kara knocks again. "Do you want me to go, so Rafe can comfort you?"

"No, just… give me a few minutes."

"We're here whenever you're ready to see us," Kara says softly.

"Thanks," Ana manages before the sob hits her chest. She turns on the shower, folds up her clothes, and hurries inside.

Lost in thought, she jumps when Rafe wraps his arm around her waist to bring her to him. "Sorry. I picked the lock. I couldn't stand the thought of you being in here alone."

"Thank you," she murmurs, wiping away her tears.

"I will never understand how you can feel so much at once."

"It's why I didn't open the door. I don't want you to feel all of this. I wasn't turning inward, I didn't want to hurt you."

"Ana, it doesn't hurt. Here." He spins her around and kisses her softly, stroking one hand through her wing. The other caresses her face, while he concentrates on how much he loves her, loves his wings. "Is that helping?"

"Yes. I wish I could feel that way about my wings, too."

"I was born with them, not traumatized like you. I'm here now, and I want to help you through this."

"I know you do, and I'm so thankful for you. I can talk to you about them because, even though you love yours, you can at least relate a little. Kara has no idea what they are like, she only sees how pretty they are."

"You are right, that I can sort of relate. After not having them for a year there was an adjustment period."

"Really?" she asks, while he washes her hair.

"I had gotten them back, sitting on the exam table, and they fluttered on their own. Startled me."

"I'm sorry you went through all of that. It does make me feel a little better about what I'm going through."

"Why are you thinking about them so much right now? Besides Kara asking, I mean."

"Because I can. I'm not hurt or recovering. I have the time to stop and focus. I am trying to be excited, with what we've done and teaching Smaug. But… it doesn't change the fact that they hurt or that I'm still kind of freaked out about them." Her eyes go wide. "I shouldn't have said that."

"You have no control over how they make you feel, but you can control what you think. We will work on this together. If flying lessons help, we'll continue. Or, if you need a break, we'll take a break. Just tell me."

"Thank you, love." She bites her lower lip. "Would you mind to wash them?"

"As you wish, Your Majesty."

He lathers soap in his hands and delicately works his way through her feathers. His hand teases the edge of one of her wings, and her head rolls back. A moan escapes her lips, and his mouth crashes on hers. He pulls back.

"I feel how tired you are."

"I'm sorry."

"No, Kara put a lot on you first thing."

Ana nods as she steps out of the shower, drying and dressing before preparing herself. She opens the door, immediately face to face with Kara.

"I am so sorry. I will never mention your wings again, until you tell me to."

Ana takes her hand, and they sit on the chaise. "It's not that I don't want to talk to you about them, but you can't begin to comprehend what I'm going through."

"I know, but I thought if I told you how beautiful they are, maybe it would help you feel that way, too."

"I know. It's why I'm not mad at you."

"Still, you're right. I shouldn't have asked you that."

"It's okay if you ask how I'm coping."

"I'll keep that in mind." Kara looks over for a

moment when Rafe steps out of the washroom. "Are you going to the morning briefing?"

"Yes. I want nothing more than to get back into a routine." She stands up. "I'll put on a crown, then we can go."

Kara watches her go into the closet. Ana steps in, walking to the shelf, and lifting up a silver crown. She pins it in then sits on the ottoman, clutching her cross. Rafe enters, but at the sight of her, rushes to her.

"What's wrong?" he asks as he takes her hand.

"Nothing. A little tired from crying, I think."

"You don't have to attend this morning's briefing."

"I want to. We'll have a light lunch and take a nap after."

"Ana, I know how tired you are."

"It's Friday. Let's get through today, and we'll relax this weekend."

"I like the sound of that." He pulls her from the ottoman and wraps his arm around her waist. "What?" he asks when she laughs softly.

"I remember you holding me like this on the battlefield. It was the only kind of physical contact we could have in public that wouldn't end in your execution."

"Ana, your mind, I swear."

"What?"

"You died and grew wings, but you were only thinking of being in my arms?"

"Always."

⁂

Audressa rises from the desk and bows. "Your Majesty."

"Chancellor, how is your family?" Ana asks.

"They are doing well, thank you."

"Any news on Remus?" Rafe inquires.

"Nothing new, I'm afraid. Still waiting on a few

guardians to check in from scouting."

"Who are you waiting for?"

"Roesh and Aylin, Majesty. They are overdue."

"I feel your worry," Rafe says softly as he grips Ana's hand. "I can tell you from experience, delays happen all the time. Do not read too much into it."

"Yes, Rafe. Thank you."

"Majesty, you are pale. Would you like to sit?"

"I'm all right, but thank you."

Rafe spins her around, studying her face. "Ana, your eyes are watering, and you feel as though you could fall right to sleep. Let me take you to your quarters."

Ana glances at Audressa. "I am so sorry—"

"Take all the time you need. Kara and I have this covered, I assure you."

"I appreciate you both."

Chapter 5

"What do you mean, Tinsley made an ass of himself?" Ana asks Kara as she takes a bite of her lunch.

"He practically demanded to know why you weren't there. Audressa reminded him that you had risked your life to save your people while he sits in comfort. Trust me, I thought he was going to cry."

Ana chuckles. "Really?"

"Yes. The people here don't know all of the details, but they know between MoonFrost and NightFall you were hurt because you defended your people. Believe me, you have a lot of admirers here."

"Thank you."

Kara stands and begins to help Evren gather dishes. "Did you want us to bring in dinner or did you want that to be private tonight?"

"Private, please. We'll do breakfast tomorrow."

"Of course."

Ana watches them leave, then goes to the small table by the large fireplace. Rafe joins her, clearly concerned. "Are you okay?"

"I am. Sitting here, enjoying the fire and listening to the rain, it's so calming for me." She lifts his hand and delicately kisses his palm. "Thank you for everything you do to take care of me. Even if it is your duty."

"Ana, not all of this is for that reason. From the moment I saw you in the café, my heart pounded so fiercely, I couldn't catch my breath. It's why I didn't walk up and introduce myself. I literally couldn't. I'm so sorry I was late. You nearly died because of me."

"You saved my life. What are you talking about?"

"After I left the café, I returned to my apartment for a long, hot shower. My back was hurting terribly. I was in there longer than I meant to be."

"If anyone can understand that, I can. It was not your fault. You saved me, my guardian angel."

"That's not how I felt, seeing you on the ground, bleeding out. I thought I lost you."

"You didn't, love. I'm right here."

"You know, I never answered your question. I think it would be nice to get married in August. It's the end of summer, the leaves are changing color, it's beautiful."

"Really?" she asks quietly.

"Yes."

"What is the spring like here?"

"So many trees and flowers different from Earth. You'll want to learn the name of each one, I have no doubt. Are you still wanting to host a spring ball?"

"Yes, the Rose Ball. Oh, is there anything in the summer? A festival or such?"

Rafe clears his throat. "Right, we haven't talked about that."

"What?"

"Your birthday is in the summer."

Ana sits up straight at his words. "What?" she repeats.

"You'll turn twenty-four on June fifteenth." He tilts his head when her jaw drops. "Are you all right?"

"I... Really?"

"Yes. There will be a parade and a festival, now that you're back."

She sighs. "I hate celebrating my birthday, yes. I will, however, because I know this is as much for my people as it is for me."

"I'm always happy to hear you plan for the future. You had me worried there for a while."

"As long as I have you by my side, I can face anything." Her eyes go wide. "Wait, when is your birthday?"

"Oh, as guardians, we don't really celebrate those. We focus on training and protection."

"Rafe, when is it?"

"It's the same day as yours."

"Really? You're exactly five hundred years older than me?" She shakes her head as she tries to take everything in. "Why did you celebrate my birthday on Earth, when you knew it wasn't?"

"I was still undercover. I was trying to keep up appearances." He squeezes her hand. "What am I feeling from you?"

"Worrying about my immortality again."

"Why?"

"Rafe, it's not normal. At least, for me it's not. Everything about me has changed, and I'm still trying to process all of it."

"That's natural. Take as long as you need."

Ana steps out of the closet wearing the silver-blue gown she knows Rafe loves. She added a diamond bracelet, necklace, and earrings with her outfit.

"You are radiant," Rafe says, taking her hand and kissing it.

"You're not so bad yourself," she teases, giggling when he turns away.

"Are we going to the dining hall?"

"No, this is for you and me. I thought we could enjoy a nice, private dinner tonight."

She walks to the table while he puts in for their meal. As he's sitting beside her, he laughs when her stomach rumbles.

"Hungry?"

"We worked up an appetite."

"With you, mia estrela, I always have an appetite."

"Hmm, keep it up, and maybe I'll be your dessert." She kisses him and caresses his wing. "See what you do to me?"

He watches as she stands up and runs from the table, giving herself room to expand her wings. He's instantly on his feet. "What's wrong?"

"Sorry, I'm okay. They were hurting."

"Wow. Seeing you in that gown with your wings is breathtaking."

She smiles at him. "Kara is right, they are beautiful, but I wish she hadn't asked me that."

"I didn't hear her question."

"She asked me why I don't love them yet," Ana replies.

"I can understand why that would upset you. She knows they hurt, and you are still adapting. She should not have asked you that."

Ana approaches Smaug, who is trying to escape his crate. She lifts him out, laughing as he runs circles around her. Rafe steps up and kisses her softly.

Smaug hisses, his wings expanding. Rafe and Ana can't hold in the laughter. "I'm not hurting her!" Rafe explains to the small, angry dragon.

"Be nice!" Ana commands.

Smaug turns away, but he watches when she lifts a few feet off the ground. He flaps his wings and manages to make it into the air, before crashing back down.

Ana picks him up. "You need your practice, but you're doing so well!" She places him gently back into the crate.

There's a knock at the door, and Rafe instructs them where to set up. Ana smiles at the meal spread out on their small table. She joins him when the staff leave.

"Dessert?"

Rafe chuckles. "I think you've earned that."

Ana takes a sip of her cocoa. "After dinner, could we go for a walk? I'd like to stretch my legs."

"And your wings?"

Her smile grows. "Maybe a little."

Rafe leads her up the stairs, and she's grateful the rain has stopped. She turns to Rafe. "This is where you want to set up camp?"

"Yes, once we're past the rainy season. It'll be warm enough. We can use sleeping bags or have cots set up."

"Hmm, I did enjoy snuggling with you in your sleeping bag. It was a… tight fit."

Rafe chuckles. "Oh, so you know what you did?"

"It was an accident, I swear."

"I know. You're lucky Roesh and Aylin were there."

"Hmm, or what would've happened?" she whispers in his ear as her hand caresses his chest.

In an instant, they are in the air, his mouth on hers. "You really love being in the air with me, don't you?"

"I do."

They lower back, when they feel a few wet drops. Rafe grabs her hand and runs to the doorway, stepping in as the heavens open. Ana pulls him back out, standing in the rain and kissing him passionately.

"Ana," Rafe says, leading her back inside. "We need to get you dry!"

"I'm sorry. I really wanted a kiss in the rain."

"Come on, let's get you warm." He rushes her to their quarters, ignoring looks from people they pass on their way.

He turns on the shower and strips her down. After gently nudging her in, he quickly undresses himself, before joining her.

"I loved that kiss, don't get me wrong. I'm worried because you can get sick."

"I'm sorry."

"No, mia estrela. It's okay. Do me a favor though and get warm." He wraps her in his arms. "You're still shivering."

After a few moments, her body finally relaxes. They

step out, dry off, and go to the closet. Wrapped in nothing but a towel, she sits on the ottoman. Rafe is drying his hair when he sees her.

"Just sitting here, wearing nothing?" he teases as he sits beside her.

"I was thinking about our first time in here. The first time you… we… you know."

"Watching you respond to me, it made me feel like a brand-new man."

"Really?"

"Yes. I know with breaking down your walls, I'm scared you'll have another bad reaction. It's one reason I'm so careful with you."

"Rafe, you have been so pivotal in helping me. Growing up the way I did, I swore to myself I would never fall in love. Because I never wanted to be vulnerable. Then you came along, with your perfect smile, amazing eyes, and beautiful soul claiming mine. Everything changed."

"Really?"

"Yes. I know I fought my feelings for you in the beginning, trying to protect myself. You brought me into your arms, into your heart, and my walls began to crumble. After I thought I lost you in the bank, I had to tell you how I felt. Never in a million years would I have guessed I'd be in a realm in a different galaxy." She trembles against him.

"You're getting cold again. Come on."

She slips on her pajamas and robe before joining him on the chaise. "My hands are still cold."

He wraps them in his own. "Better?"

"Well, my lips are cold, too."

He smiles, then leans in and kisses her softly. Her worries melt away as his finger trails her chin and neck. "You are the most beautiful woman to ever exist. You know that, right?"

She blushes as she averts her gaze. "Rafe, no, I—"

"It's true. Every time I wake up and see you, your beauty steals my breath away."

"I love waking up with you beside me. Waking up in MoonFrost, I was so empty, so lost. It was unbearable." Realization sinks in. "I forgot you can feel this!" She scoots away from him. "I won't let you hurt because of me."

"This is how we bring down your walls."

"We'll figure out a way. You can shut it off, right?"

"Ana, yes, I can, but I won't."

"Then what can we do? I see now what you mean, about how much stronger I am when sending out my emotions."

"I want to feel these things with you. Now, what else about being chained up in MoonFrost?"

"Rafe, no!" She jumps to her feet, pacing in front of the fireplace.

"I won't push you, but I think you are ready to talk about this. You only stopped because of my feelings. I want to help you."

Fighting back tears, she hangs her head as she stops walking. "It was horrible. The way he spoke to me, the things he did. I was already angry with myself for how I reacted to your gift, then to find out he killed you…" Her breathing grows ragged.

Rafe steps up beside her, wrapping his arm around her waist. "What do you mean, about the ring?"

"I was so wrapped up in it. I cried myself to sleep, then was taken. Of all the stupid things!"

"No. You had an expectation, and it wasn't met. I'm sorry I was blind to what you wanted."

"I thought I had lost you. I never want to feel that way again."

"Let's get ready to turn in."

"Yes, love."

Ana steps into the washroom, taking deep breaths and realizing he's right, that they can work together through her trauma. She will learn to focus her emotions.

When she steps back out, he smiles and leads her to bed. He tucks her in, returning her smile.

"What are you thinking about?" he asks.

"Our kiss in the rain."

Rafe sighs. "I hope you don't get sick because of it."

"I won't," she assures him. She snuggles against him, waiting like the night before, until she is certain he is asleep. "Rafe?" After receiving no response, she leans closer, whispering in his ear.

***

Ana jerks awake, realizing she is alone in bed. Rafe is with Kara and Evren, setting up breakfast. Without a word, she dashes to the washroom and slams the door behind her. She strips down and jumps into the shower, desperate to get warm.

"Have a nightmare?" Rafe asks, trailing his fingers over her ice-cold skin.

She jumps in surprise. "I didn't hear you come in. Yes, but I'm not ready to talk about it. Please, don't make me."

"I won't, but I see you trembling. Let me hold you."

"I don't want you to feel this."

"Right now, I want you in my arms."

Reluctantly, she walks to him, keeping her head down while he envelops her.

"So much shame," he murmurs, gripping her tighter. "I won't ask." He buries his face in the crook of her neck.

There's a knock, and Kara opens the door. "Ana, I'm putting some clothes for you on the vanity."

"Thank you," Rafe responds. "Mia estrela, do you think you can eat?"

"Yes."

He helps her out, watching as she dries off and dresses. While he's changing, she leans over the vanity, trying to calm her pounding heart. "What can I do?"

Her eyes meet his in the reflection. "I could really use a moment."

"Will you tell me about it?"

"When I'm ready."

They walk to the table, holding hands. Rafe pulls out her chair before sitting beside her. He and Kara watch as Ana pushes her food around with her fork.

"What's wrong?" Kara asks.

"I had a nightmare." Ana sets her fork down. "I was back in MoonFrost, chained to the ground. I was called an abomination. I looked up, but…" She shakes her head. "It was Rafe saying those things. He had a dagger in his hands, and he… I'm so sorry!" She loses the battle and weeps into her hands.

"Ana, you have nothing to be sorry for," Rafe assures her. "It's your way of trying to cope with so much trauma. Did you feel shame because of the dream, or because it was me?"

"Both," she admits.

"You did nothing wrong. You're safe now. I would never hurt you like that."

"Ana, I can't even imagine what you're going through. If you want Evren and me to go—"

"No, Kara. Please, stay."

"You know Rafe is right? You have nothing to be ashamed of. You've suffered to bring peace."

"Thank you." She takes a few more bites, grateful when her racing heart calms down.

Rafe yawns and takes a sip of his tea. "I'm sorry you had a bad night."

She smiles at Rafe. "Love, how do you feel this morning?"

"All right," he says, taking another drink.

"Rafe, I command you to leave."

He freezes, his cup an inch from his mouth. He sets it down. "Ana, what the—"

"You're still here."

Rafe looks down, as though he cannot believe he did not move at her command. "I don't understand?"

"I stayed awake the past few nights, trying to undo your indoctrination. I wasn't even sure if it would work."

"Not that I'm ungrateful, but why?"

"You are my equal. You are my lover, my partner, my other half. It was wrong for me to have so much power over you."

"Try it again."

"Rafe, I command you to go to the closet."

He jumps to his feet, pulling her up and against his chest. "This is incredible! I don't even feel the need to obey. It's so weird, but freeing." His lips are on hers, his hand stroking through her hair. "Thank you for this."

"I'm sorry I didn't do it sooner."

"You did it now. Thank you."

"You're welcome, love."

"We'll get these out of your way," Kara says, collecting dishes. "What are you guys doing today?"

"We'd like to have a lazy Saturday."

"That sounds nice." She smiles at Ana. "We'll do brunch in the morning. Call on us if you need anything."

"Thanks, sis," Ana says, watching Kara and Evren leave. She turns to Rafe. "Stuck with me today?"

"Oh, no. Whatever shall I do?" He asks with a chuckle before kissing her. Her body tenses against him. "What's wrong?"

"After my nightmares last night, I'm not up for anything like that this morning."

"Ana, you said 'nightmares' as in more than one." She turns away and hangs her head. He gently grips her chin, lifting her face. "Please, tell me."

She walks to the chaise and sits down, watching the flames lifting and falling in the fireplace. Rafe joins her. "I dreamed we had Joph run my blood, because of the way I healed myself. My life expectancy went from immortal to one hundred years. I was so scared and angry that I cheated myself out of eternity with you because of a few scars."

"Let's have Winslow run your blood to be sure."

"But what if my dream was right?" she asks softly.
"Ana, we have to know."

Chapter 6

Winslow steps into the exam room. "Morning, Majesty. How can I help?"

"Would you run my blood?"

"Of course. Is something the matter?"

"I'm not entirely sure. I used my wings of fire again, and I want to make sure I'm okay."

Winslow starts to ask, cut short by the sharp look from Rafe. "Yes, Majesty." He removed the syringe and takes the sample. After feeding it into the tray, he turns to Ana. "Joph did an amazing job updating our technology. I am grateful."

"I'm glad to hear that."

The computer beeps, and Winslow gives the screen his full attention. "Everything looks the same. Let's see. Life expectancy, immortal. Genetic markers, thirty-eight. Temperature—"

"Wait, what? How many genetic markers?"

"Thirty-eight, mi'lady."

"Joph said I had thirty-six."

Winslow scrolls through the information. "I see. You are missing two of the guardian genetic markers. The one that prevents infection and illness, and the one that accelerates healing."

"I have that, though."

"Only when you use your wings of fire, right?"

"Yes."

"It's confusing, I apologize. That is all tied in with your Crimson Queen transformation. Magic, science, I'm still not sure what caused it. It happened, and now we move past it."

"That's easy for you to say," Ana murmurs.

"Apologies, Majesty. I didn't mean to be callous."

"Everyone who never died and sprouted wings keep telling me how to deal with it. I know you are all only trying to help, but it doesn't make it any easier. I am coming to terms with it, on my own."

"How do your wings feel?"

"They feel okay. It's my back and shoulders that hurt from the weight of them. I am working with them more, and it helps a little."

"May I take a look?"

Ana starts at his question. "I beg your pardon?"

"I would like to examine your wings."

Ana wants to argue, but the look of worry on Rafe's face causes her to let it go. "That's fine."

"Would you open your wings a little?" Winslow asks as he steps up behind her. She extends them out, and he leans in for a closer look. "They are different, from the guardians, I mean."

"What? How?" Ana asks.

"Rafe's wings extend from the shoulder blades. Even tucking them in, they stick out. Your wings also come from your shoulder blades, but they are flush with your back. It's incredibly unique."

"Great. I came here for answers, only to have more questions." Ana sighs as she closes her wings.

"It's because you aren't fully a guardian," Rafe says.

"Majesty, do you have any other questions for me?" Winslow asks.

"No, thank you. You answered my main one. Do you have any for me? I'm sure, as a man of science, you are curious about me."

"Well, you said you have been practicing with them. Have you flown yet?"

"I have."

"And was it easy or hard to do?"

Rafe laughs. "She took right to it as if she were born to fly."

"Really?" Winslow asks.

"Yes," Ana responds, fidgeting with her exam gown. "Can I get dressed now?"

"I'll step out."

She watches Winslow leave, then Rafe helps her slip it off. He tosses it into the hamper before running his hand gently along her back. "I see what he means. I knew they were slightly different, but I didn't really notice it before."

"Is it bad?" she asks, slipping her dress over her head.

"No, Ana. It makes it a little easier for you to tuck them in instead of walking with them out, the way I do."

She laughs. "It was really weird, the first few days here watching you with your wings. Not that you're weird, but it was an unusual sight for me. I tried not to stare."

"I noticed." He chuckles when she blushes. "You weren't used to the sight."

"Never expected I'd be the one to be stared at," she says as he lifts her from the table.

"Ana!"

Her head goes down. "I'm sorry."

"No, mia estrela. Look at me. It's okay."

They step into the corridor, where she approaches Winslow.

"Thank you, both for your help and your discretion."

"Always, Majesty."

Once back in their quarters, Ana sits on the chaise, and Rafe kneels before her. "You didn't tell me everything about your dream, did you?"

"No."

"Will you now?"

She clasps her hands in her lap, keeping her gaze averted. "I dreamed that once you found out the results, you were so angry and… you left me."

"Ana, even if that happened," Rafe says, sitting

beside her and taking her hand, "I would not have left. I would have been determined to spend every waking moment with you, knowing how precious that time would be."

"Thank you for that."

"But you won't use your wings of fire again, right?"

"Not unless it's life or death, I promise."

"Do you feel up to some light training?"

"Yes. That sounds nice."

"Here or in the training center?"

"I could use some fresh air."

"It's too cold."

"I have warm clothes. We won't stay out long. Please?"

"All right."

She runs into the closet and slips on a winter gown. Rafe smiles when she joins him.

"What?" she asks, adjusting her collar.

"You are too precious in those gowns. My perfect snowflake."

"Oh, the snow is so pretty!"

"We'll go to the training center."

Ana scoffs as she walks to the center of the battlement. "We're already here."

"If you get sick—"

"I won't! Just a few minutes, that's all I need."

"Stretch your wings. I know you know the basics, but I have to ask. Are you sure you're okay to do this?"

"I am."

"I will be holding your hand the entire time."

"Rafe, I know how to—"

"It's nothing against you. We've seen how quickly they can give out."

He takes her hand, once she's finished stretching, and

they take off into the air. They fly twice around the battlement.

"How do you feel?"

"Good," she says with a smile.

Ana gasps when he leads her away from the palace and into the woods. They land in an open field.

"What are we doing out here?" she asks.

"I want to show you something. Keep your wings ready for takeoff."

"What?"

"Follow me." They fly up into the trees. He points to a dragon guarding her nest. Her purple scales reflect in the little light filtering in.

"Oh, Rafe!" She flies in closer but keeps some distance, not wanting to scare the dragon. Ana returns to Rafe. "She has babies!"

"I thought you would like to see them in the wild." He grows concerned when she's shivering against him. "Come on. Let's get you warm."

They fly to the battlement, Rafe keeping Ana in his arms the whole way. She wants to fly, but she knows he's only concerned about how cold she is. They lower down, and he hovers with her for a moment, kissing her as they reach the ground.

He rushes her to her quarters, turning on the shower and instructing her to step in while he orders lunch. She turns to him, smiling when he joins her.

"Thank you for showing me the dragons."

He laughs. "Speaking of which, I'm pretty sure Smaug wants your attention."

"He'll get it once I'm finished in here."

"You're still shivering."

Her teeth chatter, despite the hot water raining down on both of them. "I can't seem to get warm." Her hand touches his chest as she steps closer to him. "But I know one way I can."

"Ana, not right now. After your nightmares and the

stress of going to the Medical Center, I would rather hold you."

"Yes, love."

"In a moment, I'll step out to get us warm clothes. Stay in here until I return."

"I will."

Hesitant, he releases her and leaves the shower. She washes her hair, then shuts off the tap.

"Only get out if you've stopped shivering."

"But I want to sit in front of the fireplace and snuggle with you."

"Come on."

He dries her quickly and helps her dress. His arms envelop her as he lifts and carries her to the chaise. He settles her on it before grabbing the blanket to wrap around her.

"Do you feel sick?"

"No, but I'm cold."

Rafe starts to ask something else when he's interrupted by a knock at the door. He answers it, to find staff waiting with their lunch. They set up on the small table, then leave. Ana smiles as she sits beside Rafe.

"Looks good." The cocoa catches her eye, and she carefully takes a sip. "Thank you."

Rafe notices her glancing at him throughout their meal. When she eats her last bite, she shoots a nervous look his way before lowering her head.

"What's wrong?"

"I'm still cold."

She jumps when his palm is on her forehead. "You feel warm." He gathers the dishes. "I'll take care of these and send for Winslow."

"Thank you."

She watches the fire, biting her lower lip, as she shivers. Rafe pushes her chair from the table, moving her closer to the fire.

"You startled me!"

"Sorry."

He moves his up beside her then sits, taking her hand between his. "Winslow will hopefully be here shortly."

She looks at him when he sighs. "What's wrong?"

"It frustrates me when you get sick."

"I'm sorry."

"No, Ana. It's because I can't heal you, and it's all I want to do right now. What else is wrong, besides being cold?"

"My head and throat are throbbing a little."

Rafe says nothing, pushing down his anger that he can't help her when she needs him. Ana watches the fire, waiting patiently for Winslow to arrive.

When there's a knock at the door, Rafe rushes to it and practically pulls Winslow inside.

"Majesty, what's—"

"She can't get warm, and her head and throat hurt."

Winslow places his bag on the table and removes his machine. He takes a sample and watches the screen. When the results appear, he nods.

"What I thought. Majesty, you have andelaise. You know the routine."

"I get a shot, then go to sleep."

"Yes. Rest is the best thing you can do right now." He injects her arm before gathering up his bag.

"She will," Rafe assures him. "Thank you."

"Of course. Please, keep me updated on how she's doing."

"I will." He smiles when he sees Ana can barely keep her eyes open. "I'm taking you to bed."

"Hmm," she moans softly.

He gently lifts her up. "No, mia estrela. For sleep."

"I'm not tired," she argues while yawning.

He gets her settled in. "I'm going to check on Smaug. I'll be right back."

"M'kay." She falls asleep.

Rafe feels Ana's forehead, angry to find she still has a raging fever. Ana wakes up.

"Why are you mad?" she asks softly, turning her head aside and coughing.

"Because you still have a fever. I'm not mad at you. I'm sorry you felt that."

"Hmm, it's okay. What time is it?"

"A little after four. Do you think you can eat dinner?"

"I don't want to."

"You need it, while you're recovering."

"All right, I'll try."

Rafe steps out to request food before taking care of Smaug. He returns to Ana.

"How do you feel?"

"Tired, cold. Head hurts."

"I'm sorry I took you to the woods."

"I wouldn't have gotten sick that quickly. It was probably a combination of things."

"Like our kiss in the rain?"

Ana sits up, looking at him with tears glistening. "You're really blaming me for being sick?"

"I only meant—"

"Go away!" she cries out as she falls back onto her pillow.

Kara and Evren run into the room. "What is going on? We were nearly in our quarters when I heard her yelling," Kara explains.

"Ana has andelaise and—"

"He blames me!" she yells, her voice muffled by the pillow.

"That's not what I meant." He turns to Kara. "I don't blame her. I don't blame you," he says to Ana as he caresses her back and between her wings. "I'm sorry."

"Then why bring it up and ruin one of my favorite memories? Please, don't do that."

"I'm sorry. Will you forgive me?"

"Fine."

Her body relaxes against his hand, then he hears the light snoring. "Winslow gave her a shot, so she'll sleep through most of this. I do have dinner coming."

"Can we stay with her?" Evren asks.

"Please, I know she'd appreciate that."

"I'll get food for us," she says, giving Kara a quick peck on the lips before stepping out into the corridor.

Kara approaches Ana, running her fingers along her face and neck. "All of these changes, I wish she didn't get sick. I can't believe how warm she is."

"I feel the same way. I don't understand why she isn't protected against it like I am."

"Who knows? What memory was she talking about?" Kara asks. Rafe clears his throat, then proceeds to tell her about their kiss outside. Her eyes narrow in response. "Tell me you didn't mention that to her while she's sick?" Kara sighs when he lowers his head. "Seriously?"

"I know, Kara. I'm an idiot."

"Yes, you are." She laughs. "At least you admit it."

"Kara, I swear—"

"I'm kidding!"

Evren joins them. "Food will be here shortly." She glances down at Ana. "How is she feeling?"

"Warm to the touch. She'll probably eat a little dinner then sleep the rest of the night."

Kara gestures for Rafe to follow her. He looks at Ana before reluctantly leaving her side. "What?" he asks when they are out of earshot.

"We didn't get to finish our conversation the other day. Do you have a ring for her?"

"Kara, why are you so curious?"

"Well, Evren said you were sort of secretive in the village. I know she needs something happy to look forward to, to give her hope. She needs something good in her future to look forward to."

"She already has that. We have talked about our future, and she knows it's with me. Besides, you're the one who keeps saying we should take it slow."

"That was before… well, everything. You know I can't help but worry about her."

"I understand, and I appreciate it. All I will tell you is, I am planning a special dinner with her for next Saturday."

"I won't say anything."

"How are you and Evren doing? Ana said you were a little stressed with wedding planning."

"Evren needs a gown. She and Ana were supposed to go together, but Ana was taken instead. I swear, if it happens again, I'm going full Rambo and mowing down anyone who gets in my way."

Rafe chuckles at the thought. "She's lucky to have a friend like you." He swallows hard and turns away.

"What's wrong?"

"It's weird… having friends, I mean. My whole life has been about training and protection. The only friend I had, betrayed us all."

"Rafe, you know how much you mean to Evren and me, don't you? I know I tease, but I mean this."

"Thank you."

He looks over, when Evren lets staff in. He and Kara join her at the table.

"I'll take a plate to her and see if she'll eat," Rafe says. He walks to the bed and gently nudges Ana. "Food is here."

"Do I have to?"

"Just a little, for me?"

"Hmm, I'll try."

He sits on the edge of the bed and helps her eat most of her meal. Kara brings over her drink, then takes the dishes. Rafe returns to the table, devouring his own meal before resuming his vigil by Ana's side.

"Do you want me to sit with her while you clean up?" Kara offers.

"No, we already got a shower. I was trying everything to warm her up, she was so cold earlier."

"All right. Let me know if I can do anything."

"Thank you." Rafe takes Ana's hand, kissing it before gently laying it across her stomach. "Mia estrela, please get better soon. It hurts me to see you like this." He kisses her softly on the mouth.

"Mmm, Rafe, no. Not while I'm sick. It's gross."

"I promise you, it's not. But I'll respect your wishes."

"Thank you."

"Are you feeling any better?"

"No. My body hurts, and I can hardly swallow."

"Do I need to get Winslow?"

"No, I'll sleep some more."

"That's a good idea. Kara and Evren are staying the night, too. Like a slumber party."

Ana laughs softly. "Great." Her eyelids flutter, then she nods off. Rafe shakes his head.

Kara steps up beside him, keeping her voice low. "Rafe, I know you want to stay awake all night to watch her, but she needs your strength. Get some sleep."

"I will. Thanks."

⁓

Rafe is startled awake by Ana coughing vigorously. Her body shudders, shaking the entire mattress. He turns on the lamp as Kara runs to them.

"Ana, are you okay?" When she continues to cough, Kara grabs her a glass of water. Rafe sits Ana up, but she chokes on her drink. "I'm getting Winslow," Kara says, as she puts on her slippers, before leaving the room.

Evren stands by Ana's side of the bed, brows furrowed, and a look of helplessness drawn upon her face. "What can I do?" she asks.

Rafe shakes his head. "Same as me, wait for Kara to return with Winslow." He strokes Ana's hair, trying to comfort her as her coughing fit only grows worse. Patting her back seems to ease it, so he continues as he pushes down his worry.

Winslow rushes in with Kara. He takes Ana's wrist, feeling her pulse, before opening his bag. He pulls out a syringe and injects her arm.

"This should work on her symptoms. This is a tough case, and she may sleep a day or two while recovering."

"Thank you, Winslow."

"Of course, Rafe. I'll stop by first thing in the morning to check on her."

Rafe watches Evren escort Winslow out before taking Ana into his arms. "Oh, mia estrela. Don't scare me like that again. Sleep now."

"My love?" she murmurs.

"I'm right here."

Rafe is relieved to see Ana eat, even if only a little, before she dozes off. Winslow stopped by before breakfast, telling them to let her rest and keep her hydrated before giving her another round of medicine.

Kara walks to Rafe, who is sitting on the edge of the bed, clasping Ana's hand in his own. "Winslow said she'll sleep today."

"I know. I'm going to stay right here, in case she needs me."

"I understand. Evren is going to mend more of her clothes, and I'm going to help. Well, as best as I can," she adds with a small laugh.

"Do you think Evren could make Ana a hoodie?"

Kara sighs. "It's not appropriate."

"I don't care. After everything she has been through, I think she deserves at least one comfort item. Don't you?"

Kara relents. "But I don't have a pattern."

"My hoodie is in the bottom left drawer of my

dresser. I'm sure Evren could use it."

"I'll take a look. Oh, while we have it out, do you want it mended, for your wings?"

"That would be great. Thank you."

"A hoodie?" Ana asks, keeping her eyes closed. "I miss those. And my Chucks, too."

"I know," Kara says, stroking her hair. "Now sleep."

"Okay. But you won't make Rafe leave, right?"

Kara's face scrunches. "Where would he go?"

"Back to his apartment. Kara, don't make him leave. Please?"

Rafe meets Kara's gaze. "She must be delirious from her fever. She thinks she's on Earth, when she was shot," he explains.

"Ana, do you know where we are?" Kara asks.

"Our house, right?"

"Of course. Get some sleep. I promise you, Rafe and I will both be here when you wake up."

"Ugh, I feel like I'm going to puke."

Rafe grips her arms and hurries her to the washroom, making it in time as she empties her stomach contents. He helps her stand at the vanity so she can rinse out her mouth. She looks at her reflection when her wings open.

"What is that?" she screams, trying desperately to turn around. Rafe holds her tightly.

Kara runs in, gripping Ana's chin and holding her attention. "Ana, you're dreaming. Go back to sleep, and when you wake up, everything will be okay."

"But I have wings," she murmurs. Ana looks around the washroom. "Where are we?"

"I told you, it's a dream."

Rafe carries her to bed, and Kara tucks Ana under the covers.

"Sleep, mia estrela."

"Do… do you have wings, too?" she asks.

"Yes."

"M'kay, I guess I'm not the only one then. That's

good," she says, right before falling unconscious.

Rafe turns to Kara. "Well, that was fun. Good call, telling her it was a dream."

"I never expected that. My heart is still pounding."

"I really hope she doesn't remember any of this."

"Me, too. I'm going back to Evren. Let me know if you need anything."

He stays by her side as morning turns into afternoon. Kara shows him his and Ana's hoodies, and Rafe smiles.

Ana stirs beside him. Rafe helps her eat a late lunch, smiling when she snuggles against him once she's finished. "Ana, can I kiss you?"

"Yes."

He plants a soft kiss on her lips. "I'm glad you're starting to feel better."

"Me, too. I had the weirdest dream, though."

"Oh, what happened?"

"I don't remember."

"Ana, do you know where you are?"

She opens her eyes and looks around the room. "Our quarters, right?"

"Just making sure you're okay."

She laughs. "Rafe, you're weird."

A few hours later, Rafe takes Ana to the shower to clean up before bed. They are under the water when Kara walks into the room.

"Ana, I have fresh clothes for you. Rafe, do you want me to get you some, too?"

"That would be great. Thanks." He washes Ana, then sits her on the side of the tub while he hurries to clean himself.

Kara comes in as Rafe is leaving the shower. "I'm sorry," she mumbles, throwing the clothes onto the vanity before running from the room.

He looks at Ana when she cracks up laughing. "Poor Kara. I'm always getting on her about knocking."

Rafe joins the laughter. "Maybe this time, she'll

finally learn." They dry off and dress. He carries Ana to bed. "I'll be right back." He approaches Kara, who is looking out the window. "Thanks for the clothes."

"You're welcome," she says, keeping her eyes down.

"Kara, you have no reason to be embarrassed."

"I know, but—"

"If anything, you should feel honored."

She lifts her head and bellows with a deep laugh. "Rafe, Ana is right. You are a jerk!"

"Only to you."

Kara shakes her head before turning serious. "I am sorry I forgot to knock." She looks at Ana. "How is she?"

"She's getting better. Definitely tired. Just holding her, I was about to fall sleep. She is so powerful when it comes to sending out how she's feeling."

"I can't imagine."

He gives her a smile before joining Ana. Her hand grips his when he sits beside her. "Still awake?" he asks.

"I was waiting for you."

"How do you feel?"

"A little cold."

He rests his palm on her forehead. "I think your fever is gone, so that's good."

"Yes, love." She yawns. "Will things be back to normal tomorrow?"

"What do you mean?"

"Will my wings be gone? I don't want them anymore."

"Ana—" He stops when he realizes she fell back asleep.

Rafe can only stare, concerned at first, but anger begins to fester within him at her words. He kisses her forehead. "Sleep, mia estrela."

He goes into the washroom, splashing cool water on his face. His fists clench as her words replay in his mind, and he cries out, punching the wall.

Kara bursts in. "Rafe, what's wrong?" She sees the

blood on his knuckles. "Did you punch the wall?" His head goes down as his hand heals. "What happened?"

"Right before Ana fell asleep, she said she doesn't want her wings anymore."

"Rafe, she had a horrible fever! She probably won't even remember saying that in the morning."

"I know you're right, but it hurt me to hear her say that."

"Just because you love your wings—"

"That's not it, Kara. It hurt because I keep thinking we are getting closer to her accepting them."

"She will, in her own time. She is going through the five stages of grief, with the trauma her body endured."

"I didn't think of it like that. I remember hearing about that on Earth. And there's no time frame or particular order, is there?"

"No, and that's why she needs our patience. Even if she were perfectly healthy and said that to you, she has every right."

"Thank you, Kara."

Chapter 7

Ana yawns as she leaves the washroom, relieved to finally feel better. She slept well through the night. She smiles at Rafe, walking up and taking his hand. Immediately, she steps back.

"Why are you angry?" she asks as her eyes glisten with unshed tears.

"I'm sorry. I…" He rushes past her and goes into the washroom.

"What happened?" Kara asks.

"Why is he angry at me?"

"Is that what he said?"

"No, but I could feel it."

"Ana, what do you remember about yesterday?"

"Almost nothing. I know I slept most of the day. Why? What did I do? I'm sorry."

"You did nothing wrong. Stay here." She goes to the washroom, opening the door, and standing in the doorway.

Rafe is splashing water on his face. He scowls at Kara. "Thanks for knocking."

Kara ignores his comment. "Rafe, she doesn't remember anything from yesterday. You have to let this go."

"I'm trying."

"She is getting over being sick, and you have her in tears! I thought you were working on your anger."

"I am. Otherwise, I probably would've yelled at her for saying that."

"Why? She was delirious yesterday. I don't understand."

"You wouldn't," he mumbles.

"Breakfast will be here soon. Can we try to have a quiet, calm morning?"

"Of course. Comfort her while I shower and try to get my head on straight."

"Will do." Kara returns to Ana. "How are you feeling?"

"I'm better, but what's wrong with Rafe?"

"What's right with him?" Kara regrets the joke when Ana's face goes taut. "Sorry. He needs a few minutes to himself. You know what that's like, right?"

"Yes," she responds. "But what did I do that made him so angry?"

"Like I said, nothing. He's mad at himself."

"For what?"

"You two will talk after breakfast."

Kara and Evren set up food while Ana watches the snow falling. She hears the door open and watches Rafe step out of the closet, dried and fully dressed. Her eyes immediately go down.

Rafe steps up beside her. "They're almost done setting up breakfast. Will you eat with us?"

Ana says nothing as she goes to the table. Kara is concerned when Ana pushes her food around with her fork.

"Sis, you need to eat, after being sick."

Ana takes a few bites, glancing at Rafe occasionally as she wonders what she did. Finally, she can't take the not knowing any longer.

"Why are you mad at me?"

Everyone stops. Rafe sets down his cup before facing her. "Kara said you don't remember anything from yesterday?"

"No. Why, what did I do?"

"Last night, before you fell asleep, you told me you didn't want your wings anymore."

Ana is on her feet, backing away from the table. "Rafe, I swear, I don't remember saying that. I know I haven't accepted them yet, but how could you believe I would feel that way?"

He stands up. "I know you didn't mean it."

"Then why are you so angry?" she demands.

"Because it's something I could hear you say."

"Are you serious right now? After our training, our time alone, you really think I would say that? And on top of that, you're angry at me for something I don't even remember? It's bullshit!"

"Ana, I know you're right. I took this personally. I am doing everything I can to help you accept them, and I took those words as my failure. It's why I'm angry. For that, I am sorry."

"I'm getting a shower."

Rafe watches her walk away, wanting to say something, anything, but knowing she needs her space.

Ana strips down and turns on the tap, ignoring the tears streaming down her face. The water refreshes her. She grows angry with herself for saying what she did and with him for believing it.

She collects herself, dries off, and goes to the closet. A blue gown catches her eye, and she slips it on. Her hand trembles as she reveals the mirror. Her wings extend out, heavy and still damp.

"Ana, I'm truly sorry."

Her head snaps up, and she sees Rafe leaning in the doorway. "You know how much I love you, but I'm still hurt by your reaction."

"I know. Even if you said that, and meant it, you deserve my patience and understanding. Please, mia estrela, forgive me?"

"You know I do." She eases into his arms, her head resting on his chest. "But when it comes to my wings, I need your patience and your understanding."

"I know. I'll work on it."

"When are we leaving for the morning briefing?"

"Ana, you are still recovering."

"I am, and I crave a little normalcy right now." She pulls back, staring at him. "And that's not about my wings. Don't take it that way."

"I know. All right, we'll leave at half past nine."

Audressa bows when Ana enters the room. "Majesty, I take it you're feeling better?"

"Can't keep secrets in this palace, can we?" Ana says with a smile.

Audressa chuckles in response. "Apparently not."

"Yes, I'm recovered. In fact, I would like to lead today's briefing."

"Of course, mi'lady."

They discuss the happenings of the realm and read reports. Kara walks in, nodding for Rafe to join her. Ana stops talking, watching them intently.

"Mi'lady, are you all right?"

"Apologies, Chancellor. What were you saying?"

"I was asking if you are holding a Rose Ball in March?"

"Yes, if that's all right?"

"Majesty, you never have to ask that. This is your kingdom, your rule."

"I understand that, Audressa. But, as I am still learning things here, I will ask to confirm there isn't an event or situation that should take precedence."

"My humblest of apologies."

Ana sighs. "No, don't apologize. I wasn't scolding you but explaining."

"Thank you."

Rafe joins Ana when people begin to enter the room. "What's going on?" she asks, low enough that only he can hear her.

"What do you mean?"

"You and Kara."

"Nothing." He sighs when her eyes narrow. "We'll talk after the briefing."

"Fine." She stands at the desk, welcoming everyone

and starting the meeting. Rafe scans the room, staying nearby Ana.

Ana sets the reports on her desk, turning back to the crowd when her wings expand out. Her face flushes, and she retracts them.

"As I was saying—"

"Majesty, what was that?" Tinsley asks, getting to his feet.

"I beg your pardon?"

"Did you mean to open your wings?"

Ana looks at Rafe, unsure of what to say. He gives her a subtle, encouraging nod and smiles. She turns back to Tinsley. "Back to the latest intel, we—"

"What are you?"

Rafe steps towards him, ready to knock him out if necessary, but Ana gestures him back. "Tinsley, please sit and let me resume."

"Fine," he says as he sits. "Freak," he mutters.

Ana gasps, while a wave of murmurs pass through the crowd. Her face turns red as she composes herself. Rafe lunges forward, but Ana steps before him, gesturing him back once more, before she turns to Tinsley.

"Remind me, Tinsley. Where did you serve again?"

He's instantly standing. "I never have."

"Never fought in battle? Never bled for your realm?"

"No, mi'lady."

"I have. I rode out into battle, where I died. I woke up in the woods as these wings," they expand out as she says the word, "grew out of me. I earned them. What have you done, beside run your mouth every chance you get? You are hereby relieved of your position and dismissed from the palace."

"Mi'lady, please—"

"The decision is final. Do not try my patience. Gather your things and leave."

"Yes, Majesty." He runs from the room.

Ana brings her wings back in. "My apologies,

everyone. Is there any other business?" After no response, she dismisses them.

Audressa approaches her. "Mi'lady, are you all right?"

"I am, thank you."

"With your permission, shall I find someone to fill his post?"

"I would appreciate that. Thank you, Chancellor."

"Of course." Audressa joins Kara in the corridor.

Rafe takes Ana's hand, studying her face. "Are you sure you're okay?"

"Yes. Now, what was that about, with Kara?"

"It's nothing bad, I promise. When Evren and I went into the village, I had put in for a special order. Kara was letting me know it was delivered and asking where I wanted it. It's a surprise. Please, trust me on this?"

"You know I do."

"You were incredible, by the way."

"What?"

"The way you handled Tinsley."

"Do you believe me now, about my wings?"

"Yes, mia estrela." He leads her from the room. "Do you want lunch in our quarters or the dining hall?"

"We haven't eaten there in a while." Ana tells Kara where they are heading.

"Evren and I will meet you there."

⁕

"What did you and Evren decide, for your agenda?" Rafe asks as Ana steps out of the closet, dressed in her training gear.

"You and I will train, then we will meet her and Kara in the library for my next lesson."

He looks her over for a moment. "Are we training outside?"

"Yes."

He says nothing, taking her hand and leading her to

the battlement. Ana enjoys the walk. They make their way up the winding staircase before he leads her outside.

"If you start to get cold, or if you feel a chill coming on—"

"I will tell you. You worry too much!"

She opens her wings, stretching them out, while soaking in what little sun is filtered through the clouds. Rafe steps up beside her.

"Do you want to try on your own?"

She fails to hide her surprise. "You would let me?"

"I'll stay right beside you, but yes."

Her wings expand out, and she takes off. Rafe appears, giving her distance but staying close enough.

"It amazes me every time you do this. Meeting you on Earth, never in a million years did I imagine something like this."

"How do you think I feel?" She smiles at him. "I didn't mean that in a bad way."

"It's okay." He takes her hand, pulling her to him, and kissing her softly.

"This is incredible," she whispers. Her eyes go wide when flakes begin to fall around them. "It's snowing!"

"It's getting colder."

"Just a few minutes, please? It's so beautiful."

"Not as beautiful as you, my perfect snow queen." They lower back to the ground.

The wind is blowing, sending tufts of flakes swirling around them, as he embraces her. She leans up and kisses him softly, his fingers tangling in her hair.

"Are you ready for a shower?"

"Hmm, a shower?" she teases as she strums over his wing.

Chapter 8

Rafe and Ana enter the library. She stops abruptly before looking at him. "Rafe, I'm safe here. I feel how tense you are when we walk the corridors, and your head is on a constant swivel!"

"I have been training, and protecting this palace and the royals, for over five hundred years. This is not something I can simply switch off, nor would I even if I could."

"I understand, but I wish we could walk together, holding hands, and enjoy being together instead of you assessing every moment for a potential threat."

"I know it doesn't look like it, but I do enjoy escorting you." He kisses her hand. "It looks like Evren is ready for you. Kara and I will be back here if you need us."

"Thank you, love."

Rafe watches her for a moment before taking a seat beside Kara. "Déjà vu?"

She laughs. "Except for her wings, of course. Oh, I ordered something for Ana, for Saturday."

"Kara, what—"

"It's a gown."

"All right."

Kara cocks her head. "So, are you going to tell me or what?"

"I don't know what you mean."

"Saturday."

He smirks. "You'll have to wait."

"Hmph, fine."

He laughs, watching Ana take notes before she asks Evren a question.

"What happens if there is no heir? If I had been killed, or had not been found in time, and there was no archduke or other royal?"

"We would seek out a prince or princess, far enough from their own throne, such as fourth or fifth child, and see if they would rule here. It has only happened once, about fifteen hundred years ago. That started the new royal line, the one you are a part of."

"No one from the kingdom or this realm could rule?"

"They must be a royal or, at least, have royal blood. It is the law."

"I don't remember putting that in the treaty." Ana scrambles, looking through her bag. She finds her copy and reads a few pages. "Evren, did I make a mistake?"

"Let me see, mi'lady." Evren takes the treaty, scanning until she finds what she is looking for. "No, Ana. Here." She hands it to her. "You did include it."

"Oh, thank God. I read and wrote so much, I could hardly keep up with everything." She clears her throat as she returns it to her bag. "If Rafe and I have a child, will they be accepted as heir to the throne, since he doesn't have royal blood?"

"Yes, because they would have yours."

"Right, of course."

"Now, about your bloodline. Your father was from here, but your mother was from another realm."

"Wait, what?"

"Rosalina was from the MoonSol Realm."

"I'm a child of two worlds?" Ana asks, color draining from her face.

"Yes."

"Why didn't I know this?"

Rafe stands up, concerned at the pitch in her voice. He sits next to her, taking her hand. "Are you all right?"

"It's one thing to find out I'm from another planet, after growing up on Earth. To find out there's more…" She shakes her head, unable to continue.

"Ana, breathe with me. You look like you're going to pass out. Come on, deep breaths."

Kara runs to the pitcher on the table by the window and gets her a glass of water. "Here, sis. Drink."

Ana takes a few sips. "Why did none of you tell me this sooner?"

"Honestly, it's so common here, we didn't think about it. Why is this a big deal?" Rafe asks.

"First, I tried to ask questions about who I am and where I'm from. You all shut me down, because you didn't want to dredge up the past. Second, I grew up on Earth, where everyone was from the same planet. So yes, this is overwhelming for me."

"I'm sorry," Rafe says. "We never intended it that way. We weren't keeping it from you."

"I know. Do I have any family in MoonSol?"

"No. Even if you had, none of them could take the throne, unless they were royal by blood."

"How did my mother and father meet? Was it an arranged marriage?"

Rafe looks at Kara. "Do you know?"

"I do." She joins them. "Your mother was a baroness. He went to MoonSol to meet her and a few other members of nobility. He was smitten with her right away. He asked her to marry him after only two weeks. She said no. He returned here, heartbroken. After hearing how heartbroken he was, she came to visit. She stayed a few months, as they courted. He proposed again, and she said yes. She left her family, and everything she knew, to come here. She was sad and lonely when they first married, as she was adjusting to her new role."

"That sounds familiar."

Kara looks at her. "You and your mother have a lot in common. She set up the school system, insisting every child had the right to education. It's not law, they don't have to. However, I have yet to see anyone refuse to send their child. She focused on education, food, and wages for the working classes. She was such an incredible queen. He loved her dearly, letting her do what she wanted for the kingdom, when he saw how happy it made her." Kara looks away. "Then Killian was born."

"Kara, it's okay. You don't have to talk about it. You answered my question. Thank you."

"Ana, it's your family. You have the right to know anything. I'm sorry about before. It's not my place to decide what you should or shouldn't know."

"You were trying to protect me." She looks down. "I'm tired. I'd like to rest before dinner."

"Are you okay?" Rafe asks.

"Yes, tired. Please, help me to our quarters?" She turns to Evren. "I'm sorry."

"You learned a lot today. We can continue tomorrow, if you want."

"Yes, Evren. Thank you."

Ana slides her books and papers into her bag. Rafe takes it, slinging it over his shoulder. He places his arm around her waist as they leave the library.

Her mind reels over everything she's learned, one of the few times she is grateful Rafe is distracted by watching the corridor instead of focusing on her. Though she doesn't have an appetite, she knows he will be even more concerned if she doesn't eat. Once they arrive at their quarters, she smiles at him.

"Love, would you see about dinner?"

"Of course." He steps over to speak with a staff member.

She unlocks the door, pushes it open, and walks inside. She's almost to the chaise when there's a blade to her throat.

"Remus sends his regards."

Ana grips his arm, able to get the blade away from her enough that she can slip past him. "Rafe!" she cries out, dodging when the man slashes at her.

He grabs her hair and slams her onto the ground. While she is stunned, he pulls out a metal collar and wraps it around her neck. He lifts her up. Ana concentrates, trying to turn her wings to fire to free herself from his grasp, but nothing happens.

"Rafe!" she screams again.

He runs into their quarters, shocked by the sight of them, with the man holding his dagger to Ana's chin. "One wrong move, and I will not hesitate to kill her."

"Please, don't hurt her." Rafe's heart throbs in his chest as he tries to think. He can see no way to get her from the man without her being hurt.

"Now, Your Majesty, put this on," the man instructs, handing her a blue scarf. "Cover your hair with this. Now!" he barks when she doesn't move. Her hand shakes as she complies. "Let's go." They go towards the door when Rafe steps forward.

"Don't take her."

The man digs the tip of the blade into Ana's neck, and a trail of blood forms. "Do not test me, Guardian."

Rafe reluctantly steps aside. The man gestures for him to move away, which he does. They fly past him and out the door.

"Rafe!" Ana cries out again.

He charges after them, calling for the royal guards and guardians to stop them. Rafe finally catches up with them as they leave the palace, but the courtyard is crowded, and he loses them as quickly.

The man drags Ana, with his blade under his cloak and aimed at her side. "Say or do anything, and I will not hesitate to use this. Do you understand?"

She nods. Her heart thrums in her ribcage as she once again attempts to use her wings. When nothing happens, she focuses on another way to get away from him. As if reading her thoughts, his grip tightens.

They veer from the courtyard and into the woods. Ana grows weary after they walk for two hours, before he sets up a small camp. First, he locks her wrists in chains and gags her. He tosses her to the ground before lighting a fire.

Shivering, as the evening wind chills her, Ana glances at the sky from time to time, looking for Rafe or any of her guardians. The man eats a quick meal before relieving himself right beside her. She turns her head away, gagging.

He finishes, then attaches a chain to her bindings, which he proceeds to wrap around his wrist. "Can't have you slipping off while I sleep."

His cloak falls to the ground, where he lies down, and wraps himself up in it. Ana looks at the chain, seeing he barely has a grip on it. She slowly stands up, careful not to move it too much as she does.

She extends out her wings and flies up. He startles awake, grabbing the chain, and yanking her hard to the ground. She cries out when her wing breaks on impact, but her sounds are muted by the gag. Using the chain, he pulls her to him.

"Want to try that again?" he asks, his blade trailing over her arm. Blood drips from the cuts he is making. "I don't care that Remus wants you alive. I will kill you and not give it a second thought."

A gunshot rings out, and he falls to the ground, blood pouring from the gaping wound in his head. Ana pushes down the bile in her throat. She backs away as Remus steps into the camp with great, black shadows following him. She closes her eyes, and when she opens them, he stands before her.

"My, my. The abomination. He was under instructions not to hurt you. And he was told not to stop once he had you. If you want something done right, do it yourself. Come, I'll take you the rest of the way to my camp."

He lifts the chain from the dead man's hand, tugging on it to encourage her to keep up with him. She follows behind, whimpering in pain, and constantly looking up.

They arrive at his camp, and she hangs her head when his men stare, making lewd comments and gestures at her. They go silent when Remus raises his hand before leading her past them. Tents are scattered about, along with a few fires.

Remus leads her into his own. Noticing the table to the

side, Ana approaches it, studying it for a moment before he grips her shoulder. He forces her to sit on his cot.

"Rest for a moment." He laughs when she tilts her head, clearly confused. "Oh, you may be an abomination, but that's no reason for me to be rude." He reaches for her gag. "I will remove this, as long as you promise not to scream. If you do, I will slit your throat. Do you understand?" When she nods, he removes it. "No one can hear us out here, anyway."

"What are you going to do to me?" she asks with a tremble in her voice.

"Since you and your guardian screwed up my last plan, I had to think of something new. I will take you to the palace, once I've finished assembling my army. I am waiting on several hundred more loyal soldiers to arrive. Then we will march on the palace, hold you up to the gate, and I will demand to be let in. As soon as they do, I will slit your throat and put you on display as I take over your kingdom."

"Why not have that man kill me while we were in the palace?"

"That wouldn't do at all. I need an army to take over your throne. Then we will eradicate the guardians and the vampyra."

"Why do you hate them so much? What did they do to you?"

"Do? What did they do? They have the gall to exist! Is that not enough? Then for you, our queen, to be in love with a guardian and friends with the vampyra? It is downright disgusting!"

"You can't mean that. Why are you like this?"

"Sorry, no tragic backstory to unlock here." He chuckles softly. "It truly is this simple."

"Nothing ever is. Please, talk to me. I can help you."

He stops for a moment, staring at her in disbelief, before doubling over with laughter. "You want to help? That's too precious." Turning serious, he straightens up. "No, there is nothing you can do. Well, except die while I take over your throne."

Ana looks up when a man runs in, short in stature with dark hair, thin and agile in build. "The guardians are here!" he announces.

"Thank you. I shall be out momentarily." He smiles at Ana. "I will dispatch your beloved and get ready to gather my men. Everything is going according to plan."

"What do you mean?"

He laughs. "We'll slaughter guards and guardians here, thus weakening the palace's defenses."

"Another trap," Ana murmurs.

"You'll never learn, Your Majesty." He attaches her chain to the rail. "Stay here and rest, I insist." Before she can protest, he puts the gag on her and leaves.

Yanking on the chains, she tries desperately to free herself. Her fingers trace around the collar, but there is no way to remove it. Same for the gag. Her shoulders slump in defeat. Once again, she tries to turn her wings, crying when pain radiates through her left one.

The flap opens, and the man who stalked her at the festival steps in. "Hello, gorgeous. I was hoping we could have some time alone." His fingers trace a line from her cheek down to her neck. When her eyes go wide, he breaks out into a smile. "There it is. I love that look. The realization sinking in that you are trapped, and I can do with you whatever I want."

His hand travels lower, down her neck and to her chest. She closes her eyes, shame washing over her, as he cups her. In an attempt to pull back, she is stopped by the chains.

He chuckles. "Can't go anywhere, I'm afraid." He removes the gag. "That's better. Scream all you want. No one will hear you with the battle raging outside. I long to hear you scream."

Ana clenches her jaw shut, refusing to give him what he wants. He slaps her, but she holds her ground.

"Fine, be that way." He removes his shirt and

unbuttons his pants before sliding them down.

"No," she cries out, trying to turn away when he lies beside her on the cot. He lifts her gown and tears away her undergarment. "Stop!" she screams as his hand continues to move between her legs.

"Hmm, such a sweet girl. Are you ready for me yet?"

She nearly rolls off the back of the cot in an attempt to free herself, but he grabs her and jerks her to him. Her body is flush with shame and her stomach threatens to empty. She cries out, begging him to stop as tears stream down her cheeks.

Though she's limited by the chains, she attempts to fight back as best she can, struggling against him. He grips her arm and drags her under him. His hand raises her gown again, and she stops moving when she feels how firm he is on her thigh. When he leans in further, she cries out, bringing both of her knees up to his groin with as much effort as she can exert. He falls from the cot.

He rolls around, whimpering in pain as he clutches between his legs. "You bitch! You'll pay for that." He manages to get to his feet and slips his pants on. His smile grows as he removes his dagger from its sheath.

Approaching her, he wipes his mouth with the back of his hand before ramming his blade into her stomach. Her cries of agony fill the tent. He pulls the blade out, ready to stab her again, when Rafe appears behind him.

He turns and punches at Rafe, but Rafe grips his wrist and throws him down. Glancing at Ana, he sees the crimson pooling on her gown and down her side. He sucks in a sharp breath before lifting the man to his feet.

Rafe grabs the attacker's head and deftly snaps his neck, then drops his corpse to the ground. He sees the keys on the table and snatches them up. He undoes Ana's chains and removes the collar.

"Do you want to heal yourself or do you want me to?" he asks.

"I will," she responds with a raspy voice. "Then get me

home, please." Her eyes close as the warmth of her wing spreads to the other, healing her completely. They return to their soft plumage as she collapses into his arms.

He wraps her in his jacket, picks her up, and carries her from the tent. His worry over her current condition nearly paralyzes him, but he pushes it down and focuses on getting her taken care of.

Knowing the battle is at the front, he makes his way to the back of the camp before taking to the air. He looks for Melian, and when she sees him, he signals to her that he has the queen. She nods, before resuming battle, looking for Remus, so she can stop him once and for all.

Guardians clash against Remus's army, metal against metal, bodies dropping on both sides. Ana whimpers in his arms. He glances down, realizing that though she has healed, she is utterly exhausted and needs cleaned up.

Rafe flies as fast as he can to the palace. Once inside the safety of its gate, he lowers down by the entrance. Ana is still unconscious in his arms. He takes her to her quarters, knowing Kara and Evren will be waiting for him.

Once in the door, he nearly collapses from exhaustion. Kara takes Ana to the washroom, while Evren gets Rafe to the chaise. He gestures for her to help Kara.

Evren walks inside as Kara is stripping Ana down. She is awake, but not speaking.

"Is she hurt?" Evren asks.

"I don't think so. I don't see any wounds. Ana, are you okay?" Instead of giving any response, she simply stares straight ahead. Kara finishes pulling her gown off and gasps when she sees the torn undergarment caught on Ana's knee. "Oh, God."

"What's wrong?" Evren asks. She sees what Kara is looking at. "Oh."

Kara shakes her head. "You do not tell Rafe. Neither of us will. That is up to her."

"Yes, Kara." They finish getting her undressed.

"I will clean her in the shower. Will you bring us both

clothes?"

"I will." Evren runs from the room, returning a moment later and placing the clothes on the vanity.

Kara finishes rinsing Ana off, then dresses while Evren gets Ana into her pajamas. They help Ana into her quarters. Rafe takes Ana from them and carries her to bed, tucking her in before turning his attention to Kara.

"How is she? Did she heal?"

Kara's head goes down. "She healed, yes."

"What's wrong?"

Kara goes to the fireplace, her arms holding herself tightly as she quietly sobs. Rafe gently grips her arm.

"Please, what's happened?"

"I can't. It's not my place."

"Damn it, Kara. What happened to her?" he demands.

"I think she was… I think he…" Her breath hitches.

"What?"

"I don't know for sure." She wipes her tears. "When I removed her gown, her undergarment was wrapped around her knee, torn up."

His breath sucks in. "What? Kara, was she—"

"I said I don't know!"

He holds her. "I'm sorry. Thank you for taking care of her."

"You need to clean up, Rafe."

"I'll do so in my old quarters. I'm too angry and worried about her, and I don't want her to feel that. I'll return shortly."

"All right." Kara goes to Ana and climbs into bed with her, holding her tightly while she sleeps. She pushes down her tears, trying to comfort her friend as best she can. "I'm sorry for what you went through. I can't imagine." Kara kisses her forehead. "I'm so sorry."

"Kara?"

"I'm right here, Ana."

"I'm home?"

"You are. You're safe now." Kara swallows hard while

building her courage. "Ana, what happened to you?"

"No! I don't want to talk about the camp," Ana cries out, pulling away and sitting up.

Kara crawls to her. "Please, at least tell me."

"Tell you what?"

"Did he… Were you…"

"No. Why would you think that?"

Kara tells her about the washroom. "I was worried when I saw that."

"Well, he didn't. He was about to, but I hurt him instead." Ana looks around the room. "Where is Rafe?"

"He's getting a shower. He'll be back shortly."

"Be back? Where did he go?"

"His old quarters."

Ana is instantly on her feet. "What did you say to him?"

"I didn't—"

"You said something, otherwise he would still be here. He left because you told him that!"

"Ana, please—"

She runs from Kara and into the washroom, slamming, then locking the door behind her. Tears stream down as she sits on the edge of the tub, trying to calm her emotions.

Kara knocks. "He didn't leave, he stepped out. He'll be back any minute, you'll see."

"How could you?"

"I wasn't going to. I was crying, and he demanded to know why. Please, open the door and talk to me."

"Kara, go away!" Ana screams, falling to the floor. "You've done enough."

"What is going on?" Rafe asks as he approaches Kara. He knocks on the door. "Ana, let me in."

"Kara, please," Ana begs, crawling towards the door. "Please, tell Rafe! Tell him I wasn't—" Her breath hitches as more tears fall.

"Open the door and talk to us. We will tell him everything together. Please, sis."

Ana collapses, as the last of her strength abandons her.

"I can't."

Kara picks the lock, and Rafe barrels past her. He picks Ana up and looks her over, checking for injuries. Once assured she is all right, he takes her to the chaise. Kara sits beside her, while Rafe kneels in front of her.

"Please, Ana."

"I don't want to talk about what happened. All I will say, none of them did what you are thinking."

"Thank God," Rafe whispers as he stands up. "We're worried about you."

She gets to her feet. "Just hold me, please?"

He envelops her in his arms as he sits on the chaise, keeping her on his lap, and reassuring her, as she shivers. "You're okay now. You're safe."

"What day is it?"

"It's Tuesday, a little after nine in the morning. When's the last time you ate?" Rafe asks.

"Our snack before training."

"I'll get you a plate," Kara says, leaving the room.

Rafe studies Ana for a moment. "How do you feel?"

"Tired and scared."

"I'm sorry. I never should've let him leave here."

"You say that as if he didn't have a dagger aimed at my throat. I don't blame you. Please, don't blame yourself. I need your warmth and comfort, now more than ever. Please," she adds softly.

"Yes, mia estrela. Whatever you need."

He assures her, while they wait for Kara. When she joins them, Rafe helps Ana eat. Kara and Evren return to their quarters to give them some privacy.

"Love, take me to bed. I need to sleep now."

"Of course." He lays her down. "Give me a moment, and I'll join you." He runs to the closet and changes, then hurries to her. Climbing into bed, he gently holds her tight. "I'm so sorry," he says as she trembles in his arms.

"No, I am."

"For what?"

"What I said in the library. I see now why you constantly scan ahead."

"A lot of good it did yesterday."

"Rafe, please. I can't take your guilt right now."

He closes his eyes, burying his face in the crook of her neck, and overwhelming her with his love. "Get some rest."

Chapter 9

Ana steps out of the closet, dressed in a pale pink gown and silver shoes. Rafe and Kara are setting up lunch. Her stomach flips at the thought, but she knows she must.

"Are you all right?"

Her gaze meets Rafe's. "Sorry, what?"

"I asked if you are all right."

"I'm fine," she says, walking around him. He takes her hand but lets go when she shoots him an angry look.

"Ana, you aren't fine. What's wrong?"

"I want to eat a quiet lunch. Is that too much to ask for?"

Rafe turns away and approaches Kara, looking over his shoulder to see Ana is by the fireplace. He takes the silverware and places it beside their plates.

"We'll delay Saturday," he says.

"That's a good idea," Kara agrees.

"What's Saturday?"

They spin around to see Ana standing behind them. Rafe steps forward. "Nothing. It was—"

"You had something planned?"

"A dinner, for the four of us. Kara and I planned it outside, with the warmer weather approaching."

"We can wait a week or two," Kara adds. "While you're recovering." She puts her hand on Ana's shoulder and guides her into her seat. "You need lunch."

Ana says nothing while they eat, keeping her head down while Kara tries to keep the mood light. When she's finished, she goes to the chaise, wrapping herself in the blanket and sitting before the fireplace. Rafe joins her.

"I see you got dressed. You don't need any more sleep?"

"No. I want to sit here, if that's okay?"

"Of course."

"Where's Smaug?"

"I'll get him," Evren says, going next door. She returns a moment later with the crate and sets it beside the fireplace before lifting Smaug out. "I won't say he likes me, but he has grown accustomed to me."

She places him in Ana's arms. He sniffs Ana, then nibbles on her fingers. They all laugh when he tamps his feet before curling up in her lap.

"Thank you, Evren. I appreciate you taking care of him."

"I'm glad to. He is cute."

Rafe watches Smaug. "He really missed you."

"Yes, he did." She smiles when Smaug nips again. "Evren, I think he's hungry." She lifts him up. Evren returns him to the crate, where she gives him some fruit.

"You were right."

"What's on my agenda for today?" Ana asks.

"Your agenda for today and tomorrow is simply rest."

"Rafe—"

"No. After what you survived, I mean it. You and Evren can have a lesson in here. We can go through some paperwork. For now, stay in here. For me?"

"Yes, love. I will."

Kara sits beside Ana, taking her hand. "Will you tell us what happened at the camp?"

Rafe glares at Kara, while Ana pulls away. "Really, Kara?" he asks as Ana clings to him.

"She was in his camp. She may have seen or heard something that could help."

"As a soldier, I know where you are coming from. As her protector, I say leave it alone!"

"No, Rafe," Ana says. "She's right. I might know something important. I can talk a little about what happened."

"Only what we need to know. Anything else can wait until you are ready."

"Okay." She takes a breath, holds it, then lets it out slowly. "The kidnapper stopped and set up camp. He threatened me when Remus appeared and killed him instead. He dragged me into his camp. His plan was to bring me here, force them to open the gate, then his army would rush in. He said he was waiting on a few hundred men to join him."

"A few hundred?" Kara asks.

"No, wait. He said several hundred more. There was a map on the table, too. I only saw it for a moment." She closes her eyes, shivering as she is back in his tent. "It's marked to show he has allies coming from MoonFrost and MorningStella. But we already figured that."

"What else do you see?" Kara asks.

"Next to the map was a letter. It has a wax seal on it, with… a flower, I think. With a crescent moon underneath." Ana looks at Kara when she gasps. "What does it mean?"

Kara glances at Rafe. "He has a spy in NightFall."

"What? He hates them, and they know it. Why would any of them help him?" Rafe asks.

"Remus probably lied, offering money and sanctuary to anyone who would betray the count and their people. I'll send word to Bela, then I'll stop by and speak to Melian. You did good, Ana. I'm sorry I pressured you, though."

"No, Kara. You were right to do so. If this can prevent another war, it's worth it."

Evren approaches Kara, taking her hand, and they leave together. Rafe holds Ana tighter. "Even so, how do you feel?"

"Safe and happy, being with you."

"But?"

"Well, could we… could we still have a special dinner on Saturday? Even if it's the two of us inside? That would be really nice."

"Of course. I'll have it arranged. Will you dress up?"

"Yes," she answers with a smile.

"Anything for you." He kisses her softly.

"Thank you for saving me."

"You never have to thank me for that."

"I will though, every time."

"I hate to ask."

"What?"

"You healed yourself. Where were you hurt?"

"Why would you ask that?"

"Ana, please."

She tells Rafe about the kidnapper breaking her wing, then the man in the tent stabbing her. "Then you showed up."

"Why wasn't he wearing a shirt?"

"Rafe, please, I don't want to talk about him."

"Why did he stab you?"

"I'm not ready to talk about him!" she screams, clutching his shirt in both of her hands. "Please don't mention him again."

"I'm sorry. I promise I won't. When you're ready, we'll talk then."

"Do you want a shower before dinner?" Rafe asks, packing the pieces from the cheshire match into the box.

"Could Kara help? I think she's feeling kind of left out, since you and I spent the afternoon together."

"Of course. I'm sure she'd love to." He gestures her over. "Will you help Ana clean up for dinner?"

"Everything all right?" Kara asks.

"Yes. I'm a little tired still, from yesterday."

"Right." Kara goes with her into the washroom.

Kara removes Ana's gown when her hand brushes Ana's leg, causing her to gasp and tense up.

"I'm okay," Ana starts but has to stop when her throat constricts. Tears well up, then spill down her cheeks. She pulls herself into Kara's arms.

Evren opens the door. "Oh, sorry. I wasn't sure if you wanted pajamas or a nightgown."

"Pajamas," Kara responds and notices Rafe watching them.

Evren shuts the door, nearly running into Rafe when she turns around. "Is Ana all right?" he asks with a quiver to his voice.

"She will be. Kara is comforting her." Evren glances away for a moment. "Do you think he… you know?"

"She said he didn't. Until she says otherwise, I will believe that."

"Still, I can't imagine how scared she was." Evren goes into the closet, then returns to the washroom. Kara is standing nearby, while Ana is in the shower. "Clean clothes," she says as she sets them on the vanity.

"Thanks, Evren," Ana responds. She shuts off the water and steps out. Kara dries her off, noting that Ana is still tense.

"What's wrong?" Kara asks.

"Nothing. Just help me into my pajamas, please." Ana sees the worry on Kara's face. "I told you that didn't happen. Why won't you believe me?"

"Ana, I want to, but the way you're reacting—"

"Because I was traumatized!" she cries out.

Kara hugs her tight. "I'm sorry. It scares me to see you like this. Please, forgive me."

"I will, but please, don't bring it up again."

"I won't."

Ana gets into her pajamas and joins Rafe at the table. "I heard you yelling. What's wrong?" he asks.

"You know how stubborn she is."

"Both of you." Kara and Evren sit down. Rafe is relieved to see Ana eat without prompting. "This is what you needed. A nice, quiet dinner with friends."

"Ana, I'll probably be gone most of tomorrow, between the Communications Lounge and checking in with Melian and Ramin. Evren will be with me, but don't hesitate to call upon her. Or me."

"Yes, Kara."

"I'm sorry you'll be stuck with Rafe all day."

"Kara!" Ana exclaims with a laugh. Kara sticks out her tongue. "Grow up, sis."

"Nope." She finishes eating, then she and Evren gather dishes. "We'll take these back, then retire for the night. We'll come if we hear any news. I promise."

"Thank you." Ana stands and hugs her, then Evren. "I appreciate you both."

Evren grips her tighter, then steps back, keeping her gaze lowered. "Apologies, Ana."

"None are needed. Yes, you are my handmaid, but more importantly, you are my friend. Remember that."

"Thank you." She takes Kara's hand, and they leave.

Ana sits on the chaise, smiling when Rafe is with her. "Are you okay?"

"A little cold."

He wraps his arm around her shoulder. "How are you feeling?"

"Better, since I showered and ate."

"Kara wouldn't let it go, would she? Asking what happened in the camp?"

Her eyes go down. "I can't blame her. I had a reaction in the washroom, and it's why she asked. She wouldn't let it drop."

"I'm sorry." He pulls her in closer, then brings his hand to her neck and face. "Oh, no. You feel warm. Are you sick?"

"I don't feel sick."

"Get some rest. If you need Winslow, say the word, and I'll get him."

"I promise I will."

"Are you ready for bed?"

"I don't feel tired but, since you said I'm warm, I probably should turn in. Let me use the washroom, first."

"Let me help."

"I'm okay by myself."

"I'm right out here."

"Thank you."

Leaning against the door, he thinks about what she's endured. He takes her to bed and tucks her in.

She lies back, staring at the ceiling, as she relives the camp. The tap runs, and she knows Rafe will be joining her soon. She pushes down the memories, focusing on being in his arms, and the way he soothes her.

Ana laughs when Rafe claims her last pion. "That's not nice," she says with a playful pout.

"You left me no choice."

She studies the board for a moment, then makes a risky move. Her guard takes out his queen, leaving both of their kings vulnerable.

"Hmm, interesting."

A knock at the door, and Rafe goes to answer it. Lunch is set up.

"This morning has gone by fast."

"Well, losing to me…"

When Ana laughs again, Rafe smiles at the sound. After what she's endured, he can't help but worry. They finish their game before eating.

Ana drinks her cocoa. "Thank you for this."

"Any time." Her eyes close, and her mouth goes thin. Rafe takes her hand. "What's wrong?"

She sets her cup down. "Sorry. Having a moment."

"The camp?""

She nods as she wipes away unshed tears. "I should be stronger than this."

"You are strong. You were chained up, but you still fought back."

"I don't see it that way. I certainly don't feel it."

"That's because you are recovering. You know you'll

be okay. Let me comfort you, I will be your strength, until you find yours again."

"God, Rafe. How do you know what to say to me?"

"Because your heart speaks to mine."

She gives in, letting the tears fall, as he holds her in his arms. His love and comfort rush in, calming her.

"I have a confession to make," she says, taking another sip of her cocoa.

"What's that?"

"I'm terrified of Remus."

"It's okay to be afraid. You want the truth? I'm a little scared, too. I don't know what he's planning next. I think he's probably regrouping, which is good because it gives us time to investigate."

"I don't want to lose you," she murmurs into her cup.

"Ana?"

"Sorry. Thinking back, when he told me he killed you and showed me the bloody dagger."

"That is not going to happen. You'll see."

"I'd like a shower."

"By yourself?"

"I don't know."

"What's wrong?"

"If I have another reaction… I don't want you to see me like that."

"Do you want me in the washroom with you?"

"Yes, please."

She steps in while he gets her fresh clothes. Slipping out of her pajamas, the thought of a hot shower brings her a small measure of comfort. When she steps under the water, she lets out a sigh of relief.

Tears spill out as she fights down memories from being chained to the cot. She cries softly, realizing Rafe is in the room, not wanting him to hear.

"Ana, are you okay?"

She rinses her mouth. "Yes," she replies. "I'll be out in a minute."

"Do you need me?"

Yes, more than anything. "No, I'm fine."

She lathers the soap, fighting back tears while she washes herself. She bites her lip to stifle a sob. Lastly, she wipes her face before shutting off the water.

"Rafe, would you hand me a towel please?" She dries herself off, wraps it around her, then steps out. "Are you getting a shower?" she asks when she notices he has stripped down as well.

"I am."

"All right."

As soon as he is in, she quickly dresses and goes to the chaise. She closes her eyes, letting the fire help her dry. *Hello, gorgeous.* Her breath hitches, and she clenches her hands. Lost in her own head, she doesn't realize when Rafe sits beside her.

"Ana?" he tries again. "What's wrong?"

Her eyes open, and he gasps at the pain on her face. "I'm sorry. I was… He was…" She takes a deep breath.

"Is that why you were crying in the shower?"

"I should've known you could hear me."

"Why are you hiding?"

"Thinking of that man, of him climbing on me, it's making me think of Earth. It's too much right now. I'm ashamed."

"This is like the mugger, isn't it? You fought them both off. I know you didn't tell me everything he did, the man in the camp, but you told me enough. You saved yourself."

"I was hurt both times."

"You are alive, and the mugger and that man are both dead. You're safe now." He lifts her onto his lap. "Let me in."

"Rafe, please, all I need at the moment, is to be held like this. I don't want to talk about it."

"You don't have to."

The afternoon goes by, while Rafe comforts her. No words are spoken, but they aren't needed. His love flows into her, calming her and assuring her. He kisses the top of her head.

"Feeling better?"

She's interrupted by a knock at the door. Rafe answers, seeing Kara and Evren. They walk inside and approach Ana.

"Sorry if we're interrupting," Kara says. "I wanted to let you know, Remus broke up his army into small camps, which are scattered across the plains. We've sent patrols, but we don't know which is the main camp yet."

"Thank you for letting me know," Ana replies, keeping her voice steady, while meeting Kara's gaze.

A look of helplessness washes over Kara. Rafe notices it. "Kara, we're going to get him."

"How are you feeling?"

Ana thinks for a moment. "Ready to resume my duties tomorrow."

"Actually," Kara says, sitting beside her, "maybe it's best if you stay in here for another day. Until we get more intel. Evren and I will join you. Rafe and I can go over reports while you two have a lesson."

"That sounds nice."

"We'll bring in breakfast."

"See you tomorrow," Ana says, hugging her. Kara stands, takes Evren's hand, and gives Ana one last look before they leave.

Rafe sits beside her. "Are you upset about staying in tomorrow?"

"No, she's right. I know she wants me to open up to her, too."

"Tomorrow, Evren and I will let you two have some time together."

"That'll be nice." She leans up, kissing him softly.

Ana climbs onto his lap, gripping the back of his neck as her mouth continues to explore his.

"You need to rest."

"I am rested," she argues.

"Ana, after what you've survived, I know you aren't

ready."

"It's because of what happened in the tent, isn't it?"

"How can you ask me that? I mean, yes, but in the sense that you need time to deal with it. Not because I'm ashamed or disgusted. Don't ever think that." He stands up, gently pulling her with him. "Let's pick out a book and read together."

Ana is surprised when Yeona and Maena deliver their dinner. She says nothing while they set up. Rafe tells her to eat, while he speaks to Yeona about Saturday.

Maena stands back, watching. "Majesty, I added a dark cheese. I think you will like it."

"Thank you." Ana eats a few bites of something else, then decides to try it. "It is good." She smiles at her.

Rafe and Yeona return to the table. "Everything will be taken care of," Yeona assures him.

"I appreciate that."

"Rafe," Ana says, her breath hitching as she turns blue.

He rushes to her, not noticing when Maena flees from the room. "Ana!" He grips her tight, realizing she has been poisoned. He turns to Yeona. "Send for Winslow!"

She runs out to do as he commanded. Rafe holds Ana tight, relieved when her color slowly returns.

Rafe lays her on the chaise before rushing to the hall. He alerts the guards to look for Maena before returning to Ana, looking her over and checking her breathing.

"How is she?" Yeona asks as she enters.

"I think I got most of the poison. Now, the woman who was with you. What do you know about her?"

"She is young, but knowledgeable in the kitchen. She is betrothed to a council member. Um, Tinsley, that's his name."

Rafe starts to say something when Winslow arrives.

"What happened?" he asks as he examines Ana.

"Poison."

The machine beeps. "Hmm, interesting. Only traces left." He looks at Rafe. "You healed her?"

"I did. What was it?"

"Shadow of Death mixed with Kiss of Frost. My guess? The first one was to make her sleep, then the second would freeze her heart. I think she got the ratios wrong."

"Thank God for that."

"Do you require anything else?"

"No, Winslow. Thank you."

He and Yeona leave.

"Never a dull moment, right, Ana?" Rafe asks as he sits beside her.

She shakes her head. "Apparently not. Never did I think something like that would happen!"

"How do you feel?"

"Exhausted."

Rafe takes her into the washroom. "Get ready for bed. You need your rest after all of that."

"Yes, love."

When she's finished, he carries her to the chaise. She sits down, resting over the arm of it, as she wonders what is going on. A knock at the door pulls her from her thoughts.

"Someone's here."

Rafe opens it. "Kara?"

She runs in, hugging Ana. "I'm so glad you're okay!"

"I guess you heard?"

"Everyone's talking about it."

Evren laughs. "You should've seen Kara. She practically tackled Maena."

"She was running away! What was I supposed to do?"

"Kara, what are you talking about?" Rafe asks.

"I heard what happened and went straight to the kitchen. Maena was there, trying to dispose of the evidence."

"Kara, thank you for arresting her."

"Ana, I hate to say it, because I know how kind and

forgiving you are."

"What?"

"You can banish Tinsley, not just from the palace, but from the realm itself. I think it's best."

"Kara, we don't know if he was behind this, or if she was acting out of revenge. How can I punish him for something she did?"

"Ana, trust your gut. Do you really think he wasn't involved?"

"No."

"Then make the decree, if you wish, and we'll see him leave."

"Can I think about it? Do you need an answer right now?"

"No, but the sooner, the better. Before he hires an assassin or—"

"Okay, you're right. He's banished from the realm."

"I'll let the royal guards know. And Maena?"

Ana shakes her head. "I'm too tired to be thinking about punishing people!" she cries out. "It's too much!"

Rafe pulls her into his arms. "Shh. It's okay. Kara will take care of it for you if you're okay with whatever she does?"

"Yes, Kara. Please?"

"Of course. Rest, Ana. We'll come back with breakfast in the morning. Is that okay?"

"Sounds good. Thank you."

Kara and Evren leave.

Rafe gets Smaug out for her to play with. He smiles, watching them. Taking Ana's hand, Rafe laughs when Smaug hisses at him. "Back at you!" he says. Smaug runs and hops onto Ana's lap.

"Rafe, you scared him," she says. She pets his head, watching as he nuzzles her hand and arm. "Smaug, you need to be nice!" He curls up, falling asleep. "Oh, baby. I need to get some sleep myself." She gently picks him up and puts him in his crate.

Rafe carries her to bed. "I'll get changed."

"Yes, love." She smiles at him, getting under the covers. He changes and joins her. "What a day." She laughs. "I'm okay. Really." She kisses him, caressing his face and neck. Swallowing hard, she shivers in his arms.

"You're safe now." He pulls her to his chest. "Close your eyes and listen to me, Ana. We're going to have a quiet, private dinner Saturday. We'll dance under the stars, have our favorite desserts, then come back here. We'll sit in front of the fireplace, while you play with Smaug." He looks down as she stops trembling. "How does that sound?"

"That sounds wonderful."

He smiles at her, gently cupping her chin, as he kisses her. "Just know, you have that to look forward to."

"Thank you, Rafe." She snuggles in, clutching his shirt. "You make me happy."

"Always?"

"Forever."

Chapter 10

Rafe wakes up as she's on top of him, kissing him. "Ana—"

"I know what you're going to say. I'm recovered, really. Please, Rafe. Kiss me? Touch me?"

"Ana, I want to touch you, but not in the way you're thinking. I want to touch your heart, touch your soul, touch your very love. Will you let me?"

"Rafe, please, I—"

"I feel it, Ana. I feel your shame, your exhaustion, your pain. You are still recovering. Let me help you through this, so we can enjoy each other when you're ready. Please?"

She hangs her head. "Yes, Rafe."

He sits up and places her on his lap. "Ana, you have nothing to be ashamed or embarrassed about. I know you can feel me, too." He smiles at her. "You know what I want, but I know you are recovering. We have time to be together, to do everything you want to do. For now, rest. For me?"

She leans up, kissing him. "I will, if you'll kiss me more."

"I'll always do that." He pulls her up, kissing her hard, as his hands gently stroke her wings. "How do they feel today?"

"Better. They're not as heavy."

"Glad to hear that." He kisses her again. "It's a little after seven. Are you ready for breakfast?"

"Yes. Is it us or—"

"I'll see if they're up yet."

He steps out, going to Kara and Evren's quarters, then knocks softly. Kara answers. "What's wrong?"

"Nothing. Ana wanted to see if you were ready for breakfast."

"Yeah. We'll be over in a few."

"All right. I'll see to it."

"Thanks."

He gets the attention of a staff member, orders breakfast, then goes back inside. "They'll be over in a minute," he says, walking to her. "Do you want to get dressed?"

"Yes, please. Will you pick it out? I'm still tired."

"Of course."

He goes into the closet and looks through her drawers. Finding the hoodie Evren made her, he smiles. He takes it and a pair of pants to her.

"I think you'll like this."

Ana picks up the hoodie. "I love it! Evren made this?"

"She did."

"I need a corset or shirt for underneath it, please."

"Oh, sorry. I didn't realize. I'll grab you something."

He finds a long sleeve, cotton shirt, which he takes to her. "Thanks," she says, taking it. She stands beside the bed, slipping on the clothes, and then smiles down at the hoodie.

"You missed that, didn't you?"

She laughs. "Yes, I did." She leans against the bed.

"Where do you want to go?" Rafe asks.

"The chaise, for now?"

"Of course!" He picks her up, carrying her to it as Kara and Evren walk in. "Really, Kara? I thought you learned your lesson about not knocking?"

Her face starts to flush, but she laughs instead. "Rafe, stop. I am sorry I forgot." She grins at Ana. "Found your hoodie, I see?"

"Thanks, to you and Evren for making it. It's perfect."

Kara sits next to her. Rafe gestures for Evren to join him at the table, to give them some privacy.

"Sis, how are you this morning?" Kara asked, noting Ana's sunken eyes and dark circles.

"I'm okay. Tired, of course, from last night."

"And the camp?"

"I'm getting better." The garment bag in Evren's arms

catches her eye. "What does Evren have?"

"It's a surprise for you. I'll show you later."

"All right."

"You look good in your hoodie."

"I feel more normal," Ana says with a laugh.

"But you—"

"No, I know." Her wings extend out. "I'll never be normal, will I?"

"Ana! Are you embarrassed or ashamed of your wings?"

"No, still trying to adjust. I thought, after all this time, I would've accepted them by now. I don't know why I can't." She looks at Kara. "Please, don't tell Rafe this."

"I promise."

"There are moments that… I wish I didn't have them. I get overwhelmed sometimes, by the pain or the heaviness, and I wish they were gone. You can't tell him that. He would hate me."

"Ana, he would never hate you. Why haven't you told us this sooner?"

"I saw how he reacted after I was sick and said I wished they were gone. He was so angry, even though I didn't remember saying it! I can't take his anger, I can't. I'm telling you, because I know I need to open more, to not hide."

"I'm glad you told me. Still, I wish you would talk to him about it. If anyone could understand—"

"That's the thing. He wouldn't. He loves his wings, loves flying, loves showing them off. Everything about them. He can't understand how I'm feeling."

"I see what you mean." Kara gets up, letting staff in to set up food. She gives Rafe a look, before sitting back down. "Will you continue to open up to me?"

"I will. I promise."

Kara wraps her arms around her, holding her tight. "I've missed you, missed us. Cooking was fun, but we need some alone time. You and me."

"I know you're right. We will."

"Okay. Do you need help getting to the table?"

"Please," she says, bringing her wings in as they stand. "Thanks, sis."

"Any time."

Rafe smiles at them both. He looks at Evren, happy to see Kara happy. "Are you guys staying with us today? Paperwork and a lesson?"

"If the queen will have us," Kara says.

"Yes, Sage."

They laugh. "All right then."

"Ana, what do you want to learn about today?" Kara asks.

"The vampyra."

"What about them?" Evren inquires.

"I want to know about their homeworld and why they came here."

"Why?" Kara asks. "I'm curious to your answer."

"I want to know more about them. They are my closest allies, and I know very little of them. Is that okay?"

"Of course. I wasn't questioning you, Ana. I'm sorry if that's how I came across."

"Thank you." She turns to Rafe. "Will you help me to my desk?"

"Ana, I think you should lay on the chaise or bed."

"Rafe—"

"You're very pale. I'm worried."

She takes his hand. "I'm okay. I want to study. Please, love?"

"You can for an hour, then you're laying down."

"Really?"

"Ana, he's right," Kara says, standing up. She gathers dishes. "You need to rest today."

"Okay. We can sit here while we study."

"Ana, I'll be right back. I'm going to grab a book we need from the library."

"Rafe or Kara, go with her, please? I don't want any of us alone."

"I'll go," Rafe says. "Give you and Kara a moment together."

"Thank you."

Kara sits next to her, taking her hand. "Do you want to see your gift?"

"Yes, please!"

Kara goes to the chaise, picking up the garment bag. She walks to Ana and opens it, showing her the gown. "This is for you to wear when you and Rafe are having a special dinner."

"Oh, Kara! It's breathtaking! I'll wear it Saturday."

"Ana, what do you mean?"

"Rafe and I are having a private dinner. He said it'll be special." She admires the gown. It's navy-blue with a tulle skirt, a royal blue bodice covered with silver moons, and a star clasp across the collar. "Kara, I am speechless. It's beautiful. Thank you so much."

"Of course."

Kara puts it back in the bag, taking it into the closet. Anger flows through her, anger that Rafe would still be planning for Saturday, knowing Ana is recovering. She hangs the garment bag up, then returns to her.

"It's in the bag, so Rafe won't see it."

"Thank you. Do you know something?"

"About what?"

"Saturday."

"Ana, no, he's not. Please, don't take it personally. He wants you happy and recovered before he asks that."

"I know, and I know he's right to wait. Thank you for answering." Ana glances over when Evren and Rafe enter. He kisses her. "Missed you."

He smiles at her. "Missed you. Now, study. Kara and I will go through this paperwork that's taking over your desk."

"Thank you."

Evren sits beside her. "Where do you want to begin?"

"I want to know about our realm, too. How the

vampyra ended up here. I know a little, like how long they've been here. I know their planet became uninhabitable, but I don't know any details."

"Their planet, Sanguine, was created sometime around five hundred million years ago. We won't go into the complete history, the creatures that existed before the vampyra came into being. We'll start with about five thousand years ago, when the people noticed their crops were dying, and there was not as much rain coming through.

"They always had a rainy season, from March to June. It dwindled down to only one month. They adapted, growing new plants, and bringing in plants from drier realms. Then, about three thousand years ago, the rain stopped completely. No one could figure out why. Our queen, Celestia, bid them to come here. By this time, there were only about five thousand of them left. The NightFall quadrant they inhabit now, was uninhabited and untamed. She told them they could have it if they worked and built it themselves."

"With no aid?"

"The queen sent some people and supplies, but she knew the vampyra are fiercely proud. They would want to earn their place, not have it handed to them."

"I can see that."

"They built up their quadrant and have thrived."

"That's why I don't understand why Remus hates them so."

"If I may, he seems to hate anyone who isn't human. There is no reasoning with someone like that."

"He keeps calling me an abomination."

Evren gasps. "Ana, you are so beautiful and kind! How could anyone ever say that to you?"

"It's okay. He's not the only one."

"Ana—"

"I'm sorry. Um, the vampyra. Was Bela's father the capitol leader before he was?"

"Yes. His father, Count De Ville, was ruthless. He

wanted the throne for himself, throwing away countless lives in his quest. I am not sorry he was killed."

"Did Bela gain the position by birth or was he voted in?"

"Each quadrant elects their leader. If a leader dies, it goes to the living spouse or oldest adult child by default. If there is neither, then an election is held."

"MoonFrost goes through a lot of leaders. Is Emory still in charge?"

"Barely, I'm afraid. A lot of their people agree with Remus, wanting the vampyra gone. I don't understand why they hate the guardians."

"What do you mean?"

"They are the original race here. This planet belonged to the guardians."

"When did the first humans arrive?"

"The records are incomplete. Some say only five thousand years ago, others say a hundred thousand. There was a great war, and many relics and records were lost, thus the discrepancy."

"I see what you mean. If this is the guardian's homeworld, and they were here first, how can Remus hate them and believe he has the right to kill them?" She shivers, wrapping her arms around herself, thinking of being back in MoonFrost. "I can see how much he truly hates them."

"Ana, are you okay?"

"I'm fine."

"You're shaking."

"Evren, really," she tries, as tears fall.

"Rafe!" Evren cries out.

He runs to them. "What's wrong?" He looks at Ana. Without another word, he scoops her up and carries her to the chaise. "It's okay, mia estrela. What happened?"

"We were talking about the guardians being the original race here. It got us talking about Remus, and how he thinks he has the right to eradicate the original race. I… it made me think of MoonFrost, what he said and did. I'm sorry."

"It's okay. I'm happy you want to learn all of this, but you're supposed to be resting today. This is too much on you."

"Rafe, I am not weak."

"Ana, this isn't about strength or weakness. This is because you have such a big, loving, wonderful heart. You feel everything so deeply, so truly, that thinking of him hurting us affects you so. Even if you weren't recovering from what you went through, you would feel like this. It's empathy and compassion, something this kingdom has needed for an exceptionally long time!"

"Thank you, love."

He wipes her tears. "You have such a big heart. It's one of the things I love about you. Such a kind heart and compassionate soul. For too long, we had a cruel king. After he died, we had so much war and death, fighting for a throne that no one had the right to claim, except you. Your kindness is a breath of fresh air to us."

"I feel like I have failed as queen."

"Ana, why?"

"Because of Remus. If I can't stop him—"

"We will. He will not destroy us. I swear this to you."

Evren approaches. "Sorry to interrupt. Would you like me to see about lunch?"

"Yes, Evren. Thank you." He turns back to Ana. "You stopped the main fighting, and you will bring about a peace unlike anything this kingdom has seen. I know you will."

"I thought I was supposed to do that when I died and grew these!" she says, exasperation in her voice, as her wings spread open. "If not, then what was the point?"

"Ana—"

"No, Rafe. I didn't mean... please... I—" She closes her eyes, taking deep breaths. Her wings retract. "I only meant, I thought the prophecy said the Crimson Queen would bring about peace."

"It does say that. It doesn't say when. That's the thing

with legends and prophecies, though. How they are interpreted, who writes and rewrites them. You will bring peace. You know you will. Can't you feel it?"

"I want to. I'm so tired of battles, of lives lost. It's so senseless!"

"I know. Believe me, as someone who has fought in countless battles, I know how senseless it all is."

"Rafe, I'm so sorry."

"It's okay. You fought, too. You gave your life defending the people you love. You have every right to speak about it." His fingertips trail over her wings. "Now, what do you want to tell me about these?"

"What do you mean?"

"Something about them is obviously bothering you. Talk to me."

"I don't know what you mean."

"Ana, you opened them earlier with Kara. Then now, I could hear it in your voice. What's going on?" He holds her hand. "Why do you feel ashamed? Are you ashamed of your wings?"

"No," she replies. "I'm ashamed of how I sometimes feel about them. I've been talking to Kara about it because you can't understand what I'm feeling."

"What do you mean?"

"No, please. I'm not hiding, I'm dealing with it with Kara. Please, let me continue with her. Don't ask again."

"I won't. If she's not available or you're overwhelmed, talk to me. I won't get angry or offended by whatever you say. I know I did that day, after you were ill. It was wrong of me, and I'm so sorry for that. I don't ever want you to feel like you can't come to me."

"I know."

"Hmm. All right."

Evren lets the staff in, helping set up lunch, then they leave. "Everything is ready."

"We'll be right there," Rafe replies.

Ana leans up, kissing him. "No matter how I feel about

my wings, whatever I may think, please know that I am truly working hard to accept them. Please, believe that."

"I know, I do." They join Evren and Kara. He watches her push her food around. "Really, Ana?"

She looks at him but quickly drops her gaze. Shame consumes her, of how she thought about her wings, how she has felt about them. She turns away. "I'm not hungry." When she stands, Rafe grabs her hand, gently sitting her back down.

"What's going on?"

She picks up her fork, knowing he won't question her. She eats everything on her plate. Evren gathers dishes. Kara walks out with her.

Ana takes a moment to gather her thoughts. "I'm sorry. I was ashamed of myself, how I felt about my wings. I should do better."

"You are adjusting. Kara put it really great the other day. She said you are going through the five stages of grief, with no particular order. It will take you time."

She hangs her head. "Grief? What am I grieving?"

"Your death."

She looks at him. "What?"

"Ana, you died in battle. The person you are now is not the same woman who rode out with me. Don't get me wrong, you still have the same heart, the same love, the same soul. However, your body changed, transformed, and made you into who you are now. You're grieving the loss of who you were, trying to accept who you've become. It's okay."

"So much time has passed, though. Why haven't I?"

"Good question. Why haven't you?" He smiles when she gives him an angry look. "Seriously, stop and think. What is preventing you from accepting your wings and moving on?"

Why can't I accept them? Why do I have moments where I hate them, where I wish I didn't have them? What's causing me to feel like this?

She opens her eyes, squeezing his hand. "I've always

felt different, weird, rejected. Coming here, I still felt that way. People look at me, expecting a strong, confident queen. Instead, I was constantly under attack and fighting for my life. Then this happened. I felt even more different, more abnormal. I feel like everyone is staring at my wings, staring at the freak, because what else could I be?"

"Ana—"

"No, please. I see now, what you mean. What's stopping me from accepting myself? Me. I am. There's your answer. Because for too long, I have already been an outsider. This only made it so much worse." She wipes the tears from her eyes. "I feel like I will never belong anywhere, as long as I'm like this."

"I could understand that, if this happened on Earth, and you were the only one with wings. You know you're not, though. Why is it so hard for you, when you see me using mine? You see how much I love them and how proud the other guardians are to have them."

"You were all born that way. You grew up with them! I laid in the woods, taking my final breaths, preparing myself for death. Nothing could ever have prepared me for this to happen. Death would've been easier."

"Ana!"

"I don't want to die, that's not what I mean."

"Then what *do* you mean?"

She walks to the middle of the room. He follows her then takes her hand as she extends her wings. "I could say my prayers, say goodbye to you, and lay down. I could accept death because it's something natural. I had no preparation, no warning, nothing, that I would change so drastically. Yes, you were born with wings. It's perfectly normal for guardians to have them. I laid down and died, then grew these as I came back to life. How do you prepare for that?"

"I see. I'm sorry, you're right." He steps up, ruffling her feathers. "What aren't you telling me?"

Her eyes go down. "I don't want you mad at me. That's

why I've been talking to Kara. Your anger cuts through my heart like a dagger."

"Ana, please. Whatever it is, I won't get mad."

She swallows hard before facing him. "I have moments, when they are hurting, when they are too much. I have moments, where I wish I didn't have them." She squeezes her eyes shut.

"Ana, that's okay. Denial is a stage, it's what you're going through. I'm sure you have moments, where you feel like you could accept them, too. Right?"

"I do. When we're flying together, or when you're playing with them. When I'm happy and relaxed, showing them off."

"It's a balance, and you're working through it. That's the main thing. Let me and Kara be here for you. One day, without even realizing it, not only will you accept them, but you'll be glad you have them. You have to forgive yourself, and show yourself the same patience you do with everyone else."

She lays her head on his chest, wrapping her arms around his waist. "I love you, Rafe. I don't know how I would get through this without you."

"I will always be here for you. You know how much I love you."

She leans up and kisses him, while caressing his wings. Her other hand runs along his chest and stomach. "Rafe, I need you. Please?"

He carries her to the washroom. After locking the door, he turns on the shower. He helps her undress, folding her clothes and placing them on the vanity. She removes his shirt before pulling down his pajamas and shorts. She takes them, putting them next to her clothes. He takes her hand and brings her into the shower with him.

His mouth devours her lips as his fingertips caress her. Ana shivers as her body reacts to his touches. He picks her up, smiling as she wraps her arms and legs around him. He leans against the back wall, his hand brushing up her leg and thigh.

"Are you sure you're okay?"

"I swear I am. Please, love. Please?"

His hand moves higher, and he watches her head roll back. She grips his shoulders, sending his waves of pleasure back into him. He nearly collapses as she gives in. She kisses him, hard and hungry before gasping for air, as he puts her on her feet. Leaning against the wall, her legs tremble under her. She gives him a genuine smile.

"Oh, mia estrela. You are incredible." He gently cups her face. "You're supposed to be resting today."

"I needed to relax." She sees the light in his eyes as she says it. "Don't you?" she asks, her hand coming up. "Hmm?" she teases.

Rafe collapses against the wall, his body quaking at her touches. He grabs her arm, kissing her as the waves go back and forth between them. She falls against him, breathless, when he finishes.

He pulls her against his chest. "You are trying to kill me!" he says, when she teases along his stomach and hips. He grabs her wrists, kissing her hands. He wraps his arms around her. "Rest a moment."

"Yes, love." She lays her head against his chest.

"Ana, you are so amazing. You see how you make me feel, how you make me react. Why would you ever doubt anything about yourself?"

"Rafe, what makes you think that?"

"I see it on your face. I hear it in your voice. There are times you wonder why I'm not with you like this. When I'm telling you to rest, to recover. It's never a matter of me not wanting you. I always want you, every second of every day. I have to resist, because you have to get better. Do you see that?"

"I do now."

"You get embarrassed or feel like I don't want you when I tell you no. It couldn't be further from the truth. I know you can feel how much I want you, what you do to me. You can feel when I yearn to be with you."

"You're right. It's me, my brain. I question everything. You know this."

He smiles at her. "I do. Now let's get cleaned up so we can get a lecture from Kara about how you're supposed to be resting."

She laughs as she pulls away. His hands move over her, as he washes every inch. She returns the favor as he leans forward so she can shampoo his hair. They step out, drying off and dressing. She opens the door to find Kara on the chaise.

Ana walks to her. "Hey, sis."

Kara gives her a serious look, before laughing. "Hi, yourself. I'm not going to say anything. I've learned my lesson! Just, will you take it easy for the rest of the day?"

Ana smiles at her. "I will. I promise."

"All right. Do you want to study some more until dinner or get a nap?"

"I'd like a nap." Ana gasps when Rafe picks her up. "Rafe!" she cries out, laughing.

"I heard the queen would like a nap."

"Yes, Guardian." She smiles at Kara. "Will you be here for dinner? Please?"

"We will. We're going to see if there's any news. We'll be back with dinner at five."

"Thanks." She looks at Rafe as he carries her to bed. "Really? I was talking to her!"

"She's leaving. You need rest."

"Yes, love. Are you napping with me?"

"After what you did to me? I need one."

"Ugh! We're still here!" Kara exclaims, packing up the paperwork.

Rafe and Ana burst out laughing. "Sorry," he says.

"Bye!" Kara grabs Evren's hand and runs out the door.

Ana laughs as Rafe is getting into bed. "Poor Kara."

He smiles as she nuzzles into his chest. "She'll be okay. How do you feel?"

"Hmm." She puts her hand on his neck.

"Oh, Ana. I'm so happy."

"I feel that, too."

He kisses her. "Sleep."

"Yes, love." She grips his shirt, holding it tight.

Chapter 11

"Rafe, are you awake? We knocked."

"Sorry. We were really tired."

"I don't need to know. Dinner is set up, if you're hungry," Kara says.

"We're famished."

"Rafe, I swear—"

"I'm kidding! We'll be right there." He caresses Ana's face. "Are you awake?"

"Yes. I'm listening to you and Kara try not to kill each other."

He laughs, sits up, and pulls her with him. "Where's your hoodie?"

"I got warm." She lifts it off her nightstand and slips it on. "I love this thing!"

"More than me?"

She gasps. "Never!" She leans up, kissing him. Her stomach rumbles, causing her to laugh.

He stands, picking her up and carrying her to the table. "Sit and eat."

"Yes, Guardian."

Rafe laughs, kissing her. "Majesty."

Kara sighs. "You two, I swear." Rafe gives her a look. "Seriously, though, I'm happy to see you feeling better. I was so worried about you."

"Thanks, Kara. You too, Evren. For everything."

"We may have a lead on one of his camps, possibly the main one. We have scouts out now, so we're waiting to hear news."

"Oh, to stop this before another battle would be wonderful. I hate the thought of bloodshed but especially right on our doorstep."

"I agree, Ana. Hopefully we can end this soon," Rafe

says.

"I've reached out to the leaders of the other quadrants, to ensure they are with us. They say the men who are marching are rebels and do not represent them. Bela says they've increased the guards and have more patrols."

"I hate that he has to do this. That he feels different, hated for existing." She looks at Rafe. "You, too. No one should have to feel that way."

"It's okay. You're going to get upset again, mia estrela." He kisses her.

"Yes, love." She clears her throat. "Am I able to attend the briefing tomorrow?"

"I think you're recovered enough. It should be okay."

"If you want me to stay in quarters while Remus is out there, I'll understand."

"What do you think?" Rafe asks Kara.

"We'll go together. She'll be fine. I don't want her feeling like a prisoner in her own quarters."

"Again, you mean." Ana realizes they are staring at her. "When I first came here, it seemed I was only allowed to the dining hall, the library, the training center, and here. It felt like a prison sometimes. Where I could go, never being alone, having a set schedule. It was a little much."

"Ana, why didn't you tell me?" Kara asks. "We were only trying to protect you. We didn't want to overwhelm you."

"That's why I didn't say anything."

"Ana! What else didn't you tell us?"

"Nothing. That was it, that I felt more like a prisoner than a princess, but it wasn't all the time."

"You've adapted to your role quite well," Evren says. "We're fortunate to have an intelligent and kind-hearted ruler."

"Thank you, Evren. I don't always feel that way."

"Ana," Kara starts, leaning forward, "you are exactly what this kingdom needed. I'm sure Rafe has already said this, but after dealing with our king, we needed someone with compassion and warmth to rule. You are doing an outstanding job."

"All right, all right. Thanks, everyone. My ego doesn't need any stroking though, really." She finishes eating. "Could we have dessert and cocoa?"

Rafe smiles at her. "Of course. I'll get enough for everyone." He steps out.

"Ana, I know you know this, but you cannot wear that hoodie outside of your quarters."

"I know, Kara. I wasn't going to wear it to the briefing."

Kara laughs. "I had to be sure."

"I'll be proper and regal, don't worry." She looks up as Rafe sits beside her. "My guardian will make sure of that."

"Does she have to be dressed?"

Kara nearly chokes. "Rafe, I swear!"

"I'm sorry."

"Kara would like to keep her meal in her stomach, where it belongs."

"Yes, Ana." He winks at her, eating his food.

"Evren, thank you for my hoodie. Did you make one for yourself?"

"You're welcome. No, Ana. I don't care for them."

"Can I ask why not?"

"I don't like things touching my ears."

Ana laughs. "Oh, you don't wear the hood."

"What? Then what's the point of it?"

She turns to Kara. "Help me out here?"

Kara laughs as well. "It's more of a comfort thing than a clothing thing, Evren."

"Okay."

They finish eating. Kara and Evren gather the dishes. Kara lets staff in with cocoa and desserts, then the staff leave. Ana happily drinks her cocoa and smiles at Rafe.

"Thank you."

He returns her smile. "Of course."

Kara eats some dessert. "Everything is so good." She

turns to Ana and Rafe. "Are we doing breakfast in the morning?"

"What do you want to do?" Rafe asks Ana.

"Kara, yes. We'll eat together tomorrow, do the morning briefing, and have a lesson. Then I would like the weekend with Rafe."

"Of course. Don't hesitate to call on me when you get sick of him."

"Kara, be nice."

"Yes, Ana." They finish and gather up dishes. "We'll see you at eight in the morning."

"Night." She watches them leave before turning back to Rafe. "Seriously? You and Kara? What am I going to do with you?" She smacks his arm. "Jerk!"

He laughs, kissing her. "I'm sorry. I'll be nice."

She goes into the closet, getting fresh clothes. She checks on Smaug, who is sound asleep. Rafe steps in. Ana walks up and kisses him. "Just getting changed."

"Do you want me to step out?"

"I'm okay." She gets ready for bed, then sits on the chaise. "I'll wait for my guardian."

He smiles at her, going into the washroom. While waiting for him, she watches the flames. He picks her up and carries her to bed.

"Now, mi'lady, sleep."

"Yes, Rafe." She kisses him, clutching his shirt. "What?" she asks when he's smiling at her.

"You, holding my shirt."

"Rafe!"

"What? I think it's cute."

She smiles at him. "Well, I think you're cute!"

He's over her, planting tiny kisses. She laughs, begging him to stop. He pulls back. "Are you okay?"

"Yes, love."

"You're tense. What happened?" he asks as he lies beside her.

"Sorry."

"No, it's okay. What's wrong?"

"You laying on me, it… I was back in the camp." She closes her eyes. "I'm so sorry. This should be a happy, fun moment." She brings her hands to her face. "I'm ruining it! I'm sorry."

He takes her hands, kissing them before he wipes her tears. "Ana, it's okay. We talked about this, about good and bad moments while you're recovering. You didn't ruin anything. You're tired and overwhelmed. Get some sleep, you'll feel better in the morning."

"Thank you." She kisses him. "I know you're right."

"I'm always right."

"Rafe!" she says with a laugh. "Almost always." She thinks of Everard but closes her eyes, pushing it down. Focusing on her love for Rafe, how happy he makes her, being in his arms, brings her a small measure of comfort. "I love you."

He puts his hand on her arm, feeling her overwhelming love for him. "Yeah, you do." He smiles at her. "I love you, too."

She snuggles in, holding his shirt tighter. "Please, don't ever leave me again," she begs softly as she begins to nod off.

"I swear, I won't." He kisses her forehead, laying his head beside hers. "Now sleep." He closes his eyes, taking in her love.

Ana sits up and sees Rafe is sound asleep. She puts on her slippers and goes to the washroom. After she splashes water on her face, she decides she needs a shower. She turns on the water, and is stripping down, when the door opens. Rafe steps inside.

"Are you okay?"

She looks at him as he's studying her. "I had a nightmare. I want a shower. Is that okay?"

"Of course. Do you want me to stay in the washroom with you?"

"Please," she replies.

"Will you tell me about it?"

"After I get cleaned up."

"Okay, if you feel like it. You don't have to."

"I know."

She steps in, opening her mouth to the warm water and letting it rain over her. Tears flow down her cheeks, and she sobs uncontrollably. Rafe steps in but stands back.

"I won't do anything until you tell me to."

Wiping away her tears, she walks to him. "Hold me, please."

"I will." He holds her against his chest. "You're okay. You're safe." His grip tightens when she's trembling. "Ana, please tell me."

"I was back in his camp. This time, the man from the fair, I didn't stop him, and he—"

"It's okay. He didn't hurt you like that. He's dead, you're safe. You're okay, mia estrela. I'm right here with you."

"Can we dry off now?"

"Yes, Ana." He helps her out and hands her a towel. They dry and dress. He carries her to bed. "Can I hold you?"

"Please," she whispers.

He gives her his warmth and comfort, then kisses the top of her head. "Sleep, mia estrela. I'm here, I'll protect you."

"Yes, you will. My guardian, coming in to save me." She smiles at him. "Thank you." She falls asleep in his arms. He strokes her hair, whispering reassurances into her ear.

***

Ana opens her eyes and smiles at the sight of Rafe. She leans forward, kissing him gently. He returns her smile.

"Morning."

"Morning, love," she replies.

"How do you feel?"

"Better. Your comfort went through me. Head to toe. Thank you."

"Hmm." He kisses her again. "You're welcome." He sits up, looking at the clock. "Kara and Evren will be here shortly with breakfast." He looks up as she climbs on him, wrapping her arms around his neck. "Ana, I know you aren't ready. After your nightmare—"

"Rafe, please. I want you to hold me."

"Okay."

She kisses him, bringing her legs around. "Like this? Can we be like this?"

"Yes," he replies, kissing her as he strokes her wing. Her longing for him flows in. "Ana—"

"I'm okay. Only if you want to."

He takes his hand, placing it on her arm, closing his eyes. "I only feel love from you."

"See?"

"Let's keep it that way."

She gives him a confused look. "What?"

"Mia estrela, you are sending me your feelings of love, but your body is tense. You are still on edge. Just lay here in my arms, let me hold you. That's all you are up for right now."

She takes a breath before bringing her head to his chest. "You're right. You can read me better than I can read myself."

"Ana, we have all weekend together. Continue to recover."

"Yes, love."

He stands up, carrying her with him. He sits her on the edge of the bed before sitting next to her. "Mia estrela, I hear it in your voice. I know." He takes her hand. "Now you see how badly I want to be with you, too." He places a gentle kiss between her knuckles. "Like I said, that's never the issue. You—"

"I know you are saying this with love, but I swear, if I hear that one more time! It's all I ever do!" She looks at him, squeezing his hand. "I want to be over it. I want to be recovered, instead of recovering."

"You will be, as long as you don't push yourself."

"Rafe, you can't begin to understand."

"Help me understand. You want walls broken down? Let me in. I'll grab my sledgehammer, and we'll tear them all down. You have to be ready for it, though. It'll feel good, but it'll make a mess. Are you ready for the cleanup?"

She turns and pulls her hand away. "No," she softly replies.

"That's why we do it a little at a time. Break down the wall and recover, so it doesn't overwhelm you." He picks her up, putting her in his lap. "You know how much I want you, you know how much I love you. Neither of those should ever be questioned."

"I don't… I'm not questioning that."

"Then what's wrong?"

"Nothing," she says, standing up. "I'm going to get dressed."

"Ana—"

"No," she says, going to the closet.

She sees Smaug awake. She picks him up and carries him to the ottoman. She plays with him, as tears stream down her face.

"I'm so sorry. You must think I'm ignoring you! I've been through so much, little dragon. I never meant to be away from you. I never wanted to leave, you or Rafe." She takes a breath, not realizing he's listening outside the door. "I only ever wanted to be here, be with you and him. He doesn't understand. I was so scared. I was scared I was going to be killed or… or hurt… and I—" She stifles the sob. "All I could think of was being back here. Now I'm here, and I'm ruining everything. He's been so patient and loving. I try to show him I'm okay, to show him how much I love him, but he pushes me away. I don't know what's wrong with me."

She cries into her hands. Smaug nuzzles her leg. "I know, you love me. I love you, baby dragon." She picks him up and places him in his crate. Trying to decide what to wear, she looks up when Rafe appears in the doorway.

"There's nothing wrong with you." He watches her head go down. He takes her hands and sits on the ottoman with her. "Ana, please. Have you listened to anything I've said?"

"Yes, I have to be careful. I know. How do I know what my limits are, if I'm about to break, if you keep me encased in glass? Only to be looked at, not touched, or used, or opened?"

"You're right." He shakes his head. "I've been too protective of you. You suffered so much fear, pain, loss, that I'm terrified of causing an episode. So, you're right. I've been keeping you from doing the one thing I say you should do, which is working to bring down your walls. I'm sorry."

"Love, even if we did something this morning, then I had an episode and cried, it would still be worth it. Not only because I don't regret a single second you and I have together, but because it is helping me move on. Seriously, though, when was my last episode? I don't mean a nightmare or having an upset moment with crying. Like, a real episode? It's been weeks, at least."

"Ana, you've had some small episodes since you returned from his camp."

"And that's to be expected!" She lets out a sigh of exasperation. "It seems like anymore, I am the one who initiates physical contact. If you don't want me, tell me."

"Ana, you know that's not the case. I know you can feel it."

"You said it yourself, you're better at controlling it than I am."

He slides off the ottoman, kneeling in front of her. "Is that what you've been afraid of? Is that what you think I'm doing?"

She closes her eyes. "Yes."

"Oh, mia estrela. Why would you believe that? I've tried to give you time this week, after what you went through. Otherwise, you know how much I love being with you, you know how much I enjoy every inch of you. How could you ever believe I didn't want you?"

"Because I overthink and question everything. Because I doubt myself." Her eyes open when his lips land on hers. He sits beside her, caressing her wings.

"Ana, tell me you're ready, and I'll do whatever you want. I mean it, anything. Just say the word."

She takes his hands, squeezing them. "I can't. You're right, and I hate that you're right!"

"I meant it. We have all weekend. Let's do business today, with the briefing, your lessons, paperwork. Then you and I will do whatever you want, whenever you want, this weekend. How does that sound?"

She leans forward, kissing him. "That sounds good. You're right. After my nightmare, I should be taking it easy."

"Let's get dressed, have some breakfast, take it one task at a time. Okay?"

"Yes, Rafe."

She walks to her gowns. Looking through them, she picks up a pink one, slipping out of her pajamas and into it. She decides on a silver crown and shoes. Thinking on what Rafe said, she adds a bracelet and a necklace. He's sitting on the ottoman, putting his boots on. Approaching him, she bites her lower lip, eager to see his response. He sucks in his breath.

"God, you're beautiful."

"Thank you, love." She smiles at him then looks over when she hears a sound. "Kara and Evren are here, setting up food."

"I see. Come on." He takes her hand, stepping out of the closet. They go to the table. "Sorry we didn't hear you."

"It's all right. Ana, you look lovely. That's a great color

on you.”

“Thanks, Kara.”

Evren smiles. “Jewels?”

Ana laughs. “I’m trying a new look.”

“I like it.”

“Thanks, Evren. Everything is okay together? Nothing too formal?”

“No, Ana. You did perfect.”

“Thanks. After the briefing, will you tell me the stories behind the jewels?”

“I would love to.”

They sit to eat. Kara turns to Ana. “We caught one of Remus’s lieutenants. He’s downstairs, spilling his guts.”

“We don’t…”

“No, Ana. We don’t use torture. Maybe a potion—”

“The yellow one?”

“How do you know that?” Kara asks.

“I’ve had it used on me, a couple of times.”

“Ana! I’m so sorry. I didn’t know that, or I wouldn’t have said anything.”

“It’s okay. What’s it called?”

“Shadow of Suggestion.”

“It tastes awful.”

“I know Kane used it on you. When else—” Kara stops when Rafe gives her a bitter look. “I’m sorry. I shouldn’t ask. If you want to talk about it, you will.”

“It’s okay. Remus poured a vial of it down my throat, trying to find out how many guardians there are.”

“How did you resist?” Rafe asks.

“I used the feeling to remember Kane using it, to remember you rushing in and saving me. I was back in your arms, away from Remus. He cut me and hit me, angry that I wouldn’t tell him.”

“God, Ana!” Rafe lifts her up, holding her in his lap. “You went through hell to protect us.”

“Any one of you will lay down your life, without question or hesitation for me. Not answering a question was the least I could do to repay you."

"It was so much more than that, mia estrela. Thank you. You laid your life down for us, proving your loyalty in a way that no king or queen ever has."

She returns to her seat. "I didn't even think about it. I knew I had to refuse, whatever he asked, whatever he wanted." Her appetite fades. "Excuse me."

"Ana—"

"I need to use the washroom."

She shuts the door behind her and sits on the side of the tub, wrapping her arms around her stomach. *You're okay. You're in your quarters, with people you love. Stop feeling like this!* Her heart races along with her mind as she tries to calm both down. She washes her hands, returns to the table, and continues eating.

Rafe and Kara exchange a look. "Sis, are you okay?" Kara asks.

"Fine," she replies.

"Ana?"

"No, please. I don't want—"

"What's wrong?"

"I need a moment. Is that too much to ask for?" Ana snaps.

"Sorry," Kara and Rafe say at the same time.

She hangs her head. "No, I am. I know you're worried about me. I don't want to feel like this, to deal with this right now."

Rafe puts his hand on her shoulder before gently caressing her neck and back. "It's okay. Like we talked about earlier, right?"

"Yes, Rafe. I'm sorry. I shouldn't have snapped at you both."

"We shouldn't push you. I know you want to bring down walls, but I have this annoying habit of being persistent. Ana, I'm sorry."

"It's okay, Kara."

"At least you admit you're annoying," Rafe says, eating.

"Rafe!" Kara exclaims, watching them laugh.

"Love, be nice."

"Yes, Ana."

"What does that mean, bringing down walls?" Evren asks.

"I'll tell you later," Kara says.

"All right."

Ana sees the look of confusion on Evren's face. "Kara, it's okay. You can talk about it."

"You're sure?"

"Yes."

"Here." Kara takes Evren's hand. They go to the chaise, talking quietly.

Ana jumps, when Rafe kisses her cheek suddenly. "Are you okay?" he asks.

"Yes," she says, laughing. "You startled me, was all."

"Yet, your wings didn't pop open?"

"No. You're right, I am getting used to them."

"Really?"

"I woke up this morning, forgetting I had them."

"In a good way?"

"Yes. They weren't the first thing I thought of." She smiles at him. "You were." She kisses him.

"How do they feel?"

"Not too bad at the moment. It's usually later in the day when they start to hurt."

"Do you want to head to the meeting room?"

"Yes. Let me try and organize my paperwork." He smiles at her. "What?" she asks.

"Kara and I took care of it. It's in your bag."

"Rafe, thank you."

"It was the least we could do."

"Kara, are you coming with us?"

"Yes, Evren, too. I don't want any of us alone."

"Is she allowed in? Do I need to give her clearance? Can I?"

Kara laughs. "Yes, she has clearance."

"Thanks."

⁂

They are surprised to see the meeting room is empty. "Weird. Usually, Audressa is here at least an hour before the briefing," Ana points out.

"Maybe she left to retrieve something."

"Kara, there's some blood on the desk," Ana says. They all take a closer look.

"Let me find out," Kara says, stepping out. She flags down a royal guard and speaks to him for a moment then comes in. "They're looking for her." She turns to Rafe. "You should escort her back to her quarters, until—"

"Kara, I'm not hiding. We don't even know what happened here. She could've had a nosebleed."

"Ana, I am erring on the side of caution. Please, do the same. Don't go to your quarters because you're scared, go because I am. Please?"

"Yes, Kara."

Rafe steps out as Roesh and Aylin pass by. "Hey, guys."

They approach him. "Yes?" Roesh asks.

"We're going back to our quarters. Would you escort us and stand guard?"

"Of course," Aylin replies.

Rafe takes Ana's hand, following behind Roesh and Aylin. Rafe unlocks the door, then stays with her as Roesh inspects inside. He steps out.

"All clear."

"Thank you. If Melian summons you, please let her know you are acting under orders of the queen."

"We will."

"Thank you." He takes her inside. She trembles against him. "Ana, what's wrong?"

"I'm sorry. I'm scared, and I shouldn't be."

"It's okay. I know this is a lot and sudden. We'll stay

here until Kara brings us news."

She walks to the chaise, nearly collapsing on it. "I can't keep feeling like this."

Rafe joins her, taking her hand. "You're doing great." He puts her hand on his chest. "Feel my heart racing? I'm scared, too. It's natural."

"Thank you." She moves closer as he pulls her onto his lap.

"It's okay. You know you're safe in here. Do you want to change or stay how you are?"

"I want to get changed. Even if turns out she did have a nosebleed, I need rest. Not even lunchtime, and I'm exhausted."

"You've had a lot put on you already this morning. Come."

He picks her up and takes her into the closet. He sits her on the ottoman, bringing Smaug's crate over. She lifts him out to play with him.

Rafe gets pajamas. She takes them from him. "Thank you. I'll change in a minute."

"He missed you."

Smaug nips her fingers, then climbs into her lap and falls asleep. She gently strokes his head, smiling at him.

"Rafe? Ana?" Kara calls out.

"We're in here."

She and Evren enter the room. "Audressa was attacked this morning. She's in the Medical Center. We don't know anything yet." She sits next to Ana and sees the pajamas. "Staying here? I'll take care of the briefing, then come back and give you an update."

"Thank you. I'm sorry."

"No, it's for the best if you stay here while we're still investigating. Roesh and Aylin are right outside if you need anything."

"Thanks, Kara."

She takes Evren's hand and leaves. Rafe picks up Smaug and places him in the crate. "Get changed. We can have a lesson, if you want."

"Okay."

She strips out of her gown, hanging it back up. She removes her jewelry, placing it in the drawer. Rafe steps over to her and gently removes her crown then places it on the shelf. He helps her into her pajamas, watching her pick her hoodie up off the ottoman and slip it on.

"A hoodie kind of day, huh?"

She laughs. "Yes. Can Smaug join us?"

Rafe shakes his head, laughing. "Of course."

She scoops him up, cradling him in her arms. Rafe leads her to their small table in front of the fireplace. She laughs as Smaug goes inside the pocket of her hoodie, falling back asleep.

"Wasn't expecting that," Ana says with a giggle.

"No. Now, what would you like to learn about?"

"The portals. How do they work? How many different realms can they travel to? How long have they been around?"

"Okay, okay," he says, laughing. "Slow down. One thing at a time. The portals are combination science and magic, so I'm not a hundred percent sure exactly how they work. Probably a question Winslow could answer. As far as realms, there are fifteen realms here in this galaxy. The portals can go to any one of those that are able to sustain life."

"How were you and Kara able to use them to get to Earth?"

"We've had people from here go to Earth. You weren't the first."

"Really? Who else?"

"Socrates, Leonardo Da Vinci, Ryan Reynolds."

"Wait, what? Seriously?"

"Oh, yes. I recognized him as soon as I saw him. Didn't know he had left. He seems to be doing well for himself. Winslow went and studied, then came back. A few have done that. It's how we learned about hydroelectric power, developed some of our medicines and technology. It's why there are some things here that are familiar to you."

"Had you ever been to Earth before?"

"No. As guardians, we don't go for obvious reasons. However, when Rowenne found Kara's journal, with mentions of Earth, he knew he had to send someone he could trust. He didn't think it was a mission for just anyone."

"Did he order you or did you volunteer?"

"A bit of both. We discussed it, trying to figure out who would be best to investigate. As I said, never having an interest in anything romantic, plus knowing he could trust me with such an important task, he knew I was the prime choice. He also knew it would mean cutting off my wings, so he did not ask lightly."

"How did you feel, finding out they would have to be removed?"

"Uneasy. I had to think on it a while before I could answer. I didn't relish the thought of being without them."

"You lost your wings for me, and I grew mine for you." She smiles at him. "Made for each other."

"We truly were. Oh, as far as how old they are? I'm not sure. Again, probably another question for Winslow."

"Have you traveled anywhere else? Been to the other realms?"

"No. Our duties are to the palace and the royal on the throne. Unless they travel, we don't. I've been to all the quadrants, but never off-world until Earth. There's something about my mission you don't know. I didn't even know, until I got back."

"What?"

"Kane was the one who commanded us to find you."

"What? Why?"

"Best guess? He didn't want to wait for the kingdom to declare you dead. He figured he would either marry you or kill you, taking the throne."

"How did you find out?"

"Melian found another of my father's journals as she was cleaning out Declan's office."

She takes a deep breath. "It was Kane."

"Ana, are you okay?"

"Yes. It just… really?"

"Really. Rowenne was starting to look into it himself. Kane gave him the nudge to really pursue it."

"Oh!" She laughs, as Smaug climbs back out. "Almost forgot you were down there."

Ana picks him up and sets him on the table. He nips at her fingers. Rafe gets fruit for him. They all eat together. Smaug walks up to her, looking at his wings then back at her. She steals a glimpse at Rafe.

"If you feel up to it, go ahead."

"I do."

She scoops him up, carrying him to the center of the room then sets him on the floor. Smaug watches as her wings open and close. He does the same. Ana flies a few feet off the ground. He follows her. She goes higher, watching as he does, too.

"Rafe, do you see this?"

"I do. He's doing great."

She slowly lowers down as Smaug follows her. He lands softly, looking up at her.

"Did you like that?" She laughs when he squawks at her. "Okay!"

Rafe joins them. "Ana, that was amazing."

"I know! He's a fast learner."

"I meant you, how easily you could hover, then glide like that."

"Oh. I saw you do it once."

"And like that, you were able to do it?"

"I guess." She kneels down, playing with Smaug. He lets out a big yawn. "Okay. You need to rest." She carries him back to the closet, putting him in his crate. As she turns around, she nearly runs into Rafe.

"You do, too."

"I will, once we hear something."

"Ana—"

"I can't. Believe me, I want to lay down, in your arms, getting a nap. I'm too hyped up right now."

He takes her hand, leading her from the closet. They go to the center of the room. He opens his wings, looking at her until she does the same. Taking her with him, he hovers. Then he pulls back so she can fly on her own.

"This will help make you tired, plus you need to exercise them."

"Yes, love." She's almost to the ceiling and touches it.

He laughs. "Having fun?"

"Well, it's not like we have a lot of space in here to do anything else."

"I know. We'll train outside soon. I promise."

She slowly lowers down, sitting on the chaise. "No, we won't. Not as long as Remus is out there."

"We will. Please, believe me."

"I do."

Rafe goes to the door when he hears someone knocking. He opens it, letting Kara and Evren in. They walk to Ana.

"Audressa is awake. She went to the meeting room this morning, and a man was inside, going through her intel reports. He seemed particularly interested in what we know about Remus. She fought him off, trying to protect the reports. He was wounded, but she doesn't know how bad. She managed to get to the Medical Center before she passed out."

"She was—" Ana sighs. "She was hurt protecting paperwork?"

"Ana, those reports tell us everything we know about Remus. If he had those, he would know what we know, making us more vulnerable."

"I wasn't talking down about it. I wish it didn't happen. Is she going to be okay?"

"She'll be fine. A few stitches, but otherwise she's

unscathed. She did more damage to him than he did to her."

"Kara, I want a royal guard with her, at all times."

"Yes, Ana. I'll see to it. Would you like lunch brought in?"

"Please and thank you." Kara runs out. Ana turns to Rafe. "I'd like to go to the Medical Center after lunch and see her. Would that be okay?"

"I'm not thrilled with the idea, but I know you want to check on her and thank her for what she did. Yes, we'll go."

"Thank you."

"As long as you eat everything on your plate."

"I will." She smiles at him as she stands. "I'll get dressed while waiting for food."

She goes into the closet, where she removes her hoodie and slips on a winter gown with navy blue slippers to match. After securing her circlet, she steps out, seeing food has been brought in. She joins them at the table.

"Are you cold?" Rafe asks.

"A little."

"We're approaching spring, but there is a chill in the air. Might have one last frost."

Rafe tells Kara what they're doing after lunch. She looks at Ana. "I agree with Rafe, but we'll go there, then straight back here. Please, don't argue with me on this."

"I won't, Kara. I know how important it is."

"Thank you."

Rafe watches Ana eat, smiling at the sight.

"What?" she asks.

"Making sure you eat, after the day you've had already."

"I told you I would."

Chapter 12

Winslow escorts them back. "I know she wasn't badly wounded, but may I ask only one or two of you go in?"

"Rafe and I will. Everyone else will stay out here."

"Thank you, Majesty."

He knocks on the door before he steps inside. "Audressa, you have a visitor. Is that okay?"

"Yes," she replies. He opens the door as Ana and Rafe walk in. "Majesty," she says as she starts to pull the blanket down.

"Audressa, stay. Don't even think about getting up. I insist. You or Liara."

"Yes, mi'lady."

"I wanted to see how you're doing?"

"I'm better. Tender, but I'll be okay."

"Thank you, for what you did."

"Majesty?"

"You defended yourself and our reports. We are in your debt."

"Yes, Majesty. Just doing my duty."

Ana looks at her wife, who is holding her hand. "Now your duty is to recover."

"Yes, mi'lady."

"I insist, one week from Monday, you may resume."

"Majesty—"

"We'll take care of everything. Just rest and be with your family."

"Thank you."

"No, we are the ones with gratitude." She takes Rafe's hand. "Please, call on me personally if you need anything. I insist."

"We appreciate that, Majesty," Audressa says, smiling.

Rafe and Ana step out. Kara, Evren, Roesh, and Aylin

surround them. They return to their quarters. Roesh and Aylin stand guard outside.

Ana and Rafe go to the closet, while Kara and Evren sit on the chaise. Rafe turns to her as she's removing her gown. "Will you get a nap now?"

"Yes, I'll rest. I am quite tired." She gets into her pajamas before she checks on Smaug. "He's sleeping, too."

Rafe slips his pajama bottoms on, then a black shirt. "We have company. I guess I'll wear a shirt." He sees the look on her face. "What?"

"I have to have something to hold while I sleep."

He kisses her. "Of course, mia estrela. How could I forget?"

"Are you making fun?"

He kisses her harder. "Never. You know I wouldn't. Maybe I'm… teasing."

She smiles at him. "Yes, love."

He picks her up, carrying her to bed. "Sleep. Kara and Evren are here, we're safe. We'll have dinner and spend time with them. Sound good?"

"It does, thank you." She clutches his shirt as she kisses him. "I love you."

"I love you, too, mia estrela. Rest, knowing you're safe."

⁕

"Rafe, dinner is here."

"Thanks, Kara." He kisses Ana's forehead. "Mia estrela, are you awake?"

"Yes."

"Ready to eat?"

"Always."

He laughs. "Good. Do you want to get dressed?"

"Not yet. I want to get clean and change after dinner."

"Okay."

He gets up, helping her to her feet. They walk to the

table. Ana looks at everything, turning to Kara. "Sis, this is great. Thank you."

Kara smiles. "You're welcome." She turns to Rafe. "While she and Evren eat, could you and I have a moment?"

Ana steps in front of Rafe. "Sis?"

Kara laughs. "Nothing bad, I promise."

Ana debates for a moment. "Okay." She sits down with Evren, watching them go to the chaise. "Evren, do you know what that's about?"

"A little. She's worried about your dinner tomorrow with everything going on. She would prefer you stayed in your quarters this weekend."

"Why isn't she telling me this?"

"She wanted to discuss it with Rafe first. She will talk to you, too. The only reason I'm telling you this is so you're not worried. It's for you and Rafe, for your safety."

"I appreciate that. Thank you." She looks up as they join them. "Everything okay for tomorrow night?"

Rafe sits beside her, taking her hand. "It's fine. How did you know?"

She glances at Evren. "She told me."

"We're still having dinner. We may change the location, is all."

She hangs her head, calming herself, before she gazes at him. "If we have to have it in here, it's fine."

He squeezes her hand. "We're not."

"Really?"

"Yes." He laughs. "You'll see. Now finish your meal."

"Are you ordering me to eat?" She smiles, gasping at him.

He leans his head down, his mouth by her ear. "If I have to." When she kisses him hard, his eyes go wide in surprise. "Ana!" He laughs.

She continues eating and smiles at him. She turns to Kara. "What are you doing this weekend?"

"We're going to the village tomorrow. Then Sunday we'll relax."

"Could we do dinner Sunday? So we can go over any news to be ready for Monday's briefing? I told Audressa to take the week to recover."

"I'm sure she appreciates that. Yes, dinner Sunday will be fine. Will you be leading the briefings next week?"

"If it's safe enough."

"It should be. We'll prepare."

"Thanks, sis."

"Of course." Kara and Evren gather dishes. She sets them down, hugging Ana. "We'll be next door if you need anything. Otherwise, we'll see you Sunday at five for dinner."

"Thank you. We'll see you then." She watches them leave, then turns to Rafe. "Hmm. A whole weekend, not sick, not recovering…" She smiles at him.

"Ana, you are still recovering, but I told you, we'll do whatever you want. I mean it. You're right. I have to stop being too overprotective."

"For now, can we get cleaned up and into fresh clothes?"

"Yes."

They go into the closet. Looking at the garment bag, she smiles at the thought of the gown inside. She turns to Rafe. "Will you tell me where we're having our special dinner?"

He kisses her forehead. "Ana, it's a surprise."

"Oh, okay."

"Are you excited?"

"I am. After everything, I'm looking forward to a nice dinner, somewhere other than in our quarters or the dining hall. Don't get me wrong. I love our little table."

"I know."

They go to the washroom. He starts the shower. She smiles at him.

"Can I help you undress?"

"Yes, love."

Rafe gently removes her top. He slides her pants down,

and she steps out of them. Kissing her, he presses against her until her body tenses up.

"Ana—"

"I'm okay. Walls, right?"

"I don't want to push you. Let's get cleaned up. I want you well rested for the morning."

She smiles at him. "Hmm, what do you have planned?"

He kisses her cheek, bringing his mouth to her ear. "To taste every inch of you."

"Rafe!" she exclaims, as her heart is racing. She kisses him, her hand running through his wing. "Maybe a… taste tonight?"

He closes his eyes, focusing on how she feels. "Maybe a little. I know how tired and stressed you are."

His kiss goes from gentle to hungry as he holds her tight. Her hand teases at first, then they enjoy each other, as their pleasure builds between them. They collapse against the wall, both panting for air.

"You are incredible."

She smiles at him. "It's my pleasure."

"Ana!"

He kisses her again. He gently pushes her against the wall, kneeling in front of her. She puts her hands on his shoulders, keeping herself standing, as he overwhelms her. His body shudders, reacting to his own touches. She closes her eyes, concentrating more. He nearly falls to the floor when she finishes. He sits on the shower floor. She kneels beside him.

"How are you so much stronger at this?"

"I don't know. Are you okay?"

He laughs. "Just trying to catch my breath. It's amazing, how powerful you are. I still can't believe it!"

"Rafe, you are, too. You can control it when we're talking. I promise you, when we're doing these things, you are as powerful."

"Really?"

She smiles at him, taking his hand and placing it on her

chest. "I'm telling you, my heart is going to explode."

He laughs while kissing her. He gets to his feet, pulling her with him. "Let's get cleaned and turn in. We should both sleep good after this."

"Yes, love."

She washes and dries off. She dresses while he's getting cleaned. She sits on the vanity, waiting for him. He steps out. "Are you okay?"

She smiles at him. "Waiting for my guardian to take me to bed."

"Yes, Your Majesty." He dries and dresses, picking her up. He carries her out, puts her to bed, then snuggles in with her. "How are you feeling?"

"A little worried after what happened to Audressa. Otherwise, I'm okay. I promise."

"Ana, any reactions, any nightmares, any episodes. I'm asking, not telling, please, share with me. Don't hide."

"I promise." She kisses him, clutching his shirt. "I promise I won't hide."

"Thank you. Now, sleep, mia estrela."

"Yes, love."

She closes her eyes, falling asleep to his warmth and comfort. He strokes her hair, reassuring her she's safe.

⁕

Ana smiles at Rafe as the sun is coming in, then kisses his face and lips. "Hmm, Ana," he mumbles.

"Rafe, love, are you awake?"

"Yes." His thumb traces her mouth. "What time is it?"

"Seven. Breakfast will be here at eight."

"That's my job." He laughs.

"We have two guardians outside. I knew it would be okay."

"Yes, mia estrela. Do you know them?" Rafe asks. She shakes her head. "What are their names?"

"Deckard and Gerard. Do you know them?"

"Yes. Melian must've relieved Roesh and Aylin, to rest. They are good guardians. I've fought in battle with both of them."

"Good." She kisses him again. "Now, are we working up an appetite for breakfast?"

"Ana!" He kisses her as his hand continues touching her face and neck. "Is that what you want?"

"You are what I want."

"Mia estrela, where is this coming from?"

"What do you mean?"

"Your hunger for me?"

"Rafe, you really don't know?"

"No. What?"

She smiles at him. "We're feeding off each other's desire. I feel how much you want me right now. It grows until we have to have each other."

"Oh, Ana!" he says, when she puts her hand on his arm. "I see. I'm so sorry. All this time, I was pushing you away, thinking you needed to recover. I had no idea I was the one doing it!"

"Rafe, love, it's okay. I want it, too. It's not you, I promise."

He closes his eyes, calming himself down. He feels his love for her, thinking of her in his arms, his comfort. "Ana, we need to rest this morning. I know you want to have a special day, and we will. After last night, I'm still spent though."

She lays back down, her head on his chest. "Yes, love."

"Ana—"

"I'm okay!" She laughs. "Really. What do you want to do after breakfast?"

"We can have a lesson or tour the palace some more. What would you like to do?"

"Is it safe enough to tour the palace? Never mind. Flying in the training center sounds good."

"Will it be the two of us?"

"And Smaug. He wants to learn."

"All right."

She sits up. "I'm going to get dressed."

Ana gets out of bed and puts her slippers on. In the closet, looking at the ottoman, she smiles while thinking of their time in there. Rafe walks in and kisses her passionately.

"Missing your ottoman?" he asks with a playful grin.

"Yes. I don't miss hiding in here, but the times we had on it." She gathers clothing. "I'm getting a shower before breakfast."

"It should be here any minute." He steps out, hearing knocking as he does. They set up and leave. "Breakfast is ready."

"I'll clean up quickly, then join you."

"You don't want me in the shower with you?"

She smiles at him. "Always." He takes her hand, leading her to the washroom. "Just a shower, I know."

He laughs. "We have all weekend."

"Yes, Rafe." They clean up and dress. They sit at their table. He puts his arm around her. "I'm warm now. See?"

"I was worried."

"Like Kara said, there's a chill in the air as we're approaching the end of the month. Is there any kind of new year celebration?" She gasps. "I don't even know what year it is here!"

Rafe laughs. "I'm sorry. I shouldn't laugh."

"It's okay. I'm sure that's not something you hear often."

"It's not. Yes, we have a new year celebration. The year is 304 of the fourth era."

"I'm sorry. I don't really know what that means."

"It's okay. You're still learning about this realm. It's understandable. Unlike Earth that has centuries going into each millennia, such as the year 2000, we go one century at a time. Then we start over, in a new era. We'll get to year 999, then the next year starts year 00 of the next era."

"That's confusing."

He laughs. "You'll get used to it." He notices her eyes

go wide. "Are you okay?"

"I am. Still so much to learn. I swear, I'm never going to remember all of this."

"Ana, you will. You'll be fine. All of this history is in your library."

"It was hard enough, learning history on Earth. Here, there is so much to learn. It's not history, but art, food, culture, laws, and so much more. I feel like a child in school, trying to learn so much." She looks down when she realizes what he means. "Oh."

"What?"

She continues eating. "Nothing."

"Ana, please?"

"Just thinking about what you said, that I'll get used to it. That I'll get used to the eras, as in literal centuries going by. It's a little much to think about, being alive for… eternity… I'm sorry."

"Ana, no apologies. Remember?"

"Yes, Rafe. It's hard to think about a century going by, when I didn't even know if I was going to make it to the end of the year."

"I know, mia estrela. You are. You and I have a wonderful future ahead of us. We're so close. We'll get Remus. You'll have peace in the realm, and you'll rule with kindness and compassion. It's going to be incredible. You know that, right?"

She takes his hand. "You mean, we'll rule, right?"

He smiles at her. "Yes."

"Prince Rafe. What do you think of that?"

He chuckles, shaking his head. "I don't know. I knew I would climb in rank as a guardian. Never thought I'd do it as a royal."

Her face goes flush. "I'm sorry!"

"Ana, what for?"

"We're not even… I—"

"Ana, look at me." She raises her head, and he kisses her gently. "We are talking about the future. You know it's okay to ask and talk about it. Actually, it fills me with relief to hear you talking of it."

"Really?"

"Yes. You were so unsure of the future, as you said, not sure if you would be a part of it. Hearing you ask and talk about it, makes me happy."

"I don't want to push."

He laughs, kissing her again. "Ana, you're not. We've talked about it. We both want this. We're taking our time. It's okay." He stands up, pulling her into his arms. "You're not pushing or pressuring me or rushing anything. I swear."

She brings her arms around his neck while kissing him. "Thank you."

"Now, are we ready for training?"

"Yes!" She goes to the crate. She puts her hand in, laughing when Smaug runs up and onto her shoulder. "Oh, no. I'm carrying you."

Ana takes him in her arms, holding him. She follows Rafe out the door. He turns to Aylin and Roesh, back at their post.

"Accompany us to the training center," Rafe commands.

Roesh steps forward. "I apologize. How do I address you now?"

"Just call me Rafe."

"Yes, Rafe, we will accompany you." He stops walking, looking at Ana. "Majesty, is that a dragon?"

"It is!" She beams. "We're going to teach him to fly."

"Yes, mi'lady." Roesh and Aylin lead the way. They stand guard outside as Rafe and Ana go in.

Ana sets Smaug on the floor then proceeds to open and close her wings, watching as he does the same. Flying into the air, Smaug attempts to follower her, gaining more confidence as he approaches her. They fly together before lowering back down.

"Rest, little dragon. I didn't mean for you to do so much!"

Rafe steps up beside her. "Both of you!" he says, laughing. "You're both impressive learners."

"Really?"

"Yes, really," he says, kissing her. "I can't believe how well you're both doing. You're naturals."

Ana glances down at Smaug, then back at Rafe. "Do you think he's ready for the woods? To stay?"

"We can take him and see. It's your call. Roesh and Aylin will accompany us. What do you want to do?"

"I think he's ready. He's big and healthy enough, and he's taken to flying."

"Okay."

She scoops him up and follows Rafe. He approaches Roesh. "We're going up the battlement, then to the woods. Please accompany us."

"Yes, Rafe."

They go up. Rafe turns to Ana. "Are you okay to fly in front of them?"

Ana thinks for a moment. "Yes."

"Okay."

They take off and land in the woods. Ana puts Smaug on the ground. He runs around, sniffing everything. She laughs, watching him climb up a tree. He looks at her, then runs some more.

Rafe puts his arm around her. "I think he's ready to be out here," she says. "Oh! Evren will be upset she didn't get to see him one more time."

"They can come here any time and see him. She'll be okay."

Smaug approaches a small group of dragons. She steps up as they look at her. Ana turns to see Rafe and the guardians watching, curious. When she gives her attention to the dragons, they run up and look at her. She opens and closes her wings, then they all do as well. She kneels down as they come to her. Rafe smiles at Roesh after seeing the surprise on his face.

"Rafe, is she really making friends with dragons?"

He laughs. "Yes, she is. She'll probably make it illegal to kill them."

"Good!" Aylin says. "I know they can be pests, but I never understood anyone hunting them."

Rafe smiles at her. "You sound like the queen."

"Really?"

"She was upset at the game booth with the paper dragons."

"I was too!" she says, laughing.

"Can I ask?"

"Yes, Rafe?"

"You and Roesh?"

She laughs again. "When we went to MoonFrost, I confessed my feelings for him. As you see, he feels the same."

Rafe's smile grows. "She is so happy to see the two of you together."

"Really?"

He nods. "Yes." He walks to Ana, laughing when the dragons hiss at him. "They are all responding to you?"

"Yes," Ana replies. "Every one of them."

"It's incredible. We'll have to check the library and see if there's any mention of a Dragon Queen."

She laughs. "Rafe!" He takes her hand. "Smaug seems happy. They accept him."

"I'm glad. Are you okay?"

"Honestly, so much danger, it's better for him here."

"I hate to agree, but you're right." He grows concerned when she shivers against him. "Ana?"

"I'm a little cold."

"Let's get back. We'll have cocoa and lunch. Sound good?"

"Yes, love!" She kisses him, blushing when she realizes Roesh and Aylin are watching. "My apologies!" she says to them.

"Majesty, it's quite all right," Aylin says. "Shall we?"

They take to the air, Rafe holding her hand the whole

way. They return to their battlement, going down the stairs to their quarters. He puts in the order with a staff member, getting some for Roesh and Aylin as well. He clasps Ana's hand and leads her inside. He sits her on the chaise, wrapping the blanket around her.

"Get warm."

She smiles. "I already am."

Ana goes into the closet and looks at Rafe when he walks in. Her smile grows as she approaches him before kissing him.

"You need to rest now."

"Just a kiss before I get changed!"

"Yes, mia estrela," he says, kissing her. She slips on a winter gown and boots. "Still cold?"

"A little. I'm not sick, I promise."

"Okay."

He steps out, letting lunch service in and set up. She comes out as they leave and joins him at their table. Looking at the chaise, her heart aches at the sight of Smaug's crate.

"You miss him?"

"A little. At least I could prepare for this day. I have been, since the day we found him, knowing he would probably go back outside."

"What do you mean, prepare for this day?"

"Like we talked before, with my wings. I had no warning or preparation. If I had come here, and Evren told me I was the Crimson Queen and what would happen, I could've prepared. I've been hurt, I've faced death, I could handle that. Laying down in the woods, dying, was... awful, but natural. To come back to life, as this horrible pain sliced and burned through my back, watching wings of fire sprout out, then grow into these. It was too much."

"Ana, you're okay now. I'm so sorry it happened to you, but I'm grateful because they saved you."

"Thank you for not being angry."

"Ana?"

"That I saved you. You were so angry at NightFall."

"No, I wasn't. I was scared and hid it behind my anger. That day in battle, looking up and seeing you emerge from the woods. I saw your wings, I thought I was still unconscious and dreaming. I couldn't believe what I was seeing."

"I'm surprised I made it to the palace. I thought for sure I was going to pass out in the field. I'm so grateful for your help."

He places a gentle kiss on her lips. "Ana? Why are you thinking about this now?"

"We talked about the future. To me, the future started that day. It paved the way to the treaty, it made me into what I now am, it brought you and I closer. It was a horrible day, because I died, not because of my wings, but it was an important day."

"It brought us closer?"

"Like you said, it made me more like you. I needed your help and guidance, on how to work with my wings." Her gaze lowers. "I don't know if I would still be here, if I were the only one with wings."

"Ana!" He picks her up and holds her. "You would be. I would be with you. Hey, you found out I had wings, when you didn't. You still loved me, right? Wanted to be with me?"

"Yes."

"That's exactly how it would've been, if the situation were reversed. Feel my love, you know it's the truth. We have overcome everything together."

"We haven't stopped Remus."

"We will. We'll stop him. Kara and Melian are doing everything they can. We have too many guards and guardians for him to hurt you again." Her fear flows into him, so he decides to change the subject. "What did you think? Back on Earth when I showed you my wings? What was going through your mind?"

"I was confused, of course. I didn't believe what you were telling me, until you showed them to me. Seeing them, knowing you meant it, knowing you knew who I am and where I belong, I knew I had to see it myself. I'd always wondered about my family, about who I am." She looks away. "Then I get here, and you and Kara won't tell me about them."

"I'm sorry. Even if we didn't tell you everything, we at least should've answered questions and helped."

"I came here for two reasons. One, to learn about my past and to try and save the kingdom that I am a part of. Two, to be with you. I get here, and no one will tell me anything about my parents, and you tell me you don't love me."

"Ana, I'm sorry."

"I shouldn't tell you this. I don't want you upset."

"Tell me what?"

"The first night here, when you heard me crying and put your hand on my back?"

"I remember."

"I had been thinking of… well…" Her fingers trace her wrist.

"Ana!" He pulls her in tighter. "I'm so sorry! You were so overwhelmed and hurt and lost. I never wanted that to happen."

"Even though it was only a moment, as soon as your hand was on my back, I knew I wouldn't do it. I knew I couldn't."

"Why?"

"Because, even if you didn't love me, I loved you. I loved you too much to hurt you like that."

"How did I not see that?"

"I did everything I could to keep it down. Like you said, focusing on accepting my role and learning my place in the kingdom."

"If I could go back—"

"We can't." She kisses him. "It's okay. Now we look to the future. I'm excited for a future with us, with peace in the realm, with our love. You're right, I do want that, more than anything." She wipes a tear from his cheek. "What's wrong?"

"No, I'm happy. Any time I can hear you speaking like this of the future, means more to me than you will ever know!"

"It's been hard, but I am trying."

He smiles. "I see that. Thank you."

She kisses him. "Can I finish eating?"

He laughs, putting her back in her seat. "Of course. What are we doing after lunch? Do you need rest since we flew?"

"Please."

He tilts his head at her, as she's blushing. "What?"

"I wore the prettiest gowns I could find, with the circlets, trying to look nice… for you. Even if you didn't love me, I could see there was still some attraction."

"I knew it. I denied it to myself, thinking Evren picked out your clothes. You would step out, immediately looking at me, as if waiting for a reaction."

"I did." She laughs. "Whenever you would suck in your breath or stare, it made me feel beautiful."

"Ana, you are beautiful. You never needed a reaction from me to know that."

"Still, it was nice to see."

"I meant what I said, that I've loved you from the moment I saw you. Telling you I was performing my duty, lying to you, I would rather be without my wings than to ever hurt you like that again!"

"Oh, Rafe!" She kisses him. "No. We're okay now. You will never hurt me. I know we've fought and had our ups and down, but we've always come through it together. I'm here. I'm right here, and I'm not going anywhere."

"Ana, you are my everything. You are my future, my present, my love. You are my reason for being. You are embedded in my soul, my heart, my very life. My heart is entwined with yours, forever." He gently grabs the back of her head, kissing her with every ounce of love he has. Her arms wrap around his neck as she returns his love.

"Oh, Rafe," she sighs. "I love you so much!"

He lifts her up, carrying her to the bed. "Ana, are you okay?"

She smiles at him. "Please, love." She nods. "Whatever you want, I'm yours."

Ana sits up as he unfastens the back of her gown. Rafe helps her stand as he gently removes it. He smiles at her ruffled and lacy undergarments.

"Those are different…"

She smiles, blushing. "I hoped you would like them."

He runs his hand along her waistline, caressing the lace. "Hmm." He lays her back down, covering her, as his hand continues to explore.

Her breath sucks in as she tenses up. She forces it down, wanting to be with him while pushing the memory back. Instead, she focuses on her want and growing desire. "I need you, love," she whispers.

"What do you want?"

"Whatever you do."

"That can be dangerous," he says with a teasing smile.

"What do you mean?"

He lifts her up, laying her head on the pillow. "Do you trust me?"

"With every inch of my body."

He slowly removes her undergarments. His hand traces along her hip, then down her thigh. His smile grows as she moans. He lowers down, under the blanket.

"As you wish." His mouth explores her. She cries out when she's overcome. He pulls himself up, lying beside her and kissing her. "Every inch?"

"Oh, love! How do you do that to me?"

He catches his breath. "You have an amazing body. I love the things I can make you do!"

"Rafe, when do I get to reciprocate?"

"When you're ready. I mean it. Until then, I enjoyed that every bit as much as you did. I need a shower."

She smiles, kissing him. "Can I join you?"

"Just a shower. That's an order."

Her smile grows. "We'll see."

"Ana!" He jumps to his feet and gently pulls her out of bed. They go to the closet to gather clean clothes. She picks out a nightgown while he gets pajamas to rest in. They go to the washroom. She starts the shower.

After undressing, they step in. She grabs the soap and cloth, lathering it up and washing him all over. She hands it to him. The look on his face makes her pause, so she nods.

"I'm okay. Really," Ana assures him.

He kisses her. "If you are uncomfortable, even for a second—"

"I'll stop you."

He washes her all over, constantly looking at her and feeling for any unease. To help distract her, he plants gentle kisses on her face and neck as he washes her. Then he rinses out the cloth and hangs it up to dry.

"How do you feel?"

She smiles at him, falling against his chest, wrapping her arms around his waist. "Like a new woman."

"Really?"

"Yes. Thank you." They rinse off and step out. He watches her walk to the tub and look at it. She turns to him. "Maybe we could try another bath one night."

"Really?"

She nods. "I enjoyed the one we had in NightFall."

He steps up behind her and holds her against his chest. "When you're ready. You're shivering. Let's get dressed."

They dry and put their pajamas on. He carries her to bed, noticing she keeps her head down. When she looks at him, there is a noticeable blush on her cheeks.

"Are you embarrassed about what I did?"

"A little," she admits. "It's me, not you. I love what you did, I—" Her cheeks grow redder. "I'm not used to it, is all."

"Never be embarrassed about anything you and I do. I

know that's another wall we're bringing down."

"Yes, love." She snuggles into his chest, holding his shirt. "Rafe, thank you. I love you. You are so incredible!"

"I love you, too. Now, sleep."

"Yes, love."

He kisses her forehead while stroking her hair.

Chapter 13

Ana quietly shuts the door before walking to the vanity. She splashes cool water on her face while trying to calm her racing heart. Relief washes over her when she steps out and sees Rafe asleep. She sits on the chaise in front of the fire. She tries to push down the memories, fighting the tears threatening to escape. Rafe is standing in front of her, and she startles.

"Rafe, I—"

"What's wrong?"

She shakes her head, looking down. "Nothing."

He sits beside her. "Ana, is this because of earlier? What we did in bed? Please, mia estrela, don't hide."

"No, I—" She swallows hard. "I don't want to talk about it."

"Ana?" He takes her hand. "Fear? What are you afraid of? Please, open up to me."

"It wasn't anything we did."

"Then tell me about it, please?"

Her eyes squeeze shut. "It was our first day here. You were telling me you didn't love me."

"Oh, Ana." He pulls her in tighter. "I never should've done that! Regardless of my reasons, I should've been honest with you from the beginning."

"I'm okay. It was painful to relive, that's all."

"Why were you hiding this from me?"

"I didn't want you hurting because of it. Regardless of how you feel, it's not your fault. It was literally life and death. You didn't have a choice!"

He sighs. "Ana—"

"No! If you had told me you loved me, but we had to keep it a secret, I would've been okay with that. If you had been killed because I messed up, taking your hand, or saying

I love you, I never would've forgiven myself. You really didn't have a choice. Please, Rafe," she leans up, kissing him as tears are falling, "it was because we were talking about it. That's all."

He wipes the tears away. "I will never forgive myself for doing that to you."

"Rafe, I already have. Please, you need to as well. Bringing down walls? That's one of yours. I see and feel the guilt you still have. You need to let go. For me and yourself."

"Yes, Ana. I'll work on it." He carries her to bed. "Will you get some more sleep?"

"I'll try."

He lays her down, climbing in next to her. He holds her to his chest while stroking her hair. "Please, mia estrela. Get some rest. We have a late dinner tonight."

"Yes, love." She kisses him softly, clutching his shirt. "Please, don't ever break my heart again," she whispers as she falls asleep.

He wipes the tears from his eyes. "Never, mia estrela. I want you with me, forever."

Rafe sits on the edge of the bed. "I have snacks on the way, since dinner isn't until seven."

Ana smiles at him. "Thank you."

She goes to the closet, slipping into a pale blue gown and silver shoes. Looking herself over in the mirror, she smiles at the sight. Rafe's reflection in the doorway catches her eye, and she turns to him.

"Are you okay?" he asks.

"Yes," she replies. She opens her wings, watching them open and close. Rafe steps up behind her. She smiles at him. "I'm still adjusting, but I'm getting closer to accepting them."

"How do they feel today?"

"Not as painful. I think it's because we worked them

earlier."

"That's a relief. I know how heavy they can be on you sometimes. I hate it when you feel like that."

"So do I. It's getting better. The fact that I controlled them earlier in bed shows how much you've really helped me with them." She blushes when she's overwhelmed by an earlier memory. Rafe takes her hand.

"Why are you embarrassed?"

She laughs. "The ottoman, when they opened."

"Ana!" He leans down, kissing the top of her head. "You were still learning. They were new back then."

"I know. It doesn't make it any less embarrassing."

"You've grown so much since that time. I was worried you might never accept them. Honestly, that's why I was pushing for flying lessons. I thought if you used them, you wouldn't hate them so much. I'm sorry I pushed."

"I'm glad you did. You see now what I can do with them, how well I can control them. You were right to push. Thank you." She brings them in, turning and facing him. She expands them, wrapping them around both of them.

He smiles at her. "You are amazing!" He leans down, kissing her, as his hand gently ruffles through. His smile grows as the small moan escapes her lips.

"You are mean!" she replies, laughing. "Rafe, you know what that does to me." She leans up, kissing him hard and hungry.

"I can't help it. They're so beautiful, like you!"

"Oh, love. Thank you." She brings her wings back in. "Snacks?" she asks when she hears knocking. He leaves the closet, opening the door. He takes the tray and sets it up on their small table. She sits with him. "Cocoa! Thank you." She happily eats and drinks.

He smiles at her. "Are you the kind of person that will drink this even when it's hot outside?"

She laughs, nearly spilling it. "Asks the guy who drinks hot coffee any time of year."

"Okay, that's true." He chuckles. "I do miss coffee."

"There's hot cocoa and tea. There's no coffee here?"

"There's a similar drink, but no."

"How is Kara still alive?"

Rafe nearly drops his cup. "Ana! You're right. I think she drank more of it than I did."

She eats some cheese and bread, smiling at him. "Thank you for the snacks."

"You're welcome. I knew we both worked up an appetite." He laughs when she blushes.

She leans back in her chair, laughing. "That we did. So, where are we eating dinner?"

"Oh, no. That's a surprise."

"Is it indoor or out?" She sees the smirk on his face. "I need to know how to dress!"

"Wear a cloak over your gown, in case."

"Hmph. You really won't tell me anything?"

"Do you want me to?"

"No, you're right. I'll enjoy the surprise."

"It's not for two more hours. What would you like to do?"

"I don't know. It's not entirely safe, since we haven't caught the man who hurt Audressa. What are you thinking?"

"We could have a lesson. I could answer more questions, about the palace, the realm, anything you'd want to know."

"Anything?" she asks.

He tilts his head. "What do you want to know?"

"I was wondering, why did it become law that guardians and royals were forbidden? I understand the reasoning, as Evren explained to keep the guardians from usurping the throne and to protect the royals. I want to know, did something specific happen that forced them to make it law?"

"Ana, why are you asking about this? You don't regret—"

"No, Rafe! Of course not. I was simply curious." She

stands up and walks to the window. "How could you think that?"

"I'm sorry," he says as he approaches her. "I didn't understand why you would ask."

"Everything I went through, to work and bring this about, that you think I would regret it?"

"Please, mia estrela. I didn't mean it. I'm sorry."

Her fingers trail his jawline. "I'm sorry I asked."

"No, it's okay. You want to know?"

"Yes."

"A guardian seduced the king, then she married him. On their wedding night, she killed him to claim the throne. Instead, the other guardians killed her. It was then enacted into law. That's also when the indoctrination process began, to ensure control over the guardians."

"That's awful." She looks out the window. "Like Kane, all over again. And he wasn't even a guardian! So, see, it never should've been law. Since anyone could do that."

"It's okay. You made it right." He takes her hand when she gasps. "What?"

"If I hadn't passed the treaty, would I still be on the throne?"

"What do you mean?"

"I'm a human guardian. It was illegal for a guardian to have the throne."

He sucks in his breath. "I don't know. Or would it have made it legal for us to be together since we are both guardians?"

"Wow. I hadn't thought of any of that."

"Thankfully, the treaty was passed. You don't have to worry about it."

She laughs softly. "Have you met me?"

He hugs her. "Really. It's all said and done, in the past. We can move towards the future now."

"Rafe, but what if—"

"Ana, you read the laws. What did the law actually say about a guardian and the throne?"

"Nothing specifically, other than a royal and a guardian couldn't engage in a romantic relationship. It was on incredibly old parchment that accidentally fell apart when I was copying laws."

He gasps. "Ana!"

She smiles at him. "What?"

"Did you really?"

She laughs, turning red. "It was the only copy, and as I said, very old."

"I can't believe you did that!"

"Love, I had to. For us."

"I know. Still…"

"You're not mad, are you?"

"No! I know how much you love history and books. I can't imagine it was easy to do."

"Rafe, it literally fell apart. I didn't have to do anything."

"Really?"

"Yes. Maybe I should've been a little more careful handling it," she says, blushing. She laughs. "What?"

He shakes his head. "I can't believe you didn't tell me this."

"I didn't tell anyone. Not even Declan." Her smile fades as his name comes out. "I'm sorry."

"It's okay. I know he helped with the treaty. You can mention him."

"How could he do that to us? Want us to be together, only to kill us? It doesn't make sense!"

"You said he was conflicted."

"He was. His hatred was too powerful, and he gave in to it. He thought so highly of you. I read it in his journals. I didn't know if I should tell you or not. I'm sorry I didn't."

"You showed me his journals and told me I could read them any time. You didn't keep that from me. It's okay. He told me when I killed him I was the only guardian he ever trusted."

"Oh, Rafe!" she cries out as tears begin to fall. "I'm

sorry. I'm ruining our night."

He holds her tightly. "Mia estrela, you're not. It's okay. We're both still grieving for him. Because of him, you and I are together. Regardless of how we feel about him, I'll always be grateful for that." He wipes her tears. "Please, Ana. Don't cry."

"Excuse me." She goes to the washroom to splash water on her face and looks over to see him in the doorway. "I'm okay. I had to clean my face."

"I know. Still, I worry."

She nods toward the blades on the shelf. "Because of those?"

"No. I know you promised, and I believe you. I worry because you carry so much sorrow and try to keep it to yourself. How long have you carried this?"

Her eyes meet his. "I haven't. I swear. It's because we talked about him. I read his journals and moved on. At least, I thought I had."

"It's okay. We talked about this, about having moments. I know you cared deeply for him, trusted him even."

"He was one of few people here I trusted. Being betrayed by him felt worse than Kane's dagger going in my stomach!"

"I feel the same way." He walks in. "Are you okay?"

"I am." She takes his hand, and they go to the chaise. He sits down, enveloping her in his arms. "Really."

"I know. I want to hold you."

She lays her head against his chest. "Thank you." She takes his hand, squeezing it. "I love you."

"Oh, mia estrela. You know how much I love you." He kisses her forehead. "You haven't ruined anything. We've brought down walls, had some fun, ate snacks. Is it such a bad night?"

She smiles up at him. "No, love. You're right." Her eyes trail over to the clock on the mantle. "One hour until dinner!"

"See. We still have a great evening ahead of us. Feel better?"

"Yes, Rafe. Thank you. I'm going to get a shower at six-thirty. My hair is a little easier to manage when it's wet." She laughs. "Don't worry, it will be completely dry before we go to dinner."

"I don't need you catching cold."

"Ah-ha! It is outside."

"Ana!"

She laughs, kissing him. "Love, I figured it would be."

"What am I going to do with you?"

She caresses his face, leaning up by his ear. "Whatever you want."

"Mia estrela! We will have dinner soon."

"Yes, love."

"You're too cute."

She kisses him. "I'm grateful every single day for you."

"Me, too." He wraps his arms around her, feeling her love and warmth. "Oh, I missed this. I think Declan knew from the moment he brought me back here."

"What do you mean?"

"I told him my mission was in danger, that I had to get back to Earth. I was practically panicking about getting back to you. Pretty sure he saw that."

"Rafe, you never told me that."

"When he told me I had been here for two weeks, I freaked out, knowing you were hurting over me. When I got back to my apartment, my phone was still on the charger. I didn't read the messages, I grabbed it and came straight to you. Oh, Kara was livid when she saw me. She was trying to make me go when you came upstairs."

"I can understand. She took care of me after you left."

"I thought for sure you would hate me, that you would react like you did, hitting me and telling me to go. I couldn't, though. Even if it wasn't my mission, I couldn't leave you like that. I had to at least explain why I left. It wasn't fair to you."

"Love, we're okay now. It's in the past. Like you said, let's look forward."

"Yes, mia estrela."

"I missed that. When we got here and couldn't be together. Being called Highness or mi'lady or Majesty, but never hearing that." She closes her eyes. "I really missed it more than I thought I could."

"I nearly slipped up a time or two, almost calling you that while comforting you."

"I know. I was glad you did."

"Really?"

"It hurt, but I was happy to hear it."

"Mia estrela, I will call you that at least once a day, every day. I swear it."

"Please."

"Of course. Are you going to get ready?"

"Yes, love."

Ana takes her robe into the washroom. Stepping into the shower, she sees the cloth hanging up. Pushing down memories from MoonFrost and thinking of Rafe washing her, she smiles. She gets out, dries off, and slips on her clean undergarments before going into the closet.

She puts on the gown Kara had given her and slips on silver shoes. Looking at the shelf of crowns and circlets, she picks one out. She does her hair in a halo braid and puts on a silver crown with a crescent moon, small diamond stars dangling on the sides.

"Ana, are you almost ready?"

"Yes, love. Just another minute."

"All right."

"My hair took a little longer than I intended. My apologies."

"No, it's fine. Take your time."

She gets out a navy-blue cloak with silver stars, matching the dress, and folds it over her arm. She takes a breath and steps out of the closet. Rafe walks up to her, looking her up and down.

"Oh, mia estrela. You are my star tonight!"

She smiles at him. "Kara has good taste."

"Yes, she does. Remind me to thank her tomorrow at dinner."

"We will."

He kisses her on top of her head. "I'll get dressed. I was waiting to see what you were wearing."

Rafe goes inside as she sits on the chaise. She's nervous and doesn't understand why.

Kara told me, he's not proposing tonight. I know this. So why am I nervous? Is it because of everything that's happened? Or because we haven't really had a special date since I came here, other than the Snowflake Ball?

Her heart is racing, along with her mind. She looks up as Rafe steps out. He's in a navy-blue tunic jacket with charcoal pants. His sword is on his belt.

"So handsome! I love this color on you."

"I see." He extends his arm. She laces hers in, and they step out. Roesh and Aylin smile at him. "Guardians, will you escort us to dinner?"

"Yes, Rafe," Aylin answers. "If I may, you both look very nice."

"Thank you," Ana replies.

"Ana, close your eyes?"

She stops in her tracks. "What?"

"Trust me?"

"You know I do."

Roesh and Aylin smile at her. She closes her eyes and clings to Rafe. They continue walking. She gasps when they're going up steps.

"Ana, open your eyes."

She squeezes them a moment before opening and looking up. They're in their battlement. A firepit is in the center, with a blazing fire. To the right is a small table for two, similar to the one in their quarters. To the left of the firepit is a twelve-foot metal Eiffel Tower, covered in string lights. She turns to Rafe.

"Oh, this is incredible!" She leans up, kissing him, as he leads her to the table. He takes her cloak, wraps it around her, and helps her into her seat.

"Let me know if you start to get cold. We'll move this inside," he says, sitting across from her.

"I will. The fire is really warm."

"Yes, it is. I think we'll be okay out here." He smiles as she's staring at the Eiffel Tower. "Do you like it?"

"It's amazing! This is what you ordered while you were in the village with Evren?" she asks.

"It is."

So, not an engagement ring. That's okay. I'm still happy. This is so sweet and romantic. I won't let it ruin my night, like I did at the ball.

"What happens to it after tonight?"

"Ana, it's yours. If you want it in the ballroom, or our quarters, or to stay here. The choice is yours."

"Really?"

"Yes, mia estrela."

"I'd like it in our quarters. It could go along the wall, near the back fireplace and table."

"Good idea. We'll have it brought in tomorrow."

They finish eating. He stands up, holding out his hand. She takes it, then he dances with her around the firepit. She smiles as he sings quietly in her ear.

"Rafe, you have such a beautiful voice!"

"Thank you, mia estrela." While she sits, he pulls a lid off another dish. "Dessert?"

She laughs. "Of course." He feeds her a piece of petit cake, and she feeds him a piece of miniature pie. "Thank you for such a wonderful evening. This has been perfect!"

He smiles at her. "I have another gift for you."

"Rafe, you've already given me so much!"

"I know. It's for both of us, actually."

"Really? What is it?"

Chapter 14

He sets a ring box on the table. Her heart jumps in her throat, and she has to make herself look at him.

"Ana, we have been through so much together, good and bad, pain and pleasure. We've had our fights and our doubts, our fears and our worries. Through it all, you have shown me pure, unconditional, unending love. So, now I have one question for you, for the woman who consumes me and owns my soul. Will you be my wife? Will you be with me, always?"

She smiles at him as tears flow down her face. "Yes," she replies. "Forever."

He opens the box. She gasps at the ring, seeing the band is filigree wings holding a stone unlike anything she has seen before. He takes it out of the box, falling to one knee in front of her, as he slips it onto her finger. He leans up, kissing her.

"Do you know how happy you've made me?" he asks, taking her into his arms. She clings to him and sobs into his chest. "Ana?"

"Happy tears," she manages to get out, crying harder.

"Mia estrela, are you okay?"

"Yes! I'm so happy."

"It's radiating off you."

"Oh, love," she says, kissing him.

"Ana, you're shivering. Is that excitement or are you getting cold?"

"Both."

"Come along. We can finish celebrating in our quarters."

"Yes, love." She glances once more at the Eiffel Tower.

He smiles at her as he leads her to it then kisses her

passionately. "Is that what you wanted?"

She laughs. "How did you know? How can you read me?"

"I told you, I want to read every page of you."

"I know. You are."

They go downstairs, out the door. Roesh and Aylin come to attention. "Where to?" Roesh asks.

"Back to our quarters."

Ana keeps staring at her ring. "What kind of stone is this?"

"I'll tell you all about it, once we're inside."

"Yes, love."

Roesh goes in, checking every room. He steps back out. "All clear, sir… Rafe." He laughs. "Sorry. Habit."

"Quite all right, Roesh," Rafe says, patting his shoulder. "Thank you, both."

"Happy to perform our duties. We'll be right out here if you need anything."

Rafe takes Ana inside. "Do you want to sit and talk, or would you like to get cleaned up and comfy first?"

"Can we get cleaned up? These braids are a little tight."

"Of course."

They go to the closet. He helps her out of her gown. She lays it on the ottoman. They gather fresh clothes.

In the washroom, she turns on the water while she finishes undressing. Admiring her ring before she takes it off, Ana places it in the bowl on the vanity.

"You took your ring off?" Rafe asks in surprise.

"Love, you don't sleep or shower in jewelry."

"I didn't know that."

"As much as you wear?"

He laughs. "Not really. Just a piece or two on occasion."

"It's the only time I will ever take it off. I promise you."

"Yes, mia estrela." They step into the shower. She hands him the cloth. "Are you sure?"

"Please, love."

He washes her and cleans her wings as well. She washes him, then stands under the water, letting it soothe her wings and back.

"Are they bothering you?"

"Just a little. Like I said, usually later in the day they will."

He turns her around and gently massages them. "They don't feel as tight or tense."

"Working them definitely helps."

They dry off and dress in matching pajamas. She leans against the vanity, watching him get dressed.

"What?" he asks.

"Kara said you weren't proposing tonight."

"When I talked to her, I wasn't."

She straightens up. "What do you mean?"

"We had gotten you back from his camp. She was too worried about you recovering. I was, too."

"What changed your mind?"

"You. No, you didn't pressure me or rush me. I don't mean it like that. You brought down some walls and talked about the future. You showed me you were ready, without even knowing it was leading to this."

"Rafe, how long have you had this ring?" she asks, slipping it on.

"I ordered it right before the Snowflake Ball."

"Really?" She steps up to him. "All this time, I was so worried I was pressuring you."

He laughs. "You asked about the stone?"

"Yes. When I look down at it, I see a galaxy. I look at it from the side, it's like a cloudy sky. What is it?"

"What it's actually called, is too long to pronounce. The legend behind it though, is that a huge asteroid collided with a moon. The pieces broke off and merged, creating this stone. While that is legend, this stone is from space."

"Really?"

"Yes. That's why it took so long. It's extremely rare."

"I've never seen or heard of anything like this!"

"So, you like it?"

"I love my ring. Um, can we leave the washroom?"

He laughs, taking her hand. "Yes, mia estrela." He takes her to the chaise, where he sees her admiring her ring once more.

"I love the band. The wings are so pretty!"

"I debated it since you weren't quite as accepting of them at the time. I decided to take the chance."

"I'm glad you did. It's beautiful!"

He kisses her. "Like the woman who wears it."

She blushes, smiling at him. "Oh, Rafe. Thank you."

Rafe follows her into the closet. She goes to the drawer with the Royal jewels. She takes the key out of the small drawer, unlocks it, and opens it. Rafe gives her the ring box. She slides the ring in, putting the box in the drawer. After she locks it, she puts the key back. She turns around, stepping up to him and kissing him.

"Believe me, I wish I never had to take it off."

"I know." He takes her hand, leading her to the washroom.

Ana steps in and gets ready for bed. When she's done, she walks out and sits on the chaise. She watches the fire while waiting for Rafe. He steps out and smiles at her.

"Ready for bed?"

"Yes, love."

He picks her up and carries her. "My future wife."

Her smile grows. "Yes, future husband?"

Rafe laughs. "Hmm. Here I told you not to rush, but it seems I can't help myself. I love you, so much."

"I love you, too." She looks down.

"What's wrong?"

"I want to get married, but—"

"I know. You're still bringing down walls. It's okay. As you said, we can be engaged a year or two. There is no rush. When you're ready."

"So loving, so patient. You are such an incredible man!"

He kisses her, pulling her into his arms. "I have to be, for a woman like you. You deserve that much." He grows concerned when he hears her crying. "Ana?"

"Happy tears," she says, softly. "Thank you." She clutches him tighter. "I still can't believe this is real."

He kisses her forehead. "Your happiness is bursting out of you."

"Really?"

"It's incredible!"

She caresses his neck and face. "Rafe?"

"Yes, mia estrela?"

"Thank you for the perfect evening. I loved every minute of it."

"You're welcome. What was your favorite part?"

"The dessert."

"Really?"

She laughs. "You know I'm kidding!" She kisses him. "You put that box on the table, and I swear my heart was going to jump out of my chest. It took everything I had to look at you and not stare at it."

"Really?"

"Yes! I was so nervous."

"I was, too."

"Why? You had to know I would say yes."

"I did. Even so." He kisses her again. "Now, can you sleep?" He closes his eyes. "You feel tired, but you are still excited from everything."

"It might take me a bit to fall asleep, but I will. Trust me, I am exhausted from today."

"Once it's safe, we'll go back into the woods. I'm curious to see if Smaug remembers you. Though I'm sure he will. Plus, I'd like to see you interacting with the other dragons. They seem fascinated with you."

"Wait until Joph hears about that!"

"Ana, are we eating breakfast in the dining hall Monday?"

"I don't know. Why?"

"To announce our engagement. Do you want me to announce it, or do you want to?" He looks down when she trembles in response. "What's wrong?"

She closes her eyes, quickly thinking of the string light Eiffel Tower, the firepit, dinner, and dancing with him. She pushes everything else back. "I'm okay."

"What was that?"

"Nothing. Sorry."

"Ana?"

"Please," she begs, "I want to sleep." Ana kisses him. "I love you."

"I love you, too." He studies her face, feeling her love and warmth.

She snuggles into his chest, clutching his shirt, praying she doesn't have nightmares.

Rafe comes in as she enters the shower. "Why didn't you wake me? What's wrong?"

"Nothing, I—"

"Talk to me. Don't shut me out. Not now." He undresses then steps in with her.

"I had a nightmare. I'll be okay." She closes her eyes, knowing he's going to ask.

"What was it about?"

Tears stream down her face. "No," she says softly. "Please. I don't want to ruin our night!"

"Nothing you say or do will ruin it. We ate, danced, kissed in front of the Eiffel Tower, you agreed to be my wife. Everything is perfect. Please, open up. I'm begging you."

She says nothing as he wraps her in his arms. After taking a moment to collect herself, she begins.

"You weren't here the morning after the masquerade. Kane made me join him for breakfast in the dining hall, so we could announce our engagement. He asked me if I wanted to announce it or him."

"Ana, I am so sorry."

"Rafe, you had no way of knowing! If I had opened up sooner, told you what happened, I wouldn't be feeling like this now. It's my fault, not yours."

"No, Ana. It's his. What was your nightmare?"

"We were getting married. I was so excited. I was walking down the aisle, but once I got to you, you disappeared. Instead, I was marrying Kane."

"You're okay now. He's dead, and he'll never hurt you again."

"I wish I could believe that. It was a nightmare. I'm okay."

"You wouldn't be crying in the shower if you were okay."

"I'm sorry. Please don't be mad!"

"I'm not. Can you not feel my love? Feel my comfort?"

"Yes. I don't deserve it. I hid from you." She starts to turn away. He pulls her in tighter.

"Ana, if anyone deserves it, it's you. You were going to marry him to save Evren and me. You were willing to sacrifice yourself for us."

"I wouldn't let him kill you! I couldn't. It was bad enough, everything else he did. I wasn't about to let him have that."

"Think about what happened after. Think about falling in my arms, as we confessed our love for each other. Can you focus on that?"

"Yes. I was so grateful you were still alive. I thought I had lost you. You told me how much you loved me, how much I meant to you."

"I still do. Always."

She smiles at him, kissing him softly. "Forever," she whispers.

"Yes."

She turns off the water, stepping out and drying off. Looking at him, she gets dressed. "I am sorry I hid."

"I know. It's okay. This was a big day for you. You aren't overwhelmed, are you?"

"Yes." She smiles at him. "Only by your love."

"Don't scare me like that!" He kisses her then finishes getting dressed. "Now, how do you want to tell Kara and Evren?"

"They're coming to dinner. How long do you think it will take her to notice the ring?"

He laughs. "Knowing Kara? Less than a millisecond."

"Yeah, so that's how we'll tell her."

"All right." He takes her hand, stepping out and carrying her to bed. "Sleep, mia estrela. Please, any more nightmares, episodes, anything. Please, don't hide."

"I won't. I'll try not to."

"That's all I can ask."

"Rafe?"

"Yes, mia estrela?"

"What did I ever do to deserve you? You are the best thing that ever could've happened to me!"

"Ana, I feel exactly the same way." He leans down, kissing her. "Now, get some sleep."

"Yes, love."

Ana grabs his shirt while snuggling against his chest. He smiles down at her, happy to finally be engaged.

***

Rafe wakes up as Ana is trailing her fingers along his jawline. She moves herself over him and plants gentle kisses on his cheek and chin.

"Ana!" he says, laughing. He kisses her softly on her lips. "Good morning."

"Morning, fiancé."

"Hmm. They don't use that word here."

"Oh? What do they call it?"

"Betrothed. An older, more traditional word is entrastellar, which means entwined by the stars. It was only used by royals. I would say you are my entrastelle, and I am your entrastella."

"It's beautiful! Oh, I love it!"

He smiles at her. "But we can still say fiancée."

"Thank you. It's just, it's the word I grew up with."

"I know. It's a good word. French, right?"

She smiles at him. "Yes, like last night." She kisses him again, pulling away and taking his hand. "Come on!"

He stands up, following her into the washroom. "Ana, what are—"

Ana walks to the tub. She places the stopper in the drain while she starts filling it up. "Please?"

"Yes, we'll get a bath this morning. Are you sure?"

"Like in MoonFrost."

"Ana—"

"No! I didn't…" She gasps. "I meant NightFall! I—"

He holds her tight. "It's okay. That's why we'll have one here. I want you to have happy memories of a bath. If you still want to?"

"Yes, Rafe. I'm sorry."

"For what? You did nothing wrong. We'll enjoy a bath, like we did in NightFall, then we'll relax. Sound good?"

"Yes, love." Her stomach rumbles.

"Ana, are you hungry?"

She laughs, blushing. "I don't think I can wait until brunch."

"Stay right here." He steps out as she continues to fill the tub. A moment later, he returns with the soap from NightFall. "Roesh is getting us snacks and will bring them in shortly."

"Rafe, is that Bela's soap?"

He smiles at her. "He said to help ourselves."

"Rafe!" she exclaims with a laugh.

"Ana," he says, turning serious, "I know how important scents are to memories. I hope this will help, to make taking a bath easier, bringing up happy memories of us in NightFall."

"Oh, love. Thank you."

He pours some into the bath, then they undress. She reaches for his shorts.

"I can leave these on, like in NightFall."

"I'm okay. I promise."

He studies her eyes. "All right."

She removes his shorts. He steps into the tub, taking her hand and helping her in. They lay together, fingers laced.

"Ana, how do you feel?"

"Happy, relaxed. Is this okay? With our wings, I mean?"

"Yes, mia estrela. I've soaked a few times, after battle. My wounds can heal, but my muscles would still be sore."

"It is relaxing. I wish I could've done it sooner."

"We're here now."

"Yes, love."

She turns around to face him. Kissing him, her fingers explore his chest and stomach. He takes her hand, kissing it. "Ana, relax. We have all day. We're doing small steps, though. This is our first bath here."

"Yes, Rafe. I'm sorry."

He laughs. "Ana, never apologize for wanting to love me." He gently turns her back around. Her stomach rumbles again. "Hmm. We'll get cleaned up shortly and eat." He caresses her ribcage. "I had hoped you would put the weight back on."

"Rafe, what are you talking about?"

"No, not in here. I'm sorry. We'll talk over our snack."

"You mean the weight I lost in MoonFrost, because I didn't eat."

"Ana—"

"No, Rafe. Please. Is that what you're talking about?"

He sighs. "Yes." He runs his fingers along her side. "I can feel your ribs still. You need to put the weight back on."

"I try to eat what I can, but you know I don't always have an appetite." She takes his hand. "What am I feeling from you? You're worried?"

"There's something we haven't talked about, in regard to your immortality."

"You have me really confused right now. I thought we were talking about my weight?"

"Ana, it's tied together."

"Then tell me!"

"You get to a point where your body becomes how it is. It won't change. You won't age, put on weight, lose or change hair color, and so on. I'm scared you're going to stay this small."

"Why?"

"It's not a healthy weight! I'm worried about you."

"Rafe, love, Winslow ran my blood. If there was anything to be worried about—"

He buries his face in her hair. "Ana, please."

"Talk to me. What's wrong?"

"Please, don't take offense to this. I know you hate these words, and I promise you, I don't mean them how you think. You are so small and frail. It worries me."

She gasps softly. "Rafe!"

"Ana, I don't mean it like that, you know I don't! You aren't weak or pathetic, so please, don't even think of it."

She steps out of the tub. "I'm getting a shower."

"Ana—"

"Alone." She starts the water in the shower. As her fingers trail along her ribs, she realizes he is right. She hangs her head. "I'm sorry," she says softly.

He opens the drain and steps out of the tub. He wraps his arm around her waist. "I didn't notice because I tried to give you space after what happened. Seeing you now, I realize how much weight you had lost."

"I'm fine. I'm healthy." When he sighs, she meets his gaze. "We'll go see Winslow, if you want."

"Really?" Rafe asks.

"Yes."

"Maybe tomorrow. Let's enjoy today." He looks at the door. "Hang on." He grabs the robe, wrapping it around himself and stepping out, then returns a moment later. "Roesh brought our snack in. It's on our small table, ready for when we are."

She steps up, taking his robe off and hanging it up. "Will you shower with me, please?"

"Yes, mia estrela. You know I will."

"I'm sorry I was angry."

"No, it's okay. I hated using those words, but I didn't know how else to describe what you've been through." He takes her hand, stepping in with her. "Ana, we're getting cleaned up right now. Let's have a snack, then see how we feel."

"Yes, love." She turns to him, folding her arms around his waist. "I love you."

"I love you, too," he says before kissing her forehead.

He helps her clean, then she washes him. They rinse and step out before drying. She opens the door, making sure they're alone, then leaves the washroom.

In the closet, Ana walks to the mirror on the back wall. She opens the doors and studies herself. Rafe steps in, and Ana catches his reflection.

"I didn't realize, either. It's my own body. You would think—"

"Because you went through so much. You were focused on your scars." Her eyes close, and her head goes down. "I'm not mad about that. I'm pointing out, you were in pain from them and not paying attention to what your ribcage looked like." He steps up behind her. "Come eat with me, please?"

"I don't have an appetite." She tenses up when the anger comes from him and into her. "But I'll eat because I need to." She unlocks the drawer and removes her ring.

"May I?" he asks.

She hands it to him. "Yes," she replies softly.

His lips graze her hand as he slips it on. He kisses her mouth. "My beautiful fiancée."

Her eyes squeeze shut, as that's the last thing she feels

like. She slips on a robe and goes to their table, smiling at the mugs of cocoa. She picks up a cup, slowly drinking. He sits beside her, taking her hand.

"Thank you."

"For what?" he asks.

"Everything."

"Always."

"Forever," she says with a smile. "I mean that, you know. It's not a response, but it's the truth."

He kisses her, grabbing the back of her head. "Oh, mia estrela!" She returns the kiss and squeezes his hand. "That's all I want. Can we really have that?"

"Yes, love. I promise you, we will."

He takes a small piece of bread, adds cheese to it, and he feeds her. She laughs.

"What?" he asks.

"You," she replies, kissing him again. She feeds him a piece of fruit. He caresses her side. With worry in her eyes, she pulls back.

He tilts his head. "I'm being with you, that's all." She takes his hand to see what he is feeling. "See? Just love, no worry."

"I'm sorry."

"It's okay. After what I said, I understand."

She kisses him softly while her fingers trail his upper torso. "Rafe?"

"Yes, Ana?"

"I need you."

He smiles at her. "Eat a little more, then we'll do whatever you want. I promise."

She pouts before eating some bread. "I don't want to get too full, since we'll have brunch brought in shortly."

He leans down, his mouth at her ear. "Ana, we are going to work up quite the appetite for brunch." He kisses her cheek and laughs. "Breathe, mia estrela!"

Her face flushes to crimson as she swallows hard. "Yes, love." She eats more fruit and thinks of Smaug.

"Missing your dragon?"

"Yes. A little. He is really cute."

"You'll get to see him soon enough. If we have to take five guardians and five royal guards, I won't deny you the woods or seeing your dragon."

"Thank you. I appreciate that. I know Evren will want to see him, too." She stands up, removing her robe, as her wings expand. Concentrating on opening and closing them, Rafe is concerned by the look of pain on her face.

"Are they hurting?"

"I could feel them opening, but I couldn't stop them. I didn't want the robe to be ripped off!"

"That's my job," he says, standing up. He walks to her and examines her. "Are you okay?"

"Yes. I think I was holding them tighter, with the tension in my back. They needed to breathe." She looks up at him. "I'm okay."

He steps up, kissing her as he teases the space between her wings. Her lips part as a small moan escapes. He smiles, leaning down and kissing her again. She reaches up under his shirt and caresses his chest.

"Do you want bed, shower, or ottoman?"

"Ottoman."

He picks her up and carries her into the closet. She removes her ring, then sets it on the shelf with the crowns. He lays her down. As he leans over her, he watches her, looking for any unease.

"You're okay?"

She smiles at him and kisses him. "With you? I always will be."

"I appreciate that, but I mean it."

"Love, I'm okay."

His lips crash on hers as he caresses her chest and stomach. When he moves lower, his hand on her thigh, she writhes as desire floods her. His other hand sits her up, and he brushes his fingers through her wings, causing her to tremble.

She slowly teases him at first as he continues. Moving faster, watching his mouth open as he pants for air, she continues to stroke his desire. He kisses her as they succumb. With a shudder, she cries out.

"Rafe," she exclaims, grabbing his hands and bringing them around her waist. "Please, love. I can't!" she says, kissing him again.

"Mia estrela, the way you make me react. The power you have over my entire body."

"Same for you!" she says, laughing. His hand gently trails her thigh. "Jerk!" she screams, lightly punching his shoulder. "I can't take it!"

"I'm sorry. I didn't hurt you, did I?"

"Never. Just let me catch my breath, please?"

"Yes, mia estrela." Lying on the ottoman, he holds her to his chest. Her breathing and heartbeat return to normal. "Feeling better?"

"A little," she replies. "You've gotten stronger about sending it back to me!"

"Really?" he asks, smiling.

"That's not a compliment," she says, laughing until she sees the worried look on his face. "I'm teasing, love."

"Hmm. That's my job," he replies while touching her waistline.

"Rafe!" she says, taking his hands. She kisses him. "I need to rinse off."

He picks her up and carries her to the door. He glimpses out into her quarters to make sure they are alone before taking her to the washroom. They rinse off and dress. She slips on a blue gown and silver slippers.

They step out as brunch is brought in. She runs to the closet so she can put her ring on. As she walks out, palace staff carry in her Eiffel Tower. It comes apart into three pieces. Rafe shows them where to set up. They assemble it, turn on the lights, and leave. Ana approaches him.

"This is my second favorite present of all time."

He turns to her with confusion on his face. "What's

your favorite?" He smiles as she raises her hand, showing her ring. "Of course," he says with a laugh before he takes her hand and escorts her to their table.

When he pulls her chair out for her, she smiles as he helps her sit.

"Oh, Rafe!" she exclaims, seeing croissants, fruits, pastries, tea, and cocoa. "What did I do to deserve this?"

He kisses her. "Just being you."

"It looks amazing!"

He smiles as he watches her eat. She drinks tea and cocoa, which makes him laugh. "Really? Both?"

"They're here. Why wouldn't I?" she asks, smiling at him. "Everything tastes delicious! I didn't know they had croissants here."

"One of Yeona's chefs trained in Paris a few years ago." He watches her shake her head. "What?"

"It's so weird to think of people from here going to Earth."

He laughs. "It helped the kingdom in technology, education, medicine, and food. It's why we send someone, from time to time."

"I wonder if I ever ran into someone, besides you and Kara, of course."

"I doubt it. It's rare for someone to go."

"How did you find me?"

He looks at her. "Being a guardian, we have a sort of, hmm, internal pull to find royalty. It's a way for us to find you if you're ever lost or get hurt in battle."

"Right, you mentioned that. I forgot."

He clears his throat. "I actually found you about two weeks before we met."

She sits up and stares at him. "What? Why the wait?"

"I had to learn your routine. I didn't want to bump into you and say, 'hey, wanna go out?' I wanted to have something to talk with you about, to open you up. I'm sorry. It was my mission, and—"

"Rafe, it's okay, but I thought the first time you saw

me was that day in the coffee shop."

"I didn't want to tell you. You jokingly called me your stalker, but I kind of was. I wanted to watch you, see what kind of person you were, get to know about you, before meeting you. That day in the coffee shop was the closest to you I had been, though. It's why my heart was pounding, thinking of finally talking to you."

"I woke up in the hospital, and I was so scared. I was thinking of the mugger, what he did. As soon as I saw you, though, I calmed down. It was so weird. I told myself it was the drugs they were pumping through the IV."

He laughs. "Probably part of it."

"Rafe! Seriously. Then seeing how concerned you were, right from the beginning. I had no idea who you really were, of course."

"Ana, as I've said, even if we had been born on Earth and met that way, nothing would've been different. I fell in love with you from the start, fighting it because I knew we couldn't be together. I also let it because I knew it would help me accomplish my mission."

"Rafe, your goal was to get me to fall in love with you, right?" He nods. "Mission accomplished," she says, kissing him.

"I never expected to fall in love, especially with you." The hurt look on her face gives him pause. "Ana, because you're a royal. You know what I mean."

"Yes, love."

"I thought it would be a matter of a few dates, woo you, get you to say you love me, then we'd return here." He sighs. "I never expected to hand my heart and soul over."

"You didn't," Ana says.

"What do you mean?"

"Our hearts and souls are still ours, entwined."

He smiles. "I like that." He watches her take another bite of her croissant. "Did you get enough to eat?" Her expression sours. "Ana, I didn't mean it like—"

"It's okay. Yes, I had plenty. It was delicious."

He covers it up. "Hmm. We'll have some more in a little bit."

"What are we doing now?" She blushes when he smiles at her.

He laughs. "You're easy to tease."

"Rafe!"

He can't help but laugh harder. "Come on."

Rafe stands up, holding out his hand. She smiles as she takes it, and he leads her to the middle of the room. His wings extend out. She does the same. He pulls her into the air.

"Wanna fly a little on your own?"

"How did you know?" she asks as she puts space between them.

"I could feel them bothering you. Like you said, you needed to work them." He sees the worry etched on her face. "Ana?"

She comes back to him, grabbing him as her wings give out. "I'm sorry," she says as she clings to him. "I don't know why they do that!"

"What do you think about when you're in the air?" Her feelings flood in before he composes himself. "Ana, why are you embarrassed?"

"Please, Rafe, take me to the chaise."

"I will, but what's—"

"Please!"

He lowers down. As soon as they're on the ground, she runs to the chaise and sits.

"What's wrong? You've been doing so well. We went all the way to the woods yesterday. What happened this morning?"

She keeps her eyes on the floor. "Please, don't be mad."

"Ana?"

"I didn't mean to. I—" Her breath hitches.

"Calm down, mia estrela. You're okay. You can tell me when you want to."

"Just hold me right now, please?" she pleads softly. He pulls her into his arms to hold her tight.

"I'm right here, mia estrela."

She calms her breathing down before she works up the courage to look at him. "I was doing fine in the air. Then I thought about last night, then our bath. It took me back to MoonFrost, to Remus hurting me. It overwhelmed me. I couldn't keep my focus. I'm so sorry I'm a horrible student!"

"Ana, no. God, no. You went through so much to protect your people. I keep telling you, you're going to have moments. I don't think about those happening when you're flying. We should've talked more, prepared more. This was my failing, not yours."

"Rafe—"

"I'm teaching you, remember? This falls on me."

"I know, but I shouldn't be thinking of stuff like that while I'm trying to concentrate."

"Ana, it will overwhelm you. What you've endured, what Remus has done to you, it's going to happen. I was enjoying the moment, instead of being your teacher."

"You're still going to teach me, right?" she asks, her voice low and wavering on the last word.

"Yes. Why wouldn't I?"

"You said pretty much the same thing when you hurt me on Earth. When you were teaching me self-defense."

"Ana, even if something like that happened here, I would still teach you. You need to use your wings, learn about them, learning to use them. You know how painful it is when you don't. What about before when they gave out? What happened then?" He watches her eyes go down again. "Ana, please?"

"I was doubting myself," she admits. "I've worked on it though, and that's not what happened now!" she adds.

"It's okay."

"I didn't grow up with wings or grow up watching people using their wings, talking about them. They were kind of thrust upon me. Here you go, have a nice life! I'm using them, learning, like you say, but it's so hard for me sometimes."

"Because you make it harder."

"Rafe!"

"I don't mean that how it sounded." He shakes his head. "I'm sorry. You're right. There isn't a single person here who can give you advice about what you went through. All I can do, though, is try to help you as best I can."

"You do. I swear you do! I overthink and panic. It's how I am. So having wings with a brain like that is not a good combination!"

"Ana, you're doing fine. You act like you should be an expert by now. I've been doing it over five hundred years, while you need to practice." He gently ruffles his fingers through her feathers. "Now, how do you feel about them?"

She looks at him. "What?"

"I ask you all the time how they're feeling, if they're hurting. I don't stop and ask how you're coping, how you feel about them. I know it depends, day to day, as you're adapting. That's okay."

She stands up, opening and closing them while trying to push back tears. "Today isn't a good day for them." Tears begin to fall down her face. Rafe steps to her and pulls her against his chest.

"It's okay. Even if you hate them right now, I promise I won't be mad."

"I don't hate them or wish I didn't have them. They're a bit much right now. I want to feel normal again. Is that so wrong?" she asks, looking at him.

"No, mia estrela. I felt the same way, after losing mine. I was so ready to have them back."

She shakes her head, crying harder. "See! I can't relate to that, and it makes me feel awful!"

"Ana, why? You weren't born with them like I was. Of course, they were normal to me, and not having them was an unnatural feeling. Like you said, yours were thrust upon you. So, of course, they don't feel natural. I promise you, if you give yourself time and patience, one day they will." He strokes her hair, quietly reassuring her.

"Thank you, love," she says, wiping away her tears.

Ana retracts her wings before going to the washroom and blowing her nose. She splashes water on her face then pours herself a cup of water. She sits on the chaise, slowly drinking. Rafe joins her.

"I'm much better now. I'm sorry I had a bad reaction."

"Ana, it's okay."

"It's not. I should've accepted them by now."

"Maeriana, listen to me very carefully." She gives him her full attention. "You went through something shocking and horrifying, dying then growing wings. You will accept them when the time is right. Yes, I want you to accept them. You know how much that will mean to me. Even I know not to push that, though. You need time." He takes her hand, kissing it. "Please, mia estrela. Give yourself time and patience. Can you do that?"

"I'm trying to."

"No, if you ever want to accept them, you have to."

"Yes, love," she answers softly. "I'm sorry."

"Ana," he says, pulling her into his arms. "Please, mia estrela. Please stop being sorry for not accepting your wings! You're working through it. That's all I can ask of you."

"I did wake up this morning, thinking of you and last night. I forgot I had them for a moment."

"Really?"

"Yes," she answers, looking at him. "It's starting to happen. You were right about that."

He kisses her. "See? Just give yourself time!"

"I will, love. I promise." She blushes.

"What?"

"Can we eat a little more?"

His smile grows as he helps her to her feet. "Yes!" They sit at the table. Ana takes another bite of her croissant. "How is that?"

"Fantastic! Between the pastries and the Eiffel Tower,

I can almost believe we're in Paris! Oh, I wish we could honeymoon there."

"Don't you want to go to the beach?"

"Yes! I've always wanted to go. Do we… do we have to wait until our honeymoon? If we're not getting married for a year or two, I—"

"Ana, once Remus is taken care of, we'll go wherever you want, within the quadrants."

"Thank you." She eats more bread and cheese. "I really miss Earth," she says, softly. "I hate that I'll never go back. I came here, thinking that maybe once I brought peace, I would have a chance to return, to visit."

"Is that another reason you're unhappy with your wings today?"

"Yes. It's so stupid! Even if I didn't have them, it's too dangerous for me to go back there. I know that."

"Ana, that was your home. It's not stupid to think about going back. I'm sorry we can't. What can I do? How can I make this better?"

"Oh, Rafe, no! You've done everything, given me everything! Here, we should be celebrating, and I'm being gloomy."

"Like you said, it's all tied together. Have I told you, your wings are the most beautiful wings I've ever seen? I didn't fall to my knees at the sight of the Crimson Queen, but because I couldn't get over how stunning they are."

"Really?"

"Yes. No one has ever had wings that color, and your feathers are so soft, so unlike any I've ever felt. Your wings are absolutely incredible!"

She smiles at him, extending them. Rafe gently ruffles through the feathers. "Thank you. I… That makes me feel a lot better about them."

"Seriously?"

"Yes, love. It means a lot."

He leans in, kissing her. "I wish I had said it sooner."

"It's okay. I needed it today."

Ana stands and walks to the center of the room. She furls and unfurls them, looking up when Rafe steps in front of her.

"Love?"

"Yes, Ana?"

She smiles at him as she steps up to him. Kissing him hard, she wraps her legs around his waist. Without a word, he takes to the air, caressing her stomach.

"Yes," she whispers.

He lifts her gown but stops when she goes tense. "Ana?"

"I'm all right," she assures him. She kisses him, focusing on being in the air, his hands on her skin, his mouth on hers. "Please?"

He continues bringing the fabric up. His hand teases above her knee and inner thigh until she's trembling. "Do I need to stop?"

She smiles at him, kissing him. "No, I want this. I promise."

Seeing only love in her eyes, he kisses her, as his hand moves up. She holds him tight and cries out when she's overcome. They lower back to the ground as she collapses into his arms.

"I can't wait until I'm experienced enough to do that to you!" A smile spreads across his face, and Ana laughs. "Excited, are you?" she teases.

"No, not that. The fact that you want to use your wings and learn so much. After earlier, it makes me happy to hear." Rafe walks to the chaise, sitting down with her in his arms. He kisses her. "You are so amazing, Ana."

"Love, so are you!" She admires her ring. "It's so beautiful! I can't get over how pretty it is. What made you choose this stone?"

"We have so many beautiful stones here. That one, being so legendary, so rare, it reminded me of you." When she trembles again, his grip tightens. "Ana, what's wrong?"

Her tears fall. "How are you real?" She kisses him,

caressing his face and neck. "You're so sweet, so romantic, so loving."

He takes her hand and places a gentle kiss between her knuckles. "I'm trying to be the man you deserve."

"You're not trying."

"I am try—"

"No, love. You already are. From the moment you took me in your arms, confessing your love for me, you have been the man I deserve."

"Can I ask, how do you feel about your wings?"

She smiles. "They're beautiful. Every day, working with you, exercising them, is another day I'm getting closer to accepting them." She kisses him. "Believe me, I'm as excited as you are for the day I tell you I accept them."

"I truly hope you are doing this for yourself and not to make me happy. I want you to be comfortable, happy, and to feel normal again."

"I am doing it for me, but I am so grateful for your help. We were on Earth when you expanded your wings, and I couldn't believe what I was seeing! It was so surreal, so incredible, I thought I was hallucinating. Coming here, seeing you every day with them. I thought they were beautiful. I couldn't tell you that, though. I was angry and embarrassed, both."

"I'm sorry."

"No! No, we're not going through that. I wanted you to know, I've loved your wings from the moment I saw them. I wasn't even freaked out or anything."

"I was surprised you didn't faint." He tilts his head when she laughs softly. "What?" he asks.

"I couldn't wait to come here and have you take me in your arms to fly with me."

"Oh, Ana!" He grips her tight and kisses her forehead. "I'm sorry. The first time we did that was to save you. I wish it could've been romantic instead."

"You were so angry at me, and I deserved it. You've more than made up for it. What we did was unbelievable. It means more to me than pleasure."

"How so?"

"The fact that you can concentrate so well, while going through what we do, makes me feel confident that maybe I can be that good with my wings, too."

He gasps. "Really?"

"Yes."

"We'll practice more this week. You say the word, and we'll work with them. Yes?"

"Yes, love." She kisses him. "Thank you, for the perfect weekend! It's been so wonderful."

"Ana, do you need another day?"

"No, Rafe. I want to resume my routine tomorrow. As far as what you asked last night, we can eat breakfast in the dining hall if you want me to announce our engagement."

"Really?"

"Yes."

He glances at the clock. "Kara and Evren will be bringing dinner in a few hours. Are you nervous about Kara's reaction?"

"No. She should be happy for us, but we'll handle whatever she says. I know she loves me and worries for me." She looks down. "Rafe, I've been wondering something. I know you said why you were the best choice, but if it was illegal for a guardian and a royal to be together, why were you sent to retrieve me?"

"Rowenne and I discussed that. We knew we couldn't send just anyone because they would know who you are. We were worried they might seduce you or kill you for the throne. We knew it was tricky, with the law, but we agreed it was best for me to go. The plan was to come back here, and he would take you into his office to explain everything."

"How would that have played out?"

"He would've told you the truth. Then it would've been your choice, to keep me as your assigned guardian, send me to battle, or have me executed."

"You can't be serious!"

"It was worth the risk. We had to bring you here, restore the throne, and end the war. You've done that, and so much more. You've defended and protected your people. You are more of an amazing queen than I would've imagined."

"I bet that's not what you were thinking, seeing me hurt and scared on Earth."

"Ana, I've only ever seen you as brave and strong, as a warrior. Yes, the mugger hurt you. He had a gun, yet you still tried to defend yourself. You went hand to hand against a trained police officer. How do you not see your strength, your courage?"

"When you put it like that…" she murmurs.

"No, Ana. It's the truth. You fought and survived so much, before even coming here. You are my warrior." He smiles at her.

"Love, is it okay if we went to my mother's library?"

"Now?"

"Yes, only if you think it's safe enough."

"That should be fine. Will you do me a favor and put on a winter gown? The palace is still a bit cold right now."

"Yes, of course!"

She kisses him before running to the closet. Holding a gown in her hand, she looks up when he comes in.

"Are you okay?"

He smiles. "Yes. It surprised me to see you so excited. Do you have something planned?"

She kisses him. "I do. In a fun way, nothing romantic. Not in there."

"Ana," he says, taking her hand and kissing it, "I only meant something special for us, like a picnic and read in front of the fireplace, nothing like what you're thinking."

"I'm sorry. I know you wouldn't."

"No, mia estrela. Don't lose your smile! Please?" He leans down, planting gentle kisses on her face and neck, smiling as she laughs. "There it is."

Ana slips on the blue gown with silver embroidered

snowflakes, along with white boots. She steps up to him.

"Is this winter enough for you?"

He laughs, picking her up and kissing her. "Yes, mia estrela." He puts her on her feet and clasps her hand.

"Aren't you cold?" she asks.

"No. I don't really get cold."

"If I'm part guardian, I wish I had that part! I hate the cold."

"I know. I wish you did, too."

Chapter 15

They arrive at her mother's private library.

"Mi'lady, if I may?" Aylin asks.

"Yes?"

"I love books."

Ana smiles at her. "Let us have some time here. Have you been to the main library?"

"No, Your Majesty."

"You and Roesh will escort us there next. Okay?"

"Mi'lady, you don't have to do that for me."

"I insist."

"Thank you," Aylin says, bowing.

Rafe takes Ana inside. They go to the chairs, where she sits him down. She goes to the shelf and removes the copy of Pride and Prejudice. She shows Rafe.

"Have you ever read this one?"

"No."

Ana smiles as she sits in the other chair. She opens the book and reads to him. He closes his eyes and listens. When her throat gets dry, he takes the book and reads for her. She sits on his lap. He wraps his arm around her while continuing to read aloud. They stop and bookmark the chapter they're on before setting the book on the table.

Ana leans up and kisses him softly. "Another first?" she asks.

"Yes, mia estrela. A good one, too."

She gets to her feet. "Ready to go to the main library?"

"Ana, why now? You've been here for months. Other than your lessons, you've shown no interest in going there," Rafe points out as he joins her.

"Love, at first, I couldn't. I was too anxious and heartbroken and scared to focus on reading. I could barely concentrate on my lessons. Now that I'm calming down, I'd like to get back into reading. So much history, art, and culture to learn!"

"Heartbroken?"

From under her lashes, she looks at him. "Please, don't. We're together now. We're going to get married! Look where we are. I'm sorry I said anything."

"No, Ana. I asked a question, you answered it. Please, don't feel like you can't be honest with me." He pulls her into his arms. "I still feel guilty about all that. I'm working on it."

"Rafe, literally life and death. I've moved on. I agreed to be your wife, didn't I?" she asks, smiling up at him. He responds with a kiss. "You know I've forgiven you. The moment you took me in your arms, dying for me, I forgave you."

"I know you did, but I don't deserve it."

"Love, you do. You saved me on Earth, brought me to this beautiful realm, and even though I know it broke your heart to do it, you stayed by my side to protect me. You have spent every day, since my first day here, trying to show me you love me, even when you couldn't say it." She takes his hand and holds it to her face. "Now, can we please go to the other library?"

"Yes, mia estrela." He steps out first, seeing Roesh and Aylin. "We're going to the main library now."

"Yes, Rafe."

Ana enjoys the stroll through the palace, admiring the marble columns and beautiful woodwork on the doors and trim. Once they arrive, she turns to Roesh and Aylin.

"Please, come in. I want you to see it."

Rafe nods in agreement. They all step inside. Ana goes to the history section, watching Roesh and Aylin taking it all in. Aylin steps up to her.

"Mi'lady, this is beautiful! I only own a few books, so it's incredible to see this."

"If you don't mind me asking, why haven't you been here before?"

"We are expected to stay in, or near, our barracks on our days off."

"Aylin, you have my permission to come here, any time you are off duty."

"I—Really?"

"Yes," Ana insists. "I mean that."

"Thank you, mi'lady." She runs to Roesh and looks at various books with him.

Rafe smiles at Ana. "You made her day."

"Libraries are meant to be shared, to be open to everyone."

He smiles. "You sound like your mother."

"Really?"

"Oh yes. She loved books as much as you do. She felt the same way. That's why she had her own private library, but she made sure we had this one too. The room was already set up with a few books, but she had more books collected and gathered here, for everyone to share. Between the war and everything, most people haven't had time. I think you'll see it get used more now."

"I hope."

"Ana, you asked me to take you to your mother's library. You do realize, you've inherited that. It's your library now."

"I—" Unable to hide her tears, she turns and wipes them away.

He gasps. "I wasn't trying to make you sad. I'm sorry. I wanted you to know that it's yours."

"I do know, but I like calling it my mother's because it makes it sound like she's still here."

"Then we'll call it her library," he says. He smiles at her before kissing her.

"Thank you."

She walks to the shelf and picks out a book about the history of the palace. Rafe sits beside her at the table, watching as she flips through the pages.

"You're right! I didn't realize how big it is."

"We'll continue our tours. I know you want to see everything."

"I do, but you and Kara are right. I like seeing a little here and there, so I'm not overwhelmed. Also, I like knowing there is still so much more to see!"

Aylin approaches and bows. "Majesty, may I borrow this?" She hands her a book. Ana smiles when she sees the title.

"Of course. I love that one. It's a retelling of one of my favorite fairytales. Have you ever read a book from Earth?"

"No, mi'lady."

"If you have any questions while you're reading it, don't hesitate to ask."

"Thank you!" Aylin beams while putting the book in her pocket. "I can assure you, I'll take excellent care of it."

"Please, do. I trust you with it."

Aylin bows before returning to Roesh.

"I don't believe I've heard of that one," Rafe says.

"What? How have you not read that? It's a great book! When she's done, we'll take it to our quarters and read it together." She studies him for a moment. "How much downtime do guardians get? I know they've been short-handed with the war, but normally I mean?"

"We would work four days, twelve hours, and have three days off. During the war, we worked six days, with two off. We alternated."

"That must've been exhausting, though."

"Ana, do you forget? We're a little stronger than humans. We did okay. Now that more guardians have returned, and the war is over, they're back on their normal schedule. See? Not slaves. I told you."

"Yes, love." She continues looking through the book. Seeing a familiar sight, she smiles and holds it up to show Rafe. "Our battlement."

"Good memories, yes?" He laughs when she blushes. "Ana, I was talking about our dinner last night."

"Right," she says. "Sorry."

He laughs, kissing her hard. "Oh, mia estrela, what am I going to do with you?"

"Hmm. Marry me?"

"Yes, I will."

They laugh and hold each other. "Do you feel what I'm feeling?"

"Your love, happiness, excitement?"

"Yes, Rafe. That's all because of you."

"I want to ask something, but I don't want to upset you."

"It's okay. You can ask."

"Have you thought any more on your immortality? I'm curious, since we are talking about our future."

"Love, you know I have. We've talked about forever."

"I know. I meant, for yourself? Have you thought more on what it will be like?"

"I try to, but then I get overwhelmed. Small steps, remember?"

"Yes, mia estrela."

She smiles at him. "We should get back to our quarters. We'll have dinner soon. I'd like to clean up and change before."

Taking her hand, he stands up. "As you wish, Your Majesty."

She shakes her head while laughing. "Let's go."

Rafe gestures to Aylin and Roesh.

***

Roesh does a sweep, then comes back out. "All clear, Your Majesty."

"Thank you."

Rafe leads Ana inside. She goes to the closet, picking out a pale blue gown with gossamer sleeves and a tulle skirt. Carefully, she sets her ring in the drawer with the royal jewels. She lays the gown on the ottoman before gathering fresh undergarments and her robe.

Rafe steps in. "Am I joining you?"

"Hmm. Work up an appetite for dinner?" She kisses him and thinks of them in the air. When he shudders under her, she can't help but giggle. "Like that?"

He grabs her face and places a passionate kiss on her lips. "Shower, now."

"Yes, love."

She walks into the washroom and turns on the tap. She sets her clothes on the vanity before stripping out of her winter gown. Removing her stockings and boots, she leaves on her undergarments. She leans against the vanity, waiting for Rafe to join her.

When he steps in, she bites her lower lip. He shuts the door behind him, then comes to her. He drops his clothes next to hers, then his hand caresses the lace.

"Hmm. I do like this."

"Really?"

"Oh yes." He kisses her, moving his mouth to her ear. "I'll like it even better when it's on the floor."

"Rafe!" she cries out, kissing him as he undoes her corset, letting it fall. He slides her undergarments down, his hand tracing her hip. When her body goes tense, he stops. "I'm okay."

He stands up, pulling her in his arms. "No, you're not."

"I'm sorry," she says, trembling.

"No, mia estrela." He kisses her forehead, wrapping his arms tighter around her. "Let's get cleaned up and have dinner. You've had a busy day."

"Yes, love."

"Just think, the sooner you get cleaned up, the sooner you can put your ring on."

She smiles at him. "Yes!"

He takes her into the shower, where he washes her hair as she cleans him off. They finish. She slips on fresh undergarments, putting her robe on and going to the closet.

Ana dresses in her gown and adds silver slippers with

a matching crown. She puts her ring on, along with a bracelet and necklace.

"You look like an angel," Rafe says, stepping in. "You are so alluring!"

She breaks out into a smile. "Really?"

"Oh, mia estrela. You know what you do to me in that color with your crimson wings!"

She walks to the doors to the mirror. Opening it, her wings expand, and she admires them with the gown. "It is pretty together."

He steps up behind her, wrapping his arms around her. "It's absolutely beautiful." Her face goes flush. "Ana, what's wrong?"

"When we were in front of the mirror this morning, you called me that. I didn't feel like it, seeing my ribs. Hearing you now, I believe it."

She brings her wings in, turning around and kissing him. Her body folds into his curves, wanting to touch every possible inch of him. She gasps for air. Her lips find his again, devouring him.

"Oh, love," she murmurs. "Thank you."

"For what?"

"Your patience with me. I question myself, doubt myself, but you never do. You don't seem surprised by my accomplishments. You expect them. You expect me to be incredible. I've never known anyone to feel that way about me."

"Ana, everything you have done has been incredible. From fighting back against an armed thief, to growing wings and learning to use them, to saving your people. You do great things, without realizing how great they are!" He gently runs his hand through her wings. "Now, how are they feeling this evening?"

"A little heavy, but not too bad."

"Really?"

"Really! We worked them earlier. That helps so much. I wish I had started it sooner. They were heavy and hurt so bad because I kept them tucked in, ashamed of them. I didn't want to deal with them."

"You are doing better."

"Thank you."

"Now, I have to get dressed."

She holds him tighter, running her hand along his wing. "Do you?"

"Kara and Evren will be here shortly. Let's have a nice, quiet dinner with them. Then we'll wear ourselves out for bed."

She gives him a playful pout before kissing him. "Yes, love."

A gasp escapes when he holds her tight, closing his eyes. He feels his lips on her and thinks on her touches. She cries out, gripping him hard.

"Oh, God. How did you do that?" she asks, panting for air.

He smiles, kissing her. "Hmm. Like that, did you?"

"Do you… do you know what you did to me?"

"Oh, yes. I felt it as much as you did."

Her head rolls back, as she catches her breath. "You are incredible!"

He kisses her neck and face, his hand caressing her side. "I have to get dressed. We are having company." He helps her sit on the ottoman. "Rest. We'll eat soon."

"Yes, Rafe."

He dresses in black slacks with a pale blue shirt. As he's buttoning it up, he watches Ana bring her hand to her chest. Her eyes close while she thinks of what they did together. She desperately wants to be with him, to give herself completely. Her head hangs at the realization she isn't ready yet.

"Ana, what's wrong?"

Meeting his gaze, she lets out a deep breath. "I wish I could give you all of me. We're engaged. I feel like I should be ready, like I should be stronger."

"Ana, that's why we're engaged. You are stronger.

You've brought down so many walls! We'll have them all down by the time we get married. You know we will. Look at how much you've already come through."

"I know, but I wouldn't have had that reaction if I hadn't been taken to his camp. This is what I mean. I get a little better, only to get broken again!"

"Maeriana, listen to me," he says, kneeling in front of her. "You are not broken, nor have you ever been. You've been pushed, bent, and hurt, but never broken. That alone is a testament to your enduring strength." He takes her hands and delicately kisses them.

"Oh, Rafe," she says, falling into his arms. "Thank you, love. How do you know what to say? How do you comfort me so?"

"Like you said, our hearts and souls are entwined. I need you, the way you need me. You breathed life back into me, making me feel more alive these past few months than I have in five centuries." He stands up, pulling her with him, then leans down as she steps up to meet him. His lips consume hers while he caresses her back and neck. "I have to finish getting ready."

"Yes, love," she says, sitting down.

Rafe gets his shoes on then joins her and escorts her into the main chamber.

There's a knock at the door, and he lets Kara and Evren in, along with dinner service. Everything is set up, then the staff leave. Kara and Evren sit with Ana, while Rafe runs to the washroom.

"Did you go to the village yesterday?" Ana asks.

"We did. It was nice. It wasn't too cold or busy. How was your dinner?"

"Wonderful. Thank you again for the beautiful gown."

Rafe sits beside Ana. He squeezes her hand, then begins to eat. Ana reaches for her cup when Kara grabs her hand and examines the ring before looking at Rafe.

"Congratulations," she says, letting go. She resumes eating.

"Sis, please—" Ana starts as Kara gets up and walks to the window.

Ana starts to stand when Rafe gently pushes her back into her seat before approaching Kara.

"What's wrong?" Rafe asks.

She turns to him. "You lied to me. You told me you weren't going to! Not while she's still recovering. Everything she went through—"

"I didn't lie to you." He sighs when Kara scoffs. "I didn't. When I said that, I was going to wait. You weren't here yesterday. We flew out to the woods, she talked about our future together. She is happy and accepting herself. I saw she was ready for this. You know that I am the one who has been waiting, not her. Now, she should be so happy, sharing this wonderful news with her best friend. Instead, she's over there wiping away tears because of you."

Kara hangs her head. "I'm sorry."

"Tell her you are."

"It's not that. I'm jealous. I've felt like she was replacing me with you. Now, the two of you will get married, start a family. She doesn't need me anymore!"

"Kara, you know that is not true. She opened up to you about her wings, even after you humiliated her with them. She tells you all the time how much she loves you, how important to her you are."

Ana joins them. "What did I do wrong, Kara?" she asks.

Kara grabs her and hugs her tightly. "Not a damn thing! I'm so sorry. I was jealous and angry. Please, forgive me?"

"Why were you jealous? You're engaged, too."

"I felt like you were replacing me. It was petty and stupid." She squeezes tighter. "Please, Ana, please forgive me! I am so happy for you, so excited for you and Rafe to get married. I truly am."

"Kara, you know I forgive you, but what am I doing wrong? How else can I show you that you're still my sister and my best friend?"

"You didn't do anything wrong! This was all me, all my doing. I got so focused on protecting you, on worrying over keeping you safe, instead of being with you!" She looks at Rafe when he chuckles. "What?"

"I said basically the same thing to her. We have been too worried about protecting her, instead of spending time together."

Kara turns back to Ana. "Do you want to resume your duties tomorrow? You have two guardians, and starting tomorrow you'll have two royal guards, as well."

"Why all the extra security?"

"Come, let's sit and eat. We can discuss this over dinner," Rafe says, taking Ana's hand. They return to the table.

"We still haven't found Remus. He is planning an attempt to take the palace, but his lieutenant didn't know when. We have doubled our scouts and have more patrols."

"Kara, I'm sorry. You were supposed to have a weekend off."

"We did. We went to the village yesterday, spent time together today. I went to the Communications Lounge and gathered intel before coming here. Really."

"All right. Is that all we know about Remus?"

"Unfortunately, yes." Kara sighs. "Knowing he is out there is so frustrating. I want him brought to justice, after everything he has done to you." Kara watches as the color drains from Ana's face. "I know we will. In the meantime, can I see your ring?" Kara hopes changing the subject will help put Ana at ease. Ana lifts her left hand, holding it over to Kara. She takes it and studies the ring. "Rafe, is that—"

"Yes."

"How in the world did you ever acquire one?"

He laughs. "I know the right people."

"Oh, Ana. It's absolutely beautiful!"

Ana turns to Evren, who is blushing. "Evren?"

"I'm so sorry. I don't know what's going on?"

"Oh, right. This isn't a tradition here. At dinner last night, Rafe asked me to be his wife. I said yes, and he gave me this ring."

"Congratulations!" Evren leans up to see. "It is beautiful. Is the band made to look like wings holding the stone?"

"Yes."

"Rafe, it's stunning."

"Thanks, Evren."

Kara turns to Ana. "Have you set the—"

"No, Kara," Ana says as she stifles her giggle. "We're waiting a year or two. Speaking of which, have we started the new year? I hate this, still learning everything here! I feel like an idiot because I don't even know the date."

"Don't," Kara says. "You're doing fine with your lessons. No. The new year starts Saturday. That's why there is a ball on Friday, from nine to one in the morning."

"Kara, how are we planning a ball on such short notice?" Ana asks.

Kara laughs. "We're not."

"I don't understand?"

"The guardians host it. It's a new tradition that Melian and I decided to start. I wanted to surprise you."

"Oh, thank goodness!" Ana laughs. Turning serious, she swallows hard. "It's not a masquerade, is it?"

"No. For security purposes, we thought it best. I thought you loved the idea of a masquerade ball?"

"I did," she says softly.

Rafe takes her hand. "Ana?"

"Sorry. It still brings up painful memories. Does this one have a theme?"

"No," Kara replies.

"Then I'll wear the gown I wore last night, since you and Evren haven't seen me in it."

"That sounds perfect. We were supposed to help you get ready, weren't we?"

"I did okay."

"Ana, you were absolutely gorgeous. Your braids were perfect."

She blushes. "Thank you, Rafe." Ana stops eating when she sees Kara staring straight ahead. "What?"

Kara gets to her feet and rushes to the corner of the room. "What is that?"

Rafe joins her and turns on the lights. "It's a replica of the Eiffel Tower. It was at our dinner last night."

"That's what you had delivered?"

"Yep."

"Rafe, you are something else. This is beautiful!" She smiles at him, until noticing how serious he appears. "What's wrong?"

He glances back to be sure it's the two of them. "Ana misses Earth. She wants desperately to go to Paris. She understands why she can't, between the danger and her wings, but I wish there was something I could do."

"I'm sorry. I agree, it's too dangerous."

"She says she's always wanted to go to the beach. I told her a little about MorningStella."

Kara nods. "I'll help you on selling that to her. Once she sees the pink sand and emerald water, she'll forget all about Paris!"

"I can only hope. Of course, we can't do anything until we get Remus." Ana stands up, catching his eye. "Ana, please sit. We're coming back over." He nods to Kara, and they return to the table. He sits, taking Ana's hand.

"Everything okay?"

"Yes, mia estrela." He notes the worry on her face. "Everything is perfect."

"Okay." She finishes eating. "Kara, is there anything else we need to know to prepare for the briefing tomorrow morning?"

"Everything is running smoothly. Audressa is back in her quarters, our royal guards are doing a good job with patrols, and there seem to be no issues at the moment."

Ana sighs in relief. "I was so worried about being

crowned and stopping the war, I never really stopped to think about what it would be like after, to run a kingdom. It was too overwhelming to think about. Kara, thank you for everything. You and Evren have taken on so much!"

"We really haven't—"

"No. I feel like I've neglected my duties." Rafe can't hide his disapproval as his brows furrow. Ana struggles to stay serious, though a bubble of laughter nearly escapes her at the sight. She focuses on her words. "I know, love. I know that I've defended our people and needed to recover. Still, I feel like I should be doing more."

"Ana, don't take this the wrong way. This kingdom basically runs itself. As Kara said, everything runs smoothly. Your advisors, chancellor, and captains oversee so much, you truly do not have to worry. I would not have brought you here, if I thought you couldn't handle it."

"Thank you, Rafe. You have always seen me as more than I can see myself. You and Kara both do."

"Sis, you know you're amazing."

The laughter escapes Ana. "Okay." She looks up when she realizes she's being serious. "Kara—"

"No, don't. I mean it."

"Thank you."

"Evren, what say you and I gather these, so Kara and Ana could have a moment together?" Rafe asks, holding up his empty plate.

"Yes, Rafe." They collect dishes and leave.

Kara stands and takes Ana's hand. They go to her Eiffel Tower. "I can't believe he had this made for you. It's absolutely incredible."

"I know. I can't, either."

"Sis, Rafe said you're missing Earth. Anything I can help with?"

"No. When I first came here, I thought maybe after the war ended, I could go back and visit." She expands her wings. "I know now I can never go back. It made me sad, but I'll be okay."

"I miss it, too."

"Really?"

"Yes."

"The coffee?"

"Oh, God! Especially the coffee!" They both laugh. "How are they today?"

"They're good. I'm getting closer to accepting them. Rafe has been so patient about that."

"Can I see you fly? If it's not too much for you?"

"Of course!" Ana goes to the middle of the room. Her wings extend fully, then she's up in the air. She hovers for a moment before she lands in front of Kara. "Well?"

"He's right. You are a natural. It's incredible to see you do that. How does it feel?"

"So weird." They laugh. "I'm getting more used to it, though. I've started waking up in the morning, forgetting I have them. Rafe said that's a good thing, a sign that I'm starting to accept them. I do think they're beautiful, too."

"Really?" Kara asks, smiling.

"Yes. Rafe and you have both told me so."

"I don't want to embarrass you…"

"What?"

"Have you kissed in the air?"

"We have, with snow falling. It was so beautiful."

"Okay, I'm a little jealous now."

"Kara, do you want to fly with me? When I've had more training, I mean?"

"Yes. I didn't want to ask because I know it can be a difficult subject. I never meant to embarrass you about them, or what you've done with Rafe."

"I want to tell you something, something really personal. Only because I know you'll understand. You'll see how he's helping me with walls."

"I swear, no jokes or embarrassment."

"Rafe and I have taken a bath together."

"Ana! Really?"

"Yes."

"I thought you would never take one. After what you told me, about when you were growing up. I'm so grateful you have each other."

"He is amazing. If he feels me tense up, or sees a look in my eyes, or anything, he immediately stops and makes sure I'm okay. He's held me after my nightmares, and he reassures me when I have an episode." She pulls Kara into her arms. "I'm sorry."

"Ana, for what?"

"You already feel like I'm replacing you, and here I am—"

"Stop. I never thought you would fall in love with a man, after the hell you've endured. Believe me, I am happy for both of you."

"Thanks, sis."

Rafe and Evren step up beside them.

"We'll retire for the evening. Breakfast at eight?" Kara asks.

"Yes, thank you."

She bows. "Your Majesty."

"Sage."

They laugh and hug. Kara walks to Evren, taking her hand. They say goodnight to Rafe and leave.

"You two okay?" Rafe asks as he stands beside Ana.

"We are. Thanks for giving us some time."

"Of course. You are exhausted."

"I'm sorry."

"No, it's okay." He kisses her. "You've had a busy weekend. We'll change and turn in soon." He looks at her ring. "A beautiful, unique stone for a beautiful, unique woman." He laughs when she blushes. "What?"

"Rafe, really?" She kisses him. "Thank you for this weekend."

"Always."

Her smile grows. "Forever."

"Now, let's get changed for bed."

"Yes, love." They go into the closet. She sits on the

ottoman, barely able to keep her eyes open.

"Ana, are you okay?"

"Yes. I'm really sleepy."

He runs his hand through his hair, debating if he should ask. "What did you and Kara do while we were gone?"

"We talked about Earth. She really does miss coffee. I told her how much you've helped me by bringing down walls and comforting me."

"Anything else?"

"I flew up to the ceiling and around the room. She asked to see."

"Ana, I really wish you wouldn't do that when I'm not around. That's not against you, but after what happened earlier, I worry."

"I know. I'm sorry. I was trying to make her happy, after everything."

"That's how you wear yourself out, worrying about everyone else. I'm not mad, I swear. I want you to rest now."

"I will."

He gets her pajamas, and she changes into them. Gently taking her ring, he puts it in the box and closes the drawer. They go to the washroom.

"You'll be okay by yourself?"

"Yes. I'm tired."

"Okay."

She gets ready for bed, then steps out. He carries her and lays her down. "I'm going to get changed. Give me a minute, and I'll join you."

"Yes, love."

He goes into the closet, changes into pajamas, and uses the washroom. Then he climbs into bed with her. She snuggles into his chest, clutching his shirt.

"I love you, mia estrela."

"Hmm. I love you, too."

The shower running wakes Rafe. He sees it's a little after three. He puts on his slippers and goes into the washroom.

"Ana?"

"I'll be out in a moment."

"What's wrong?" He leans against the vanity but straightens up when he hears her crying. "Ana?" He strips down before stepping in with her. "Nightmare?" She shakes her head. "What?"

"I had an episode."

"Oh, Ana." He holds her close and grows concerned when she's trembling against him. "Do you want to talk about it?"

"Not yet. Help me get warm, please? I can't seem to get warm."

He moves her under the water, holding her tight. "Bad, huh?"

"Rafe—"

"Feel me, feel my comfort."

"I've been doing so well. I'm sorry!"

"No, mia estrela. No apologies. This is going to happen as we continue to move forward, breaking down walls. Why didn't you wake me?" When she starts to move away, he tightens his grip. He kisses the top of her head. "I'm not angry. I'm worried. Please, Ana."

"I was too ashamed. I was going to wake you, after I was done in here. I swear. I needed a moment to collect myself."

"It's okay, but let's get you warm."

"Yes, love." She pulls herself in tighter, holding him with everything she has. The warmth and comfort comes off of him in waves. When she stops trembling, calming her racing heart, she reaches to turn off the water.

"Another minute?"

"Yes, Rafe." She leans back into him as his arms enfold her. "Thank you."

She turns, facing him, then laying her head on his chest. He caresses her neck and back, sending out all the love and comfort he can. When she's trembling again, he brings his hand up, feeling her tears.

"Oh, Ana."

"I'm sorry!"

"No, mia estrela. Please, stop apologizing." He kisses her forehead. "Let me comfort you right now."

She wipes her tears away and turns off the water. Taking his hand as they step out, she towels off. They get dressed. She goes to the chaise and wraps the blanket around herself. Rafe sits beside her, taking her hand.

"Are you okay? You don't have to tell me anything you don't want to, but I want to know if you're okay now."

"I am," she replies, her voice a whisper in the air. She traces her finger over his hand. "I don't know what triggered it. It wasn't anything from this weekend, I promise."

"It's okay. Ana, we can go back to bed. You don't have to tell me."

"I know that, and I know you mean that. It feels wrong, though, to not tell you, after everything you've done for me."

"I want you to tell me because you want to open up, to bring down walls. Not because you feel like you have to." He sees her lip quiver, as her eyes fill with tears. He moves over, wrapping his arm around her. "It's okay. You're safe now. Whatever it was, you're safe."

"It was my foster brothers," she says softly. "I'm not really ready to talk about it. I'm so sorry!"

"No, Ana. When you're ready, you know that."

"What caused this, though? I don't understand."

"Sometimes it happens. You were relaxed, and we had brought down some walls. It's going to happen again. It sucks, but it shows you're moving forward, moving past what's happened."

"Can we go back to bed?"

"Of course." He picks her up and carries her. "Thank

you," he says as they snuggle.

"For what?"

"Opening up. I'm going to ask a question. You absolutely do not have to answer it. Okay?"

"Okay."

"Was there anything else, after they tried to hurt you?"

"I told you about the sixteen-year-old coming in, when I had the knife."

"Yes."

"He came in, but I didn't hear him. There were other beds in the room, and mine was away from the door. I felt him on me. He…" She closes her eyes. "He pulled the blanket off, running his hand between my—" Her breath trembles. "He—I brought the knife up then."

"Oh, mia estrela. Why are some boys so awful? I'm grateful you survived, that I have you here. You are my everything."

"Rafe, thank you." She snuggles in closer, clutching his shirt with both hands. "Please, love, don't ever leave me."

"Never, Ana. We're going to get married, we're going to rule the kingdom, and we're going to have a wonderful forever. I swear this to you now."

"I love you."

"I love you, too. Can you get more sleep?"

"Yes," she replies, yawning. "I will."

He sings softly in her ear and is overwhelmed with happiness because she is comforted.

Chapter 16

"Rafe, I think Kara is here with breakfast."

He lets them in and helps set up the food. He returns to her. "Ana, are you okay to eat?"

"Yes," she says as she gets up, putting on her robe and slippers.

She sits at the table. Kara watches her, studying her for a moment before speaking.

"Ana, are you okay?"

"Yes, Kara. Why?"

"You look like you could use more sleep."

"I had a rough night. I'm okay now." She looks up, seeing worry on their faces. "Maybe I'll get a little more sleep before the briefing."

"About that," Kara says. "I know you want to get into your routine. You can skip this morning."

"No, Kara. I'm okay. I promise."

"All right."

"Ah!" Ana exclaims.

"What's wrong?" Rafe asks, jumping to his feet.

"No, no. It's okay. I realized, we were supposed to eat breakfast in the dining hall so we could announce our engagement. I wasn't thinking."

"You were exhausted," Rafe says, sitting back down. He kisses her. "Don't scare me like that."

She laughs. "I'm sorry. It hit me!"

"Honestly, dinner is when it's busiest," Kara suggests.

"You're right."

"Will you announce it at the briefing?" she asks.

"No. We'll wait until dinner."

"All right. We'll get dishes taken care of so you can get a little more rest. We'll come over around nine-thirty."

"Thanks, Kara. See you then," Rafe says, helping them

get dishes together. He watches Kara and Evren leave then turns to Ana. "Did you wake up again last night?"

"No. The episode wore me out. I'm okay."

Rafe takes her hand, focusing on how she's feeling. "You are exhausted! Why didn't you say anything?"

"I'll lay down. Wake me at quarter after nine. Please?"

"Hmm. If you're sleeping good, I'm not waking you up."

"Fine." She laughs when he picks her up to carry her to bed. "Are you laying with me?"

"Of course," he says, crawling into bed with her. "I won't sleep, but I'll snuggle with you. I want to."

"Thank you."

He kisses her forehead. "Get some rest, please?"

"Yes, love."

She falls asleep in his arms. He holds her tight, staying with her until almost nine-thirty. There's a knock at the door, and he opens it to find Kara.

"She's still sleeping. You can update us at lunch."

"Of course. I hope she's okay." She sees the look on Rafe's face. "What?"

"She had a bad episode last night, about her foster brothers. She's okay now, but it wore her out."

"Thank you for telling me. We'll be back at eleven with lunch."

"Yes, Kara. See you then."

He closes the door, then slides back into bed. Ana mumbles in her sleep, and he pulls her in tight. Her exhaustion washes over him, and he falls asleep with her.

***

Rafe glances at the clock and sees it's nearly eleven. He caresses Ana's face and smiles when her lips part. He leans down, planting a soft kiss.

"Hmm," she moans. "What time is it?"

"Almost time for lunch."

She sits up. "The morning briefing!"

"Ana, you were practically passed out. You needed your rest."

The worry is obvious on his face. She sighs. "Yes, love. Are you getting dressed with me?"

"Or undressed?"

She laughs. "Come on."

They go into the closet, where she picks out a long sleeve lavender gown. She lays it on the ottoman when Rafe grabs her hand and spins her to him. He kisses her hard while stroking his fingers through her hair.

"I love you, mia estrela. Recover today, then tomorrow will be back to routine."

"Yes, Rafe. I love you, too."

She slips on her ring and changes into her gown before approaching the mirror, where she opens her wings. Rafe steps up beside her.

"Are you okay?"

"Yes. I wanted to see them." She sees the look of confusion on his face and smiles. "I woke up, forgetting I had them. It's a good thing, but then it kind of freaks me out when I see or feel them. I'm glad I'm starting to accept them, but it's still weird sometimes."

"I understand."

She looks in the mirror, furling and unfurling them. They still don't seem real, as though she can't believe she has them. She thinks back on the battle and lying down in the woods. Memories seep in, from growing cold to everything going dark as she lost blood. She gasps, remembering the pain that brought her to her feet as the wings began to form.

"Ana, what's wrong?"

"Nothing. Remembering the day I got them. I lay down to die, then I was in pain so intense it literally brought me to my feet."

"I had no idea it was that strong."

"It only lasted a moment, before they went from fire

to feathers. Then it didn't hurt as bad."

"No wonder it was so traumatic. Ana, why didn't you tell me how much it hurt?"

"I thought I did when I was telling you what happened. I'm sorry."

"No, no, mia estrela." He kisses her, caressing her neck and jawline. "It's okay. I'm worried, is all."

"Don't worry. Really. It was so much to take in. I don't remember much immediately after, as I was so wore out. I remember lying in bed with you behind me, touching my wings." She sees him blush. "What?"

"I thought you were asleep. I was so curious about them, still in shock myself. I'm sorry."

"Rafe, it's okay. Of course you would want to look at them."

"Kara joked that I was violating you by checking your wings."

She laughs. "That sounds like her. No, love. I promise you, you weren't." She steps up, kissing him as she wraps her arms around his neck, holding him tight. "Thank you for your patience with me and them."

"Ana, anything for you. You know that."

She turns back to the mirror, opening them again. "I can't believe I ever tried to bind them. I don't know what I was thinking."

"You weren't," he says, stepping up behind her. He gently ruffles through her feathers. "You were scared and traumatized. Understandable."

He extends his wings, watching her. She turns around, gently teasing his wings and smiles when his head rolls back.

"Please, love?" she asks, stepping up and kissing him. "I'm okay now."

He can't hide his concern. "I'm torn right now. I know what you said about keeping you encased in glass. However, what you went through last night…"

"No, you're right." She lays her head on his chest, holding him tight. "Tomorrow?"

"I promise." He kisses her again. "They should be here any time with lunch."

Ana laughs when they hear a knock at the door. "Good timing."

Rafe lets Kara and Evren in, then helps set everything up. "How was the briefing?" he asks as Ana joins them.

Kara sighs. "We have a problem."

"What's wrong?" Ana asks.

"We have intelligence there is an assassin here."

"Remus wouldn't do that. He doesn't want to simply kill me. He wants to make an example of me, then take the throne. Someone who knew Kane? Or is it Tinsley?"

"We don't know. It's early in our information, and I'm waiting for more. I'm only telling you because you need to be aware of the threat. You have two more guardians outside and two of the royal guard."

"Thank you, Kara. So much for dinner in the dining hall."

Rafe takes her hand. "You decide. You know that. Say the word, and we'll eat wherever you want."

"We'll stay in quarters. I don't want to needlessly endanger anyone."

"Ana, we don't have to hide in here, either. You can think about it, and let us know later."

"Thank you, love." She looks at Kara. "Are we still having the ball on Friday?"

"Yes. Unless anything significant happens, we're on schedule for that. It's been taken care of."

"I wish I could invite Bela and Joph. I know they aren't travelling right now, either. Not with the threats." She shakes her head. "I thought I had brought about peace! I want this over. I know, I shouldn't complain. This has only been a few weeks. You had to deal with the war for ten years. I'm sorry."

"It's okay to be frustrated. Believe me, we all want peace. We feel the same way as you."

"Ana, we have several scouts out now. We're getting

closer to finding him. We'll stop him."

"Thank you, Kara. Is there anything I can do to help?"

"Just stay alive. Your people need you."

"Kara—"

"Ana, I mean it. You're not some figurehead or symbol, you literally laid your life down for your people. Because of that, they turn to you now. They need you."

"Yes, Kara." Ana turns to Evren. "I'm so sorry, Evren. We took Smaug to the woods, to see how he would do. He was accepted by the other dragons and stayed with them."

"It's okay. We'll see them, once it's safe."

"How did they react to you?" Kara asks.

"The same as him. They opened their wings with me and let me pet them."

Rafe turns to Evren. "Any legends or prophecies of a dragon queen?"

"Not that I'm aware of. I'll have to check. I'm very curious, now."

"We all are!" Ana says, laughing. "I don't know why they like me so." She looks at Kara. "Did you find anything out about the seal I saw in the camp?"

"Oh, I knew there was something I wanted to tell you! Yes. His name is Neven. He was a friend of Bela's. As we thought, he was offered gold and sanctuary if he betrayed them. Bela messaged me and informed me of this. He has him now, in his dungeon. They're trying to use him to lure out Remus. We can only hope it works. Thank you, for your critical intel."

Rafe smiles at her. "See, Ana? I told you, you're incredible."

She smiles back and finishes her meal. Her eyes close, and she's on the cot, bound and gagged.

"Ana?" Rafe asks. "Ana, are you okay?"

She swallows hard, opening her eyes and looking at them. "I was back in his tent, I'm sorry."

"No, mia estrela," Rafe says, taking her hand. "No apology. Are you okay now?"

"Yes, love. I was having a moment."

"Ana, do you need us to go?" Kara asks.

"No, sis. Please. Really. I'm sorry." Seeing the look of disappointment on Rafe's face, she hangs her head. "Rafe, please—"

"No, no. I am sorry. I don't mean to do it. It's okay if you apologize. It hurts me because you have nothing to apologize for."

"Kara, will you and Evren sleep in here tonight?"

"Of course. Everything okay?"

"I want us together, with everything going on."

"Thank you."

"For what?" Ana asks.

"Your concern."

"Kara, you and Evren are my closest friends. Of course, I'm worried."

"Thank you," Evren says. "By the way, my brother Royse is coming to the wedding. He's asked if he could arrive a few days before?"

"Should we postpone our wedding, until Remus is apprehended or killed?"

Ana glances from Evren to Kara. "I see no reason to, unless there is something impending or definite you know."

"I don't," Kara says, "and that's the problem."

"I think it will be all right. Royse is most welcome." She sees the look of concern on Evren's face. "What's wrong?"

"I apologize, Ana. He is a member of the high court. Where can we put him?"

"Caelum's chambers."

"Ana—" Rafe tries.

"No, I mean it. Have them cleaned. Any clothes can be donated, sold, or burned. I don't care. I truly don't." She sees Kara and Rafe exchange a look. "What?"

"What's changed?" Kara asks.

"I want nothing to do with my father or his cruel legacy. I want a fresh start, as the Crimson Queen who brings love and peace. Is that wrong?"

"Not at all," Rafe exclaims. "You're right. That's exactly what this kingdom needs. We'll see it done. Right, Kara?"

"Yes, Rafe."

"Evren, can we have a lesson in the closet, to learn about the jewels and crowns?"

"Yes, Ana. That's fine. We'll take the dishes back then return."

"Thank you."

Kara and Evren collect everything and leave. Rafe leans forward. "Ana, are you sure you're okay?"

"What do you mean?"

"I understand wanting to start a new legacy. Do you not want to learn anything about your family?"

"I would like to learn more about my mother when Kara is up for it. My father? No. I have no interest at all."

"Can I ask what's changed?"

"I don't want to."

"Why not?"

She walks to the fireplace and sits on the chaise, bringing her knees to her chest. She doesn't look at him when he sits beside her. "Rafe, please."

"You don't have to tell me what changed your mind. I want to make sure you're okay. Threats of Remus, an assassin, a ball. I don't want you overwhelmed again. I love you, and I worry for you."

"I know, Rafe. I'm sorry. I love you, too. Thank you."

He moves closer. "Ana, you look tense. Are your wings hurting?"

"A little."

He pulls her to him, gently massaging her shoulders and around her wings. "You are tense! Why didn't you say anything?"

"I honestly didn't feel it because I'm so worried about all the things you mentioned. I am overwhelmed." Her gaze meets his. "I hate feeling like this."

"It's going to be all right. You brought back intel that may be crucial to finding Remus. An assassin? Pfft. You've dispatched plenty of those. The ball? We'll dance, we'll eat, we'll sleep all the next day. You know everything is going to be okay."

"Yes, Rafe. Thank you. You are so amazing."

"I know I am."

"Jerk!" she says, laughing. Her tension eases under his firm grip. "Thank you. This helps so much."

"Do you need to work them?"

"In a little while. I'm enjoying being with you right now."

"What do you know about Evren's family?"

"Nothing," she admits. "She's never really talked about them. You?"

"No. I want to ask, since we'll be meeting them."

"I know. I do, too. You don't mind that I'm having them stay here tonight, do you?"

"Of course not. Everyone's safety is a priority right now. Are we sleeping on the ottoman?" he asks with a teasing smile.

"Yes, love. Is that okay?"

"I guess. I hope it's… relaxing enough."

"Rafe," she says with a laugh. She leans up, kissing him while caressing his face. "My fiancé. I love you, so much."

"Oh, mia estrela. I love you, too."

"Je t'aime beaucoup."

"Ana, what does that mean?"

She smiles. "It's French. It means I love you a lot."

"You speak French?"

"Mais oui. Yes."

"Why didn't I know this?"

She laughs. "I don't know. I guess it didn't come up. I studied it in high school and college, hoping to go once I had graduated. I'm glad I did because, even though I can't go, I got to learn about the culture, enjoy traditional dishes, and learn a beautiful language. This isn't me being sad that

I can't go." She looks at him. "What?"

"I just… I can't believe I didn't know you spoke French." He nuzzles into the crook of her neck, kissing along up to her mouth. "Any other secrets in there?"

She laughs. "Probably still a few. When you came to Earth to find me, how close were you?"

"What do you mean?"

"Were you in the US? Or Europe? Where did you arrive?" She sees his eyes go down. "What?"

"Ana, I don't want to talk about it."

"I'm sorry. I didn't know it was a difficult topic."

"No, it's not that." His shoulders sag. "I actually arrived in Paris." He notes the pained look on her face. "I hate that I got to see it, and you didn't. I'm so sorry."

"Rafe, it's not your fault. Please, don't feel guilty. I'm glad you did."

"Really?"

"Yes, because you gave me a perfect evening in NightFall, in the tub. Honestly, after hearing you describe it, I had a feeling you had been there. If you didn't know the language, how did you get around?"

"I had on a universal translator. Rowenne had acquired it, knowing how many different languages Earth has. I traveled a little through Europe, before finding myself stateside. As I said, using the internal pull to try and find you. Something about Earth mutes magic, so it made it a little harder."

"I didn't know that."

"I think it's why Kara picked it, to make it harder to find either of you."

"So, if the coffeeshop the day I was shot wasn't the first time you saw me, when was it?"

"It was almost two weeks before when I found you. I was at the bistro, having brunch with Lauren, when you walked past. You were going to your café. I knew immediately who you were when I saw you. I apologized to Lauren, told her I wasn't feeling well, and started following you."

"Stalker!" She laughs, kissing him again. "I'm glad you did. You saved my life. I wouldn't be here, engaged to you, if you hadn't." She admires her ring. "I'm still in shock."

"Why?"

"Kara said you weren't. I heard you say you were going to delay it. Everything told me it wasn't going to happen."

"I'm glad I was able to surprise you."

"With everything! I think Kara is jealous of my Eiffel Tower."

"Oh, she is."

They laugh. Ana takes his hand, going to the middle of the room. She opens her wings as Kara and Evren come in. Kara stops.

"We'll go if you're training. I don't want to interrupt."

"No, please. I want us together right now, until we know more about the assassin in the palace. We'll work my wings, for a moment, then Evren and I will have a lesson about the crowns."

"Okay. We'll go on into the closet to give you some privacy."

"Thank you."

As soon as they shut the door, she turns back to Rafe. She takes his hand as they fly up towards the ceiling. He takes her around the room a few times, before lowering back down.

"Better?" he asks.

"Yes. They needed the exercise. Thank you." He takes her to the closet, where Kara and Evren are sitting on the ottoman. "Are you joining us?"

"I am," Rafe says. "I am curious to know the history behind some of these."

"I'll go to your desk and work on paperwork," Kara says.

"Are you sure?"

"I know most of the history. Please."

"Okay."

Kara steps out. Rafe and Ana sit. Evren walks to the shelf and picks up various crowns. She explains which queen they were made for, when they were made, and notable events that occurred.

"Your coronation crown is the most valuable, most important piece in the collection." Evren carefully picks it up. "This was made for Celestia herself and has been handed down ever since."

"When Rafe and I get married, he'll be crowned as Prince, right?"

"Yes."

"Which crown do they use for that?"

"It's in your father's chambers, along with all of the other men's crowns. We'll have them brought in when we have the room cleaned."

"Evren, may I ask about your family?"

"Of course."

"You said your brother is coming. Do you have other family?"

"My mother and father are deceased. I have a sister, but she won't come. She's still too ashamed that I was a slave."

"Evren, I'm so sorry."

"It's okay, Ana. I have a few cousins and other family."

"Are you going to Vulcara for your honeymoon? Or did you decide on somewhere else?"

"Kara insists on taking me there."

"Do you want to go?"

"Yes and no. I want to because it's my homeworld. I am curious to see it. I don't relish seeing some of the other elves there."

"What do you mean?"

"Even though I am a member of your court now, they do not see that as a high honor, since it's a human court and not an elvish one."

"Is there anything I can do to help?"

"Ana, you have done more than enough for me. I want

to apologize in advance, for my brother. He is quite snobbish and even though you are queen, he may try and talk down to you. I am hoping he will be on his best behavior."

"Do you and he not get along?"

"Oh, you don't know. He is the one who sold me."

"What?" they both ask.

"My father had acquired gambling debts. Once he died, it fell to my brother. He couldn't afford to pay them. He knew as an elf, I was quite valuable, so he took me to another realm and sold me."

"Evren, if I may. Why did you invite him to your wedding?"

"He reached out to me once my status was raised. He says he wants to make peace. I'm giving him a chance."

"You are more forgiving than I am."

"It was a long time ago. I'm hoping he truly has changed. We'll see."

"Have you met him before?" Rafe asks. "You said you hadn't seen much of your family, because of your status."

"Before I came here, I was serving on a realm not too far from Vulcara. He visited me a few times, checking up on me. I believe he felt guilty for selling me. He wanted to make sure I was okay. I had not spoken to him since, until recently."

"Evren, I am so sorry. We were supposed to look at gowns."

"Ana, you went through so much. Don't worry about it. We can look at your gowns, and if I find something I like, maybe I'll make my own."

"Of course! That's a great idea." She looks at Rafe. "We're going into the other closet."

"Is it far?"

"Really?" Ana laughs at the confused look on his face. She takes his hand, leads him over, and opens the door.

"Okay, I did not know this was here." He kisses her. "You two go ahead. I'll see if Kara needs help with the paperwork."

"Thank you, love."

He steps out.

"Where to begin?" Evren asks.

"Hmm. Do you know what color you want?"

"Honestly, I don't know."

"Well, let's look and see." Ana looks around. She pulls out a lavender gown, with a cinched bodice and ballroom skirt. "What about this?"

Evren shakes her head. Ana continues her search until she sees a pale blue gown. She holds it up. It has off shoulder sleeves, with a cinched bodice, and a tulle and lace ballroom skirt. Along the hem are white lace roses.

"Evren?"

She lets out a small gasp, walking up to Ana to inspect the dress. "Oh, this is perfect."

"I think it will fit you too. Would you like to try it on?"

"Yes, please."

"I'll step out to give you privacy. Let me know if you need help."

"Thank you."

Ana sits on the ottoman, waiting for Evren. She stands up in awe when she steps out of the closet. "Oh, Evren. It's beautiful!"

She turns around. "Thank you. Would you help with the back?"

Ana cinches up the corset. "How does it feel?"

"It fits me well. I can't believe it. Most other gowns are for your height. Why this is in here, is beyond me."

"I'm grateful it was. Do you need anything else with it?"

"No, Ana. Thank you. I have shoes and jewelry to wear."

"We'll keep it in here, for the time being, so Kara doesn't see it."

"I appreciate that. Thank you. I know it's not tradition here, but she did tell me about not seeing the gown until the day of the wedding. We are having a mixture of our traditions for the wedding."

Ana undoes the backing. "Get changed, and I would love to hear about some of your traditions."

"Yes, Ana." She steps back in, changing. She hangs the gown up, looking at it once more, before stepping out. They sit on the ottoman. "One of our traditions is for me to write her a ballad and sing to her. This is done in private, on our wedding night."

"Are you nervous about any of your wedding stuff?"

"No. Kara has been handling a lot of it. The only thing we really have left is deciding on a menu."

"Because you can't agree or you're still deciding?"

"A bit of both, really." She laughs. "Otherwise, everything else is picked out and ready. Now, it's waiting."

"We haven't set a date yet. I don't want to rush, but I don't want to wait too long, either."

"Can I ask, when would you like to?"

"Rafe said August is his favorite time of year. If we could get married in August, I would be really happy. I don't know if that's too soon for him, though. He doesn't want to rush."

"Waiting for your nightmares to end." Evren gasps. "I'm sorry. I shouldn't have said that."

"It's okay, Evren. What do you mean?"

"He and Kara talked about him marrying you, but that you still have nightmares, from Earth. He wants you better before he marries you. I apologize—"

"It's okay. He's told me this. I didn't know you all had discussed it."

"Kara was concerned."

Ana laughs. "Isn't she always?"

"Yes." Evren looks at the clock. "Are you ready for dinner?"

"Please." She watches her step out.

He is waiting on me. She closes her eyes. *What can I do? How can I move past everything to make myself ready for him? I love him and want to be with him. How can I show him?*

"Ana, are you okay?" Rafe asks as he walks in.

She wipes her tears. "Yes."

He kneels in front of her. "What happened?" She shakes her head, burying her face in her hands. He stands up, pulling her into his arms. "Please, talk to me, mia estrela."

"I'm overwhelmed."

"About what?"

"Rafe, please."

"I'm sorry. Feel my love, feel my warmth. Let me comfort you."

She clutches his shirt, crying harder. "I'm sorry. It's so stupid. I shouldn't be feeling like this."

"Will you tell me what happened?"

"Talking to Evren about her wedding, realizing what I still have to do so we can be together. I've overcome a lot, but I still have walls to bring down. It made me upset that I'm not there yet."

"Ana, I told you when they got engaged to please not feel like we have to rush."

"That's not what I'm talking about," she snaps, putting distance between them.

"Then what do you mean?"

She takes a deep breath, then lets it out slowly. "I don't want to discuss this right now. I'm done with this conversation." She leaves the closet, going to her desk, where Kara is working. "How's the paperwork?"

"Ana, what's going on?"

"Oh, you heard that?"

"Some of it."

She hangs her head. "I need to be alone right now."

"Ana—"

"I'm okay. Just, please, can I have five minutes?"

"I don't want to leave you alone, not with everything going on. What can I do?"

"Talk to Rafe, distract him. Let me have a few minutes

in the closet to get my head together?"

"All right."

Kara walks to Rafe, taking his hand and leading him to the chaise. Ana goes into the closet, shutting and locking the door. She sits on the ottoman, trying to push down her anger.

He was worried. I had no reason to react like that. I want to tell him what I'm feeling, why I want to move past everything. He thinks it's so we can get married. He doesn't understand how much it still hurts, how I bury it every day, because it's too painful to deal with. I want to be with him, I want to marry him, but more than anything, I want to be free of these memories!

She lies back on the ottoman, pulling the blanket over herself, and cries herself to sleep.

Chapter 17

Ana wakes up, realizing she's in Rafe's arms. She looks up at him when he caresses her face.

"Hi," he says in a low whisper.

"Hi back."

"Ana, what happened?"

She sits up, keeping her gaze on the floor. "I want to get married, please don't misunderstand. You think I want to break down walls to be with you. I do, more than anything. It's just, I want them down for me too. I want to be free of what he did to me, of what he put me through. You acted like I was only doing it for you, like I was rushing to marry you, because of Evren and Kara. It made me angry. I felt like you should know by now that's not why I would rush."

He wraps his arm around her. "I'm sorry. I should know better. Even if you told me you wanted to get married tomorrow, I should understand it's because you love me and want to be with me, not because you're jealous of them or feel like rushing. I didn't see that. Ana, why didn't you tell me that?"

"I got angry. I didn't want you feeling that. I'm sorry."

"Why were you angry? Why not tell me?"

"Rafe, please. You know how I get when we discuss this. You're pushing me, and I don't want to right now. Please, stop!"

"I had no idea. You're right. I was pushing you, instead of letting you have time."

"It's too much sometimes, because when we're talking about the wedding, I'm thinking of the wedding night. I'm wondering if I can truly overcome what I've been through. I'm scared I won't, and you deserve more than that."

"Ana, please. We've had that discussion. You are all I

have ever wanted. We will get married when you're ready. I don't care if it's next year, or ten years from now. Let's enjoy being engaged, enjoy being together, and work on healing together. Can we do that?"

"I want to."

"Then what's wrong?"

"How can I prove myself to you? You give me all of you, without hesitation. I know how much you love me."

"Ana, I know how much you love me. We know that is never in question. We are made for each other, soulmates, destined to be together, forever. You know this is true. Why are you questioning it now?"

"I guess seeing them making their wedding plans, seeing something real, is making me think of ours."

"Should I have waited to propose?"

She gasps. "What?"

"Am I putting too much pressure on you, is what I mean?"

"No, love. I'm so grateful you did. I was overwhelmed. I'm okay now. Is dinner here? We can eat." She stands up.

"Ana, stop." He gently pulls her to him. "Just stop. It's okay. Please, don't hide from me. Don't tell me you're okay when you're not. It breaks my heart when you do. I'm sorry I pushed. We can go eat. When you're ready to talk more, we will."

"Do you regret proposing?"

"Ana! Absolutely not. That is not what I'm talking about."

"I'm sorry."

"No, mia estrela. I am. I can understand why you thought that. We still have walls to bring down and hurdles to overcome. We will, together. That's what's important, right? You know I love you. I'm not going anywhere."

"Yes, Rafe. I love you, too. Thank you."

"Now, are you ready for dinner?"

"Yes, love. I'm sorry about everything."

He kisses her, holding her tight. "Ana, it's okay. It's an

emotional topic. I understand. Just please, try to let me in?"

"I will. I don't mean to get so upset with you. It's me, not you. I don't know why, when we talk about a wedding, I feel like I'm pressuring you, making you do something you don't want to."

"Really?"

"Yes. I don't know why it upsets me so!"

"Was your foster father ever married?"

"Yes. She died a few months after they had taken me in."

"What? Why didn't you tell me this?"

"They brought me to their home when I was six years old. I was with him nearly four years. I didn't think about it."

"What did he say about her?"

"He hated that she died, blaming her for getting sick. He said he regretted marrying her."

"Ana, this is why it upsets you so."

"What do you mean?"

"You grew up hearing a man say horrible things about his wife. Even if you didn't understand all of it at the time, it has stayed with you. This explains so much."

"Really?"

"This is why we talk, how you bring down your walls."

"I'm so sorry I didn't tell you sooner. I didn't realize it."

"It's okay. God, you went through so much hell because of him. Ana, you will take all the time you need to handle this. I will help any way I can. I am not going anywhere. I know how much you love me, and you know how much I love you. Please, don't question that."

"Rafe, I—"

Kara steps in. "I don't mean to interrupt, but are you eating with us?"

Ana laughs. "Yes, Kara. We'll be out in a moment. Sorry."

"It's okay."

She turns back to Rafe. "My gown is wrinkled. I'll change and be right out."

"Yes, mia estrela."

He steps out. She removes the gown, lays it on the ottoman, and picks out the pale pink gown he likes. Her heart races as she tries to push down the memories brought up by their discussion. She walks to the table. Without a word, she begins to eat.

"Ana, what's wrong?"

"I don't know what you mean."

"I asked you if you enjoyed your lesson with Evren earlier."

"I did. It was interesting, learning the histories. I'd like the king's and prince's crowns brought in here, whenever possible."

"We'll have it taken care of today."

The worry is etched on Rafe's expression. "I'm okay," she assures him. "Talking about them was a little much. I know I have to, though."

He kisses her hand. "Bringing down walls."

"Yes, love."

"Ana, did you mean you wanted to get married this coming August?" Evren asks. They all look at Ana as her face flushes.

"Evren!"

"I'm sorry. Was that in confidence? I didn't mean to embarrass you."

"Deep breaths, Ana," Rafe says, squeezing her hand. "It's okay. We've talked about getting married in August."

"I know, but you and I hadn't really discussed a date. Evren asked when I wanted to, and it slipped out."

"It's okay. I like the idea of getting married then."

"Really?"

"Yes."

She looks down. "What if I'm not ready?"

"Ana, it's seven months from now. We'll plan towards it, and see what happens. How does that sound?"

"That sounds good. Thank you."

"Evren and I will get dishes taken care of, then see about getting the crowns moved in here."

"Thank you. Please, be safe."

"We will. We have royal guards, too."

"Oh, thank goodness. I meant to ask you to do that."

"It's covered."

While Evren and Kara gather dishes, Ana goes into the closet. She rearranges the crowns, moving them together, and emptying the bottom two shelves for whatever they bring in.

Rafe lingers in the doorway. "Are you excited to see the men's crowns?" he asks.

"I am. I haven't seen any of them. I know Evren will teach us their history, too. What I want to learn, that is."

"You're not mad at her, are you?"

"No. It's okay. I know she didn't do it on purpose." She sits on the ottoman. She takes his hand when he sits with her. "I didn't talk about my foster mom, because when she was alive, it was actually kind of nice there. She got sick and didn't last long after. Then he started drinking and things got bad. It was still too painful for me. Plus, I was so young, I think I repressed a lot of it, not wanting to deal with it."

"Are you okay now?"

"I am. I don't want to talk about it right now. I want us to have a nice day together. We'll continue dealing with it, I know. I need a break from so much."

"Then a break you shall have," he says, pulling her up with him.

"Rafe?"

He holds her as he sings softly. They dance around the closet, stopping as he plants gentle kisses over her face and neck. She laughs, playfully crying for him to stop.

"Better?"

"Yes, love. Thank you."

They look up when Kara and Evren walk in, carrying

two wooden crates. They set them on the floor. Ana carefully lifts each crown out.

"Evren, tell me if it's a king or prince, so I know which shelf to put it on. Please?"

Evren guides her through the process. She puts the king's crowns on the bottom shelf, knowing Rafe will not be wearing them. She looks at the prince's crowns, some simple silver while others are jewel encrusted. They put them on the shelf, admiring them.

"What?" he asks when her eyes meet his.

She laughs. "Do you see yourself wearing these?" He clasps her hand. "Prince Rafe… hmm."

"I think so. It will be quite different for me."

"How do you think I feel?" she asks, laughing. "I never wore head bands or tiaras, hats, or anything on my head. I'm still trying to get used to wearing these."

"You look so pretty in them," Kara says. "You wear them well."

"Thanks, sis. I prefer these circlets because they aren't as heavy and are easier to wear."

Rafe laughs. "I don't have that option."

"No, I'm afraid you don't. Sorry."

"It's okay. I'm sure I'll adapt fine. It's the least of my concerns for being crowned as Grand Prince."

Evren and Kara exchange a glance before stepping out to give them privacy. Ana turns to Rafe. "What concerns do you have?"

"Oh, no. I didn't mean it like that."

"Rafe, love. Now it's my turn. Don't hide."

"Yes, mia estrela. It is weird to think of, becoming a prince. I never gave it a thought since it was forbidden. Having no interest in romance anyway, I never gave marriage much thought either. You came crashing into my heart, and you have changed how I see everything."

"Love, how do you feel about becoming a prince?"

"Honestly? Yes, I'm nervous of course. Otherwise, I've been in battle and faced assassins. What's putting a crown on?" His voice wavers on the last sentence.

"Rafe, what's wrong?"

"Being the first royal guardian in two thousand years is a little bit… unnerving. I'm supposed to protect the royals, remember?"

"You do, love. You have saved my life more times than I can count." She kisses him. "Technically speaking, aren't I the first royal guardian?"

"Yes, I guess you are."

"See? No big deal."

He laughs. "Ana, what am I going to do with you?"

"Hmm…" She nuzzles into his chest, her hand working around to his wings.

"We are having company tonight."

"They won't be in the washroom with us."

"Ana!" He leans down, kissing her hard. His hand caresses the space between her wings, and her head rolls back. He gently cups her face and kisses her again. "Are you ready for a shower?"

"Hmm," she softly moans. "Yes, please."

"Let's get our pajamas."

They gather clean clothes. She puts her engagement ring in the box, locking it in the drawer. He takes her hand as they step out of the closet. Kara and Evren are admiring the Eiffel Tower. Kara nods at Ana.

Rafe takes her into the washroom, locking the door. They put their clothes on the vanity. He turns the water on, when she spins him to her, kissing him hard. They undress each other as they're kissing, trying not to bump into the vanity.

She laughs, picking up their clothes and throwing them into the hamper. Her gaze meets his, and she presses her chest into his stomach. He carries her into the shower.

"Ana, are you sure you're okay?"

"Yes, love. Please?"

She bites her lower lip before his mouth crashes on hers.

Rafe takes her against the wall. "What do you want me to do?"

"Love, my body is yours. I know we are saving that one thing until our wedding night. I trust you. You can do anything you want."

"I'm going to try something different. If you aren't comfortable, if it overwhelms you, if—"

"Rafe, I will tell you immediately. Please, love?"

He stands her up before kneeling in front of her. His hand trails along her waistline, down her hip. He moves his fingers along her thigh then reaches up. She gasps at the feeling, looking at him as she pushes down the memories, then nods.

He slowly moves his hand, stroking in and out. She leans against the wall as her body trembles from his touches. Her grip on his shoulders tightens while she sends everything back into him. She cries out, collapsing on him when she is overcome. He picks her up, sitting on the floor of the shower, holding her in his lap.

"Hmm. I'd say you liked that."

She smiles at him, kissing him. "It was different."

"It wasn't too much for you?"

"No, love. It was wonderful."

She turns around, kneeling with him, and caresses his chest. He grabs her hand.

"Let's get cleaned up."

"Rafe—"

"I promise you, I enjoyed that every bit as much as you did." He kisses her before helping her to her feet. "It was amazing."

He washes her, then washes himself, while she puts shampoo in her hair. She rinses off, steps out, and sits on the vanity to wait for him. He wraps the towel around himself as he steps up to her.

"Ready for more?"

She blushes. "Oh, no, love." She jumps down. "I wanted you to see me."

"What do you mean?"

"I made myself eat more yesterday and today. You can already see a slight difference."

He is happy to see her ribs aren't as visible. "Oh, that's wonderful! I've been so worried about you."

"I told you I'd be okay."

She gasps when he suddenly pulls her into his arms. He kisses the top of her head, holding her tight. "Oh, mia estrela."

"Really, Rafe. I'm okay now."

"I see that," he says. They dress and step out. "Still, I was worried. You had lost so much weight."

She sits on the chaise, looking at him when he sits with her. He laughs when she blushes.

"What?" she asks as he takes her hand.

"You are too cute." He plants a gentle kiss.

"Rafe," she says, turning even more red. "Kara and Evren are in here!"

He notices they are at the small table in front of the fireplace. "They are at our table, not paying any attention."

"Yes, love."

"How are you feeling?"

She squeezes his hand. "I'm okay. We did a lot today, even staying in."

A loud commotion outside the door gets their attention. She gets to her feet, and Rafe takes her to Kara and Evren.

"Stay here!" he says, grabbing his sword and opening the door. Aylin is fighting an assassin, when Roesh grabs them from behind. He quickly has him in magical bindings. He turns to Rafe.

"We'll take him down to the dungeon."

"Bring him in here."

They turn and see Ana at the door, dressed in a winter gown and boots.

"What?" Rafe asks.

"I want to question him myself."

"Then we'll go to the dungeon and interrogate him." He takes her hand, following Roesh and Aylin.

⚓

Roesh chains the assassin's bindings to the table. Ana goes to the cabinet, seeing all the bright colored poisons and potions. She gets out a yellow one, smiling when the assassin's eyes go wide.

She walks up to him, holding it in front of his face. "I'm no stranger to this one. Do I have to use it, or will you tell us who sent you?"

"I'm not telling you a damn thing!" he hisses at her.

She smiles at him. "I had hoped that would be your response." As Rafe holds his head back, she removes the cork. She pours it down the assassin's throat, watching as he swallows it. "We'll wait a moment for it to kick in. How are you feeling?"

"Relaxed," he says, his words starting to slur. "Very relaxed."

She gently strokes his face. "Now, what were you saying?"

"What?"

"You were telling me who hired you to assassinate the queen. You were proud of that."

"Oh, yes. His name is Tinsley. I have the letter from him in my pocket. He offered me a lot of gold to kill the freak."

Kara and Rafe exchange a glance, watching her continue to work him. "I see. How did you sneak into the palace?"

"I bribed a guard. Her name is Ginnerva. She let me in."

"You are so brilliant!" Ana gushes. "Were you going to kill the queen? Or were you going to kill anyone else?"

"Just her. Then leave and return to Tinsley."

"Where were you going to meet him?"

"It's supposed to be a secret…"

"Oh, sweetie," she says softly, her breath warm on his face. "You can tell me. Please?"

"He's back in our realm. I was going to meet him at the market at seven tonight."

Ana turns to Kara, who nods. "Thank you for the information. For your reward, you will be executed first thing tomorrow."

"What?" he cries out as Kara leaves the room.

She smiles at him. "You tried to kill the queen. The punishment for that is death. We don't take assassins lightly here. You will make a fine example!" Ana looks at Rafe, who is unable to hide his surprise. She gives her attention back to the assassin, leaning down, her face mere inches from his. "Enjoy your last night." She smiles and approaches Rafe. "Love, I'm tired. Can we return to our quarters now?"

"Yes, Majesty," he says, taking her hand.

* * *

Rafe and Ana go into the closet, where she changes back into pajamas. "Ana, are you okay?"

"Of course. Why?"

"You interrogated a man and sentenced him to death."

"Okay. And?"

"Ana!"

"What? I've killed assassins. I've been interrogated, so I knew how to do that. Now, Kara and the royal guard can get Tinsley. He'll be executed, and he'll be one less threat we have to deal with."

"You never cease to amaze me. How could you ever think you are small or weak, when you do these incredible things? I was in awe watching you back there."

"Really?"

"Yes. You handled that perfectly."

"Thank you."

"How you can go from so shy and soft spoken, to

facing down an assassin, is beyond incredible."

"You are so sweet and gentle with me, yet you snapped that man's neck without hesitation. We do what we must, to survive and protect those we love."

"I'm telling you right now, Kara is very worried about you. She saw a side of you she hadn't seen, and she doesn't know what to make of it."

"I'll talk to her when they get back. She knows some of what I've been through, but I haven't really talked to her like I should. She'll see for herself that I'm okay."

Rafe steps up, taking her hand. He closes his eyes as he concentrates. "You really are. I don't know what to say."

She laughs. "I won't be intimidated, and I won't let you or my friends be hurt or killed because of me. He will be made an example, and maybe someone will think twice about trying to kill me. It has to be done."

"Do you know how they do executions here?"

"No."

"Beheadings."

She gasps. "No wonder Kara said it wasn't funny when I told her it was her head if the new chancellor didn't work out! I was kidding, I had no idea."

Rafe laughs. "Poor Kara." He leads her out of the closet, sitting with her on the chaise. "You are tired. Will we go to bed soon?"

"Yes. I want to see what happens first."

"I know." He looks at the clock. "They should be back shortly. Hopefully, they are able to capture him." He debates his next question before facing her. "Will you interrogate him, too?"

"No. One tonight is enough. Once we hear what happens, we can go to the closet and sleep."

"They're still staying the night?"

"If that's okay? I'd like them to."

"Of course." He smiles, leaning in and kissing her. "I think you want an excuse to sleep on your ottoman."

She blushes. "That might be part of it." She yawns. "I

am tired."

"I know. I feel it coming off you. Go on and rest." He lays her on the chaise, covering her with the blanket. He sits on the edge. "I'm right here. I'll wake you up when they return."

"Yes, love." She turns onto her side, falling asleep.

Rafe watches her, still unable to believe how well she handled the interrogation. He cannot believe that's the same shy, quiet, timid woman. The thought of it causes him to shake his head.

Kara and Evren walk in.

"Ana, they're back."

She slowly sits up, yawning. "What happened?"

"Tinsley is dead. He battled the guardians who accompanied me."

"Oh, I'm so relieved!"

Kara approaches Ana then sits beside her. "Can we talk?"

"Yes."

Rafe gets up, gesturing to Evren to follow him to the table. Kara turns back to Ana. "What happened earlier?"

"What do you mean?"

"Ana, you poisoned a man and sentenced him to death!"

"He was going to kill me. What would you suggest, a tea party?"

"Ana, this is not a joking matter!"

"Kara, I have been stabbed, shot, poisoned, strangled. I have been kidnapped, tortured, interrogated. I see what I have to do, in order to survive and protect the ones I love."

"I'm worried about you. I don't know if I like this person you're turning into."

"How so?"

"Ana, you literally cried because you couldn't find your class. Now, you can sentence a man to death without blinking an eye!"

"Kara, I've served in war, I've laid down my life for my

people. I've worked too hard and sacrificed too much to let someone think they can get away with trying to kill me!"

"I understand that. I do. Please, sis, I'm worried that you're losing your heart, losing your empathy. I don't want to see you cold and stoic! You're too good for that."

"Kara, you were there. Did I hurt him? Did I torture him?"

"No, but—"

"I can't bear the thought of that. Even though he was going to kill me, I still couldn't bear the thought of hurting him. Does that sound like someone with no heart?"

"No, you're right. I'm afraid you could still lose it if you continue like this."

"Continue like what? Defending myself and my people?"

"That's not what I mean. Of course not."

"Kara, I will always have empathy and compassion. It's who I am. I've gotten stronger, able to defend myself, my loved ones, and my kingdom. I'm still me, I promise you. That's not going to change."

"Ana, I've never seen you like that. I felt like I was watching someone else down there. It scared me to see."

"I'm sure you've had to do things on my behalf, either while I wasn't here or while I was recovering."

"Yes, I did. I've done things I'm not proud of, things I've had to do. Like you, to protect myself and others. That doesn't mean I'm happy about it, or that I wanted to do it. You seemed to be enjoying yourself!"

"Kara, is that what you think? I smiled at him because I know one of the effects of the potion is that it makes the subject… um… romantically interested. I smiled, speaking quietly and pretending to be his friend, to open him up. I knew if I was cruel or mean, he would clam up. I was not happy while I was doing it, nor did I enjoy it. I can't believe you would think I would!"

"Ana—"

"No, Kara!" she cries out, standing up. "How could

you believe that? What is wrong with you?" She runs to the closet, slamming and locking the door.

"Ana?" Rafe tries. "Please, at least let me in. I don't want you alone right now. Just me, no one else. I promise." When she opens the door, he steps inside and takes her hands. "What happened?"

"Kara was worried because she thought I enjoyed interrogating him!"

"She should know better. I could tell what you were doing, see the way you were thinking, working him over. I never thought for a second you were enjoying it. I know you were trying to get the information out of him."

"I'll be happy if I never have to do it again! I could tell, the way he looked at me, that the yellow potion would work on him. Otherwise, I would've let them do it instead. Because I did, Tinsley is no longer a threat."

He envelops her in his arms. "I'm sorry about Kara. I don't know how she could believe that."

"Thank you. It took everything I had to push down my fear, to not tremble in front of him. I did what I had to, in order to protect us."

He kisses the top of her head. "Let's step out. You and Kara can talk some more. I won't say anything, but I'll stay by your side."

"Thank you."

They walk out of the closet. Kara is sitting with Evren on the chaise. At the sight of them, she stands.

"You're right," Kara says as she approaches Ana. "I'm sorry. I never should've thought that."

"How could you think that?"

"You've been through so much, endured so much. I've been worried, how you are handling everything. Honestly, I thought you had snapped."

"Kara!"

"You've been through hell and back. How anyone could stay sane after all the things you've endured, is beyond me!"

"I have you and Rafe and Evren. You three have been my hope in everything. Rafe has shown me unending love and patience. It's because of you all that I am still here and still sane. How can you question that?"

Kara hangs her head. "I'm sorry. You are so strong, and I doubted you."

Ana pulls her into her arms. "We've both had to make changes here. We have to carry so much responsibility. You are always worried about me being overwhelmed, I never stopped to think about if you were. I'm sorry."

"No, Ana. You told me you knew how much responsibility I was carrying. You checked in on me. You asked if I needed help. Don't feel guilty." She steps back. "I promised your mother I would protect you from this life. She didn't want you to grow up here, to endure the war and death and political intrigue. She wanted you to have a normal life. Instead, you were shot and hurt on Earth, nearly killed how many times here, laid down, died, and grew wings! I failed your mother, and I failed you."

"Kara, stop right now. I am happy with who I am, how I am, and who I am with. I love my wings, I love my fiancé, I love the life I have. Is it normal? No. I still love everything about it. So no, you haven't failed either of us."

"Do you mean that?" Rafe asks.

She turns to him. "I mean every word of it."

"I know, but you said you love your wings. Do you mean that?"

"I do. I really do."

"Oh, Ana!" He holds her tight. "I've been waiting so long for you to say that. I know you will still have bad days with them, and I understand. Please, don't feel like you have to hide that from me."

"I won't." She yawns. "I am beyond exhausted. Kara, are you and Evren still sleeping here tonight?"

"If you want us to."

"I do. Please?"

"Yes, Ana. We will. Are you sure you'll be—" Kara

stops as they're going to the closet. "Okay then." She turns to Evren. "Let's get ready for bed."

Ana pauses at the door. "Night, guys." She takes Rafe's hand, leading him in. She shuts and locks the door. She slips into a nightgown as he changes into pajamas. They lie down on the ottoman, covering up with the blanket. "I love you, so much. I meant what I said, that the only reason I'm still here, still me, is because of your love."

"Oh, mia estrela. I love you, too. Sleep, and please don't have nightmares tonight!"

"I'll try," she says, clutching his shirt. She falls asleep listening to the sound of his heartbeat.

Chapter 18

Rafe's eyes open when Ana is on him, planting soft kisses on his face and neck. He smiles at her. "Mia estrela, what are you doing?"

"Hmm. What does it look like?"

"You are so beautiful." He kisses her lips. "How are you feeling?"

"Happy and loved." She leans down, kissing his cheek and ear. "I need you," she says softly.

"Ana!"

He flips over and leans above her. His hand caresses her leg, bringing the fabric up with it. Love flows between them. She kisses him as his hand continues to explore. He tugs on her undergarments. She nods and smiles. He gently pulls them down until she tenses up.

"What's wrong?"

"I'm okay. It was a moment."

His hand traces her upper leg and thigh but stops when she is trembling. Tears stream down her cheeks. He lowers her gown.

"Oh, Ana." He holds her tightly.

"I was back in his camp. I'm so sorry!"

"Shh. It's okay, you're okay. Just rest with me. You're safe now."

"Yes, love," she says softly, clutching his shirt. "I'm sorry. I really thought I was past it. I didn't mean to."

"Ana, we're bringing down these walls. You're doing so well with it. I believe if you want to get married by August, we will."

"Really?"

"Yes, mia estrela. I truly do," he says, wiping her tears.

"That would make me so happy!"

"I can see that." He laughs then places a gentle kiss on

her forehead. "Are you ready to get dressed and join our friends?"

"Yes, love. Thank you." She walks to the gowns, surprised when Rafe is right behind her. "What?"

"Could I pick out what you wear today?"

"Of course."

He finds a dark purple gown, with tulle sleeves and skirt. Lavender roses are embroidered along the bodice and hem of the skirt. He holds it up.

"How about this?"

She laughs. "How have I not seen that one? It's absolutely beautiful!" She pulls her nightgown off then goes to the drawer, getting out a corset. Rafe helps her into the dress. "My crown?"

He picks out a silver crown with small diamonds. He gently places it on her. He gets her ring and kisses her as he slips it on.

"Anything else, my queen?"

"That is all, Guardian."

She slips on silver shoes, while he changes into charcoal pants with a black shirt. He gets his boots on, then takes her hand. Kara gasps at the sight of her when they step out from the closet.

"Ana, that color is fantastic on you!"

"Thanks, Kara. Evren, thank you for taking such great care of all my clothes. I deeply appreciate your hard work."

"You're welcome. Breakfast will be here any minute."

"Thanks!" She turns to Kara. "This gown is okay with my wings? The colors don't clash?"

"Oh, Ana," Kara says, laughing. "No, it doesn't clash. It's beautiful."

She turns to Rafe. "You did good, picking it out." She smiles at him as she takes his hand. They sit on the chaise. "I want to talk about last night."

"Are you okay?"

"Yes. I was terrified the whole time I was interrogating him. I've never done that before, and I truly hope I never have to again."

"You did a fantastic job, but I understand. If we can avoid it, we will."

Kara walks to them. "I'm relieved to hear that."

Ana smiles at her. "I know. I did what I had to do, in the moment, to protect all of us."

"I'm sorry for how I reacted."

"Kara, it's okay. It was my fault, too. I've turned to Rafe, and you and I haven't really talked like we used to. We'll work on that."

"I want that, too." She goes to the door to let breakfast service in. They set up and leave. She turns back to them. "Ready to eat?"

Everyone sits at the table. Ana looks at Kara. "How did you all sleep?"

"Very well. You?"

"Good."

Kara laughs. "You and that ottoman!" She sees Ana blush. "I didn't mean—"

"I know."

"I know what it means to you." Kara sees the look of confusion on Ana's face. "When you and Rafe were forbidden. That was your secret."

"It was. It also became my sanctuary." Now it's Kara who is confused. "When I was being hurt or tortured, I thought about being in there, in his arms, safe. It helped me through everything."

"I am so glad you have him. I know I was jealous, but I really mean it."

"Kara, I know you've cared for him longer than you will admit. When I was worried for his safety and spoke of getting another guardian, you flipped out. Remember? I know how much we both mean to you."

Rafe flashes Kara a smile. "Fine," she begrudgingly says, "yes, I do care for him." She smiles back.

Ana laughs. "I guess that's good enough."

"Kara, you said Rafe was really good for Ana, and that

you were happy she has him," Evren says.

Ana turns to Kara. "Really?"

"Evren!"

"I'm sorry."

They all laugh. "No," Kara says, "it's okay. Rafe, yes, I was jealous thinking she was replacing me with you. Seriously, though, you know I am grateful you found each other and that she has you."

"Thank you, Kara. I appreciate that." He turns to Ana. "Are we going to the morning briefing?"

"I'd like to."

"Then we'll go."

"Thank you, love."

Rafe kisses her hand and looks at her ring with a smile. "I am so grateful you agreed to be my wife. I've loved you from the moment I saw you." He kisses her.

"I love you, too. Now, will you stop trying to embarrass Kara?"

He laughs, turning to her. "Sorry."

"Nope, it's fine. We are in your quarters." Kara gets to her feet. "We'll take dishes back and meet you in the meeting room at nine-thirty for the briefing."

"Yes, Kara. Thank you," Ana says, standing up. "We'll see you then." She watches them leave, then walks to the middle of the room, opening her wings. Rafe steps up beside her. "They were a little tight. I need to stretch them."

He runs his fingers through them. "They are so beautiful."

"Rafe—"

"Not as beautiful as you, mia estrela."

She smiles at him as he kisses her. "Thank you."

"Are you self-conscious about them today?"

"A little. I don't know why."

He takes her hands as his wings open. "Are you ready for some outdoor practice?"

She tilts her head. "I thought we couldn't, until Remus is caught."

"We won't go into the woods yet, but we are safe enough in our battlement. We can practice after lunch if you'd like. I can feel your happiness."

"Yes! I want to practice outside."

"We will. As long as you'll wear warm clothes."

"I promise." She steps back, furling and unfurling her wings. "This used to feel so weird to do."

"It doesn't anymore?"

"No. It… it almost feels normal."

"Really?"

"Yes." She's surprised when he pulls her to him again, kissing her hard. "Rafe!"

"I'm sorry, mia estrela. I've waited so long to hear you say that."

"Love, you are beaming with happiness! I knew it was important to you, I had no idea it was this important. I would've worked harder—"

"Ana, no. This was for you, not me. Remember?"

"Yes, Rafe."

He gingerly runs his fingers through her feathers. "How are they?"

"Better." She glances at the clock. "We'll leave in a few minutes."

"How are you feeling, after this morning?"

"I'm okay. I was having a moment, was all."

"Ana, no. It was an episode." He sees her eyes go down. "Nothing to be ashamed of. We're working through it, remember?"

"Yes, love."

After retracting her wings, Ana goes to her desk to gather her paperwork. She opens the bottom drawer and removes her laptop bag. Rafe approaches her to see what she has.

"Missing it?"

"No, and I'm not going back to using it." She laughs. "I wanted to see it." She opens it up, goes through the front pocket, and takes out a small, leather notebook, and nearly drops it in surprise. "I don't remember grabbing this. We were leaving and—" Her voice trails off as she locks it in the top drawer of her desk.

"Ana, what was that?"

She shakes her head. "A notebook I wrote in when you were gone. Please, please don't read it."

"I will respect your privacy. I hope one day you can trust me enough to let me see it."

"It's not about trust, Rafe. I was sad and heartbroken, but I got really angry, too." She retrieves the journal. "You know what?" She walks towards the fireplace, but Rafe grabs her arm.

"You don't have to do that. I won't read it. I promise you."

She debates for a moment before making her decision. "I don't want to take the chance." Then she throws it into the fire.

"That bad, huh?"

She hangs her head. "I—"

"Ana, no matter what you wrote in there, I left you. I told you I loved you, then I left. You had every right to be angry, pissed, heartbroken, upset, whatever you were feeling."

"I was devastated," she says quietly. "I didn't know if you left, if you'd been hurt or killed. Not knowing nearly killed me!"

He pulls her to him. "I didn't think about that. I am truly sorry."

"Rafe, it wasn't your fault."

"Still, you were dealing with all of that for me to lie to you."

"Love, we're here now. We're getting married in August, we're happy. That's what matters. I'm sorry I'm dredging up the past."

"Ana, that's the point. You're supposed to be, remember? To work through it."

She goes to her desk and picks up her laptop bag. It's

her last remnant from Earth. She goes through once more, making sure it's empty. Satisfied, she throws it into the fire.

"Ana!"

"I don't want any reminders from Earth." She takes his hand. "Feel? I'm not angry or hurt. I'm ready to leave it in the past and move forward."

"Am I not a reminder of Earth?"

She smiles at him. "Love, you are a reminder of my past, my present, and my future. That's why I wear your cross, that's why I love waking up and seeing you every morning."

He kisses her. "I love you, so much."

Her smile grows. "Rafe, you are my everything. I love you, too." She takes a breath. "Now, shall we go to the meeting?"

"You know once we step out, you will be surrounded by guards."

"I know. I'm ready."

"Okay." They go out as Roesh, Aylin, and two royal guards make their way around them. "We're going to the meeting room," Rafe explains.

Roesh steps inside and finds Kara alone. "Sage, is everything all right in here?"

"Yes, Roesh. The queen may enter."

He steps back, gesturing Rafe and Ana inside. "We will be in the corridor, until you need us."

"Thank you," Ana says. She walks to Kara. "Such an entourage to go from my quarters to another room!"

"It's necessary right now."

"I know. I hate this. Have we heard any more on Remus?"

"I'm afraid not. At least, not about him. His troops seem to have scattered, with several of his people returning to their quadrants. I don't know what he's planning."

"Why would they return? I know he's not giving up."

"No, he's definitely working on something."

Ana turns to Rafe. "Any thoughts on what he's doing?"

"I could come up with a hundred scenarios and still be wrong."

"I wish I had killed him in MoonFrost!"

Rafe pulls her to him. "Ana, calm down. We're going to get him. Please, I know it's frustrating. Try to be patient?"

"Yes, Rafe. I'm sorry."

"It's okay." He looks at Kara. "Any other news or business?"

"The assassin was executed this morning."

"Have we heard any more from NightFall? From Neven?"

"No. Bela is supposed to message us if anything comes from that," Kara explains.

"I need to message him. I'm sure he and Joph would want to hear about our engagement. I'd give anything to tell him in person."

Rafe glances at Ana when her sadness flows into him. "I know, mia estrela. I promise you, hearing about it will make them happy." He squeezes her hand.

"Thank you."

"Ana, are you leading the briefing this morning?" Kara asks.

"I can."

"Ana, you don't sound like you want to."

"Would you? I'd greatly appreciate it."

"Of course. It's no trouble."

They look up as people start to come in. Ana sits at the desk, with Kara and Rafe on either side. Kara gestures for everyone to quiet down. She leads the briefing, answering questions and addressing issues. She adjourns the meeting.

"Where do you want lunch?" Kara asks when everyone is gone.

Ana sighs. "In our quarters."

"Ana, we can eat wherever you want. We can go to

your mother's library or—"

"No, Rafe. It's fine."

Kara puts her hand on her shoulder, kneeling beside her. "We don't want you to feel like a prisoner again."

"Let's eat lunch in our quarters, then we can do dinner in the dining hall."

"Sounds good," Kara says, smiling at her.

"Where's Evren?" Ana asks.

"She's in our quarters, making an engagement gift for you and Rafe."

"She didn't have to do that."

"She wanted to."

"Okay, I feel bad. I didn't do that for you guys."

"Ana, you didn't have to. Do you not understand, you gave us your gift when you granted her freedom, then made it so she and I could be together? I promise you, that is the greatest gift we could've received. I know you've already heard this, but I need to say it.

"You could've made it only about you and Rafe, a guardian and a royal, to be together. You didn't. You thought of your people, bringing them freedom." Kara hugs her tight. "I know I said thank you when the treaty was signed. I never told you how much I appreciate everything you did. You worked so hard to set her free, and I am so thankful for that."

"Kara," she tries as tears stream down her face, "please."

"Ana, what's wrong?"

"No, I'm happy. You never mentioned dating on Earth, never had any romantic interests. Coming here and seeing you in love with her, knowing you couldn't be public about it, nearly killed me. I had to do something."

Kara smiles at her. "And you did." She hugs her tighter. "Thank you."

Ana wipes her tears then glances at Rafe. "Can we check on Audressa, before returning to our quarters?"

"Yes, Ana." He takes her hand.

She turns to Kara. "We'll be there shortly."

"Go ahead."

Rafe leads her out, and they are surrounded by guards. "We're going to the chancellor's quarters for a moment."

Roesh steps forward. "I'll lead." They follow him there. He knocks. Liara opens the door, surprised to see such a group. "Her Majesty would like to see the chancellor, if she is up for company," Roesh explains.

"Please, she and Rafe may come in."

Roesh looks at Rafe, who nods. "All right." He steps back, letting them inside.

"I apologize," Ana says to Liara. "Trust me, I do not enjoy having so many people around me. I wanted to see how Audressa is."

"I'll get her."

"If she's up for company."

Liara smiles. "She is, Majesty." She walks into the other room and returns with Audressa on her arm.

"Majesty," Audressa bows.

"Chancellor. How are you?"

"Much better. I'm mostly healed. If you need me—"

"Audressa, please. Take this week. I mean it."

"Yes, mi'lady. Thank you."

They look up when a door opens, and the girls run out. Little Kara approaches Ana. She bows. "Majesty."

"Good morning, Kara. Do you have wings yet?"

"No," she replies, clearly disappointed.

"Hmm. Maybe one day?" Ana turns to Karliah. "And how are you this morning?"

Karliah bows. "I'm good, Majesty. Thank you."

Little Kara slowly approaches Ana. "Can I see your wings again?"

"Kara!" Audressa scolds. "We've talked about this."

"It's okay," Ana says, laughing. "My friend Kara is as obsessed about seeing them."

"Really?" Little Kara asks, looking up.

Ana nods. "Oh, yes." She steps forward to give herself

more room. She opens her wings, seeing everyone is watching.

"They're so beautiful!" Kara exclaims. "Can you fly?"

"Kara!" Audressa says. "She—"

Before she can finish, Ana is a few feet off the ground. "Well, Kara. What do you think?" she asks, lowering back down.

"It's amazing! I wish I could fly." With eyes as big as saucers, she looks at Rafe. "You have wings, too, right?" He nods in response. "I'm so jealous!"

Everyone laughs, but Ana sees Audressa is getting tired. "We'll go now. I know you need your rest, as you're recovering."

"Thank you, your Majesty. This means the world to my girls. I appreciate the time with them, and you showing them your wings." She bows.

"It's the least I can do for what you've done, protecting our intel. Thank you."

Rafe takes her hand as they leave. "Back to our quarters," he instructs Roesh.

"Yes, Rafe."

<hr>

"All clear."

"Thank you, Roesh," Rafe says as he takes Ana inside. "Are you okay?"

"I am. Just, walking with this entourage, seeing the fear on some of the people's faces at the briefing, I want this over."

"I know. It will be. He might go underground for a few months. We will be okay. You know that."

"I do."

Rafe smiles. "Hmm. I can't wait to hear you say that in August."

She caresses his face. "Rafe, are you excited about getting married?"

"I am. Why wouldn't I be?"

"Growing up on Earth, there was so much negativity from men about getting married. Hearing about the ball and chain or game over. To hear a man wanting to get married, excited even, is unusual to me."

"Are you saying I'm unusual?"

"Well, you do have wings…" She smiles at him.

"So do you," he whispers, his lips on her ear.

"Rafe!" She laughs. "Seriously, though, I want to be ready by August."

"I will do everything I can to help you. You need to understand something."

"What?"

"If you aren't ready, it's okay. We will get married when you are. There is no rush. Yes, I want you as my wife. I know you want me as your husband. As I've said, we will enjoy our engagement, and the time we have together, leading up to it."

"I'd like to freshen up."

They step into the washroom and take a shower. After getting dressed, she steps up to Rafe.

She kisses him as her arms cling around his neck. "Thank you." She smiles at him. "And you're right. I am excited to be your wife."

His kiss grows in hunger as he strokes her wing. A moan escapes her lips, and she whimpers softly when he pulls back.

"How do you read me like that?"

He smiles. "I told you, you are very powerful, what you send out."

"I'm sorry."

"It's a good thing, I promise. We can work on controlling it, but I enjoy everything you give me."

Her eyes go down. "Not everything."

"When you're feeling like that, I can control it on my end. I'm okay, really."

"If you're sure? I never want to hurt you—"

"You won't."

"Yes, love."

Lunch is being set up by Kara when Ana walks into the main chamber. She approaches the table.

"Kara, I think we're okay with two guardians. We stay in the palace and—" She sees the smile on Kara's face. "What?"

"One of our scouts has brought news. Remus has a camp set up between NightFall and MorningStella. We're sending a battalion now."

"Oh, please, let this be over soon!"

"It will be. We outnumber him." Kara takes her hand. "As far as your entourage, I think you're right. We'll reduce it to two guardians, unless something else comes up."

"Thank you."

Kara laughs. "Never big on crowds, were you?"

"No," she says. Rafe joins them. "Kara, I need to use the washroom before we eat. Please, fill him in?"

"Of course!" Kara sits with Rafe.

Ana goes into the washroom and shuts the door. She sits on the edge of the tub, pushing down the memories. *I wasn't even in his camp that long! I fought off that man, and Rafe killed him. I should not be getting this upset.*

She holds her head in her hands, trying to calm her pounding heart. Turning on the faucet, she splashes cool water on her face while taking deep breaths. Looking at her ring, she thinks of Rafe and smiles. She steps out, joining them at the table, as Evren comes in.

"What have you been doing?" Ana asks.

Evren blushes. "You'll see."

"Okay. You don't have to tell us. I was kidding," she says.

"I know. It'll be ready by tomorrow."

"Kara, how many men are in his camp?" Rafe asks.

Ana squeezes her eyes shut, trying to fight the memory. She can't breathe, as she's chained to his cot. The man from the fair comes in and sits next to her.

"Hello, gorgeous."

"Ana!" Rafe calls out, picking her up and placing her on his lap. "Ana, please. What's wrong?"

She opens her eyes. "What?"

"You cried out. Was it an episode?"

"Yes," she says as her eyes water up. "I was back in his camp."

"I'm sorry. We should not be discussing this during lunch. I never meant to cause this!"

"It's okay," she says softly.

"No, Ana, it's not." He wraps his arms around her. "I'm so sorry." Her fear seeps in, and he feels her racing heart. "Ana, breathe with me." He takes slow, deep breaths and watches her match him. "There you go."

She lays her head on his chest. "It's okay, Rafe. I'm okay."

"What happened?" Evren asks.

"Rafe mentioned his camp, and it brought up memories of what I went through there. It's not his fault."

"What happened at his camp?"

Kara turns to her. "Evren!"

"Kara, please. You are my friends, my family. You have every right to know what happened."

"No, Ana. Not right now. Not while you're dealing with it. When you're ready to tell us, you can."

"Thank you. I'm okay now. Can I finish eating?"

Rafe studies her face. "You sure?"

"Yes, love."

He stands up to help her into her seat. He sits down, taking her hand. "I'm right here, mia estrela."

"I know." She takes a drink and clears her throat. "It's okay, Kara. You can answer his question. How many men?"

"We're not sure. Less than five hundred, we know that much. NightFall and MorningStella are sending battalions, too. By this time tomorrow, hopefully all of this will be a bad memory."

"Oh, NightFall! I was going to message the count. I'll

wait, since they have all of this to deal with. Speaking of the engagement, I'd like to wait until Friday to announce it." Rafe's brow furrows, and Ana can't stifle the laugh. "I'd like to announce it to the guardians first. Since they know you. I think it's appropriate."

"Really?" he asks. "That means a lot to me."

She smiles at him. "Yes."

He kisses her. "Thank you."

She turns to Kara. "So, are you and Evren going to be self-conscious? Being the only ones there who don't have wings?"

Kara laughs. "No, Ana. We'll be fine. It will be different to see, that's for sure!"

"Is it only guardians?" Rafe asks.

"Yes. It's a ball for the guardians, hosted by us and Melian."

Rafe turns to Ana. "Will you be okay?"

"What do you mean?"

"I know you said you love your wings, and I know you're doing so much better with them. To be in a room full of people with their wings out, won't you feel self-conscious? Will you feel like you belong?"

"I don't know," she admits. "I want to say yes, but I don't really know any of them. You were born with wings, and I wasn't. I still feel different." She takes a breath. "I'll be okay. I will."

"Are you okay for training after lunch? We don't have to."

"I'd like a nap after lunch. Maybe some training later this afternoon."

"Yes, mia estrela. You do need to work them today."

"We will." She smiles at him and finishes her meal. "See? I'm okay now."

"Ana, please. You don't have to reassure me. You're the one who needs—"

"No, don't. Please, don't."

"What's wrong?"

"It makes me sound weak."

"That's not what I mean, and you know that. Mia estrela, let me comfort and reassure you, please?"

Ana stands and walks to the window. She buries her head in her hands, jumping when Rafe wraps his arms around her. "I'm sorry," she says.

"It's okay."

She turns, folding into his chest, as her tears fall. "I should be over this. Why is it still affecting me so?"

"It wasn't that long ago. Healing takes time." He kisses the top of her head. "Please, mia estrela, let me comfort you."

"Thank you, Rafe."

Kara approaches her. "What can I do to help?" She gasps when Ana grabs her and pulls her in. "Ana, you're making me hug Rafe." Kara looks at him when Ana giggles. Rafe smiles at Kara. "Okay." She steps back. "Ana, you know I'm here for you, too."

"I do know. Thank you for everything." She clutches him tighter, fighting back tears. She sighs as they continue to fall. "Why can't I stop crying? I hate feeling like this!"

Kara grabs her a linen and brings to her. "Here."

She wipes her face. "Thanks, sis."

Rafe picks her up, carrying her to the chaise. She snuggles in while enjoying his warmth.

"I'm right here. Just stay with me, okay?"

"Yes, love."

"I'm sorry. We shouldn't be discussing his camp in front of you, especially not during lunch."

"Rafe, I promise you, this wasn't your fault."

"What aren't you telling me?"

"No, please. Just hold me."

"I am."

Kara kneels in front of her. "We're going to take care of a few things. We'll be back in a little bit."

"Okay. Thank you."

Kara smiles at her. "Of course." She takes Evren's

hand and leaves.

Rafe strokes his fingers through Ana's hair. "I'm sorry," she says softly.

"For what?"

"I was already upset before you asked Kara that. Because she mentioned him. I went to the washroom and tried to calm myself down." She hangs her head. "I hid from you, after I promised I wouldn't."

"Why?"

"I'm still ashamed of what happened in the tent."

"He tried to hurt you, and you fought back. You have nothing to be ashamed of!"

"He had his hands on me, and he…" She stifles the sob. "It was too much."

"Ana, did you tell me everything he did?"

"I swear, he didn't do that! Why won't you believe me? You and Kara both!" She tries to pull away.

"Ana, tell me to let go, and I will. Please, I am sorry for everything you went through. I believe you. I swear, I do."

Giving in to the pain, she collapses against him. "Please," she begs.

"Shh. I'm right here. We don't have to talk about anything. Just stay with me. Stay here." He picks up the blanket, wrapping it around them.

"Rafe, I'm sorry I hid. You have every right to question me when I'm not being open with you."

"Ana, no. You will have moments, and you will need time to yourself. I worry for you, and I don't give you space."

She runs her hand along her wrist. "You have every right to. I can't be trusted alone. You were right."

"Hey, you were alone in the washroom. Did you hurt yourself?"

"No. I didn't even think about it."

"See? I can give you space when you need it. I have to stop being overbearing and overprotective."

"Honestly, I love that you are. I get upset, I know, but

I know why you worry. You do it because you love me. I shouldn't hide from you. I shouldn't turn inward. It's that sometimes it feels like it's too much, and I don't want you to feel it."

"Ana, if I do, it's only for a moment before I start sending you my warmth and comfort. You are powerful at sending it out, but I am good at controlling it. That's why I ask you not to hide. I can calm you."

"You do." She smiles at him while caressing his face. "You truly do."

"Would you like to train a little bit? Or do you need to rest?"

"We could train a bit. I'm okay. I'll change into warmer clothes."

"Okay."

Ana goes into the closet and changes into a pale green winter gown. Looking through her dresser, she finds a pair of wool tights. She slides them on then slips into her boots before joining Rafe.

"Ready?"

He takes her hand. They enter the corridor, where Roesh and Aylin await their command.

"We're going to the battlement," Rafe says.

"Follow me."

Rafe glances around before looking at Ana. He opens his mouth to ask, but Ana beats him to it. "Kara reduced the guards at my request."

"Ana—"

"Remus is far away, preparing for battle. It's okay."

"I don't like it, but I won't argue with you."

"Thank you. It was too many people."

Roesh and Aylin stop at the door. "We'll stay here."

"Thank you." They go up the stairs. Stepping out, Rafe watches the snow falling. "Ana—"

"Look!" She lifts her gown to her knee to show him the stockings. "I'm plenty warm, I promise."

"Okay."

"Rafe, really. I will tell you if I start to get cold."

He takes her hand while expanding his wings. Ana does the same. They stretch together, then they fly above the palace.

"Do you want to try a little on your own? I'll stay right with you."

"Yes," she says, pulling away. He follows her as she flies around the palace, staying near their battlement.

"Do you want to see your dragon?"

"Not today. You're right, it's too dangerous." She sees relief on his face.

"Okay."

Ana takes his hand. "I am getting cold."

"Let's return. We'll have hot chocolate brought in."

As they lower down into the battlement, he lets go as she lands on her own. He arrives next to her. Roesh and Aylin come to attention when Rafe and Ana join them in the corridor.

"We're going back to our quarters."

"Yes, Rafe." Roesh leads the way. Rafe stops a staff member to request hot chocolate. He holds Ana's hand tight as she starts to go into their quarters. They stay back as Roesh walks in. He steps out a few moments later. "All clear."

"What's wrong?" Ana asks Rafe as they enter.

"I didn't want you in here until he checked it."

"Because last time I came in while you were talking to a staff member, I was taken. You're right. I wasn't thinking."

"You want to get warm. That's understandable."

She goes into the closet to gather clothes before going to the washroom.

Rafe steps in. "Do you want to shower alone?"

"You can join me."

"Just to clean up?"

"Yes, love."

Chapter 19

Ana sits on the chaise to wait for him. When he walks out, she stands.

"Hoodie?"

She smiles at him. "Yep!"

"Okay." He takes her hand, and they go to their table. While she takes a sip of cocoa, Rafe puts some cheese on the bread and feeds her. "Better?"

"Yes."

"How do your wings feel?"

"Not nearly as tight. Thank you for the exercise." She hesitates and takes another sip. "Do you think they'll kill Remus?"

"I can only hope."

"I desperately want us to be free of him. The guardians and vampyra should not be hated simply for existing! How can anyone be like that?"

"Unfortunately, evil exists in many forms. Kane was selfish and greedy. Remus? There is no understanding someone like him."

"He keeps calling me an abomination."

"Ana—"

"No, I'm okay. I don't understand why he is so full of hate. He also wants the throne."

"What?"

"I asked him to let me help him. He laughed, saying the only thing I could do was die so he could take the throne. I'm not saying he doesn't hate us, but he has ulterior motives. He wants to rule."

"Just more greed."

"Yes. I never wanted a throne, never wanted to be a princess or queen. You told me who I was, and I thought you were on drugs. Or that you were crazy, until you showed me your wings. Why anyone would want this so badly that they would hurt and kill so many innocent people, is beyond me."

"The fact that they are proves why they aren't meant to. Being a leader is about putting your people first. You have done that. You have been hurt, protecting us and the vampyra. You never had to prove you were queen, but you have so many times."

"I did it without hesitation, without a second thought."

"That's why I know you're the right one to lead. I knew you had the natural right, being born into it. I wondered what sort of leader you would be, once we got here."

"Did you ever think you made a mistake bringing me here?"

"Of course not! Why would I?"

"I couldn't even defend myself against Kane, much less—"

"You could, and you did. You went into battle when you didn't have to. You defended the vampyra. You refused to answer questions about the guardians, taking the torture. Why would I ever think I made a mistake? Do you?"

"No. Everything I went through, good and bad, I would go through again, as long as I knew it would end with me here, being with you. It was worth all of it to have you take me in your arms and tell me you love me." She examines her nearly empty mug, refusing to meet his gaze.

"What?"

"If you stopped the assassin, and Kane had been arrested, you would not have told me you loved me, would you?"

"Ana, let's not play the 'what if' game. Everything happened for a reason. Honestly, if I didn't tell you that day, which I probably would have since you were sacrificing yourself for Evren and me, I'm sure I would have told you before we went into battle. I was at the point where I couldn't keep it in any longer."

"Really?"

"Yes. It was too much, not telling you how I felt. It hurt me to not say the words. I came into the closet and told you I never loved you because I heard your conversation with Kara. I thought I was making it easier for you to get over me. It nearly killed me to say it, but I did it to help. I had no idea you were going to try and kill me at sword training." He looks up when she laughs.

"That I did. I was so angry about everything, I guess I snapped. I'm embarrassed by how I behaved, but I had so much building up in me."

"I didn't help with that. I'm sorry. I thought I was."

"Rafe, it's in the past. I'm sorry I brought it up. You're right. Let's focus on the future."

"For the record, you did best me with your sword." He smiles at her.

"Really?"

"You did. You are amazing with a sword. You're amazing at everything you do. I've never seen anyone learn to fly as quickly as you. Trust me, I've taught a lot of guardians."

"You're a great teacher. I know our first lesson wasn't what we wanted, but it's okay. You've more than made up for it. I feel safe when we're in the air. I trust you, with my wings, with my life, with my heart."

"If I could go back—"

"Rafe, let's focus on the future, remember?"

"Yes, mia estrela. Speaking of which, since you put on your hoodie, does that mean we're eating dinner in here?"

"Please? I would like a nice, quiet dinner."

"We can do that."

"Thanks. After everything today…"

"Ana, you never have to explain why you want to stay in here. It's okay."

"Thank you," she says with a kiss on his cheek.

He caresses her face. "I mean it when I say I want to help you heal. I want to be with you as you overcome everything." Her eyes go down. "Ana, look at me, please."

She meets his gaze. "I'm not scolding you."

"I'm sorry about earlier."

She stands and walks to the middle of the room, where she opens her wings. Rafe joins her. He clasps her hand in his.

"Why are you so happy?" he asks.

"Because I love my wings."

"It makes me happy when I hear you say that." He kisses her hard. "You will still have a difficult day. When you do, don't hide. I won't get mad, no matter how you feel about them." Her head rolls back when his fingers tease her feathers.

"Rafe, please—"

"I'm sorry. I know you're recovering."

She steps up, kissing him, as her hand ruffles through his wing. "Rafe, I'm okay." She smiles at him.

"Ana, you had an episode and did training. I know you are tired."

"You're right."

She laughs when he pulls the hood over her head. He joins the laughter as he lowers it down.

"You love your hoodie, don't you?"

"Yes. I know what I said about reminders from Earth. This is a comfort item, so it doesn't count." They sit on the chaise before the fireplace.

"Ana, you don't have to get rid of all reminders. I know you're upset you'll never go back. I can't begin to imagine what you're going through. It's okay to reminisce, to have a reminder." He hears someone knocking. Opening the door, he finds Kara and Evren standing before him.

Kara looks at Ana. "I'm guessing we're eating dinner in here?"

"If that's okay? It's been a long day."

"I'll see to it. Evren will get your gift."

Kara turns and leaves. Evren runs to her quarters, returning a few moments later with the blanket she made. Ana runs it through her fingers. It's navy blue with silver stars and moons.

"Evren, it's beautiful!" She holds it up. "It's huge!"

"I wanted you to be able to share it."

"Thank you, so much." She lays it on the chaise then gives Evren a hug.

"You're most welcome, Ana."

Ana spreads it over the bed. "We'll use it tonight!"

Rafe walks up to Evren. "Thank you for our lovely engagement gift."

She smiles at him. "You're welcome. I'm glad you like it."

Kara returns. "Dinner will be here shortly." The blanket catches her eye. "I see you like your gift."

"I love it!" Ana beams.

"You and your blankets. You always had a horde of them."

Ana laughs. "Yes, I did. It's like I collected them." She winks at Kara. "They were good for covering ugly couches."

Kara gasps. "Take it back! That couch was not ugly!"

Rafe laughs. "Seriously, Kara, was it that bad?"

"It wasn't!"

Ana laughs. "It was horrible! Why won't you admit it?"

"I loved that couch, and nothing you say will make me change my mind."

"Why?"

"Because it was the first thing we bought together for our house."

Ana turns serious. "Kara—"

"No, it's okay. You're right. It didn't match anything. Just, we had hand me downs or college friends bought us a few things. That couch was the first thing you and I went and purchased together, after the house."

"Now I feel bad."

"Ana, don't! It's okay. You can joke all you want. I mean it."

"Why didn't you say anything before now?"

"You were having fun with it. Really, it's okay. It was a

couch."

"Kara, it was more than that. It showed that you and I were moving in together. I was so excited to finally move out of the dorm and into a house."

"Ana, you made it into a home. You took such great care of me, after I would travel for work or have a bad day at school."

"I miss you, Kara. I miss the time we had together. Coming here, we've drifted apart. So much put on both of us at once." Her eyes meet Rafe's. "That isn't against you. I'm glad you brought me here. I'm glad for the things I've done, to help the people."

"I know, Ana. It's okay."

"Kara, we have to set aside a day and do something, the two of us. Whatever you want."

"What if Thursday, after lunch, I took you on a little tour of the palace?"

"That would be wonderful!"

Rafe looks at Kara. "Roesh and Aylin will be with you."

"I know. That's okay."

Ana walks to Rafe, putting her hands on his chest. "What will you do while I'm with Kara?"

"Evren and I can go into the village." Rafe steps over to let dinner service in. They set up and leave. "Shall we eat?" he asks, taking her hand.

She smiles and nods. He leads her to the table, sitting her down. He sits beside her. Relief washes over him when she eats. When Ana catches Rafe staring at her, she tilts her head at him.

"I was worried, Ana. After the day you've had."

"I'm okay now. You three have made me feel a lot better. I don't know what I would do without you."

"We're all here for you. You know that, right?" Kara asks.

"Yes, sis. Thank you."

"We've got Caelum's quarters cleaned and ready. I know the wedding is still a month and a half away, but it's one less thing to worry about." Kara glances at Evren when she sighs. "Are you okay?"

"Yes. I'm excited for our wedding but nervous about seeing my brother."

"Evren, sweetheart, you know everything will be fine. I will be with you."

"I know, Kara. Thank you. I'm worried he's going to embarrass me or be rude."

"Whatever happens, we'll deal with it," Kara assures her.

"She's right. Hopefully, he is coming in the spirit of making peace with you. Focus on that?"

"Yes, Ana. Thank you."

"What is your sister's name?" Rafe asks.

"Cassandra. She is my twin. Having grown up away from me, knowing I was a slave, she is ashamed. She will not come. A lot of my family feel the same as her."

"Kara, do you have to go to Vulcara? Wouldn't you rather go somewhere happy for your honeymoon?"

"Evren and I have discussed it, in length. We are going to Vulcara for a few days, then we are going to the MoonSol realm."

"Where my mother was from?"

"Yes. It's beautiful there. We'll spend the rest of our honeymoon there."

Ana turns to Rafe. "Will I ever get to see it?"

"You're not really supposed to go off-world."

"I understand. Forget I asked." Ana takes a sip of her tea, swallowing the tears threatening to escape.

"Maybe we can find a way."

She shakes her head. "Don't worry about it."

"Oh, Ana. I'm sorry."

"It's okay. I guess I'm stuck here." She gasps as her eyes go wide. "I didn't mean—"

"Ana, shh. Calm down. I know what you mean. Everyone else is traveling, and you can't. I understand how you feel."

"Wait until Rafe takes you to MorningStella," Kara says, nodding to Rafe, and hoping the thought of traveling somewhere new will bring a smile to Ana's face. "It's absolutely beautiful. You are going to love it."

"She's right, Ana. You have your own cottage on the beach."

Her head jerks up. "What?"

"You do. Your grandmother had it built when she was queen. Our own private beach getaway. Doesn't that sound nice?" Rafe asks as he squeezes Ana's hand.

"It sounds amazing. I wish we could go now."

"If we're getting married this coming August, don't you want to wait? Make it our honeymoon destination?"

"Yes, Rafe. It sounds perfect." She kisses him softly. "Thank you. Thank you for bringing me home, thank you for asking me to be your wife, thank you for everything you have given me."

He smiles as a tear slides down his cheek. She wipes it away. "Ana, I could say the same for you. Thank you for giving me a home, for agreeing to be my wife, and for giving me all of you. It's more than I ever thought I would have."

Kara and Evren gather dishes and quietly leave. A minute later, Ana realizes they are gone. "I guess they thought we needed to be alone."

Rafe laughs, pressing his forehead to hers. "You told me you were deeply, desperately, madly in love. I don't think I've told you, I am too. You are so incredible, so beautiful, so full of life. Everything about you exudes love, peace, and happiness. You unlocked my heart, let yourself in, and made your home. I wouldn't want it any other way." He kisses her, wrapping his arm around her.

"Rafe, I know we are still bringing down walls, but I want to be with you. I want to give myself to you."

"Ana—"

"We're waiting until our wedding night. It's okay. I wanted to tell you, so if you want to."

"Mia estrela, you aren't ready. I know you aren't. I can

see it. We'll wait, and it will be perfect. Just think, our wedding ceremony, the reception. We'll stay here that night and travel the next day. I have a surprise in mind for our wedding night here."

"Really?"

"Yes, mia estrela."

"Oh, love. I'm so excited. I know, we're waiting until August. I won't rush it, I promise."

"Can we talk about the wedding night?"

Confusion sweeps across her face. "What do you mean?"

"I know it can upset you."

"I'm okay."

"Have you thought about it, the wedding night?"

She smiles up at him. "Yes. I envision us holding each other. You remove my gown, smiling at what I'm wearing underneath. You gently remove it before bringing your hands around my waist. Then we kiss. You carry me to the bed, laying me down. You undress. You climb into bed, pulling yourself onto me. We kiss again as my hands are on your chest. Our bodies join as we become one."

He lets out a soft gasp, lifting her out of the chair and holding her in his arms. "Oh, Ana. The fact that you did that, without getting upset, without having bad memories, shows me how hard you've worked to bring down your walls!" He kisses her and runs his fingers through her hair.

"I told you, love. I am working so hard on it. I won't ruin our wedding night."

"Ana, no matter what happens, it will not be ruined. Please, mia estrela, tell me that."

She caresses his face, kissing him. "Yes, love. It won't be ruined." She takes his hand and leads him to the bed. "Rafe, I need you."

Smiling as her love and happiness rush in, he lifts her onto the bed before climbing up with her. He removes his shirt and pants as she strips her hoodie off, throwing it onto her nightstand. His hips lift so she can remove his shorts, which she tosses to the floor. As she's on her back, looking up at him, he slowly lifts her shirt. Each kiss to her chest and neck send desire burning through her. He tugs on her pants, and she can only nod. Slowly, he lowers them with her undergarments. He climbs over her, and she devours his mouth with hers. Her hands grip his hair as her passion builds up between them.

"Oh, mia estrela, what you make me feel!" he cries as he kisses her again.

His tongue probes inside as her hand works down to his chest and stomach. She gently grips him, stroking slowly at first. He kneels as she parts her legs. His mouth is on her neck, her cheek, finally her lips as she moves faster. Her hips writhe as he continues to caress. He devours her lips as he is overwhelmed by her. Her head rolls back as she cries out. They snuggle together while catching their breath.

"How was that?"

"Oh, love. Thank you."

Ana wraps her legs around him as he sits up. She clings to his chest, kissing him hard. They look up when Kara and Evren step in. Rafe grabs the blanket and wraps it around them.

"Kara!" she cries out.

"I'm so sorry!" She grabs Evren's hand and rushes out.

Ana collapses against Rafe, laughing. "She is never going to learn to knock."

Rafe joins in the laughter. "You're right." He kisses the top of her head. "Clean up and change for bed?"

"Yes. Poor Kara. How red do you think her face is?"

He laughs harder. "I can't imagine. We probably won't see her again until breakfast."

"Love, be nice in the morning."

"I'll try."

"Rafe!"

"What? She came in without knocking. It's not my fault."

"Hmm. Can we clean up?"

"I don't know. Can we go to the washroom without someone else coming in? Is it possible?"

"Oh, love. Yes."

He picks her up and carries her. "Start the shower. I'll grab us clothes."

"Thank you."

The water warms up, and she steps in. She closes her eyes, feeling his mouth on her body, her hand stroking him. When he joins her, his arm wraps around her stomach.

He gasps at her feelings. "Mia estrela, really?"

She turns, smiling at him. "You are so incredible."

Wrapping her arms around his neck, she kisses him with all the fire she has. His hands caress her sides. The water washes over them as he pulls her to the wall. He kneels in front of her as his mouth teases along her hip and thigh. When she nods, he continues.

His mouth is on her while she holds his shoulders, sending all of his passion and pleasure back into him. Her passion erupts against his tongue, causing her to fall against the wall, her body spent. He holds her on his lap.

He kisses her as she wraps her arms tighter. "Rafe, love, thank you."

"It goes both ways." When she laughs in response, he can't hide his confusion. "What?"

"It literally does."

"Yes, it does."

Helping her up, they stand and rinse off before getting dressed. When she steps into the main chamber, Ana is surprised to see Kara sitting on the chaise.

"Ana, I am so sorry," she says as she stands. "I never meant to—"

"We're going to have a latch installed, so when we are in here, we can have privacy."

"You shouldn't have to do that because of me."

"I want you to have access so when we're recovering or need you, you can get in here. You forget to knock. It's okay. It's an easy remedy."

"I didn't know you were… that you could do that in bed. I'm glad to see it." Her face flushes red before she lowers her gaze again. "I don't mean—"

"Kara, I have never seen you this embarrassed! Really, it's okay. I know what you mean, that you know what I went through on Earth. I told you Rafe is breaking down walls, helping me get over what I've endured."

"You're already so self-conscious, that for me to make my comments after your shower, then to walk in today. I am so sorry."

"You asked me once why we still used the closet since it wasn't forbidden. I told you I wasn't comfortable yet with the bed. That was the truth. I also feel more exposed out here. I don't really feel like this is my room. Everyone comes in, from food service and staff, to housekeeping, to you and Evren. I'm not at all complaining, I want you to understand."

"This doesn't feel like yours?" Rafe asks as he steps up beside her.

Ana shakes her head. "It's so open and exposed."

"Why didn't you tell me? We could've moved the bed, brought in privacy walls."

"Because I have a huge, beautiful chamber. I didn't feel right complaining, especially with so much going on at the time."

Kara steps up, taking her hand. "Thank you for not being mad or embarrassed about earlier."

"We laughed, wondering how red your face was."

She smiles. "It was pretty red. I'm going to turn in. Are we having breakfast here in the morning?"

"Yes. Then the briefing. I hope we have news of the battle by then."

"Me, too." She hugs Ana. "Night, guys."

"Night, Kara," Ana says. "It's okay. Really."

Kara laughs softly as she leaves. Ana wraps her arms around Rafe's waist. He studies her for a moment.

"What can I do to help?"

"With what?" she asks. He gestures around the room. "Oh, love. No. It's okay."

"Tomorrow, we'll have breakfast, then I'll see about a latch while you and Kara prepare for the morning briefing."

"Thank you."

She uses the washroom, then sits on the chaise to wait for him. Looking around the room, she remembers her first day. The size alone overwhelmed her. She thinks about stepping up to Rafe to kiss him, when he pulled back. She looks up when he sits beside her and takes her hand.

"What's wrong? Why are you sad?"

"I was remembering our first day in here."

"Oh. Ana—"

"Stop. I didn't mean to dredge up the memories. It's okay." She closes her eyes, thinking of him proposing at dinner, of their upcoming wedding, then smiles at him. "See? I'm okay."

"What were you thinking of? So much happiness!" She tells him, and he helps her stand. "Are you ready for bed?" He laughs at the look on her face. "To sleep, Ana. We need to go to sleep."

"Yes, love. I need a minute."

"Are you okay?"

"Yes," she answers as she steps away to extend her wings. "They needed to stretch." He watches her walking around furling and unfurling her wings. He smiles at her. "What?" she asks.

"You've taken to them so well." She turns away. He takes her hands. "What's wrong?"

"They're hurting a little. It's why I needed to stretch them."

He begins massaging her back and shoulders. "You're not as tight as you were in the beginning. I'm so grateful they are getting easier for you to handle, not hurting as much."

"Oh, they were horrible in the beginning."

"I remember. I'm grateful you survived. Knowing you

gave your life, sacrificing everything to save me, not even knowing if I was dead or alive, was more than I ever wanted. Thank you, for saving my life."

She smiles at him, caressing his face, as her wings retract. "I would do it again and again, without hesitation, because I will not lose you."

"You've saved my life, my heart, my soul. I give them all to you."

"And you have mine." She looks at her ring. "I'll put this up."

"You really don't like taking it off, do you?"

"No. I know I have to, though."

"Hmm."

They go into the closet. He opens the drawer as she removes her ring, and he locks it in before leading her to the ottoman.

"We're sitting for a minute, then going to bed."

"Rafe?"

He smiles at her, sitting down and bringing her onto his lap. "I brought you in here, in my arms, as the poison was raging through you. I knew I wouldn't lose you. I didn't know if you would forgive me, if you would accept me, but I had to save your life. Kissing you, telling you I loved you, was the best thing that ever happened to me.

"We have died for each other, but then we brought each other back. I never truly felt alive, until that day. When I came to, and you pulled me into your arms, telling me you loved me as well, I was so overcome with joy."

"You scared me. You told me you were immune to poison, then I watched you die! I was so angry, so scared, so devastated. Having you back in my arms, feeling your love and warmth, was everything I ever wanted."

"I'm sorry I questioned that, thinking you would want more than what we had in here. I know now you meant it when you said having me was more than enough."

She smiles at him, kissing him gently. "Love, I am exhausted. Can we turn in?"

"Yes, mia estrela." He stands up, carrying her out with him, and placing her in bed. "Every beat of my heart is yours," he says as he climbs up beside her.

She clutches his shirt while pushing down her tears. "Every inch of my body, my heart, my soul, is yours."

He kisses her forehead. "Sleep, mia estrela. I love you."

"I love you, too."

⚜

Ana wakes up, breathing hard. Rafe is sound asleep. She wants to slip away to the washroom. While calming her breathing, she remembers her promise to him. She caresses his face. "Rafe?"

"Hmm. Go back to sleep."

"I… I can't."

His eyes open as he quickly sits up. "I'm sorry. What's wrong?"

"I had a nightmare."

He turns on the lamp, then wraps her in his arms. "What happened?"

"You died on the ottoman. I sat and waited, but you never woke up."

"Oh, Ana. I'm alive and right here."

"Please, love, don't ever leave me!"

"Shh. I won't. You know I won't." He strokes her hair gently, reassuring her. "I'm never leaving you again. I am so sorry I ever did." He wipes away her tears, kissing her gently. "What can I do? How can I help?"

"Hold me like this, please."

"I will. Feel my comfort, let it penetrate through, warming you and reassuring you. I'm right here, mia estrela."

"It was so real. I thought I had lost you. I can't—" She gives in, her tears falling fast. "I'm sorry."

"No, Ana, it's okay. We shouldn't talk of things like this before bed. This was my fault. Thank you for waking me."

"I almost didn't," she admits as shame washes over her.

"I'm glad you did. Let me comfort you now."

"Yes, love." He strokes her hair as he whispers reassurances into her ear. Her heartbeat slows down as her tears stop. "Thank you."

"Will you get more sleep?"

"Yes."

"If you can't—"

"I'll wake you."

"All right." He gently guides her onto her back. "I'm right here, mia estrela."

"Yes, love."

She clutches his shirt. He kisses her forehead, seeing the peace wash over her face. One last glance, and he closes his eyes, praying she falls asleep.

Chapter 20

Rafe wakes up, realizing Ana's not in bed with him. He turns on the lamp as he sits. He sees her on the chaise in front of the fireplace. Wrapping the blanket over his shoulders, he approaches her.

"Are you okay?" he asks.

"Yes, love. I did get more sleep."

"Then why aren't you in bed?"

"I had another nightmare. I was back in his camp. I didn't want you feeling it. It was too strong."

"Ana, we've talked about this. I can handle it."

She shakes her head. "No, you couldn't."

"What do you mean?" he asks, sitting beside her.

"I was holding you when it happened. Tears ran down your face. You didn't feel that?"

"No."

"I wiped your face and quickly pulled away. It was too much for you."

"Because I was asleep."

"I'm sorry. I didn't think of that. Seeing you like that, I didn't want to hurt you!"

He holds her. "It's okay. Now you know for next time, wake me up. I can't help you if I'm asleep." He opens the blanket, wrapping them both in it.

"Yes, love."

"It's six o'clock. Do you want a little more sleep?"

"I can't. I'm too wired now."

"Ana—"

"No. I'm going to get a shower and get dressed."

"Do you want to shower alone? I know sometimes you are self-conscious, thinking about being back in his camp. I'll give you space if you need it."

"I need to be with you. Please? Just a shower, but with

me?"

"Yes, mia estrela."

He helps her up and follows her to the closet. She picks out a gown and undergarments, laying everything on the ottoman. She slips into her robe before going to the washroom. After turning on the tap, she strips down then steps in. She cries in the shower, gasping when Rafe pulls her into his arms. He presses her head against his firm torso.

"I… I don't mean to get so upset!" She wipes her tears away.

"Ana, please, it's okay. You were hurt and traumatized. You are coping with it and owe no apology or explanation."

She kisses him. Their passion flows back and forth as their lips consume each other.

"Ana, you need to take it easy."

"I know. Just kiss me, please?"

His mouth crashes on hers as he holds her tighter against him. He runs his hands along her sides, then gently strums through her wings.

She jumps up into his arms, and her legs wrap around him.

"I love you."

He kisses her again before putting her on her feet. "I love you, too. Now, do you want a shower or the closet?"

"Really?" She bites her lower lip when he nods. "Closet."

He carries her in, takes her to his dresser, and gently places her on it. Kissing her, he stands between her legs.

"Ana, what do you want?"

"You. Just give me all of you."

"We're not—"

"No, I know."

Ana nudges him back then stands. She kisses along his neck and chest before moving lower. His head rolls back when her mouth is on him. He trembles, panting, as she moves slowly at first, then speeds up.

He kisses her as he finishes. She goes to the dresser

and gets a towel for him.

"How was that?" she asks with a grin.

"Oh, God. I still need a minute," he says, cleaning up. She falls into his arms, lying with him on the ottoman. "How do you feel?"

"It was incredible. I've never felt anything like that before!"

He laughs. "Neither have I. How did you—"

She blushes as she sits up. "I read a lot back on Earth. Sometimes romance novels were the only books available. I'm glad I read them." She lowers down, kissing him as her hand traces along his chest. "I've been waiting a long time to take care of you like that." She smiles at him. "Another first."

"Hmm. You are amazing." He gasps when she lowers down on top of him. She lays on him, kissing him. "Ana, we need to get dressed."

"Yes, love."

Wrapping the towel around his waist, Rafe runs to the washroom. Ana slips on her corset and gown. The crimson matches her wings, and it is adorned with embroidered black roses. She puts on a pair of black slippers with a matching tiara before lifting up her engagement ring.

She goes to the mirror and admires her reflection, looking herself over when Rafe walks in. He is dressed to match her.

"This is different."

She smiles at him. "I hope it's appropriate. Evren will tell me if it's not."

"Love, open your wings." He gasps when she does. "Oh, with that gown. It's more than I can take!"

She glances at the mirror. "It is incredible together." She blushes. "I feel beautiful this morning."

He steps up behind her, kissing the top of her head. "Ana, you are beautiful. Don't you know that?"

She brings her wings in before facing him. "You make me feel that way."

He laughs. "I'm glad, but surely you see how gorgeous you are!"

She steps up, kissing him. "Thank you. I love you."

"Oh, mia estrela, I love you, too." He sits on the ottoman. She climbs on his lap and kisses him. "What's wrong?"

Ana laughs. "I think we are a little overdressed for breakfast in our quarters."

"What would your Highness recommend?"

"Breakfast in the dining hall? We haven't done that in a while."

"Kara and Evren?"

"Would you see if they'll join us?"

"Of course!" He stands up, putting her on her feet, then kisses her forehead. "Be right back."

She steps out of the closet and goes to her Eiffel Tower. After turning on the lights, she's admiring it when Rafe walks in.

"Well?"

"They're getting dressed and will be over in a minute."

"At least you knocked, right?"

"Of course." He steps up to her. "May I?"

Rafe takes her hand and dances with her. She laughs, holding him tight. They look over as Kara and Evren come in.

"Really, Kara?"

"I thought since he was dressed—"

"I'm teasing, sis. It's my turn now to make fun."

"Yes, Ana. I'm sorry."

Ana kisses Rafe's cheek then approaches Evren. "Is what I'm wearing okay?"

"Uh, well, it's considered evening wear."

"Oh."

"Ana, you are the queen. Wear what you want, when you want. If I may, that dress is absolutely beautiful on you! Why so fancy this morning?" Kara asks.

"I don't know. It was what I picked out."

"Are you announcing your engagement at breakfast?"

"No, the ball. I wanted to look pretty."

"You are pretty. You know how nice you look in any of the gowns you wear. Even the simple cotton ones we wear to the village."

"Thank you, Kara. Are we going to breakfast?"

Rafe takes her hand and leads her from the room. Roesh turns. "Where to, your Majesty?"

"Dining hall, please."

"Of course."

She catches Aylin staring. "Aylin?"

"My apologies, Majesty. That gown is exquisite!"

"Thank you."

They sit at their table. Ana ignores some of the looks she gets from the ladies of the court. Kara sees it, too.

"They're jealous. You have a good-looking man on your arm, you are beautiful, and you are the queen. Of course, they're going to stare."

Rafe turns to Kara. "You think I'm good looking?"

"For a man."

They all laugh. "I know you're right," Ana says as she butters her toast. "It's... once I'd like to fit in somewhere. I never really feel like I belong."

She watches Rafe stand up and go to the table. He speaks with the women, making them smile and laugh. Then he sits beside Ana.

"What was that?" she asks.

"They would like to meet you, after we've eaten."

"What?"

"Ana, you said it yourself, you need to get around the palace more, meet your people. You want to feel like you belong, that's how you start."

She takes a deep breath. "Yes, love."

When they've finished eating, he takes her hand, and

walks with her. The ladies come to their feet, bowing.

"Your Majesty," says a young blonde woman, in a lavender gown. "I am Countess Dianna. It's a pleasure to meet you."

"Countess," she nods. The other ladies are introduced. "I apologize that I haven't met you sooner."

"Majesty, if I may?" Dianna asks. "You have battled for your kingdom and your people. We understand. When you came in this morning, we were surprised to see you is all. Between that and your beautiful gown, we did not mean to stare. Our apologies."

"Quite all right. Thank you." Ana's face flushes when her wings open. "Oh, I'm so sorry."

"No, your Majesty. Please, they are absolutely incredible. We still cannot believe you are the Crimson Queen." The countess gasps. "It slipped out."

"Dianna, it's okay." She opens her wings further. "Apparently, that's what I am. I didn't believe it myself when it happened." She retracts them until they are resting on her back.

"Thank you, Majesty. You are so gracious and kind. You are what this kingdom needs. We are so grateful you have returned to us."

Ana takes Rafe's hand. "Then thank my guardian. He is the one who found me and returned me."

Dianna smiles at them. "Thank you, both. Majesty," she bows. "Guardian," she says, nodding to Rafe.

"Countess, excuse us."

They turn and return to their quarters. Ana sits on the chaise, calming her heart. "I'm okay. It's a little nerve-wracking sometimes, meeting new people. And then for my wings to open!"

"You handled it well. I was extremely impressed," Rafe says, kissing her. He kneels in front of her. "Now, how are you feeling?" He takes her hand. "Hmm. You really don't like meeting new people, do you?"

"No. I know I have to, it's in the job description."

"I didn't mean to put you on the spot."

"I'm glad you did. I would've felt more self-conscious wondering why they were staring. Meeting them actually helped. Thank you." Ana looks over when Kara laughs. "What?"

"You could interrogate an assassin but get nervous meeting new people?"

"I was terrified the whole time I spoke to him, but I could hide it."

"I know. Still. Sis, you are weird."

Ana smiles at her. "Thank you."

"We're going to the Communications Lounge to see if there's any news. We'll meet you for the morning briefing."

"We'll be in there at nine-thirty." Ana watches them leave. Rafe sits next to her. "They seem nice. She said she was a countess, but she's not a royal?"

"No. There are higher nobility classes from other quadrants, such as Count Bela, and even from other realms, such as Royse. He is Lord Royse."

"Does Evren have a title?"

"She is Lady Evren, as your handmaid and member of court."

"So, basically the same level as him? I hope it's enough that he doesn't ruin her wedding day."

"You're worried, aren't you?"

"I never had to deal with that kind of family drama, and I really hoped I never would. I pray he doesn't start anything with her."

"All we can do is wait and see. Now, your paperwork is done. What would you like to do until we leave for the briefing?" He glances at the clock. "We have an hour until we leave."

She smiles at him, kissing him. "Rafe—"

"Ana, we need to rest since we are training later this afternoon."

"Yes, love." She walks to her tower and admires it. "I still can't believe this is real!" she says when Rafe is beside her.

"I'm so glad you like it." He sees her blush. "What?"

"There's something about me you don't know."

"What?"

Ana leads him into the closet. She removes her gown before extending her wings.

"What's going on?"

"Come up behind me." Rafe does as she asks. "Lift my left wing and look at my shoulder blade."

He carefully moves it, seeing a small butterfly tattoo below where her wing extends out. "Ana! How did I not know you had this?"

She laughs. "You hadn't really seen me naked, at least my back, until after I had grown my wings. Honestly, I wasn't sure if the tattoo was still there."

He studies it closer. "Does it say Paris underneath?" He leans forward, kissing the tattoo.

"Yes. It was my way of saying one day I would fly to Paris." She brings her wings in.

He shakes his head while laughing. "You are full of secrets! Does Kara know you have that?"

"Yes. Who do you think took me?" she asks as she gets dressed.

"I can't believe I never noticed it!"

"The wings hide it now."

"Is that your only tattoo?"

She laughs. "Yes."

"How come you never learned to drive?"

"No one would teach me. Kara offered after I met her, but by then I didn't see the point. Where our house was, I could walk to work, the store, the café."

"It's funny, I learned how to drive, and you didn't."

She smiles. "Yes, it is funny. You miss your pretty car, don't you?"

"It was nice."

"Rafe, you mentioned training."

"Yes?"

"After lunch, could we take Kara and Evren to the woods and see the dragons?"

"That should be okay. We'll see what they have planned for today."

"Are you ready to head to the briefing? I know it's a little early, but maybe Kara will be there with some news."

"Yes, we'll head on." He shakes his head.

"What?"

"You have a tattoo. I have to wrap my brain around that."

"Rafe!" She takes his hand, smiling. "I have other secrets, too, you know."

He gasps, laughing. "I will find them all out."

She smiles as she opens the door. Roesh turns to her and bows.

"We're going to the meeting room."

"Yes, Majesty." He leads the way. He looks in and sees Kara and Evren. "Everything all right in here?"

"Yes, Roesh, thank you. It's okay for the queen to enter."

He steps back as Rafe and Ana walk inside. "Any news?" Ana asks as she approaches her desk.

Kara smiles at her. "We received word. Remus is dead. He fell in battle, and his men are scattered."

"Oh, thank God!" Ana declares.

"We can breathe again. Still, will you keep two guardians with you?"

"Yes, Kara. Thank you." She turns to Rafe, hugging him tight. "I'm so happy we are free of him."

"I am, too."

"Ana, do you want me to lead today?" Kara asks.

"If you don't mind. Oh, do you and Evren have plans after lunch?"

"No, why?"

"We want to go into the woods and see the dragons."

Evren smiles at Kara. "Can we?"

Kara sighs, then laughs. "Yes, we'll go."

They go over intel from the battle, look at reports on the treasury and supplies, then get ready as people start entering the room. Ana sits at the desk with Rafe standing beside her.

Kara stands on the other side, papers in hand. She gestures for everyone to quiet down, then leads the briefing. Once it's over, Rafe escorts Ana to their quarters for lunch.

"I'll get changed before food gets here."

Ana goes into the closet, slipping on a winter gown, wool tights, and boots. Rafe changes into black pants and a simple button up shirt. They step out, seeing Kara and Evren come in, dressed in warm clothing. Lunch is delivered and set up.

"What?" Kara asks when she catches Ana smiling at her.

"Rafe saw my tattoo."

Kara nearly chokes on her roll. "I almost forgot about that! Your wings—"

"He could see it."

"What's a tattoo?" Evren asks.

Ana laughs. "It's a permanent picture put on your body. Mine is a butterfly."

Evren shakes her head, unable to hide her confusion. "Like a mothra," Kara explains.

"Oh! Those are pretty."

Rafe looks at Kara. "Do you have any tattoos?"

"No, believe it or not. I was quite shocked when she told me she wanted one! Honestly, I only agreed to take her because I thought she would lose her nerve once we got there. I never would've, if I had known she was actually going to go through with it!"

"Kara, why not?"

"I may not be your mother, but you know how I feel about you."

"Yes, Kara."

"You surprised me when you said you wanted a tattoo. That was the last thing I expected from you!"

"Any other deviant behavior?" Rafe asks.

"Rafe!" Ana exclaims, laughing. "Having a tattoo is not deviant behavior."

"I was kidding."

"Yes, love."

Kara laughs as well. "Hmm. Should I tell him about the night we went to the club?"

"Kara, I swear to God. If you do, I will tell him why you taught me how to do embroidery!"

"Ana, no!"

They burst out laughing, seeing the confusion on Rafe and Evren's faces. Ana holds Rafe's hand. "Seriously, it's not a big deal."

"I'll tell you later," Kara mouths to Rafe.

He smiles and nods before returning his attention to Ana. "Are we ready to go into the woods?"

"How are we going?"

"We'll walk."

"Not used to that, are you?" Kara teases Ana.

She laughs. "No. We usually fly."

They step into the hallway. Rafe looks at Roesh. "We're walking to the woods."

"Yes, Rafe."

Ana takes Kara's hand, smiling at her. "Sis, are you excited to see the dragons?"

"No. They don't like us, remember?"

"You'll be fine!"

Kara gently pushes her to Rafe. "We'll see."

Chapter 21

Arriving in the woods, they listen for the dragons. Rafe leads them when they hear squawking. As soon as Smaug sees Ana, he runs up and circles around her.

"I knew he would remember you," Rafe says.

They watch as the dragons interact with Ana. She opens and closes her wings as they do the same. She flies up, and they follow her around. She gently lands, watching them. She kneels down, and they run up to her.

"Well, is she a Dragon Queen?" Rafe asks.

Evren laughs. "I can't find any prophecy. There must be, though. I mean, the way they react to her!"

"If I may," Aylin says. "There is a prophecy." They all turn to her. "I have a book back in my quarters, of myths and prophecies. There is one story, but it's not about dragons, specifically. It's about the Crimson Queen, and how all creatures react openly to her, not hostile."

"Really?" Evren asks. "What book is it?"

"Isidora's Book of Myths and Legends."

"Oh, I haven't read that one yet! Is there much mention of the Crimson Queen inside?"

"There is. When we return, I'll get the book."

"That would be great!"

Kara laughs. "Crimson Queen is her favorite story. It was before this happened, actually."

Aylin gasps. "You must've been so surprised!"

"We all were."

"Aylin, we are on duty. Keep your eyes open."

"Yes, Roesh. My apologies."

Rafe looks at her. "Ignore him. You're doing an excellent job," he says quietly.

She smiles at him. "Thank you." She takes to the air and patrols.

Rafe turns to Roesh when he clears his throat. "What?"

"Rafe, I know you have more rank and experience than me, but I am her instructor. Please, don't do that again."

"Roesh, while it's important that she remembers her duty, it's also important to keep morale up, especially with everything that has happened. There are three guardians out here, not two. I am also keeping watch."

"Yes, Rafe."

He steps up to Ana. "Are you ready to head back?"

"Almost." She picks up Smaug and brings him to Evren. She smiles while she pets him, then Ana sets him on the ground. "Okay."

⚊⚊⚊ ❦ ⚊⚊⚊

Aylin delivers the book to Ana's quarters. Evren looks at her. "I'll return it to you soon. Thank you."

Aylin nods while stepping into the hallway.

"What's that?" Ana asks.

"A book of myths and legends, similar to the one you had. This is a different author, from a different time. I'll be curious to see what his stories say."

"Will you do me a favor?" Ana asks, placing her hand above Evren's elbow. "Take it to your quarters and read it later. Then you can tell me what's in it, if you want? After the last book—"

Evren nods. "I understand. I'll be right back!" she leaves.

Ana walks to the closet and changes into a simple pink gown. She slips on a silver circlet. Rafe watches her intently when she steps out.

"What?" she asks, checking her outfit to see what is wrong.

"Kara is right. Even in a simple gown, you are beautiful."

She smiles. "Thank you. It's not comfortable, but it's better than the dressier gowns."

"Missing your yoga pants?" Kara teases.

"Shut up!" Ana says, laughing. "Yes."

"I know. I do, too."

"Kara! At least you can wear comfortable pants. I have to be in gowns or dress slacks, regal and appropriate. It is a little much, sometimes. Plus, having to constantly wear a crown or circlet, too."

"I'm sorry. I tease, but I know you're still trying to get used to wearing the fancy clothes."

"It's okay." Ana walks to the chaise and grips the armrest as she leans over it.

Rafe steps up beside her. "Are your wings bothering you?"

"A little."

"Do you want to stretch them?"

"I can go," Kara offers.

"No, sis. It's okay."

She straightens up then takes his hand, leading him to the middle of the room. Kara watches Ana expand her wings and go to the air. Rafe follows close behind. They fly a lap, then they land.

"Ana, it's incredible how you do that."

"Thanks! As you see, I'm getting less self-conscious about it."

"As you should. Can I ask, how are they? How are you coping?"

Ana goes to her and hugs her. "Thank you." She pulls back. "You can. They were a little tight, but better now. I've accepted them, knowing they are a part of me."

Rafe steps up to her. "Really?"

"Yes—" He envelops her in his arms, kissing her. "Rafe!"

"I'm sorry, but I'm so happy to hear you say that!"

"You heard me tell her that I love them."

"Yes, but to hear you finally say that you accept them, when it was so hard for you to even think about, is wonderful."

"Love, please." Ana smiles at him then looks at Kara. "Wait, where is Evren?"

"Hmm. Knowing her, she probably started reading the book! I'll get her," Kara says as she leaves.

Ana faces Rafe. "Love, I can feel how happy you are, without even touching you!"

"I told you, I've waited a long time for this. From your first day, when you were so scared and angry. I tried my best to comfort you."

"Rafe, you did comfort me. You couldn't make me accept them, though. I told you I would in my own time."

"Did you forget you had them when you woke up?"

"I did. Then what happened at breakfast and seeing them with that gown this morning. It took little moments for me to be able to see."

"I remember your first day, you called yourself a freak."

"Did I really?"

"You don't remember?"

"I was in shock and so exhausted, I remember bits and pieces, but not that."

"What do you remember?"

"Hmm. I remember how much it hurt when it happened, you helping me into the palace, you kissing me when I asked you to. Um, I remember you touching them. Up until we sat down and ate, I don't remember a whole lot. I was tired and trying not to deal with it."

"You've come so far since then."

She takes his hands, pulling him to her, then flies with him up to the ceiling. "Like this?"

"Ana, you are incredible."

He extends his wings then kisses her. She wraps her legs around his waist as his kiss grows in hunger.

"Kara and Evren could be back any moment."

"Oh, right. I need to see about a latch," he says as they lower down. "I'll do that when they return."

"Private dinner tonight?" she asks, smiling. "We'll

celebrate my wings?"

His smile grows. "Absolutely."

Kara and Evren enter. "I was right!" Kara exclaims. "She had started to read."

Ana laughs. "I don't blame you, Evren. I'm the same way, whenever I would get a new book."

"My apologies!"

"No, Evren, it's okay. Did you read anything good?"

"Like Aylin said, all creatures respond to you."

Ana walks up to Kara. "Could Rafe and I have a private dinner tonight?"

"Of course. Are you okay?"

"Yes. He's so happy about me and my wings."

"Let's do lunch here tomorrow, then you and I will tour the palace. How does that sound?"

"Sounds great."

"We'll see you tomorrow, at eleven."

Ana sees them out. She turns to Rafe. "What?"

"I was going to see about a latch."

"I can go with you."

"I tell you what." He leans down by her ear. "Why don't you get a shower and go into the closet? I'll join you shortly."

"Yes, love."

Ana kisses Rafe then watches him leave before gathering a special outfit to wear for him. She goes into the washroom and starts the water while undressing. The hot stream relaxes her while she cleans her hair.

Visions of Rafe pinning her to the wall before ravaging her with his tongue invade her senses. She trembles as she rinses off, every nerve on fire while she brushes her teeth and goes into the closet.

Slipping on the corset, her desire continues to grow. She sits on the ottoman, leaning back with her legs crossed, as she waits for him. He returns only a few moments later.

"Ana?"

"I'm in here," she responds.

Rafe shuts the door and locks it before he turns to her. "Oh, mia estrela. What is this?" he asks, taking her all in before approaching her.

She blushes. "Do you like it?"

"Hmm. It's beautiful." He leans down. "I'm afraid it has to come off, though," he says, gently tugging on the corset.

Rafe's fingers move deftly, unsnapping it and letting it fall to the floor. He brushes over the exposed skin. Ana reaches for his belt.

"Not yet," he says in a low voice. "Allow me to take care of you, first."

He helps her lift up as he finishes undressing her. His lips crush hers as he strokes through her wing. She moans in response, and he caresses between her thighs.

"Rafe, please," she murmurs as each wave threatens to drown her.

He smiles down at her before lifting her and holding her against his chest. She wraps her arms and legs around him. His wings open, and they take to the air. She gasps, holding him tight.

"Trust me?" he asks.

"Yes," she breathlessly replies.

His hand continues touching her desire, and her body shudders as she pants for air. The pleasure continues to build between them. Her head rolls back as she cries out, each sensation overtaking her. She kisses him hard, clutching him, as they lower down to the ottoman.

"Oh, love," she whispers. "That was absolutely incredible!"

He smiles at her. "Another first?"

"Yes, a very good one at that." When his hand teases her hip, she trembles. "Rafe!"

"What?" he asks, feigning innocence before doing it again.

"Jerk!" she cries out, hitting his arm. "It's too much!"

Rafe plants kisses on her face and neck. He lies beside

her, pulling her against his chest. "How do you feel?"

"Oh, Rafe. I feel happy, beautiful, and loved. Thank you."

"You're welcome, your Majesty."

"Guardian?"

"Yes?"

"Kiss me."

He's on her again, his mouth finding hers. "Hmm. I think you need more kisses," he says, smiling. "Your body is absolutely perfect. I love everything about it. All of it."

She smiles at him, kissing him again. "You know it's yours. Everything about me is yours. I belong to you."

"I know. And you know I belong to you." He lifts her hand, kisses it softly, and traces it with his other hand. "When I was sent to find you, never in a million years did I think this was where we would end up." He looks at her. "Do you know what you've done?"

"What do you mean?" she asks, trying to keep her voice steady so as to hide her worry.

"You made me fall in love. I never thought it possible."

"Neither did I."

"Made for each other."

She smiles at him. "Yes, we were." She sits up. "Now, I need another shower." When he chuckles softly, she shoots him a funny look. "No, I am spent. Just cleaning up."

"Yes, mia estrela."

They shower, then sit on the chaise.

"I wish I could've met your father."

Rafe clears his throat. "I do, too."

"I'm sorry. I didn't mean to put you on the spot."

"What do you think you would've said to him, if things had gone to plan and he was here?"

"I was angry and hurt, so I don't really know for sure. I probably would've kept you as my guardian, like I did. Would you have told him the truth? That you love me?"

"I've given it a lot of thought, and I honestly don't know. Probably not, only so he could have deniability. I wouldn't want to see him hurt because of us."

"I can understand."

"Once you passed the treaty though, I wonder what his reaction would've been. He gave up on me finding someone long ago."

"What was he like?" Ana asks as she squeezes his hand.

"Similar to me. He put duty and the kingdom first. He was tired of the war, ready for peace. It's a shame he died in battle. He should've retired his commission long ago."

"Rafe, I'm so sorry."

"It's okay. It's not your fault." Ana pulls her hand away and looks down. "What's wrong?"

"My father was responsible for the death of yours. We should've had peace, instead of his cruelty and greed!"

"Ana, it's in the past."

"I know. Still, I feel bad."

"Don't. I've grieved and moved on. Being with you has brought me a peace and happiness I never knew existed. Believe me, you have given me love and comfort." He lifts her onto his lap, wrapping his arms around her.

"Same for you."

He breathes her in. "You are my whole world."

A single tear runs down her cheek. "You are mine." She kisses him while wrapping her arms around his neck. Her stomach grumbles. Biting her lower lip and clearly embarrassed, she moves away from him.

"Ana, are you hungry?"

"Yes, love."

"Why didn't you say so?"

"How much food do you need to eat?" she quietly asks, wrapping her arms around herself.

"Ana?"

"Sorry. I didn't always get enough to eat. Sometimes my foster father would forget to feed me. I would get hit or yelled at if I asked for food, so I learned to go without. I would eat breakfast and lunch at school. Sometimes I would have lunch at school on Friday and not eat again until breakfast at school on Monday. Once I was a little older, I learned how to sneak food in, so I could eat over the weekend."

"Why didn't you tell me about this?" He pulls her onto his lap, holding her. "Mia estrela, what hell you've suffered!"

"It's okay. It was a long time ago. It doesn't bother me now," she says with a hollow laugh.

"Yes, it does. Otherwise, you would've told me you're hungry."

Unable to stop the tears falling, she trembles in his arms. "Please, don't be mad."

"Mad is the last thing I'm feeling. I am so sorry for everything you went through because of him. You should've grown up here, in this palace, with two loving parents who would give you everything you need."

"I'm here now," she says softly, tracing the veins in his hand. "See? I'm okay."

He gently wipes away her tears. "Ana, no. This is part of your walls. Everything dealing with your foster father, not what he did at night, has to be dealt with."

"I'm sorry!" Burying her face in his neck, she clasps his shirt in her hand.

"For what?"

"I wasn't hiding this. I didn't think about it. You're right, I should've told you."

"You are telling me. This is what we're working on. Shh. Close your eyes, mia estrela. Please?" he asks, looking at her. She does as he asks. "Can you imagine growing up here? Running through the palace, your mother reading to you in the library, having every meal in the dining hall with her and attending school. Can you see that?"

Ana lets out a soft gasp. "That's part of why Kara is so sad. She didn't lose my mother that day, she lost a future with me and my mother, all of us together. Then she lost me on Earth. She grieved for both of us."

"Ana, please. I know how important Kara is, but let's focus on you right now."

"But don't you see? It's tied together. I would've grown up with Kara, like an aunt, as close as she was with my mother. I would've had her and you in my life." She opens her eyes, looking at him as her breath shudders. "I can't... I can't do that. It's too painful to think of the life I should've had. Please, don't be mad at me."

"For what?"

"Because I can't think about this right now."

"I'm not mad. I promise. Feel me, feel my love." He squeezes her hand, sending everything he can to her. "It's okay now. You're here, happy, safe, and loved. I will get us food." He stands, sits her on the chaise, kisses her forehead, then steps out. He returns a moment later. "See? Just that easy now."

"Thank you, love." She looks down. "I'm sorry."

"Ana, please. Stop apologizing. Stop blaming yourself, stop feeling guilty. You were literally only a child trying to survive. Let me take care of you now. Will you let me?"

She swallows hard. "I want to," she softly replies.

"What's stopping you?"

"My overthinking. That you'll get tired of taking care of me and see I'm not worth the effort. I know you love me, that's not the issue."

"Ana, I am telling you, here and now. I am here to stay. I will never leave you, I will never desert you, and I will never stop loving you. Listen to what I am saying, because every word of it is the absolute truth. Do you believe me?"

"Yes," she says, crying. She pulls herself into his arms. "I do believe you."

He holds her hand up, so she can see her ring. "Do you know what that is?"

"My engagement ring?"

"Yes."

"It's a way of letting people know we intend to get married, right?" she asks.

"It's much more than that. It is a symbol, my promise, that I want to marry you and be with you forever. When you start to doubt, when you start to question, look at that ring and know I am always here for you."

"Yes, Rafe. Thank you."

A knock at the door interrupts their kiss. Rafe answers, letting in staff to set up for dinner. He sees them out then leads Ana to the small table.

"Thanks for getting dinner."

"Always."

Drinking her cocoa, a memory hits her. "I only had this once as a child."

"What?"

"The older lady who lived next door made me a cup one time. I didn't have it again until Kara made it for me in college. It's my favorite drink."

"I'm glad we have it here."

"Bela! I'm sure Kara messaged him about Remus, but I still want to announce our engagement to him."

"Do you want to invite him here and do it in person since Remus is dead?"

"After dinner, we'll message him and see. If he's not wanting to leave yet, then we'll tell him via message."

"Good idea. You're still touring the palace with Kara tomorrow, after lunch, right?"

"Yes. Why?"

He smiles at her. "Just curious."

"Hmm. Okay." She finishes her meal. "Could we—" She shakes her head.

"What?"

"Could we take our dishes to the kitchen and see if there's dessert?"

"That's a great idea." He stands up, gathering the plates and cups. "Are you ready now?"

"Yes."

They step into the corridor, where they are greeted by Roesh.

"We're going to the kitchen, then the Communications Lounge."

"Yes, Rafe."

Ana notices there aren't a lot of people milling about, realizing they are probably having dinner themselves. Rafe glances around and occasionally checks on her as they walk.

Once in the kitchen, Rafe hands Yeona the dishes. "By chance, is there dessert?"

Yeona smiles at him and gestures him and Ana to a side table. "Yes." She smiles when they eat some petit cakes.

"Thank you," Ana says.

"You're very welcome, your Majesty." Yeona bows.

Rafe escorts Ana to the Communications Lounge. She messages Bela, asking if he and Joph can visit for the weekend since Remus is dead. She knows it's last minute and understands if he has other obligations. She seals it and sends it through.

"I guess we're going back to our quarters?"

"How are you feeling?" Rafe asks.

"Good."

He takes her hand, steps into the hallway, and looks at Roesh. "Our battlement."

"Yes, Rafe."

When they arrive, Roesh and Aylin remain at the door, as he takes her up the stairs.

"Are we flying?" Ana asks as they step out.

"Yes."

"Where?"

"We can stay around here. I thought you might like to stretch them before bed."

"That sounds nice."

Ana opens her wings as she approaches the center of the battlement. After stretching for a minute, she soars into the air. Rafe joins her, and she kisses him as snow falls around them.

"Are you cold?"

"Not yet. I promise, I'll tell you if I start to feel it."

He takes her hand as they fly over the palace. She looks down at the village, smiling at the view. He pulls her closer before returning with her to the battlement.

"Thank you."

"Always, mia estrela."

"Forever, my love." She takes his hand as they go into the palace.

"To our quarters," Rafe instructs Roesh.

They follow behind, waiting in the hall with Aylin as he inspects inside.

"All clear."

"Aylin, will you go inside with Ana for a moment? I'd like a word with Roesh."

"Yes, Rafe." Aylin gestures her to come inside.

"Roesh, I want to apologize for what happened in the woods. You are correct, she is your pupil."

"I appreciate that. You were right, too, though. I can be a little hard on her sometimes, harder than she deserves. She's a good student."

"You're a good teacher. I see how you are with her, and it reminds me of my days teaching guardians."

"Can I ask? Is it weird, being with the queen? I don't mean, you know, but that we spent our whole lives being told it was forbidden, that we would be put to death."

Rafe laughs. "Yes, it was weird at first. Now, it's as natural as you two."

"I find that hard to believe."

"Really, I swear. Looking at the crowns and thinking of becoming a prince is a little weird though."

"Are you getting married?"

"We're announcing our engagement at the ball. Please, don't tell anyone? Not even Aylin?"

"I give you my word. Congratulations."

"Thank you." Rafe steps inside, seeing Ana and Aylin admiring her Eiffel Tower. "Everything okay in here?"

They turn and look at him. "Yes, Rafe. Your tower is beautiful."

"Thank you, Aylin."

"Your Majesty," she bows to Ana then leaves.

Rafe takes her hand. "What did you girls talk about?"

"She started reading the book she borrowed. She likes it so far. I answered a few questions for her. She says she wishes she had more time to read. Even off duty, Roesh drills and quizzes her. He sounds like he's too hard on her."

Rafe chuckles. "That's actually what we were talking about. He's going to ease up."

"Oh, I'm glad. I understand training and discipline, but you need time to yourself, too."

"Ana, do you need time to yourself?"

"No! You know I don't like being away from you."

"I'm sorry," he says, pulling her in her arms. "I didn't mean it like that. I was making sure you were okay."

"I should know better. I'm sorry for how I reacted."

"That's okay. I'll punish you now."

"No!" she cries out, laughing, as he buries his face in the crook of her neck, then plants kisses all over her face. She turns to him, taking him in her arms. "Oh, Rafe. I love you so much."

"I love you, mia estrela."

There's a knock at the door, and Rafe answers it. He takes the message from the squire, thanking him. He hands it to Ana.

She reads it. "Bela and Joph will be here Saturday afternoon. They are eager to visit."

"Good! We'll plan a nice dinner with them, Kara, and Evren."

"That would be wonderful!"

"You're really excited about telling them, aren't you?"

"Love, I'm excited to tell everyone." She sees a look of guilt on his face. "What?"

"I'm so sorry. I let it slip to Roesh. He swears he won't tell anyone."

"It's okay. The ball is in two days. Even if everyone knows by then, it will be fine. Really."

"Okay."

"What?" she asks.

"Did you tell Aylin?"

"Nope!"

"Ana, I swear."

"I know how to keep a secret."

He runs his fingers over her shoulder blade. "Yes, you do."

His touch elicits a shiver from her. "Seriously?" She laughs. "It wasn't really a secret. Just, I honestly didn't know if it had survived the wings or not. With everything going on, I forgot I even had it."

"Really?"

"Yes. I had it done a few years ago. It's not in a place I would see it every day, so yes. I forgot about it."

"Why there? Why on your shoulder blade?" Her eyes go down. "I'm sorry. You don't have to answer."

"No, it's okay." She prepares herself before answering. "It's the one place I hadn't been hit."

"Ana!" He grips her tighter. "I'm so sorry."

"It's okay, love. It was a long time ago. I'm here with you, happy and loved." She kisses him to reassure him.

"Ana, you told me what he did at night. Now you've told me about food. What about hitting you? How often did that happen? Why?"

"Rafe, it's so close to bedtime."

"No, you're right. I'm sorry. You'll talk about it when you want to."

"Look, he didn't do it that often. I learned quickly what to say or do to avoid it. I've moved past that." She caresses his face. "Love, forget about it. It's in the past."

"Ana, how did you live with all of this? You obviously didn't tell Kara everything, so how?"

"I wrote in my journals, I practiced self-care, and I binge read books or watched shows."

"I never had many friends, given that my life was dedicated to protecting the palace and the throne. Still, being around guardians, sharing our experiences, I had that. I don't understand how you survived being so solitary."

"It was lonely. I found solace in books, in reading about brave knights and magical schools. Books became my escape, my home." She looks at him. "Until I found you. You are my home."

"Ana, you are mine. You are everything to me." He crushes her to his chest, holding her tight. "Now, are you ready to turn in?"

"Yes, Rafe."

"Ana—"

"I swear, any episodes, nightmares, anything, I will wake you. I give you my word on that."

"Please, do."

They go into the closet and change into their pajamas. Ana kisses him.

"Thank you."

"For what?"

"Being you."

He laughs then kisses her forehead. "You're welcome." He picks her up and takes her to the washroom. "Get ready, and we'll turn in."

"Yes, love." She goes inside. Rafe leans against the wall while waiting for her. Once she steps out, he kisses her. "I'll wait," she says, sitting on the chaise.

After finishing getting ready for bed, Rafe leaves the washroom, and carries her to bed. She snuggles into his chest.

"Get some sleep."

"Yes, love."

He looks down as she falls asleep in his arms. "My little warrior, having survived so much. Please, sleep through the night."

Chapter 22

Rafe wakes up at seven in the morning. Ana is beside him, and he smiles at the sight before snuggling with her. She plants gentle kisses on his mouth and face.

"I didn't mean to wake you."

She laughs softly. "You didn't. Can we get breakfast?"

"Of course." He gently lays her down and goes to the door. She pulls the blanket up and waits for him to return. He climbs into bed. "It will be here shortly. Are we getting cleaned up before breakfast?"

"I don't need to. I'd like to get dressed to stay in this morning. We're seeing Kara and Evren at eleven for lunch."

"Okay."

They go into the closet, where Ana is happy to see her hoodie has been washed. She slips on black pants and a shirt, then puts her hoodie on. Rafe walks in.

"Is it a hoodie kind of day?"

"Just this morning. I'd like to be comfortable before putting on a gown to tour the palace."

"I can understand." He slips into black pants and a matching shirt before putting his hoodie on as well.

She laughs. "Thank you."

Breakfast arrives, and Rafe helps with the setup. The staff leave as Ana joins him at the table. "Sit, mia estrela."

"Yes, love." Seeing the NightFall pancakes, she can't help but smile. "My favorite!"

"With cocoa."

"Thank you."

"What do you think Kara is going to show you today?" he asks, wiping away crumbs from his shirt.

"I haven't the slightest idea. It was her suggestion, so I'm sure she has something in mind. What will you and Evren be doing?"

"Oh, I have a few errands to run. She'll help."

"Okay."

"Ana, are you all right?"

"Yes, why?"

"You don't sound very enthusiastic about today."

"I love Kara, and I know I need to spend time with her, but I hate being away from you. I feel better at least, since Remus is dead."

He takes her hand. "Ana, I feel the same way. It's for an hour or two. I'll miss you the whole time."

She smiles at him. "Really?"

"Yes, mia estrela. But you're right. You do need to spend some time with Kara."

"I will."

"Do you want to practice with your wings this morning, since you're spending the afternoon with her?"

"Wow."

"What?"

"I forgot I had them this morning. And again now. They really are becoming a part of me, of something I'm not always self-conscious about. Yes, I would like to practice in a bit."

"Then we will."

"How long was it, for you to adjust to having them, when you got them back?"

"About a week. They were heavy at first and hurt a little. Not like what you went through, but I'd had them over five hundred years and the muscle memory was there. It took me a bit to get used to flying again."

"I can't imagine. Why didn't your scars heal, with your accelerated healing?"

"Earth mutes powers like that. It's why our healing wasn't as strong as it is here. I didn't know that. I thought they would heal, then I would get my wings back when we returned."

"I'm glad you had them. I don't think I would've believed you, otherwise. I thought you were high or crazy."

She smiles at him.

"I can understand. It was a lot to take in. You took it all in stride, I must say. I didn't expect you to be that calm about everything. Can I ask, what convinced you to come? To say yes?"

"When I was thinking about it. Stay on Earth, playing video games and eating pizza, or come here and make a difference."

"And that you have, bringing peace and freedom to the quadrants." He leans down, kissing her.

"It was hard, and there was loss and sacrifices along the way, but everything was worth it. And no, I'm not talking about my wings. I'm talking about losing Declan, losing you when I thought you didn't love me, not my wings."

"I know. It's okay."

She walks to the center of the room, where she extends them out, furling and unfurling them. Rafe sees her flinch. He runs to her.

"What's wrong?"

"They're a little tight this morning."

"Ana, did you sleep okay last night?"

"Yes, love," she says, extending them again. She goes into the air, slowly moving around the room. He stands and watches, amazed at the sight. "What?" she asks when she catches him staring.

"Just watching you, as if you've been doing this for a hundred years."

Lowering back down, she smiles at him. "I have a great teacher." She steps up, planting a soft kiss on his lips. "Thank you."

"Always."

Her smile grows. "Forever."

"Yes, mia estrela. Forever." Pulling her into his arms, they go into the air. He kisses her as she wraps her arms around him.

"I love flying with you. It's wonderful."

"I'm happy to hear that. How do you feel when you're flying?"

"I'm still adjusting. It's so weird to even think about, much less actually do. I've accepted my wings, don't get me wrong. I'm still processing flying."

"That's understandable." He lowers them back down. She smiles at him.

"Give me a moment?" she asks.

When he nods, she steps out and speaks with Aylin for a moment before sitting on the chaise.

Rafe stands beside her. "Everything okay?"

She smiles up at him. "Oh, yes. You'll see." A minute later, there is a knock at the door. Ana takes something from Aylin, thanking her before shutting the door. She turns to Rafe, holding up a book. "Read a little this morning?"

"Yes, mia estrela."

Ana snuggles in beside Rafe, reading until her throat goes dry. While she's drinking water, he continues to read. He places the bookmark in and sees they are nearly halfway through the book.

"Do you like it so far?" she asks.

"Yes. Mr. Darcy is quite the character! She is a brilliant author."

"This has been one of my favorites for as long as I can remember. Then I was excited to read it again for English Lit in college!"

"I don't know that I've read any book more than once."

"I usually don't. This one is worth it, though."

"You really do love it, I can tell."

Ana looks at the clock. "I'd like to get cleaned up and changed for Kara and Evren joining us. Touring the palace, I guess I'll wear something… regal."

"Ana, everything is regal on you," he says, turning her to him and kissing her. "I mean that."

"Thank you."

They go into the closet, and Ana rifles through a few

gowns before she sits on the ottoman.

"What's wrong?"

"I finally feel comfortable, dressing down like this. I'm not relishing the thought of putting on a dress and crown."

"I'm sorry. It's only for a little while, then when you get back, you can put on your hoodie again. We can snuggle in front of the fire."

"You are so sweet, so amazing. You always know what to say. Thank you." She stands up and walks to the gowns. "Hmm. They're all starting to look alike to me."

Rafe helps her look. "You have a lot of blue and pink gowns."

She laughs, "I see that. I need some different colors!" She sighs. "Ones that won't clash with my wings."

"Ana, everything you wear is beautiful with your wings. I'm not just saying that, it's the truth." He takes her hand, going into the smaller closet. "Maybe we'll find something in here."

"I don't need a winter gown, but I do want long sleeves. It is a little chilly still in the palace."

"Okay. Let's see what we can find." She stands back, watching him go through them. "What?" he asks when she laughs.

"You, picking out a gown for me."

Rafe gives her a confused look, then continues. He pulls out a long sleeve black gown, trimmed in silver, with silver stars and moons embroidered along the bodice and hem. "How about this?"

"It's beautiful." She takes it and turning it over. "And it's been mended. Thank you, Evren." She laughs. "Okay. Let's get cleaned up."

She lays it on the ottoman then gather clean undergarments. They go to the washroom. She turns on the water. Helping him undress, he kisses her before he does the same for her. She caresses his neck and chest. He takes her hand, then kisses her hard.

"Rafe," she says as his lips crash down on hers.

"What's wrong?"

"No, nothing's wrong. I'm sorry. Can we get cleaned up?"

"Yes, Ana." He takes her into the shower. "Are you sure you're okay?" he asks while washing her hair.

"I'm saving my energy for whatever Kara has in store."

He laughs. "Who knows with her?"

Ana steps out of the shower and dries off before slipping into her robe. She goes into the closet and dresses, adding a black diamond tiara with black shoes. As she's admiring her reflection, Rafe comes in. He loses his breath at the sight of her.

"That gown is stunning."

"Really?"

"Yes, mia estrela. Especially with your wings."

She goes to the drawer, getting her engagement ring out. Before she can do anything, he takes it from her and gently slips it on, kissing her hand. She kisses him in response.

"Thank you for a wonderful morning."

He smiles, thinking of the surprise he has in store for her. "Hopefully, a wonderful day."

She tilts her head. "What?"

"You'll see."

"What do you and Kara have up your sleeves?"

He laughs. "Oh, no. This is all me. Kara knows nothing about it."

"Okay. I trust you… I guess." She smirks up at him.

"Ana! How dare you?" He leans down, planting gentle kisses all over her face, loving the sound of her laughter. "Now, I have to get ready for lunch. I don't think Kara wants to see me in a towel."

"Hmm. I like the look, myself."

Walking to his dresser, he lets out a chuckle. He changes into black slacks and a matching shirt, then slips his boots on. He wears the ring and cuff she bought him. He goes to her and wraps his arm over her shoulder.

"Well?"

"We look good together."

"Open your wings again?" They look in the mirror as they each expand their wings. "Made for each other."

Turning, she retracts hers in and takes him in her arms. "Yes." She sighs when she hears knocking. "I think lunch is here."

Rafe goes to the door to let Kara and Evren in. Lunch service is behind them. Kara runs to Ana.

"Oh, this gown is so pretty on you!"

"Thanks, Kara. Evren, thank you for everything you've done in my closet. That was a lot of gowns to mend, so I appreciate your hard work."

"Ana, you're very welcome. Please let me know if you come across one that hasn't been mended or if you need help with anything."

"Thank you," she softly says. "You and Kara are such wonderful friends."

"Ana, are you okay?" Kara asks.

"I am."

After studying her for a moment, Kara decides to let it go. "Are we ready to eat?"

"Yes," Ana says.

"Ana, you and Evren go ahead. I'd like a moment with Kara. We'll be there shortly."

"Yes, love. Evren, look. We have cocoa."

"I'm coming, Ana."

Kara looks at Rafe as they step away. "What's wrong?"

"Nothing. Just, did you know about her food issues?"

She gives him a confused look. "What do you mean?"

"She told me last night there were times her foster father wouldn't feed her, or she wouldn't get enough to eat."

"I wondered why she would take such small bites sometimes. Then she would save a cookie or crackers, wrapped in a napkin. I would find them in her room." She brings her hand to her face. "God, I'm glad he's dead."

Rafe cocks his head at her. "So, you know what she

did?"

"What?" she asks, shock in her voice. "She said he died of a heart attack."

He sucks in his breath. "Oh. I mean, technically—"

"Rafe, tell me."

He shakes his head. "You can talk to her about it, but I'm not saying anything. You were right, though. She does still have a lot of issues from growing up with him. We're working through them, but I know you're her best friend, and she needs you, too."

"Thank you, for trusting me with this and letting me help her. I appreciate you thinking about me."

"Um, are you guys joining us?" Ana asks.

Rafe smiles before facing her. "Yes, Ana. We'll be right over." He turns back to Kara. "Let's eat."

"Thank you," she says as they head to the table. He nods at her. They sit and join Evren and Ana.

"Everything okay?" Ana asks.

Rafe takes her hand, kissing it. "Everything is fine. Are you excited to tour the palace with Kara today?"

"I am. Where are we going?"

Kara laughs. "You'll see. I promise, it's stuff you've wanted to see."

"Okay."

They eat their meal then Rafe walks Ana to the chaise. "I'll miss you." She turns to Kara when she lets out a small cough. "What?"

"No, I'm sorry. We won't be gone long, I promise. Just a few hours. Is that okay?"

"Yes, Kara."

Rafe hugs her. "Ana, you'll be safe with Kara, and it's only a little while. I'll miss you, too." He kisses her. Reluctantly, she goes to Kara.

"I'm sorry, Ana. I really am. I wasn't thinking."

"Kara, it's okay. We need this time together. I'll be okay. Honestly, a little time apart might be a good thing."

"What do you mean? Is something the matter?"

"No, it's just, I had an episode last night. He gets so upset, seeing me like that. I promised him I wouldn't hide, but after his reaction, I don't want him to see that anymore."

"What happened?"

"Can we tour the palace, please? We'll talk once we're alone in a study or room. I know Roesh and Aylin are behind us."

"Yes, Ana. Come." They go through a corridor she doesn't recognize. Kara turns to her. "We're going into to a classroom with kids. Are you okay?"

Ana takes a deep breath. "Yes."

Kara knocks, and the teacher opens the door. "Sage, your Majesty." She bows. "I am Professor Kinney. Please, welcome," she says as she gestures them inside.

The class is made up of thirty students, about eight to ten years old. She stands in front with Kara and the Professor.

"Students, this is our queen."

Audressa's daughter stands up, bowing. "Hello again, your Majesty."

"Hello, little Kara. How are you?"

She giggles. "I'm okay." She quickly sits back down.

The professor steps forward. "Does anyone have a question for our queen?" Nearly every hand is up. "Hmm. Not about her wings?" The hands go back down.

Ana turns to the professor. "It's okay. They can ask."

"Majesty?" She sees Ana nod. "Okay, class." She calls on a young boy. "Mikael? What's your question?"

He stands up, bowing. "Majesty. Can we see your wings?"

Ana can't help but notice each child staring at her, eyes wide and expressions of curiosity on their faces. She smiles. "Yes." She turns around, extending them then retracting them. "Any other questions?" She points to a young girl.

"Majesty." She bows. "Thank you for ending the war and bringing my mother home."

"You are most welcome. What is your name, little

one?"

"Rosie."

"That's a very pretty name."

"Thank you, Majesty." She bows again and sits.

Ana turns to the professor. "We don't want to take up any more of your time."

The professor bows. "Thank you, Majesty, for your visit today."

Ana winks at little Kara. She giggles and covers her face. Ana notices big Kara rolls her eyes. She takes her hand as they leave the classroom. Kara looks at her, once they are in the hall.

"Was that too much?"

"No, it was fine. Where to next?"

They continue further into the palace, to corridors and arches Ana hasn't seen. Ana is in awe of everything she sees.

"Here," Kara says, gesturing into a study.

After Roesh inspects it, they step inside. Roesh and Aylin stand guard in the corridor.

"Now, we can talk. I also wanted to show you something." Kara leads her to the back, where there's a small fireplace, bookshelves, and a painting of Rosalina. "This was when she first came here. Your father had this commissioned for her."

Her mother is dressed in a beautiful lavender gown, silver crown, and smiling. "She's happy in this one."

"She was, at first."

"Kara, I know this is hard for you. Thank you."

"She was your mother. I don't have the right to keep her from you." She takes her arm, sitting her at the table. "Can we talk a minute?"

"Of course. What's wrong?" Ana asks.

"Nothing, with me. What happened last night?"

"What do you mean?"

"With food."

Her eyes go down. "Oh. Rafe told you?"

"Yes. Please, look at me. You have nothing to be

ashamed or embarrassed about. I want to make sure you're okay. How come you never told me any of that?"

Ana meets her gaze. "I was past it by then. You always kept plenty of food and snacks around the house."

"Ana, you aren't past it. Not if something happened last night. Rafe didn't tell me, that he thought you and I should talk."

"He heard my stomach and was confused why I didn't tell him I was hungry. I would get hit by my foster father if I did. I know Rafe loves me and would never hurt me, it was hard for me to say anything."

"Because you aren't past it."

"Kara—"

"Ana, please. It's us. I want to help you."

"I know you do. I thought we were having a fun day today, is all."

"Let's talk a bit, open up. Then we'll continue our tour. Please?"

"Okay. What do you want to know?"

"How are you? I know you and Rafe are happy, but how are you doing?"

"I'm okay. I still get a little overwhelmed sometimes, but I keep it together. I've gotten better with my wings, and you and Evren have done so much to help with my duties."

"What else?"

"Kara, I'm sorry. What do you want?"

"I know you and Rafe have been working to overcome everything you went through on Earth. How are you doing with all of that?"

"It's coming. I want to get married in August, so I have to be ready by then."

"Ana—"

"What, Kara? I'm dealing with things, not pushing them down. I cry, I have nightmares. What do you want?" she asks, tears falling.

Regret floods Kara, and she hugs her. "I'm so sorry. I thought we could sit and talk, that I could help you deal with things. I see now, I'm only making it worse. We'll continue our tour."

"You are helping," she says, squeezing her. "I do have things I should talk to you about, things that I'm embarrassed or scared to say in front of Rafe."

"Like what?" she asks, pulling back. "If you want to talk."

"Well, I don't know how knowledgeable you'll be."

"You're worried about your wedding night."

"Is it that obvious?"

"Ana, it's okay. I'm nervous, too."

"What? Why?"

"Because it's a special night. You want everything to be perfect."

"Yes! I've never… well, you know. And I'm scared it won't be good or he won't like what I do. Or that I'll have an episode." Her eyes remain fixed on the floor. "I don't know what to do, how to prevent that."

"Ana, keep doing what you're doing. Keep bringing down your walls. I know I'm clearly not the expert on men, but Rafe seems to love everything you do, and he loves you. Talk to him about your concerns. What about him? If it's not too personal, what kind of experience does he have?"

"Um, same as me. None, really. His life has been protecting the palace and royals, fighting in war. We're learning a lot together." She blushes.

"Ana, please, don't be embarrassed! It's okay. Well, that's good then. As you said, you can learn together. As it gets closer to your wedding day, I'll check in with you, see how the walls are doing. Is that okay?"

"Yes, Kara. I would really appreciate that. Thank you." She hugs her. "Now, can we see more of the palace?"

"Of course!" Kara helps her to her feet. They step into the corridor. "We are going to the King's Chambers," Kara informs Roesh.

"Yes, Sage. Follow me."

Ana looks at Kara, confused, but says nothing. She

follows them. Kara opens the door. "Are you okay to come in here?"

"Yes," Ana responds. "Should I ask you that?"

Kara laughs. "It's fine. Come on."

They step inside. "Why are we in here?" Ana asks.

"We both have demons to face. I needed to come in here, myself. I thought we would do it together."

"Will you tell me about him?"

"I will. Anything you want to know. As I've said, it's not my place to keep your family history from you, good or bad."

"No, I really don't want to know about him." Looking around the room, a memory hits her. "This is where they took me from."

"What? What are you talking about?"

"I came in here, and Roban and Regan found me. Then they took me to MoonFrost."

"I never would've brought you in here had I known that."

"It's okay. I wanted to see it again." She walks to the nightstand and opens the drawer, removing her father's journals.

"Are you going to read those?"

"No. They're going into the fire, once we're back at my quarters."

"If that's what you want to do."

"It is. I want to have my legacy, and I want to continue my mother's legacy, caring for the kingdom and its people. I want all traces of my father removed, except their portrait in the library."

"You don't have to decide anything right now."

"I've been thinking about this. It's not a rash decision."

"Okay."

"I do have one question about him."

"What's that?"

"Did he really hate me?" she asks, her voice hitching.

"Ana, no." Kara pulls her into a tight embrace. "He

was angry and grieving. Do you remember when Rafe disappeared, some of the things you said when you became angry?" Ana can only nod. "He never hated you. Your father was so excited about you. It was the heat of the moment, the loss and heartache."

"Will you tell me about it, the day I was born? If it's still too painful, or you don't want to—"

"It's okay. Here, let's sit." They go to the sofa, and Kara takes her hand. "Everything with your birth went so smoothly. Your mother held you in her arms, kissing your head. She told you how much she loved you, then she was trembling. I grabbed you away as she died on the bed. Your father was there. He started yelling for the guards. He was going to have me executed, blaming me for your mother's death."

"Kara, you don't have to continue."

"I mean it. I'm okay. It's your birth, your family. I still had you in my arms. I used my magic and disappeared. I packed a few things, then got us to the portal. I didn't go straight to Earth. I had to go to a few realms, to lose our trail.

"It's why I was knocked unconscious. You really shouldn't travel that much in such a brief time. I had planned to raise you as my own. I never meant for us to get separated."

"We're here now. Like I tell Rafe, when he apologizes for our first day here, we survived, and we're here. That's what matters."

"Like your mother, with love and patience. You remind me so much of her. Your beauty, your kindness, your grace. She would be proud of you."

"Thank you, Kara. That means a lot to me."

She smiles at Ana. "Now, one more room I want to show you, then we'll get you back to Rafe."

Ana follows Kara into the hallway. Roesh steps forward.

"We're going to the observatory."

"Yes, Sage." He turns and leads the way. They continue further into the palace.

"How far are we from the main hall and our quarters?"

Kara laughs. "Quite a ways. And there's still so much more to see. I figure you and Rafe can tour some, too."

"Thank you."

Roesh opens a door as Kara and Ana go up the steps. They walk into a room with a giant telescope. The walls are dark blue with gold suns and silver moons, and constellations paint the ceiling.

"Really?"

"Yes."

Ana can't hide her excitement. "This is incredible!"

Kara laughs. She shows Ana how to use the telescope, guiding it towards the next planet. "Can you see that?"

She gasps. "I can! What is that?"

"That's MoonSol, where your mother was from."

"Really? I know Rafe said I'm not supposed to go off-world, but do you think there's a chance, maybe someday, I could go there?"

"If you have an heir to take the throne, you could," Kara says. Ana's smile fades. "What's wrong?"

She sees Roesh and Aylin are out of earshot. "I don't want children. I know we'll have to, in order to continue the royal bloodline."

"You don't have to do anything. Who knows? You feel that way now, maybe twenty or thirty years down the road, you'll want children? That's the wonderful thing about being immortal, no rush."

"Yes, you're right."

"Ready to head back?"

"Yes, please."

Kara smiles. "I can see how much you miss him. Let's go. Back to quarters, please," Kara says to Roesh.

"Yes, Sage."

"Roesh, call me Kara."

"Um, yes, Kara."

Arriving at her quarters, Ana sees a guardian she doesn't recognize standing guard.

"Kara, who is that?" she quietly asks.

"I don't know."

"Majesty, if I may," Aylin says. "That is Mira."

"Thank you, Aylin."

They approach their quarters. Mira bows. "Majesty. Rafe is still working inside. Please, give me a moment."

"Yes, Mira," Ana says, looking at Kara, who is as confused as she is.

Mira steps in and comes out a moment later. "He says the queen may enter." She opens the door.

Ana and Kara step in, seeing the room has been rearranged. Where the bed was, the desk now is. The bed has been moved to the back wall, with a privacy divider set up. A small sofa with end tables is in front of the window. The art she had bought from the market is hanging around the room. She walks to their small table, seeing a shield and their two swords hanging above the fireplace. She turns to Rafe.

"This is what you did today?"

"Yes! Do you like it?"

"No."

"What's wrong with—"

She smiles at him. "I love it. It's perfect!"

He kisses her face and neck. "Don't do that to me!" He takes her hand. "Follow me." They go to the door. He closes it then checks to be sure Kara is watching as he pulls the latch across. "So now we can have some privacy, as well."

Kara blushes before bursting into laughter. "Yes, Rafe. My apologies."

"This is incredible," Ana says as she continues to take everything in. "I feel like this is my own room now, our own room. Thank you."

"Evren and I wanted everything to be perfect, but if there's anything you want to move or change—"

"Oh, no. Truly. I love it exactly how it is."

Kara walks around, admiring the dividers and artwork. "Rafe, you did a good job."

"Thank you, Kara."

Evren steps out of the closet. "You're back!" She runs to Kara and kisses her. "Sorry, Ana."

"Evren, please. Quite all right. Now, what were you doing to my closet?"

Rafe grips her hand. "Come on."

He takes her inside. Her ottoman is covered with a beautiful blanket and more pillows have been added. Her gowns have been organized by type: day, evening, formal, and so on. The crowns are on one shelf, with tiaras on the next.

"Oh, this is wonderful! It will make getting ready so much easier." She looks at Rafe and Evren. "Thank you both."

Evren steps in. "Any questions or changes, please don't hesitate."

"I won't."

Kara smiles at Ana. "What say we have private dinners tonight? We'll see you at eight in the morning for breakfast."

"Thank you, Kara. For everything today. I had a lot of fun."

"I did, too."

Ana watches them leave, then faces Rafe. "Well, you did amazing for such short notice."

"I had been wanting to make some changes, but I wanted to talk to you about it first. Then, hearing what you said about it being so open and not feeling like you have privacy, I knew I could do this. If you walked in and hated it, it would have been nothing to put it back."

"Oh, Rafe. You know I wouldn't hate anything you did here. It's our quarters, our space. I want you to be comfortable, to feel like it's home, too."

"I already do. Just being with you."

She looks at him, her heart pounding, as he brings his head down. His lips are softly on hers, gently kissing. She grabs the back of his neck, kissing him harder.

"Rafe—"

"Yes, mia estrela?" he asks, smiling at her.

"Washroom. Now."

He laughs and picks her up, before carrying her to the door and closing the latch. They go into the washroom, where he strips her down.

"You are so alluring, so sexy."

"Rafe!"

"What? You know it's true."

"Hmm. You are gorgeous."

He turns on the water, then undresses. Caressing her neck, he leans in and asks with a husky voice, "What do you want, mia estrela?"

Ana surprises him when she grabs him and pulls him in for a passionate kiss. She jumps into his arms.

"I missed you," she says, gasping in air. "I need you now."

He swallows hard, trying to contain himself, as he takes her into the shower. "Yes, Ana. Whatever you need."

Their lips meet as her hand is on him. He strokes her needs. They send their pleasure into each other as each wave grows stronger and stronger.

"Ana!" he cries out, collapsing against the wall, as they finish together. He holds her tight, trying to calm his pounding heart.

"How was that, love?" she asks with a teasing smile.

"I need a moment."

"Me, too."

He laughs before putting her on her feet. He gently presses her against the wall as his hands explore. "Hmm."

"Rafe!" she cries out. "Please."

"Are you spent?"

"You know I am, you can feel that. Oh, love. Please, I can't," she says as she trembles from his touches. She cries out again.

He leans down, kissing her. "Yes, Ana. Recover, then we'll clean up." She holds him for support. He envelops her in his arms. "I've got you. I will always have you."

"Forever," she whispers, trying to catch her breath.

"Yes, mia estrela. Forever."

Once she's caught her breath, she rinses off then dries. She goes into the closet. While she wants to be comfortable, she decides instead to look nice for dinner.

She pulls out a silver gown with a tight bodice and ballroom skirt. The bodice has silver stars, with gold suns along the hem of the skirt. She slips the gown on, goes to the shelf, and decides on a crown with thin diamond edging and stars on the top. She slips it on.

After she finishes dressing, she steps into the main chamber the same time Rafe emerges from the washroom. He stops and admires her.

"My God, you are beautiful! Are we eating in the dining hall?" he asks as he approaches her.

"No, this is for us tonight."

"I'll be right out."

Rafe goes into the closet and dresses in charcoal pants with a silver shirt and a black tunic jacket. He slips into his shoes and looks up when Ana comes in.

"I forgot to look." She walks to the full-length mirror, expanding her wings. Her breath sucks in at the sight. "Oh, my," she says softly.

Rafe is instantly behind her. "What's wrong?"

She shakes her head. "No, I feel beautiful in this gown."

"Ana, you are beautiful! How many times do I have to tell you before you believe it? Oh, mia estrela, you are more heavenly than the stars, more beautiful than the galaxies, and more radiant than every sun." He gently spins her around, concerned as he wipes her tears.

"Happy tears," she whispers.

He gingerly raises her face, bringing his mouth down to hers. "You are the most beautiful, amazing woman I have ever met."

She falls into his arms, holding him tight. "How do you do that? How do you break me down with your words? You make me feel loved, beautiful, and whole, by the things you say. Do you know how incredible you are?"

He kisses her forehead. "Ana, you made me into the man I am. You gave me everything, simply by being you. I will spend every day of our life, telling you how beautiful you are."

"Rafe, kiss me."

He watches her lips part for him. He teases first, softly tracing his lips along hers. When her tongue is on his mouth, he cannot hold himself in any longer. He holds her tight, kissing her with everything he has. She pulls back to catch her breath.

"Ana, you know you are my everything, right? You know you are my reason for being, my purpose, my destiny?"

"Yes, Rafe. I truly do. As long as you know, you are mine, too." She kisses him. "You are the sun, making me warm, bringing me comfort, and bringing light to fill my darkness."

"Ana, you are the moon. You are exuberant, only to be seen by those loyal enough to wait. You wane and phase, as you change and grow in your beauty and kindness. You eclipse me with your love, your heart, your very being." His mouth is on hers again as she desperately clings to him. "Now, we need dinner."

She smiles at him. "Yes, love, I am hungry. Will you see to it, please?"

"Anything for you."

He steps out. She sits on the ottoman while trying to calm her pounding heart. Her hand trails over the blanket, admiring the deep blue color and how soft it is.

"Ana, are you all right?"

"Yes. My heart is still pounding in my ears," she admits, a small laugh escaping. "The way you make me feel is incredible."

He takes her hands. "Because you are incredible."

Rafe helps her to her feet and escorts her from the closet. She looks around, still trying to adjust to her quarters.

"It's so different, but in a good way!" She walks to the bed and sits on the edge. "To finally have privacy when meals are brought in, or if I don't feel well. Thank you for this." A small bell rings. "What is that?"

"So we know if someone is here. You can't really hear knocking back here. Evren suggested it."

Ana laughs. "It's brilliant!"

Rafe lets dinner service in. After they leave, he escorts her to their table. She glances at the sofa in front of the window.

"So, we can watch the rain?" she asks.

"Yes, or the snow, or look out and admire our kingdom." He sees her smile grow. "What?"

"You called it *our* kingdom. I like that."

"August first? It's on a Saturday if that's when you want to get married."

"Yes, Rafe, more than anything."

"Then we have the date. Now, where all did you and Kara go?"

"We went to one of the classrooms to meet some of the children. She took me to a study and showed me another portrait of my mother. Then we went to the observatory, where she showed me MoonSol in the telescope."

"Sounds like you had a good day."

"It was. We talked and toured the palace. We needed it. I had no idea she was so nervous about her upcoming wedding."

"Really? She doesn't show it."

"That's the thing with Kara, she doesn't really show how she's feeling. She's kind of hard to read sometimes."

"Are you excited about the ball tomorrow night?" Rafe asks, growing concerned when her eyes go down. "What?"

"I am very excited, but nervous too."

"Ana, why?"

"You were kidnapped and tortured the night of the masquerade, then I was taken after the Snowflake Ball."

"Oh, mia estrela. We are both safe now. I promise you, nothing like that is going to happen. Remus is dead, his men scattered. We have guards everywhere." He takes her hand. "You are safe."

"I know, but I'm still worried. I'm sorry, it's how I am."

"You have every right, after what you endured. Please, believe me, when I tell you that you are safe, and I ensure you nothing will happen to you."

"I believe you, I do. Don't take it personally that I'm still worried, that I'm afraid."

"I won't. Talk to me, let me help."

"Yes, love. Thank you." She continues eating.

"Would you like to take the dishes back and tour a little bit, after dinner? Are you up for that?"

"Yes. Are you excited to see Bela and Joph Saturday?"

"I am. I am grateful we are able to host them here."

They gather their dishes, greeted by Roesh and Aylin as they step into the hallway. "Roesh, we are going to the kitchen."

"Yes, Majesty."

"Majesty, that gown is fantastic."

"Thank you, Aylin. Do you have your gown for tomorrow night?"

"Mi'lady, we are your escorts. We will be in uniform."

"My apologies, Aylin. I did not realize."

"It's all right."

Ana looks at Rafe, wishing Aylin and Roesh could be dressed for the ball. He squeezes her hand, smiling at her, and scans ahead as they walk.

They go into the kitchen, where Yeona has a basket made up. "I had a feeling you would be coming here. These are various desserts and pastries for you.”

"Oh, thank you!” Ana exclaims. Yeona nearly drops the basket when Ana hugs her. “We appreciate this.”

"Yes, your Majesty.”

Ana takes the basket, beaming at Rafe. “Hmm. I guess we’ll return to our quarters then,” he says.

"Yes, love,” she responds while eating a petit cake.

"Ana, can you wait until we’re back?”

"I’m sorry.”

He thinks of the night before and takes a mini pie from the basket to eat. “I’m teasing. Help yourself.”

"We’ll head back. Thank you. Everything is delicious!” They bow to Ana as she leaves with him.

They return to their quarters. Roesh inspects inside. Ana turns to Aylin. “I wish you could dress up for tomorrow.”

"Majesty, don’t worry about it. We’ll be off for three days after, and he says he has something special planned for us.”

"Oh, that’ll be nice!”

"Thank you.”

Ana holds up the basket. “Would you like anything before we go in?”

Aylin smiles, taking two petit cakes, one for her and one for Roesh. “Thank you, Majesty.”

Rafe smiles, taking Ana’s hand and leading her inside. “You are so kind, so sweet, to every person around you.”

"I told you, everyone should feel important, thought of, cared for. I wish I could make everyone feel that way!”

"You try,” he says, leading her to the closet. He takes the basket and sets it on the table. “Let’s get changed into something more comfortable, then we’ll have treats.”

"Okay.”

Ana slips the gown off and lays it on the ottoman. While removing her corset, Rafe gets her out pajamas. They change and leave the closet. He stops at the table but watches as she continues toward the center of the room, opening and closing her wings.

"How are they?"

"A little tight still."

"Did you have a bad night?"

"Why do you ask?"

"I think you did. Because of it, you kept them tucked in, and that's why they're hurting."

"No, love. I told you earlier, I didn't. You said it yourself, the more I use them, I would have moments where my muscles would be sore."

He doesn't believe her but doesn't want to push. "Okay."

Ana hears it in his voice. "I'm fine."

He approaches her and massages around her wings. "They are tight!"

"I told you, I'm fine." She retracts them and walks to the washroom. "I'll be right out."

The door shuts behind her, and she sits on the edge of the tub, where she buries her face in her hands. Rafe enters.

"What are you—"

"Ana, please. What's wrong?"

"I needed a moment. Nothing is wrong." She smiles as she takes his hand. "See?"

He concentrates on breaking down her wall. She tries to pull her hand away, but his grip is too tight. "Ana, what is this?"

"Please, love. Let me go!"

He releases her hand. "Fine."

The door slams behind him. Ana hangs her head, then starts the water. After getting undressed, she steps in and cries. She gasps in surprise when Rafe envelops her in his arms.

"I'm so worried about you. Why won't you open up to me? What happened?"

"I saw how upset you got last night, talking about my foster father. I didn't want to do that again so I decided to keep it in and deal with it myself."

"It's my fault?"

"That's not what I mean, please."

"We're supposed to be a team."

"Rafe, you were so angry and upset when I told you what he did. You didn't mean to, but it hurt."

"I'm sorry. Why didn't you tell me this? How can I help if you pull away and hide?"

"I didn't want you to feel that way again. I could see and feel how much it upset you, how much it angered you. I thought I was helping you." She turns to him, clinging to his chest. "Please, don't be mad."

"Oh, mia estrela. What am I going to do with you?"

She smiles at him. "Please, don't punish me with tiny kisses. Anything but that!"

Laughter fills the shower as he attacks her face and neck, before he turns serious. "Ana, let me in. Work with me, no matter what."

"I will. I know my promises don't mean much since I keep breaking them. Please, believe me, that I am working on it."

"You are overcoming so much. I can't even imagine how hard it is. Yes, it hurts me when you turn inward, but I know what you are dealing with." He caresses her face, brushing wet hair away. "Just please try. That's all I can ask."

"I will. I really will." She steps up and kisses him. "Can we get out now?"

"You sure?"

She smiles at him, kissing him again. "Please. I'm tired."

"Yes, mia estrela."

He turns off the water as she steps out. She dries off and slips back into her pajamas. Remembering their snacks, she goes to the table and sits. Rafe joins her.

"You really like your desserts."

"They're so good! Yeona is amazing in the kitchen."

"So are you. Are you ready to cook again?"

"I would, but no."

"What do you mean?"

"Kara doesn't like to cook."

"You could teach me."

"Really?" she asks, sitting up.

"Yes."

"I would love that! We'll plan to, one day next week. Anything particular you want to learn? Or shall I surprise you?"

"I'll let you pick."

"Sounds good. I'm going to use the washroom, then we'll turn in."

"Ana, you need to stretch your wings. I could feel how tight they are."

"Okay."

Ana returns to the middle and expands her wings. Rafe approaches her as she furls and unfurls them. He takes her hand and pulls her into the air. They circle a lap, then lower down.

"Better?"

"Yes. Maybe tomorrow we can have proper training in our battlement? I know we have the ball tomorrow night, but if we trained after breakfast, we'd have all afternoon to recuperate."

"That sounds good."

Ana uses the washroom, then waits for Rafe on the chaise. He picks her up and carries her to bed, lying beside her and stroking her hair.

"Do you like the bed here?"

"Yes. I really like the privacy dividers you put up. I don't feel as exposed. And I love how you did our swords! It looks great."

"I hoped you would like that. I pray that's where they will remain."

"To have peace and keep the peace, is my greatest hope for the kingdom."

He holds her against his chest. "So far, you have." He studies her face.

"What?"

"Looking at how gorgeous you are."

She blushes. "Rafe!"

"What? It's the truth. You are so beautiful, so caring, so compassionate."

"Thank you, love. I never felt beautiful until I met you. I saw you, and I was too afraid to speak to you. I thought you were way too good looking for me."

Rafe laughs. "Really?"

"I did! Sitting there, in your black leather jacket, drinking a cappuccino. I couldn't stop staring."

"You remember that?"

"I will never forget the first time I saw you." Her fingertips trail over his cheek. "I never imagined I'd be here now."

"Always?"

She smiles. "Forever."

He moves forward, kissing her. "I love you, Ana."

"I love you, too, Rafe."

"Now get some sleep."

"Rafe, are you awake?"

He laughs. "No. What time is it?"

"A little after three. I'm sorry."

He sits up and turns on the lamp. "Nightmare?"

"Yes."

"Come here." He lifts her onto his lap, wrapping his arm around her waist. "Will you tell me about it?"

"I was back in my childhood home. I was in bed, and I—" Her breath hitches in her throat.

"Shh. You're safe now. Feel my love and comfort. He's never going to lay another hand on you again."

She trembles against him. "I'm calming down. It's taking me a minute." As his warmth pushes through, her trembling stops. "Thank you." She looks at him. "I should never have hidden from you. I'm sorry."

"Just let me in now. Thank you for waking me and letting me help you."

"I told you I will try, and I meant it. Can we get more sleep?"

"Do you think you can?"

"Yes."

He snuggles with her and smiles when she clutches his shirt. "I'm right here. I'm not going anywhere." He holds her tight, sending his comfort and assurances into her. He watches her fall back to sleep. "Get some rest, my little warrior."

Chapter 23

Rafe knocks on Evren's door. Kara opens it, still half asleep.

"What?" she mumbles.

He laughs. "Morning, beautiful. Are you joining us for breakfast?"

"Yes, we'll be over."

He catches a staff member and requests breakfast. He goes inside and walks to the bed. Ana watches as he sits on the edge.

"Kara and Evren will be over shortly, along with breakfast."

"Thank you."

She goes into the closet and changes into a rose-pink dress. It has long lacy sleeves, a tight bodice, and a floor length skirt. Lace roses cover the gown. She slips on silver shoes and a silver circlet. Rafe steps in, getting dressed in charcoal pants and a red shirt.

"You look so perfect in that gown," he beams.

"Thank you, love. Pink is okay with my wings?" She opens them up.

"Yes. I mean it."

"Thanks."

She goes to the drawer, getting out her ring. He takes it and slips it onto her hand. The bell rings as she steps out. She lets everyone in. Kara helps set up while Evren is admiring her gown.

"Ana, that is a great color on you!"

"Thank you. Evren, could we go into the village one day next week?"

Evren looks at Rafe, who nods. "Yes, Ana. What for?"

"I would like to have a few gowns made up."

"For what?" Kara asks. Ana shoots her a sharp look.

"I'm sorry. I just, you and fashion." She laughs. "I was surprised, is all."

"It's all right, Kara."

They sit to eat. Kara takes a sip of her drink. "It looks like we've dispersed the last remaining camps. Any talks of Remus, or his ideology, and we will take swift action. His men know now that their hatred will not be tolerated. Especially by their leaders."

"Thank you, Kara," Rafe says. "Truly."

"Yes," Ana agrees. "We will have training this morning, if you'll hold the briefing. I don't want to do it too close to the ball tonight."

"I understand. Then are we having dinner in here?"

"At six, please. Nine is a little too late for me."

Kara laughs. "You always were the early one. Are you sure you'll be awake at nine?"

"Kara," Ana exclaims while trying to stifle her laugh. "Yes, I will. We'll train and get rested before the ball. I don't know that we'll stay until one, but we will stay as long as we can."

"Evren and I will help you get ready."

"Thank you." She hugs Kara. "We'll have a day next week, you and me?"

"Yes, Ana." Kara pulls away then takes Evren's hand. "We'll see you at six. Then I can't wait to see you in your gown!" They turn and leave.

Ana glances at Rafe, biting her lower lip. "I know we talked about flying this morning, but could we do something else, first?"

He walks to her with confusion written across his face. "What did you have in mind?"

She takes his hand, and they go toward the middle of the room. Placing his hand on her waist while holding the other, she nervously glances at him. "Dance lessons?"

He smiles. "Of course!" He studies her for a moment. "Is that why you put this gown on?"

"Yes. Do we have to lead the first dance?"

"Hmm. Kara didn't say anything about that. We'll find out when they come to help you get ready. Will you be okay if we do?"

"Yes. I'm nervous, but I'll be fine."

He leads her around the room, dancing and singing. She smiles at him and rests her head on his chest. "Ana, you are a natural at this. Why are you worried?"

"Because I'm me." She laughs. "It's how I am. I think of a million different ways it can go wrong."

"Like what?"

"Really?"

"Yes."

"I could trip, my wings pop open, I could end up in the air."

"Ana, none of that will happen. Think of the last ball. Your wings popped open, you quickly retracted them, and no one noticed. Try thinking of what will be good about tonight. Announcing our engagement, meeting your sworn protectors, dancing with me. Can you do that?"

"I'll try," she softly replies.

"Ana, what else are you worried about?"

She keeps her eyes closed as she pushes her fears down. "Nothing. I'm excited about going tonight."

"Ana, please tell me?"

She swallows hard before meeting his gaze and kissing him. "Really. I'm excited to meet more guardians."

He decides not to push. "Okay. Are you ready for flying?"

"Yes!" She smiles at him. "Um, no. I'd like to change first." She goes into the closet and dresses in black pants with a pale blue shirt and black boots. She steps out. "How's this?"

Rafe's brow furrows. "Are we not training outside?"

"Training center. Look," she gestures to the window. He sees it's snowing again. "Probably too cold," she says.

"Good catch. I was so excited, I didn't even notice."

"I am, too." She takes his hand. They go to the

corridor. "Roesh, please escort us to the training center."

"Yes, Majesty."

They stand guard outside as Rafe and Ana step in. "At least this has a much higher ceiling than our quarters."

"Yes. I'm sorry we're stuck inside today."

"It's okay. It's getting exercise and stretching them that matters." She smiles at him. "Come spring, you might have to drag me back into the palace," she says, stretching her wings.

He laughs. "I'm sure we'll both enjoy being outside." He sees the joy on her face. "What?"

"Thinking of spring. I can't wait to see it!"

She extends her wings and soars to the ceiling. He flies up to her.

"Are you okay?"

"I am." They fly a few laps before landing. She furls and unfurls her wings.

"How do they feel today?"

"Okay. A little tight still, but I know that's why we're working them. I'm still ashamed—"

"Ana!"

"No. I'm still ashamed that I hid them away at first. I should've been working with them from the beginning, instead. I thought if I didn't deal with them, they wouldn't be real. It's stupid, I know, but I was still so scared from what had happened."

"You worried me."

She smiles at him. "I'm not ashamed of them. I love them. See?" She smiles as she takes off again. He chases after her, laughing as she evades him. She flies to him, letting him take her in his arms, as they slowly lower down. "Thank you. I needed this."

"Are we ready to head back?"

"Yes, please. I don't want to overdo it, not with the ball tonight."

"Good idea."

He takes her hand, stepping into the hallway. Roesh

and Aylin come to attention. "Our quarters, Roesh."

"Yes, Rafe."

They follow behind. "Mia estrela, you are quite happy!"

She laughs. "I enjoyed that. My wings needed it." She sees Aylin glance back at her. "Aylin, do you need something?"

"I'm sorry, mi'lady. I was going to ask, but I don't want to be rude."

"Aylin, please."

She looks at her. "Did you really get your wings like the prophecy said?"

"Aylin," Roesh snaps. "Really?"

"I… I'm sorry!"

"No, Aylin. It's okay. Roesh, please. You don't need to be so hard on her."

"Apologies, your Majesty," Roesh says.

"To answer your question, Aylin. Yes, it happened like the prophecy. I jumped on Rafe, saving him. Kane dragged me to the woods and left me to die. Then I sprouted wings. Please, Aylin. You can ask me anything, any time."

"Thank you. I apologize if I was out of line."

"You are literally protecting me with your life. I don't mind any questions you have. I mean that."

"Yes, your Majesty." She turns to Roesh. "My apologies."

"Mine, too."

They return to their quarters. Rafe takes Roesh in, leaving Ana and Aylin in the hall.

"Aylin, is Roesh always so gruff with you?"

"Sometimes. I am young and still learning."

"You battled Remus in NightFall! You are an incredible guardian."

"Thank you, mi'lady. I genuinely appreciate that."

"I am honored to have you both protecting me. I do not understand the way he speaks to you."

"It's how most guardians are with those they are training."

Roesh and Rafe step out. Rafe takes Ana's hand, leading her into their quarters. She looks at him.

"It's not my business, but did you have a talk with Roesh?"

"I did. He apologized and said he will work on not being so harsh with her."

"I swear, if you spoke to me like that, I would be in tears!"

"For starters, I wouldn't speak to you like that."

"I told her what an incredible guardian she is."

"High praise! Thank you. It means a lot to us, to hear that."

She kisses him. "You're an incredible guardian, too."

"Mia estrela, thank you."

"I need to get clean, after training."

"Hmm. Making ourselves hungry for lunch?"

"Yes, please." She kisses him again, holding him tight.

"I'll see about lunch."

"I'll meet you in the washroom."

Ana smiles at him while going inside. She starts the shower then undresses. Stepping under the water, she lets it wash over her. She closes her eyes as her heart is pounding and her head swimming. She goes to the back wall, leaning against it.

"Ana, what's wrong?" Rafe asks as he steps inside.

"I'm sorry. I closed my eyes, and I was back in that house."

"You're safe." He holds her against his chest. "Feel my love, let it soothe you. Let's calm your heart."

"Yes, Rafe." She holds him tight and matches his breathing, calming down. "I have no idea what set that off. I'm sorry."

"It's okay. Let's get cleaned up. Lunch will be here shortly."

She washes and dries off, wrapping the robe around her. She goes to the closet, putting on her hoodie and black pants. She sits on the ottoman as the memory tries to overwhelm her again. Rafe steps in, dressed in his pajamas. He rushes to her, pulling her onto his lap.

"I'm sorry," she says softly.

"No, no apologies. Just stay with me, let me comfort you."

He holds her while she sleeps in his arms. After an hour, he lays her down then puts in for lunch. Once it's set up, he debates waking her. He stands over her and watches her when she opens her eyes.

"Hmm. Rafe?"

"Ana, how are you feeling?"

"Better. I'm hungry."

"Okay. We have food." He helps her to her feet. He takes her to their table, getting her a plate. "Eat, mia estrela."

"Yes, love. How long was I out?"

"About an hour. Are you okay now?"

"I am. I have no idea why it was so strong, why now."

"Will you tell me about it?"

"You know what it was. I was back in the house, in my bedroom. I thought I was doing better, moving past it."

"You are. You will still have episodes and nightmares as you're dealing with it. I told you, it will get worse before it gets better. The main thing is that you are dealing with it. Thank you for being open with me, for not hiding."

"I said I would do better."

"You are. Now, eat."

"Yes, love." She finishes her plate. "What are we doing until the ball?"

"We can have a lesson if you want. Anything in particular you want to know?"

"Why am I not allowed off-world?"

"Ana, what—"

"No, I'm simply curious. Kara said I could if there was an heir. Why?"

"The portals aren't always reliable, plus it's more dangerous, traveling. You aren't forbidden to go, it's preferred. Do you want to travel?"

"No. I think of what happened to Kara and me, getting separated. I wouldn't want to chance it. I am excited to see MorningStella. To finally go to the beach would be wonderful! And to do it with you, makes it that much more special."

"I'm excited to go as well. I've never been to the cottage, but I have been to the quadrant. It was a long time ago. Would you like to read some more? I am most curious to see what happens with Ms. Bennett and Mr. Darcy."

"Okay." She takes the book, reading a few chapters with him. "What do you think so far?"

"Hmm. I am a bit perplexed by his behavior, but I see now that they both have what the title says."

She laughs. "Very good! We'll finish reading it this weekend, then return it to my mother's library."

"Okay."

Ana yawns. "I think I would like to get some more rest before the ball. I'm going to use the washroom. Will you lay with me?"

"Yes, mia estrela. I think a nap is a good idea, after our training!"

She goes to the washroom, then waits on the chaise for him. He steps out, taking her into his arms. He carries her to bed.

"Rafe, thank you for earlier."

"For what?"

"When I had my episode. Having you around helps me so much. Thank you."

"You're welcome. Now, get some sleep. We have a ball tonight."

"Yes, love." She grips his shirt, snuggling in. He caresses her face as she falls asleep.

"Hmm. My warrior, battling so many demons. How do you not see how strong and brave you are?"

Chapter 24

Rafe wakes up and smiles as Ana continues to sleep peacefully, his shirt still in her hand. He lays his head next to hers, gently trailing his fingers along her mouth. Her lips part at his touch. He plants a soft kiss.

"Hmm. My love."

"I'm right here."

She opens her eyes, looking at him. "Hi," she says softly.

"Hi, yourself. How do you feel?"

"Much better." She stretches, pulling back into his chest. "How do you feel?"

"Good. I enjoyed our training. I'm impressed at how well you're doing. I enjoyed chasing you."

"That was fun!" She laughs. "Once I've had more training, we'll do that outside."

"All right," he says with a chuckle. He leans forward, kissing her. She wraps her arms around him, then sits on his lap. "Ana—"

"I'm okay." She caresses his face, gently placing her hand. "See?"

"We have a late night tonight. Let's rest today, then we'll have time tomorrow before Bela and Joph arrive." She tries to move away. "Ana, please. Tell me to let go, I will. Otherwise, I want to hold you like this. Will you let me?"

She holds him tighter. "Yes, love. Please, hold me."

"What happened earlier, in the shower?" he asks. She looks at him, her eyes narrow with hurt on her face. "I know it was an episode. You told me you were back in the house. Will you talk about it?"

"Rafe, please. I was feeling so much better. Why would you ask that?" she asks, falling against his chest.

"I'm sorry. I worry about you." He kisses the top of

her head. "You're right. What do you think the ball will be like tonight?"

Thinking of it makes her smile. "Beautiful! I hope I can stay awake," she chuckles. "Kara was right. I've never been one for staying up late. I always went to bed early and woke up early. She's the night owl. Though, sometimes I did stay up late reading."

"My smart, funny, bookworm. There were some nights I would stay awake until dawn, unable to put down my current read."

She laughs. "Hmm. I forgot you love to read. We'll do that in my mother's library. She has such an amazing collection!"

"When she was pregnant with you, she would sit in there and read to you. Well, read to her pregnant belly."

"What? How do you know that?"

"Kara told me, when I told her we had been going there. She said that was her favorite room, especially when she was pregnant with you."

"Maybe that's why I feel such a connection in there. Kara is starting to open up more, talking about my mother. I don't want to push her though."

"You're not. I can tell she is sorry for how she reacted before."

"It was her grief. I can understand." She kisses him. "I need to use the washroom."

He helps her up then sits on the chaise while waiting for her. When she's finished, she walks past him to open her wings.

"Are they bothering you?"

"No. I'm trying to feel less self-conscious about tonight. I love my wings, I do. Please, don't get me wrong. Still, I've never been in a room full of people with wings. I'm trying to prepare."

"That's understandable." He massages her back and shoulders. "You're not nearly as tight."

"Working them earlier took care of that. Thank you."

"Ana, we don't have to go tonight."

"Rafe, what do you mean?"

"You aren't obligated to be there."

"I want to go. These are the very people who are willing to lay down their lives for me, the people I was tortured to defend. Why wouldn't I want to go?"

"You're right. I'm worried."

"I'm going to be okay. I'm excited to go, and I'm curious to see all the different wings. I know you resigned your commission, but since you are still a guardian, are you wearing a uniform tonight?"

"No. I'll be in what I wore to our dinner."

"Oh, good! I love the uniforms, don't get me wrong. I was hoping you wouldn't be in one." She smiles at him, kissing him. "My own personal guardian."

He leans down, by her ear. "It's my pleasure to serve my queen."

"Rafe!" she gasps, stepping up and kissing him. "I need you."

"What do you need?"

She brings her hand up under his shirt, caressing his chest. "You," she softly answers. He scoops her into his arms, taking her to the bed.

"Wait," he says, running to the door. He locks the new latch, then returns. "Hmm. You're wearing too many clothes, Majesty."

She smiles at him. "Then do something about it."

"Ana!" He laughs, climbing into bed. He helps her out of her hoodie and pants. "Better?"

"Yes, love. Now, you are the one wearing too many clothes."

He quickly undresses, then climbs back into bed, pulling her into his arms. "What do you want?"

She blushes, taking his hand along her stomach. "I want you," she says.

His fingers trail from her neck down her chest, teasing her stomach, then stroking between her legs. She trembles as his hand moves faster, her breathing in short gasps. He kisses her hard and hungry while continuing to build her up. Stars blur her vision as she succumbs to him.

She rolls with him, lying on his chest. "Hmm. I think your heart is going almost as fast as mine."

"We need to clean up. Dinner will be here shortly."

"We worked up an appetite, didn't we?"

Rafe laughs as they stand and go into the washroom. "Yes, we did." He starts the water, looking at her. She bites her lip. He kisses her again. "We are getting clean."

"Yes, love."

They step in, letting the water run over them. She lathers up the soap and washes him as he holds onto her. She leans against the wall as he washes her.

"Ana, are you okay?"

"My legs are still shaking," she admits, laughing. "Only you can have such an effect on me!" She grabs his arm, thinking of what they did. She kisses him, feeling him tremble at her thoughts.

"Ana!" he says, leaning against the wall, catching his breath. His mouth crashes on hers. "Hmm. We need to get dressed."

She dries off, wraps the robe around herself, and goes into the closet. Slipping on a pale blue gown and silver shoes, she next puts on the circlet with the small star dangling on her forehead.

Rafe walks in, going to the drawer. He gets out her ring and places it on her finger. He changes into black pants and a black button up top. When she steps up to him, kissing him, he returns her passion.

"Thank you, love. We needed that."

"Ana, I always need you. You know that, right?"

Her smile grows. "I do now."

"I hear the bells. Dinner must be here." He steps out, going to the door to let them in. Kara and Evren follow behind. Everything is set up and the staff leave. Ana steps out, smiling at Kara.

"How is everything?"

"Good," Kara replies. No whispers or mentions of Remus' men. We're hoping with him dead, and his men scattered, that they will give up on his mission."

"That's what I'm hoping for, as well. Are you and Evren excited about tonight?"

"We are. We came from the ballroom. Everything is perfect! I think you'll enjoy tonight."

"I already am."

"Ana!" Kara cries out. "You and Rafe, I swear!" She takes her hand, leading her to the table. "Now eat. I don't need you passing out at the ball."

"Yes, sis."

Rafe laughs as he joins them. "Don't make me separate you two!"

Kara turns to him. "You can try!"

Ana smiles while eating her food. "Okay, okay. Let's call a truce."

"Since the Crimson Queen commands it," Kara says, winking at her. "Ana, are you okay?" she asks when she loses her smile.

"Yes, sorry. It's still weird to think of, that I am the Crimson Queen."

"As long as you don't call it the Crimson Curse again, I'll be happy."

"What? When did she say that?"

"Oh, it was a long time ago, when I was still trying to deal with everything. Yes, Rafe, I know you're right. It's not a curse. I'm sorry I ever said that."

"As you said, you were still trying to come to terms with it."

"You don't have to answer, but can I ask? How are your wings?"

Ana smiles at Kara. "They're fine. According to my flight instructor, I am doing very well with them."

"She is," he agrees, smiling. "Like a natural. Watching her now, you would think she's had wings her whole life!"

"How do you feel about them?"

"They are feeling more… normal, more natural. A little bit every day."

"That's good! I've been so worried, ever since I humiliated you."

"Are you jealous I have wings?" She watches her head go down. "Kara, really?"

"I am. I don't know why! I swear, I didn't humiliate you on purpose, though. I would never do that!"

"I would never think that. It's okay. Why are you jealous?"

"Just, everything. You are the Crimson Queen, and I've heard so much about the legend and for so long. I never wanted wings myself, but seeing you with yours, it made me jealous. I'm sorry."

"It's okay. For so long, I was jealous of you."

Kara nearly drops her fork. "What?"

"You are so pretty, and confident, and strong. When we were on Earth, I looked up to you. You were everything I wanted to be."

"Ana, I promise you, you have surpassed me in every way. That's a good thing. I want that for you."

Rafe looks at Evren. "Let's gather dishes and take to the kitchen, shall we?"

"Yes, Rafe," Evren agrees, getting to her feet. They collect the plates and leave.

"I guess they thought we needed a moment."

"Kara, you know how much you mean to me, right? You will always be my protective big sister. I love you for that."

"I love you, too, Ana. There's another reason I asked about your wings."

"What do you mean?"

"I told you, I felt like I had failed you and your mother. With everything you've been through, what you've become. Seeing you now, happy with your wings, makes me feel better."

"Kara! You have never failed me. I am grateful to be here with all of you. I think my mother would be proud of my accomplishments, of who I have become."

"I don't think so."

"No?" Ana asks, looking down.

"Sis, I *know* so. She would be amazed at everything you have done. She would be so proud of you, so happy for you."

Ana pulls her into her arms, hugging her tight. "Thank you!"

"Rafe told me you've been going to her library. I will go with you one day, if you want me to."

"I don't want you overwhelmed. I know the grief is strong in you."

"It's okay. I want to help you, I want you to know everything you can about your mother. I owe you that." She stands up, helping Ana to her feet. "Now, let's see about your gown for tonight!"

"Yes. I sent it out Thursday to be cleaned. It was supposed to be returned yesterday. I forgot to check."

"Ana, with everything going on. Come on." They go into the closet. "Evren organized this?"

She laughs. "How can you tell?"

"She did the same to ours. She is neat and organized!" She walks around, looking through the gowns. "Ana, please don't panic. I don't see your dress."

Her shoulders sag. "Shit."

"Ana!"

"I'm sorry."

"It's okay," she says, chuckling. "Just not used to hearing that from you!"

"What am I going to do? I must have a gown for tonight!"

Chapter 25

"Ana, breathe. We are literally in a closet full of gowns."

"The closet!" She takes Kara's hand and leads her into the other closet. They go to the back, to the gown on the model. "Is this too much?"

"Oh, Ana. I think it's perfect!"

The gown is silver-blue, covered with a silver sparkle and grey embroidered roses along the bodice. Ana walks around it and gasps at the back. Kara runs to her.

"Oh, my! It doesn't even need to be mended. What's wrong?" Kara asks when she sees Ana frown.

"It's such a low back. My wings will be completely exposed." She shakes her head. "I don't think I can wear this."

"Ana? Kara?"

"We're in here," Kara says, taking Ana's hand. They step into the main chamber. Kara goes to Evren. "I need your help with something." They go into the closet.

Ana opens the window, letting the frigid air hit her face. Rafe sees how flush she is.

"Are you okay?" he asks as he steps up beside her.

She nods. "I am. My dress wasn't returned from the laundry service. I have a gown to wear, but, it's a bit much." She sees the look of confusion on his face. "The back is completely open. I'd feel so exposed."

"Ana, wear whatever you want. I want you comfortable and feeling safe. I don't want you too self-conscious."

"I know, thank you." She looks over as Kara steps out.

"Ana, come see."

"Whatever I end up wearing, you'll be fine in your proposal outfit."

Rafe smiles. "Yes, mia estrela."

She goes into the closet and finds the gown on the ottoman. She picks it up and examines the back.

"How did you do this? You are amazing!"

Evren created a backing with the same material, leaving room for her wings.

"Ana, I made that gown."

She nearly drops it. "What?"

"Your mother planned to wear it for a ball in your honor, to welcome the new princess. She heard I made clothes, and she asked me to make her this."

"Oh, Evren! I—" She pushes back the tears. "Thank you. It's such a beautiful gown. I can't wait to try it on."

Ana strips down. Evren helps her get the new gown on. Ana walks to the mirror.

"It's perfect!" She opens her wings, looking at her reflection. She brings them back in, turning to her. "Thank you."

Evren smiles. "You are welcome. Now, what crown are you wearing?"

Ana goes to the shelf, looking them over. She finds a tiara with diamond stars, lined with two rows of diamonds that will rest across her head. She holds it up to Evren.

"This?"

"Oh, Ana. It will look amazing with that gown." Evren leads her to the ottoman. "We're going to do something different with your hair tonight. Let me know if it hurts or it's too tight."

"I will. I trust you, Evren."

She laughs. "It's just hair."

"No, Evren. You don't understand. No one ever styled or braided my hair, until Kara then you. It means a lot to me."

Evren turns serious. "Yes, Ana. Thank you, for letting me do it." Evren gathers her hair, brushing through it. She makes a few braids, then wraps them around the back of her head. She pins them in place, creating a halo circling the back. "Is that okay?"

"Yes."

She finishes pinning the braids, then gets the tiara. She puts it on, pinning it into place. Ana stands up, going to the mirror and smiling.

"You're right, Evren. It does look great with this gown." She gets out a pair of silver shoes and slips them on. She goes to the drawer with Royal Jewels. "I know we aren't meeting ambassadors or dignitaries. Is it still okay if I wear these?"

"Yes, Ana."

"Thank you." As she tries on the diamond choker, it reminds her of the metal collar she was forced to wear. She nearly yanks it off and places it back in the drawer. A beautiful diamond teardrop on a platinum chain catches her eye. She puts it on. "What do you think?"

"It's perfect. Kara and I are going to get ready. We'll be back over in a few minutes."

"Thanks, Evren. For everything!"

"You're most welcome." She leaves the closet.

Ana admires the gown in the mirror. She gathers her thoughts, trying to be excited for dancing with Rafe, ringing in a new year.

"Year 305 of the fourth era." She shakes her head. "It's too much, too different. Like me." Her heart races, and she sits on the ottoman. A knock on the door startles her.

"Ana, are you okay?"

She takes a deep breath, pushing all of her fears down. "Yes, Rafe. I'll be out in a moment." She stands up, collecting herself. She walks to the door, keeping her head up as she opens it and steps out.

His mouth opens as the air is knocked out of him at the sight of her. "Oh, mia estrela!"

"I take it you like it?"

"It is fantastic!" He takes her hands. "Would you please open your wings?" His smile grows as they extend out. "Oh, my!" She smiles at him, but he sees fear in her eyes. "What's wrong, mia estrela?"

"I'm overthinking again. I'm nervous about the ball, about being around so many new people, people with wings." She takes a breath. "I'll be okay."

He holds her with all of the love and compassion he can. "Ana, you are going to be brilliant! They are going to love you. They're excited to meet you, as well." He looks at her. "What is it?"

"I feel like, I don't fit in with humans, since I have wings. I don't fit in with guardians, since I wasn't born as one. I don't belong anywhere."

"Ana, here, in my arms, is where you belong. I'm telling you right now, they are going to accept you. They know what you've endured, protecting them. They are so grateful to have you as their queen. Please, mia estrela, believe me."

Kara and Evren walk in, laughing and talking. They stop upon seeing Ana. Kara approaches her. "What's wrong?"

Ana shakes her head. "I don't… I'm not—" Kara leads her to the chaise. "I'm not a human or a guardian. Where do I belong?"

"Ana, do you know what I am?" She shakes her head. "I am a witch. We are born that way. I am immortal and have magic. I am revered by some and hated by others, for having powers. Witches are extremely rare. I'm the only one in this realm."

"Really?"

"Yes. Evren is immortal and has magic. She and I aren't the same, but we're similar. Like you and Rafe, right?"

"Well, yes, but—"

"Good. Now, you were born here, this is your home. Evren and I are the outsiders, the strangers here. However, everyone has been so kind, so welcoming, we both know this is our home. What will it take for you to feel that way, too?"

Rafe joins them, curious to hear her answer. Ana shakes her head. "I don't know. Having you three here has definitely helped, I mean. I've accepted my wings, I know they are a part of me. After Remus and Tinsley—"

"They were bigots. There are still some of those here, don't get me wrong. Trust me when I tell you, your kingdom, your realm, is honored you are their queen. You have brought peace and freedom, and your people love you for it. So, what's wrong? Why are you feeling this way now? Because you'll be in a room full of guardians?"

"Yes," she answers quietly as her shoulders go down. "I was trying to mentally prepare myself, to know I was going to be in a room full of people with their wings out. I was trying to make myself believe I belong."

"What happened?"

"I did what I always do. I was overthinking."

Rafe kneels in front of her. "Ana, say the word. Say what you want to do, and we'll do it. Kara and Evren can go to the ball while we have snacks brought in and have a quiet new year. Or I can get dressed, and we'll all go together."

"It's your call," Kara adds. "I will understand if you want to get comfortable and stay here."

"No. You all have worked so hard to make this a wonderful night. I won't ruin it. Please, Rafe, get dressed."

"Yes, mia estrela." He stands up, kissing her on the way. "Be right out."

"I'm sorry, Kara."

"For what?"

"I hope I didn't ruin the night. You and Evren look great!"

Evren is wearing a lavender gown. Kara is in black dress pants with a lavender shirt.

"Ana, you haven't ruined anything. Don't forget, you are going to make an announcement tonight, remember?"

"Oh, yes! How could I forget? Thank you, sis."

She hugs her. "Ana, you know we are always here for you."

"Kara, do Rafe and I have to lead the first dance?"

"It would be tradition, but with everything you're feeling, you don't have to do it."

"No, we will. It's okay. Really." They look over as Rafe steps out. Ana gets to her feet. He's in black dress slacks, with a black shirt and silver-blue tunic jacket. "Oh, Rafe! You look so handsome!" She takes his arm. "We'll be perfect to lead the first dance, won't we?"

"Yes, Ana." He turns her to him, taking her hands. "Deep breaths, and we'll go." His eyes go wide in surprise when she steps up and kisses him.

"I'm okay. Let's go."

"All right." He leads her out the door. Roesh and Aylin come to attention.

"Aylin, you got to dress up!"

"Yes, Majesty, thanks to Rafe. He spoke to Melian." She turns to him. "Thank you, love."

"I could see you were disappointed she couldn't dress up. Melian made an exception."

"Your Majesty, if I may, that gown is exquisite!"

"Thank you. One of my dearest friends made it." She looks back at Evren, smiling at her before looking at Aylin. "That pale blue is fantastic with your hair and wings!"

Aylin turns to her, surprised. "Thank you, Majesty."

***

They arrive at the ballroom, which is already filling up. Kara leads them to their table then takes the sound amplifier to welcome everyone.

"This is our first New Year's Ball. A few things before we begin. Food will be served shortly. One minute before midnight, I will make an announcement. Then, a ball will drop, counting down. Once it is midnight, you may hug or kiss your lover and friends, as is an Earth tradition. You do not have to partake, but anyone is welcome to. Now, her Majesty has an announcement, then the ball will begin."

She hands Ana the sound amplifier. "Good evening,"

she says, getting to her feet. "I am so honored to be in a room with fellow guardians. Every one of you has my utmost respect. I thank each of you for what you do, to protect me and the palace. As Kara said, I have an announcement to make."

She takes Rafe's hand, gently nudging him to stand. "I'm sure you all know Rafe, my personal Guardian." A few laughs and whistles erupt. "We have been together for a while now. Last weekend, Rafe asked me to be his wife, and I said yes. We are now betrothed." Cheers and applause break out through the ballroom. "Thank you," Ana says, handing Kara back the amplifier.

"I'm okay." She looks at Rafe, taking his hand. "See?"

Kara announces the first dance.

Rafe leads Ana out to the dance floor, grateful when her tension eases. He holds her close, concentrating on sending her love and comfort.

"You are my little warrior. Did you know that?"

She looks up at him. "What?"

He smiles. "All these battles you've fought and won."

"Rafe, I've only been in one battle."

"Ana, battling Tinsley, Kane, Remus. You have fought in many. Battling your demons, your fears. You are my warrior queen."

"Thank you, love." She sees all eyes on them as they dance around the floor. A sigh of relief escapes her lips as more couples join them. "Can we eat?"

"Of course." He takes her hand. She fills her plate, sneaking bites off his. "You are hungry." He laughs. They go to their table. "Eat, then we'll dance some more, if you want."

"I'd like you to take me around, if you don't mind. Introduce me to the guardians you know best."

"I would be honored." He smiles at her. "Any chance to show off my beautiful fiancée!"

Aylin sits beside her. "Aylin, if I may, how old are you?"

"I am only thirty-two."

"You are older than me, but so young compared to the other guardians!"

"Yes, Majesty."

"How old is Roesh?"

"Two hundred and twelve."

"Such a difference! Although, Rafe is five hundred years older than me, so I guess that's normal with guardians?"

Aylin laughs. "Yes, Majesty. It's rare for two guardians of the same age to end up together. By the time you go through training, lessons, and battles, you are more like siblings than lovers."

"I see. It is a tight-knit group, isn't it?"

Aylin sees the worry on her face. "Ana—" She blushes. "I'm so sorry! Your Majesty, it is. You have earned your place amongst us; I promise you that."

"Thank you."

Ana finishes eating. Rafe takes her hand, walking around and introducing her to various guardians. Each one bows, addressing her, then introductions are made. They see a group of young female guardians at a table.

"Shall we?"

She sees them staring at her. "No, thank you."

"Ana—"

"Please," she quietly begs. "I can't."

"All right." He takes her back to their table, sitting her down. "I'll get us some desserts. Stay right here."

"Yes, Rafe.

He walks away, and she sees the girls are still watching her. She goes to their table. They immediately jump to their feet and bow.

"As you were," Ana says. "If I may, how old are you?" she asks as her eyes drift across the different guardians at the table.

"We're fifteen and sixteen, your Majesty."

"So young! Are you enjoying the ball?"

"We are. Your gown is lovely, your Highness."

"Thank you. What are your names?" They go around the table, introducing themselves. "It's nice to meet all of you."

Yvonne stands up. "Majesty, if I may. We are curious about your wings, but don't wish to offend."

"What do you want to ask?"

She looks at the other girls, then back to Ana. "Is it true? Did you get them like the prophecy said?"

"I did." She sees Rafe and waves her hand, telling him to go on to their table. "I fell in battle, went into the woods, thinking I was dying. Instead, I came to as wings of fire erupted from my back. Then they turned into what you see now." She sees awe and surprise on the girls' faces.

"Thank you," Yvonne says. "I can't imagine how scary that was, your Majesty."

"It was scary at first, but I have learned how to use them and to accept them. Having a guardian to help."

"He is handsome." She blushes. "I'm so sorry!"

Ana giggles. "Do me a favor, don't tell him that? He already has a big head on his shoulders!" Everyone at the table laughs. "I'll be returning to him now. Please, enjoy the ball."

Yvonne bows. "You as well, your Majesty. Thank you, for everything you've done for us and the kingdom."

"You're most welcome." She turns and goes to the table with Rafe. "I apologize. I wasn't going to get up, but they wouldn't stop staring."

"Everything okay?"

"They're young and curious. They're very friendly."

"Good."

Kara walks up to them. "It's almost midnight. I'll be making the announcement momentarily. I wanted to give you a head's up."

"Thank you!" Ana says. She takes Rafe's hand. "Ready to celebrate the start of a new year together?"

"Yes, mia estrela. A new year, and a new life, with

changes ahead of us.”

She smiles at him. “Yes, love.”

Kara stands up, announcing there is one minute to midnight. The dance floor clears, as a silver ball is slowly lowered down. They count down to midnight. Rafe grabs Ana, kissing her hard. She holds him tight. He pulls back.

“Happy new year, mia estrela.”

“Happy new year, my betrothed.”

He smiles at her. “I like that.” He kisses her again. “Now, are we staying a little longer? I feel your exhaustion.”

“I am quite tired. We’ll stay a few minutes, then slip away.”

“Yes, that’s fine.”

“Ana, are you okay?” Kara asks.

“We’re exhausted. We’ll leave in a few minutes.” She stands and hugs her. “Happy new year, and thank you for this beautiful ball!”

“I’m glad you’re enjoying it.”

“Could Rafe and I have the morning to sleep in? We can have lunch at noon, if you want. Then Bela and Joph will be here for dinner.”

“That sounds good. We’ll see you at noon.” Kara goes back over to Evren.

Rafe looks at Ana. “Are you ready to go?”

She laughs. “I am. I’m so tired.”

“I can feel it. All right.” He gestures to Roesh and Aylin. “Will you accompany us back to our quarters?”

“Yes, Rafe. Then Gerard and Deckard will relieve us shortly after.” They stand up, walking them out.

“You’re off for three days, aren’t you?” Ana asks Aylin.

“Yes, Majesty.”

“Enjoy your time off! You’ve earned it. Please, feel free to come see me to talk about books or anything else.”

“Thank you,” Aylin says. They arrive at the quarters. Roesh goes in, checking every room. He steps out.

“All clear, your Majesty.”

“Thank you. Both of you, happy new year.”

"You as well, Majesty," Aylin says, bowing.

Rafe takes Ana inside. She goes to get clean clothes, but as she's removing her jewelry, memories flood her from the last ball. Tears prick her eyes as she pushes everything down.

She undoes the ties around her neck and gently places the gown on the ottoman. While she finishes undressing, everything becomes too much, and the memories consume her. She collapses onto the ottoman and sobs into her hands.

Rafe walks in, but at the sight of her, he runs and sits next to her. He takes her hand. "Ana! Why are you so afraid? What's wrong?"

She shakes her head. "Memories from the last ball. Coming in here, cleaning up, then going to bed. I woke up, being taken from here. I—" The sobs strangle her breath.

He picks her up, putting her on his lap. He wraps his arms around her. "Shh. You're safe now. He's dead, and we have guardians outside." He strokes her hair. "Would you want to sleep in here tonight? We can lock the closet door and sleep on the ottoman, if you want."

"Could we?" she asks, looking at him.

"Of course! We'll get cleaned up and sleep in here."

"Thank you."

They go to the washroom. He holds her up as they clean. She's so tired, she can barely stand. He helps her dry and into pajamas, taking her to the closet. He locks the door. He picks her up, carrying her to the ottoman.

"Sleep, mia estrela. In the morning will be a new day, a new year."

"The start of our new life," she says softly, yawning.

"Yes. A life with hope ahead of us."

"I love you, Rafe."

"Oh, mia estrela, I love you, too."

She clutches his shirt. "Please, don't let him take me," she mumbles sleepily.

"Ana, you are staying right here with me, always."

"Forever," she replies, falling asleep.
"Yes, my little warrior, forever."

Acknowledgements:

Thank you, Kevin. You are my Rafe, bringing down my walls, and helping me in battle.

To Traci, Bonita, Ronda, and Jess, thank you for being my dedicated readers. I could not do this without you.

To Lisa, my sister, thank you for being there for me.

To Kat, Brittany, Steve, Misty, Emily, and Sherry. You are such wonderful friends, and I appreciate your support!

Thank you, God, for my love of writing and reading.

<u>Also Available from A.R. Kaufer</u>

The Courtship Saga:
Courting Fate
Courting Destiny
Courting Eternity

The Stolen Royalty Series:
Kingdom of Forgotten Curses
The Sword in the Roses (Novella)
Court of Lies & Cinder (Coming October 2024)

The Unexpected Queen

About the Author

A.R. Kaufer lives in Indiana with her husband and furbabies. When she's not playing video games or watching movies, she is reading or writing. She can be found on Twitter, Instagram, Threads, TikTok, & Pinterest, and she is happy to hear from her readers.

Author Photo By:
Kevin Kaufer